"*The Wandering Season* is a delightful journey of self-discovery, romance, good food, and a little magic. I devoured every word and, although the ending was perfectly satisfying, I can't deny wanting just a little bit more. I eagerly looking forward to Runyan's next offering!"

—KATHERINE REAY, AUTHOR OF
The London House AND *The Berlin Letters*

"Aimie K. Runyan has knocked me out with *The Wandering Season*, a lyrical book about a young woman's modern-day quest to find out who she really is and how to fulfill her creative dreams. Rich with exquisite descriptions of food, family, international travel, as well as fully believable instances of magical realism, this book has everything I love in a story. Brilliantly written, Veronica's journey will stay with me for a very long time."

— MADDIE DAWSON, BESTSELLING AUTHOR

"It's a rare book that feeds both your soul and your body, but that's exactly what Aimie K. Runyan's *The Wandering Season* accomplishes. For anyone who has ever looked in the mirror and wondered where they really came from, this story combines the realities of modern DNA testing with a sprinkle of magical realism to bring the past to life. *The Wandering Season* is the perfect palate cleanser and an utterly delicious tale of self-discovery."

—SARA GOODMAN CONFINO, BESTSELLING AUTHOR
OF *Don't Forget to Write* AND *Behind Every Good Man*

"Some books are simply a joy to read. Aimie K. Runyan's *The Memory of Lavender and Sage* is one of them. Sensuous . . . dreamy . . . romantic . . . *The Memory of Lavender and Sage* is a mélange of tastes and smells, magic and romance. Aimie K. Runyan weaves a sumptuous tale of mystery and magic, family and friendships, reminding us that it's never too late to find the home of our heart.

—LORI NELSON SPIELMAN, *New York Times* BESTSELLING AUTHOR OF *The Life List*

"In Aimie K. Runyan's signature heartfelt voice, *The Memory of Lavender and Sage* is a warm, generous, and utterly satisfying novel about the power of kindness, character, and finding purpose and love where you least expect it."

—ANN GARVIN, *USA TODAY* BESTSELLING AUTHOR OF *There's No Coming Back From This*

"Aimie K. Runyan wows in her latest atmospheric novel . . . *The Memory of Lavender and Sage* reminds readers that every moment should be savored and that, sometimes, the simplest pleasures are the greatest gifts. Runyan has proven herself as a standout voice in women's fiction. I was captivated from the very first line."

— KRISTY WOODSON HARVEY, *New York Times* BESTSELLING AUTHOR OF *The Summer of Songbirds*

"*The Memory of Lavender and Sage* is an enchanting novel that sweeps you away to France on a journey of self-discovery, uncovering family secrets, and learning how love lives on. Friend-ships are forged, romance is cultivated, and magical moments abound in the captivating small French town. For readers who love *Under the Tuscan Sun* and *Chocolat*, this is your next heartfelt, delightful read."

—JENNIFER MOORMAN, BESTSELLING AUTHOR OF *The Magic All Around*

The Wandering Season

THE
Wandering
SEASON

A Novel

AIMIE K. RUNYAN

HARPER MUSE

The Wandering Season

© 2025 by Aimie K. Runyan

Published by Harper Muse, an imprint of HarperCollins Focus LLC

This novel is a work of fiction. Names, characters, places, and incidents are either products of the author's imagination or used fictitiously. All characters are fictional, and any similarity to people living or dead is purely coincidental.

Library of Congress Cataloging-in-Publication Data
Names: Runyan, Aimie K., author.
Title: The wandering season : a novel / Aimie K. Runyan.
Description: Nashville : Harper Muse, 2025. | Summary: "Unraveling the tangled roots of her family takes her places she never expected"--Provided by publisher.
Identifiers: LCCN 2024049351 (print) | LCCN 2024049352 (ebook) | ISBN 9781400237289 (paperback) | ISBN 9781400237296 (epub) | ISBN 9781400237302
Subjects: LCGFT: Novels.
Classification: LCC PS3618.U5667 W36 2025 (print) | LCC PS3618.U5667 (ebook) | DDC 813/.6--dc23/eng/20241021
LC record available at https://lccn.loc.gov/2024049351
LC ebook record available at https://lccn.loc.gov/2024049352

Printed in the United States of America

25 26 27 28 29 LBC 5 4 3 2 1

To Kimberly Brock
for your unwavering support when I need it most

and for your invaluable help in naming
The Book That Would Not Be Named.

Every writer should have a friend as dear as you.

*It's around the table and in the preparation of food
that we learn about ourselves and about the world.*

—ALICE WATERS

The stove is the shrine where I convene with my ancestors.

—ADAM RAGUSEA

Chapter 1

Colorado snow was charming in December, as winter was just making herself at home. Rarely was there more than a heavy dusting—a few inches at the outside—and it had the good manners to depart within a day or two. The more insistent snow, the kind that wore out its welcome in a hurry, was reserved for March: the time when every sane person wanted to vacate the state of Colorado in favor of a beach and a rum-based cocktail. Preferably with a magenta paper umbrella in it. Instead, most of us went skiing, which at least made putting up with the snow feel worthwhile.

I loved the wintery whimsy of the tree-lined drive up the mountains, and as I pulled in front of my parents' cabin, I was glad I'd made the trek alone. At least that's what I told myself. I certainly felt relief that Jonathan wasn't turning seven shades of Kermit-the-Frog-green in the passenger seat, but at some point someone would question his absence.

My boyfriend of four years had always hated the windy drive

up Highway 36 from Denver, even though he'd always been the one behind the wheel. He was a California boy, lured to Denver by good jobs and scenery. He loved Colorado but was more comfortable in LA gridlock than on a mountain road. He had usually opted out of trips to see my parents since he was so prone to motion sickness, preferring to see them when they came down to the city where we lived and worked. I sensed he was low-key baffled as to why they'd retired to such a place. Yes, it was the gateway to Rocky Mountain National Park. Sure, it had world-class hiking and some of the most stunning mountain views in the world. But a lot of great hiking and scenery could be found elsewhere in the state on four-lane highways that didn't twist like a fine Laguiole sommelier's corkscrew.

He never understood our attachment to Estes, and that was okay. Some things could only be explained by a childhood full of memories. But his barely veiled disdain for the small mountain town was just another reason why our recent split didn't hurt as much as it should have. This place didn't *have* to be important to him, but it should have mattered that it was important to us. To me. The breakup was ultimately the right decision, but it would bring the conversation to other areas of my life that didn't quite sit well with the rest of the family. I was almost twenty-seven, and they'd all expected me to have graduated culinary school and be well on my way to a Michelin star by now, but I'd subverted their expectations.

I took a steadying breath and went to the cargo area of my nine-year-old Toyota SUV. I hoisted out the heaviest of the boxes, trying not to grunt under the weight of small-batch Hawaiian vanilla pods, ethically sourced cocoa, and a ton of freshly ground almond flour and quinoa for the gluten-free menu at my mother's bakery. Left to haul in was a case of Colorado wine Mom was partial to, a bottle of locally distilled whiskey for Dad, and Avery's favorite truffle chips.

Those things weren't for the shop, but rather because my parents had become like family to my vendors.

Dad rushed over from the front porch to relieve me of the box. "Holy cow, shortcake, did you leave any food in Denver?"

I kissed his cheek in greeting before grabbing another load from the cargo area. "A bit. But I have to help Mom replenish her stock of vanilla."

"Just don't let it eat too far into your profit margins, kiddo."

My heart tugged a bit. He wanted to press further, but he wasn't going to because of the holiday. He was always more than a little worried that my niche business ran too close to the red. And some months that was true. But the more time that passed, the larger and more impressive my client list became. I didn't hold my breath when the rent came due anymore, and there was no better feeling than to have that small sense of security.

My little venture was called The Kitchen Muse. I was a food broker but more specialized. I wasn't the person to get you a dozen hundred-pound bags of brand-name flour, but I could be counted on to let you know what farm had the best spinach this year and would drive to Hatch, New Mexico, for a client to ensure the best pickings during green chile season. I liked to consider myself a food matchmaker. If a restaurant or gourmet boutique shop was in need of truffles from a specific region of Italy, I was the girl to call. Closer to home, I could work magic. If a mom-and-pop kitchen out of Boulder was making standout artisanal cheese and charcuterie meats, I would help them find outlets to sell their goods and, hopefully, expand their business. For this reason, my SUV often smelled like a farmers' market stall rather than a store-bought air freshener. And I loved it.

Inside, the decadent aromas of Mom's toffee interlaced with her famous cinnamon rolls proving on the counter for morning enveloped me just as tightly as her embrace. "You have to let me pay you like any other client, Vero." Mom shook her head as we unloaded the rest of the boxes. Hers wasn't the only bakery in the small town, but the ingredients I sourced for her made her menu unique. No one else had hibiscus croissants or Napoleons made with hand-whipped crème anglaise, flavored with extract she'd made herself. She paired the vanilla pods I sourced with alcohols that would tease out the best flavor and perfume. She loved soaking the spicy Tahitian pods in a top-shelf rum or the floral Madagascar in brandy. I wasn't sure what she'd do with the Hawaiian varietals I'd found for her, but I was excited to find out.

I took my familiar arms-akimbo stance. "You're not like any other client. You're my mom. I accept payment in samples only."

Her hands were already busy dusting the top of her famous Christmas Eve lasagna with a final layer of Parmesan before putting it in the oven, but she angled her cheek for another kiss. "I owe you a bakery's worth of samples at this point, darling. You're too good to me. What did your client think of my vanilla?"

"Fairbanks has taken my ideas and run with them." I was unable to conceal my pride. He was one of the most prestigious chefs in all of Denver and was hungry for a Michelin star. My idea for him to stack his holiday menu with dishes inspired by my mother's assortment of homemade vanilla extracts had infused him with some much-needed inspiration. Not just desserts, but some sauces for the savory dishes and a whole line of out-of-this-world cocktails I was particularly proud of.

"Well, it was a brilliant idea, my dear. I'll get all these lovely vanilla beans soaking in a few days. They'll be ready by next Christmas if he wants more."

"If his receipts were what I expect they were, I'm sure he will."
I whisked in next to her to toss together the vinaigrette I made every
year to go on the salad that accompanied the meal. "Every time I've
gone past 540 Blake this month, it's been packed."

"Just think how well your own place would do," Dad chided.

I felt the enamel of my teeth begin to strain as my jaw clenched,
which it did whenever this topic bubbled to the surface.

Mom shot him one of her infamous *looks*. "Martin James Stratton,
don't you dare. Veronica doesn't need your prodding today. It's
Christmas Eve for heaven's sake." The rest didn't have to be said:
*And she's just been through a breakup and is living in that tiny apartment
all by herself. She's three cats away from being the punchline of a joke.*

I leaned over and planted another kiss on her cheek in wordless
thanks.

Dad held up his hands in defeat. "I know, Elena. I know."

I put on a falsely bright voice. "Hey, we got it out of the way
early. What's a family meal without the 'when is Veronica opening
her own restaurant' spiel? It's refreshing to have it over so early in
the day."

This was Veronica-speak for *please drop it already*. The argument
was an old one, and there was no good to be had from rehashing it.
Mom and Dad had been fortunate enough—privileged enough—to
craft the life of their dreams. I got the feeling that my not having
met some of the same benchmarks by the age of twenty-six worried
them a bit. Not because they had many specific expectations for my
future but because they were so adamant that whatever bent my life
took, it should be as happy as theirs had been.

We'd lived in the suburbs in a spacious house, usually with a
lovable cat or two underfoot. Mom didn't have to work, so she spent
her days making Martha Stewart and Paula Deen look like talented

amateurs. It was an idyllic upbringing. But the agreement was, once Dad retired, it was Mom's turn to call some shots. Most of them. She had put all her energy into supporting the three of us for so long that when she said she wanted to leave the 'burbs and move to the small town where we'd vacationed two weeks every summer, Dad put our childhood house on the market and found a rambling cabin before the month was out.

Once settled, Mom never adjusted to the reality of her empty nest. She needed to occupy her time, her hands. Dad helped her secure a bakery on a prime spot of real estate on the bustling downtown avenue that served as the tourist hub, and The Summit Sweet Shop was born. In the four years she'd been in business, she'd created a zealous following of the carbohydrate agnostic. My sister, Avery, helped her with social media and marketing, but really, the food stood for itself. It seemed like an SUV load of high-quality ingredients was the least I could do to support her dreams.

Half an hour later, a short, friendly burst of a car horn sounded from outside, causing all eyes to turn to the door. "Sounds like Hurricane Avery is about to make landfall." Dad made a motion like he was bracing himself for impact against the counter. Mom swatted his shoulder and dashed to the door, where Avery was striding up the walk, dragging a suitcase large enough for a six-month expedition in the Antarctic behind her with one hand and a couple of train cases likely loaded with cosmetics and hair products gripped in her other hand.

I hung back as my parents got swept up in the wake of her exuberance and the cloud of her Burberry perfume. Avery had finished at the Parsons School of Design four years before—coinciding with Dad's retirement—and was already becoming a name in New York's fashion industry. And it was no shock to anyone she was so successful so early in her career. She'd commandeered Mom's be-loved Bernina sewing machine when she was twelve and had begun wearing her own designs ever since.

To know Avery was to love her, but it was just as easy to be eclipsed by her. Literally. I stopped growing at five-foot-three and was lean with red hair I kept in a bob. She was closer to six feet with long, wavy black hair like Mom's and had the sort of figure one found on marble statues of Greek goddesses. She was the boisterous one, while I was more reserved. I was the sort who holed up for weeks studying, while she was the one who breezed into class and aced the test without a backward glance at her notes.

She was the perfect blend of Dad's brains and business sense and Mom's magnetic charm and impeccable people skills. It was hard not to be dazzled by the trio of them at times. Dad was a finan-cial genius. Mom was a veritable kitchen wizard. Avery, at barely twenty-five years of age, was the next Valentino in the making. I never begrudged them their successes, but at times I felt small by comparison.

"Mom, it looks amazing!" Avery enveloped me in a hug before gliding into the living room, which was decked out in the same Christmas decorations my parents had been using for decades. The same ornaments on the tree, the same set of reindeer statues on the coffee table, the same light-up ceramic tree with three missing bulbs that Avery and I had both adored so much that Mom found us each a replica of our own when we moved out. Mine was in a place of honor, the only holiday decoration I bothered with in my little one-bedroom Denver apartment.

My very favorite of their decorations was the display of fifteen little ceramic Santas from all over the world from various points in history. It had been a gift to Dad from some client at his firm when

I was a baby, and I'd been enamored with it since the time I was old enough to understand the holiday.

I walked to the wall where it hung and traced a finger on the bottom of the wooden display case with fifteen tiny nooks. From the 1925 pudgy American Santa, looking like he'd just finished shooting a Coca-Cola ad for *The Saturday Evening Post,* to the especially lean and regal Czech Father Christmas circa 1882. I loved how each culture had their version of the spirit of giving wrapped up in one man. I'd made up stories about them when I was a child. More specifically, I'd envisioned the treats each one would have brought to good children each year. The English Santa brought marzipan and toffees, the French one, almond nougat and chocolate truffles. The American one, of course, brought classic candy canes and Hershey's bars.

My nature-loving dad always insisted on a living tree that could be replanted after the holidays. Back when we were kids living in the city, he had donated the trees to the Forest Service, but now that he had enough land, each Christmas tree was planted in a place of honor on their acreage in the new year. The piney perfume it diffused in the living room was a million times more vibrant than the freshest cut tree. Mom and Dad's ability to make this place a haven left me with a tingling in my chest.

Avery linked her arm in mine. "Let's put our stuff under the tree."

"You got it." I grabbed the pile of wrapped gifts for the family from the corner where I'd deposited them. We got down on our hands and knees to add the presents to the beautifully wrapped packages Mom and Dad already had in place. Avery arranged and rearranged everything so she could get Instagram-worthy photos. Of the tree, of me in front of the tree, of us together, and a dozen selfies . . . so many I worried for the space on her phone's hard drive.

"People in New York will love this." I assumed she spoke to me, but her eyes were still glued to her screen. She was forever creating content for her social media feeds, and I knew I ought to be doing the same to help boost The Kitchen Muse, but I could never bring myself to be online nearly as much as she was.

She looked up and breathed contentedly, taking it all in without the phone as a barrier between her and the room. "A shop in the city would spend a fortune to bring in decorators who would spend months searching for vintage decor to replicate this vibe, and they'd never come close."

"Well, Mom and Dad have had about thirty-five years to curate their collection." I chuckled, as not a single piece had been "curated" to create an aesthetic. They were gifts or purchases made with love. "And you have to admit there isn't a store window in Manhattan that can compare to this—" I gestured to the expansive views of Longs Peak and Eagle Cliff out the window.

"Not even close. But the city does have a few charms. Not to mention some of the best restaurants in the world and a sleeper sofa always at your disposal. If you don't come see me, I'm going to start taking it personally."

I felt bad about that, as she'd been asking for three years now. I'd tried explaining to her a zillion times that money was tight and I couldn't afford travel that wasn't work related, but there was no convincing her.

As if hearing my thoughts—an annoying habit of hers—she prodded. "I'd buy the ticket. And if you won't take it from your kid sister, Dad would buy you one in a heartbeat."

"Are you spending more of my money, Avery?" Dad's mock-warning baritone rang from the kitchen. His hearing was uncanny when it came to his finances.

"To promote familial bliss and strengthen the bond between your daughters," she called back.

His tone lightened. "Carry on. You know my Amex number."

I rolled my eyes. Dad's joking reply wasn't really a joke at all. Avery was welcome to punch in the numbers to his Platinum Card whenever she needed it, and she had no compunction about doing so. There was no other way she could have lived in comfort and safety in New York, especially when she was first settling in, and Mom and Dad were glad to supplement her wages even now that she was more established.

"Things were different in the eighties and nineties when your mother and I were your age and getting started. I'd rather you spend your inheritances now and get ahead while you're young. It'll pay better dividends in the long run." Dad had repeated some version of this mantra regularly in the days when Avery was still hesitant to accept the money he offered freely.

That same offer would have been open to me, but I could never bring myself to accept it. I'd not asked Mom and Dad for a penny since college, beyond a few very candid answers about what I wanted for birthdays and Christmas when I was first starting out and desperate. I was adamant that I wouldn't start asking for cash, no matter how bleak the ledgers were. On some level it would have felt like my accomplishments weren't my own.

I nudged Avery, who just finished photographing the nativity set from her seventh angle. "To turn the tables back on you, I could have easily picked you up from the airport. You didn't have to get a rental."

She waved a hand dismissively. "Oh, I have so many travel points, they basically gave it to me. And I like having a car of my own, you know?"

I saw the logic. The likelihood a friend from Denver or Boulder would summon her to dinner was almost guaranteed. And it wasn't bluster that she'd already climbed the ladder to the point where trips to Milan and Paris were regular occurrences for her, and she was savvy enough to put all the expenses on a credit card with all sorts of travel perks before submitting her receipts to her company for reimbursement. She could probably get me a ticket to New York without making a dent in her frequent-flyer miles, but it didn't change the principle of the thing.

"It's hard for her to get away," Dad chimed in, trying to take my side. "Now that Denver is a Michelin city, her client list is apt to start booming more than it is now."

He cast me his best "I got you" glance, and I returned a smile. The recent addition of Denver as a Michelin city couldn't help but be a boon to business. Chefs who struggled to stand out in New York or LA, where the dining scene was so established, might have a shot at being noticed in Denver, where the competition was growing but there was room for fresh blood. We'd already seen a few promising restaurants set up in the last year, and there was bound to be more.

Avery got to her feet, offered me a hand, and hoisted me to my feet. "Come on, it's not like you wouldn't be able to network while you're there. What if some amazing restaurant in the city was dying for just the thing one of your artisans produces? It could be the making of them. Think of your clients, Veronica."

"Heaven forbid the girl just goes for a few nice meals and a Broadway show or two." Mom sighed and gestured for us to come to the table and tuck in. The lasagna was tradition because it used to be something Mama could make in advance and freeze so she could focus her time preparing for the main meal on Christmas Day. But we grew to love it even more than her fancier dishes, so she made more of a fuss over it. As time went on and our Christmas Day meals grew more casual, she insisted on making the lasagna fresh on Christmas Eve with her own homemade pasta and marinara. The mozzarella she bought from the local pizzeria that made their own, and she always used plenty of fresh basil.

"You must be glad the holidays are finally here." Avery accepted a helping from Dad. "I bet the lead-up is chaos."

"For sure. From Halloween to New Year's Eve is insane, same as retail. People go out to do their holiday shopping and stop for lunch. They get tickets to *The Nutcracker* at the Performing Arts Center, so they make a night of it with a four-star dinner before-hand and dessert and drinks after. Of course, with all the boost in business, the restaurants want to bring their A game. And that's not even getting into the boutique gourmet shop demand. Everyone becomes Julia Child over the holidays. I only get a few days to breathe because I got my clients stocked up early for the last push today, and they're mostly all closed tomorrow. My January 2 is like Dad's April 16 used to be."

"The best day of the year." Dad lifted a glass, clearly without much nostalgia for the office.

It was true: January was the doldrums for me. The kind that I looked forward to during the height of the summer tourist season and dreaded when it actually arrived. Some people were able to shift between the frenzied panic at work and downtime. My dad was one of those. Every single year, Dad took a long weekend off right after Tax Day, slept, and watched crap TV. He'd go fishing if he felt really ambitious, which wasn't often. Once the long weekend was over, one set of grandparents or the other would come to watch Avery and me for a week, and Dad whisked Mom someplace tropical to get out of the late-spring gloom. They counted down the minutes to it every year with the same enthusiasm Avery and I had anticipating Christmas morning.

For me, January was just when I tried to plan for the year ahead and hoped my clients would all weather the seasonal downturn with their businesses intact. There would be a small flurry of tourists coming for the famed National Western Stock Show, but they mostly flocked to either the dreaded chain restaurants or, in the best-case scenario, the nicer steak houses. They mostly gave the more adventurous upscale restaurants, my clients, a miss. There wouldn't be tropical vacations to celebrate the quiet season just yet, but I clung to the hope the time would come.

After dinner, so full we could barely walk, we gathered in the living room around the tree. Mom and Dad on their favorite chairs, I on the sofa, and Avery on the ottoman, poised to play Santa as she did every year. She'd had little patience for it as a kid but loved doling out presents slowly now that she was grown. She drew the evening out, giving us time to admire one another's gifts before moving on to the next. Add to that Dad's newer Christmas Eve tradition of serving a very nice bottle of champagne to enjoy as we opened the gifts, and it made for a lovely evening.

Mom loved the silk robe, and Dad was chuffed with the golf polos Avery had brought for them from her swanky contacts in New York. I gushed over the shoes she procured for me, even though the heels were so high I would probably never wear them. Part of me loved that she thought I was the sort of person who *would* wear them.

I'd done my best to supplement the food items I'd brought with real gifts, but there was no keeping up with Avery. The department store sweater, the little wooden house from the Denver Christkindlmarkt, and the alpaca scarf from the Estes Park Wool Market were received warmly enough, but I simply couldn't afford to be as generous as Avery, at least not with gifts. But, as always, Dad won at gifting. The photo album he'd had made of the heaps of photos from our summer trips to Estes over the years had Mom in tears.

"That looks like it," Dad proclaimed, unable to see anything left under the tree from his vantage point in the recliner. "A good haul. Apparently we fooled Santa again this year."

Avery sprung to her feet. "Not quite. I have one last gift for you all to finish off the evening." She rummaged in her massive purse and pulled out four small boxes, all brightly colored with vaguely science-adjacent graphics all over them. "A new DNA company, FamilyRoots, just rolled out home kits in time for the holidays. We share a building, and they gave us all a slew of these to be neighborly. They'd love reviews but probably don't expect them. Lots of good health info apparently. I thought you'd think they were fun . . . We can all take them."

Mom's and Dad's faces blanched. "Avery, I don't think this is a good idea." Mom stood and made a move like she wanted to take the tests from Avery's hands.

Avery swooped them away before Mom could intercept them. "Why? They keep the data secure. From some of the protocols their floor has in place, I believe them."

"It's not that," Dad said.

I took a hefty gulp of the champagne, which was likely a crime punishable by flogging in several *départements* in France, and set the flute aside. "It's because I was adopted, right?"

Chapter 2

S o how long have you known?" Avery asked later that night. She was dressed in pajamas, probably designer but not fussy, and her long dark hair was up in a messy bun. She didn't look so much like the New York fashionista but more like my kid sister this way. I liked her so much better like this. Less polish, more Avery. Mom had gone to bed, too upset to cope with the rest of the evening. Dad had enveloped me in a hug, then went to tend to Mom.

I'd assured them both that I was fine with it, but it didn't seem as if they liked the idea of my knowing after all these years.

"I began to suspect in high school when we learned basic genetic inheritance in science. My college science classes backed it all up. I have dimples, a dominant trait, and our parents and grandparents don't. The red hair is recessive, but it's rare to have no others with it in the family. Same with green eyes. Height, body shape . . . It all added up."

She reached over and grabbed my hand. "Why didn't you say anything?"

"Because, honestly? I didn't really care. Mom and Dad raised me. They're my parents. Biology doesn't matter." I'd said those words to myself a million times over the years, figuring if I repeated the line often enough, I might convince myself it was true.

I leaned back on the mountain of pillows in the room designated as mine when I came to stay in Estes. It boasted a rough-hewn log bed and a comforter adorned with black bears. Mom leaned into the cozy mountain motif without being kitschy, and I'd always found the room restful.

A knock on the door preceded my best friend since grade school, Stephanie Conway, breezing in without waiting for a reply. She was dressed for a chic Denver party, in a red sequined 1920s retro dress, but had a posh weekender tote, which probably cost as much as a year's worth of my rent, slung over her left arm and a high-end bottle of Australian Shiraz in her right hand. Armed for battle. She was only two months my senior but seemed ages more sophisticated than I was.

"You did *not* have to leave your Christmas Eve party and drive almost two hours in the dark for me." My words were muffled into her shoulder. Like Avery, she was tall, but she was all golden blonde and Nordic features to Avery's Italianate beauty.

"This seems like a level-ten crisis. And is it not in the bestie handbook that any emergency level eight or higher requires immediate personal attention and decent liquor?"

"Point well-taken," Avery responded for me, patting a space on the bed for Stephanie.

The two got on so well, I was surprised that *they* weren't best of friends, but the two never bonded to that degree. Was it simply too much personality between the two of them to spend extended amounts of time in the same room? They needed the freedom to absorb the light, so they surrounded themselves with people who could eke out survival in the shadows. People like me.

"I want every detail you didn't cram into the text." Stephanie's face was solemn as she went into damage-control mode. Calculating and rational at all times. Given that she was in PR, it was more or less her natural state. While Avery and Stephanie had loads in common when it came to clothes and lifestyle, Avery was more of the calm, creative "things will work out better if I don't get in the way" type when it came to anything that wasn't her work. Stephanie was always on duty, always problem-solving, even when she was supposed to be having fun, and I knew firsthand her consumption of black cold-brew coffee was more than any doctor would consider healthy.

I stammered out the whole embarrassing DNA-kit ordeal, complete with Mom and Dad practically needing CPR at the sight of them.

"Okay, so that is a huge thing to be going on with." Stephanie gently swayed back and forth as she did when pensive. "The fact that you haven't spontaneously combusted is amazing." Always lead with a positive. Boardroom Rule #1.

"Oh, I'm sure Avery has had to throw water on me a couple of times when she saw the smoke billowing from my nostrils."

Steph glared, impatience rippling off her like steam off a hot sidewalk. "Ha ha. Seriously. Are you going to be okay?"

I shrugged. "Yes. I mean, it is what it is, and I've had a long time to adjust to the idea."

"But have you really?" Stephanie widened her eyes in her signature *I could smell your BS all the way from Denver* look. "You never once mentioned this to me, your best friend since fifth grade. That doesn't seem like particularly 'fine with it' behavior."

"You're close to the family," I reasoned. "I didn't want to make things weird."

"So you just bottled it up and didn't process it at all," Stephanie countered. "This is too big to hold in. I don't care how strong you think you are, Vero. That's too much for anyone."

"It was hard, okay . . . I mean, it was a million slow realizations. It didn't happen all at once. What kid doesn't go through an 'I must be adopted' phase? Mine just didn't present any contradictory evidence when I searched for it. I mean, sure, Mom and Dad's names are on my birth certificate, but they amend those after adoption. Thanks to the internet, I learned that years ago."

"But surely you have other questions," Avery prodded.

I shrugged again. "To what end, really? I don't need to know the details about why Mom and Dad chose to adopt me when clearly they were capable of having kids." I nudged Avery for emphasis. I'd been too little to remember kissing Mom's expectant belly or Dad holding me up to see Avery in her little plastic bassinet at the hospital. But they had pictures of it all. Pictures of Mom with a baby bump with Avery, but none with me. That had been one of the clues that tipped me off.

"I never cared what agency they used, or if they met my birth parents. Maybe that makes me weird."

Stephanie exhaled. "There has to be *something* you want to ask."

"I *do* want to know if my birthday is accurate. That one has gnawed at me a bit."

"I get it. I mean what if you grew up thinking you're a Gemini only to find out you're really a Cancer? The world would cease to make sense." We dissolved into a pool of giggles, none of us being all that keen on astrology but fond of blaming our foibles on it all the same. Avery was the classic social Libra and Stephanie the visionary Leo. I was passionate Aries, and it did feel like a fit.

"Go ask. You know they aren't asleep yet." Avery pushed on my shoulder.

I gripped one of the bedposts so I didn't slide off. "It's not that big a deal. I can ask after Christmas."

A knock sounded at the door, which wasn't fully closed. Dad swung it open a beat later. "I came to ask if Stephanie needed anything to eat before bed, but I couldn't help but overhear the last bit of what you were saying. What do you want to ask, Veronica?"

I tossed a pillow at Avery, which she expertly dodged. "If someone had a volume setting slightly lower than a jackhammer, you might have been able to help overhearing."

Dad looked like he wanted to chuckle but wasn't equal to it. "I've missed the sound of you three laughing more than I realized. Your sister emitting a sonic boom notwithstanding, what is it that you want to know? Your mother and I want to help you through this."

I looked down at my hands, as if somehow I might find courage in the speckles of green glitter in my drugstore holiday nail polish. "Is my birthday really April third, or was that the day you adopted me?"

"Yes and yes," Dad replied. "We met you minutes after you were born and stayed with you overnight in the birth center like any other new parents and brought you home on the fourth. It was a three-way tie for the best day of my life, along with the day your sister was born and the day I married your mother." His head bowed to punctuate his sentence, the emotion thick in his voice.

I stood from my bed and enveloped him in a hug. "It doesn't change anything, but it's nice to know you were both there from the beginning."

"Thanks for that, shortcake. We wanted to tell you a long time ago, but all the records are sealed, and we had to fill out one hell of an NDA. No photos were allowed until we left the birth center grounds. It was a whole thing. We only met your birth mother for a few minutes and were never given her name for privacy reasons. You look just like her."

"So why adopt?" I couldn't help but ask.

"Well, your mom and I tried for a long time with no result. Then we let them run a few tests and we tried a few medications, but nothing worked. Rather than putting ourselves through an emotionally draining series of more invasive fertility treatments, we decided being parents was being more important than being pregnant, so we started the ball rolling with adoption."

I cocked a thumb in Avery's direction. "So explain that one."

Dad's face split into a genuine grin for the first time since Avery had produced the infernal kits. "Common enough tale. If a fertility-challenged couple adopts, the worry about having a baby goes away. When worry goes down, fertility goes up. We'd resigned ourselves to being a family of three, but Avery wasn't having it."

Avery winked at Dad. "Hey, I knew even then I wanted in on this party."

I tossed a pillow she'd deflected earlier back at her and turned to our dad. "Thanks, Dad. I appreciate hearing this from you."

He nodded, his voice still husky as he croaked out, "I'd better go check on your mom."

Avery wrapped an arm around me as I reclaimed my place on the bed. "You're taking this really well."

"Too well," Stephanie interjected. "Listen, I get that you're in shock, but you *will* need to process this at some point. If you bury it, it will eventually demand to be dug up. And it will be so much worse. Trust me."

Stephanie knew of what she spoke. She'd lost her dad when she was in her final year of college and was so focused on graduation, internships, and jobs that once she'd helped her mom and siblings manage the funeral, she "powered through" her grief and graduated summa cum laude in public relations from USC. She also had a breakdown a year later that nearly ended her career, but in true Stephanie inimitable fashion, she spun it and came out with her career intact.

"I know," I said. But it was mostly to appease them. It wasn't the same as losing a parent suddenly, like Stephanie had. I'd adjusted to the idea over a number of years.

"Have you texted Jonathan about all this?" Stephanie asked. "I'm amazed he's not here, despite hating the drive."

"Yeah, no. We broke up a few weeks ago."

"What?!" Avery sat up at attention, nearly upending her glass of wine on my bed. "I just thought he had stuff with his own family."

"Nope. It was hard, our schedules always being at odds. Retail and finance don't play nice together. It was wearing us both thin, really."

"Okay, I'm going to pass over the fact that you didn't tell your sister and best friend some pretty heavy news right away . . . but that is a pretty shoddy excuse for ending a four-year relationship."

I leaned my head back against the pillows. "We got to the 'all or nothing' precipice of our relationship, and we decided 'nothing' was the right path for us. Better now than five years down the road with a kid or two in the mix."

"That's true, but why do I get the feeling that 'we' is really just 'he' in this case?" Stephanie leaned forward, giving me her trademark no-nonsense stare.

"He initiated things," I admitted. "But that doesn't mean he was wrong."

"Maybe not, but you'd have tried if he wanted to, right?" Avery took another sip of Shiraz.

"For sure." I didn't hesitate, because that's how I was made—one didn't just bail on a relationship, especially a long-term one, without heroic efforts to make things work. But I was pragmatic enough to know I couldn't be the only one making them if it stood a chance of working.

Avery sat up straighter, indignant on my behalf. "All the better, then. Not to be mean or anything, but I always thought you were selling yourself short. He was okay, and I'd have loved him like a brother for your sake, but he was never worthy of your level of awesome."

Stephanie raised her glass and clinked it against Avery's. "Amen to that. Keep fishing, Vero."

"If either of you gives me a single platitude about all the fish in the sea, I will personally tie-dye those ritzy pajamas in red wine." The glare I shot Avery could have probably turned her to stone.

"Oh gawd don't. She's in fashion. I could not handle if wine tie-dye became a thing." Stephanie rubbed her temples, as if the very idea was threatening to give her a migraine.

"Well now I have a concept to pitch in January, thanks." Avery flashed me a wink that earned her yet another pillow in the face from Stephanie. Stephanie's expression warned that if the designer labels were carrying a line of wine tie-dye next spring, there would be consequences.

Despite their levity, my head drooped onto my bent knees. "I'm sorry I've screwed up the holidays."

"Come on." Stephanie now lobbed the pillow at my bowed head. "You didn't ask for any of this crap. Jonathan is an idiot and doesn't know what he's missing. And we have to credit Avery with bringing up the adoption issue."

"I *do* feel like an idiot." Avery's expression grew somber. "I knew you and I looked different, but I never thought of you as anything other than my big sister. It literally never occurred to me."

Tears threatened in my ducts, and I was losing the battle to keep them at bay.

"Love blinders," Stephanie supplied. "You saw the family as you imagined it."

"I saw the family as it was." Avery's tone was absolute. "It doesn't really matter what the test says. Vero is one of us. She's a Stratton with some borrowed DNA."

I wrapped an arm around her. "That means a lot. Thank you, Stinkerbell."

She stuck her tongue out at me, but Stephanie was pensive. "Why don't you take the test, Veronica? I'm not saying you need to go make Hallmark-esque memories with your birth family, but it could be interesting to know some of the details. Medical history if nothing else."

"Why not?" I wiped my face on the pillow, making a mental note to wash my linens before I left to spare Mom the trouble.

Avery fetched the box I'd left, long abandoned in the living room. "I'll take your sample back with me and pull some favors to get it run quickly."

I accepted the box, peering dubiously at the bright colors, then took a steadying breath. "You don't have to go to any trouble."

"Oh trust me, they would love to do this for me." She batted her eyelashes demurely, and I could all too easily imagine a bevy of genetics nerds tripping over themselves for the honor of being in Avery's debt. It had been that way since middle school.

I opened the box and read the directions. Ugh. I would have to fill a vial with saliva. Not a fun process. I waited thirty minutes for the wine residue in my mouth to dissipate and prepared my sample for Avery to take back to New York. All while Avery and Stephanie laughed hysterically at my attempts to produce enough spit.

"So, thanks for hauling my drool back to New York," I said lamely, handing her the sealed tube with my sample.

"It seems like the least I can do, given that I basically sent Mom into vapors like someone out of an Austen novel." She tucked the pouch safely in her bag.

For the rest of the night, I thought about the sample and what it might reveal and hoped I wouldn't be too disappointed with the results—whatever they might bring.

Chapter 3

By mid-January I was convinced the DNA result would come up as part bear, so adept I'd become at hibernating. I'd spent the entire afternoon in my favorite faded flannel pajamas, eating ice cream and watching the most recent season of *The Great British Bake Off*, which I'd largely missed due to the holiday rush. As I binged, my mind wandered to Jonathan, who always seemed irritated that I had my low season when he was heading into tax season.

When my work was too busy to accommodate his plans, he had a tendency to pout about how the other wives and girlfriends in his office were able to schedule their vacations to coincide with their partners'. All of them were either stay-at-home mothers, had otherwise flexible jobs, or were in finance themselves, making the sync easier.

Unless I left the food business altogether, there was no way I could have been that accommodating. And the truth was that he shouldn't have expected me to be. Of course, it wasn't Jonathan who designed the fiscal calendar or set the timetable for Tax Day, but there was no denying that his schedule in finance and mine more closely aligned with retail, were always—and by design—at odds. It made sense that the retail and finance sectors would have complementary calendars so each could serve the other, but it didn't facilitate the running of a relationship at all.

For four years, we'd been a bird and a fish trying to build a home together. We'd always told each other that we'd find a way to make our disparate lives mesh, but it was a ridiculously optimistic notion. The more I considered it, the more foolish it felt.

But despite being only responsible for half the implosion of our relationship, I still felt like a failure.

And the naked truth was that I missed Jonathan. Or at least the idea of him. Something was unsettling about feeling isolated in the world, and even if the rational part of me knew that our relationship had a lot of barriers, I couldn't help but wish we'd been able to sort things out.

On the fifth episode of *Bake Off*, my attention began to wander as they fumbled over an ice cream–based dessert. Ice cream episodes were usually painful to watch as the challenge always seemed to fall on the hottest day of summer. The result was soggy desserts and lots of tears on what was usually a low-drama show. I hated seeing good bakers set up for failure. I thought about clicking it off to go test some recipes in the kitchen, but I just didn't feel up to it. I let myself tune out for this segment of the show and pulled out my phone. An email dinged on my screen from my business account:

Hi Veronica,

The bespoke vanilla was a genius idea, and it was an absolute hit. Record profits for the restaurant. Please thank your vendor for us. We'll be in touch about a consult for the late spring and summer menus. Looking forward to hearing more of your ideas—you've got great instincts there, Stratton.

All the best,

E. Fairbanks

Edward Fairbanks was the chef and proprietor at his restaurant, 540 Blake, which was fast becoming one of the trendiest restaurants in the city. And, like every restaurant in town, Fairbanks used Valentine's Day as a lure after the January slump. Denver Restaurant Week, on the other hand, was its own special mess. The first week of March, every restaurant worth its real estate showed off its best moves to the local crowd of avid restaurant-goers in an event designed to bolster the dining scene. It was when chefs tested new dishes and experimented with new menus for the upcoming tourist season.

I loved and hated Restaurant Week. It was great for business, and it was an opportunity to entice people to try new restaurants in hopes they'd become regulars. But the constant one-upmanship between the restaurants, all trying to outdazzle one another, was usually exhilarating but occasionally mean-spirited. The latter grew tiresome, and I was in the thick of it. They all wanted the inside track on the best, the freshest, and the most innovative ingredients. And I'd done just that for Edward. I'd procured a massive stock of homemade vanilla in all sorts of flavors from Mom's cache and sold it to him at a premium. Mom pocketed the bulk of the profit, but my cut had helped see me through December.

But more than that, I'd spent weeks with Edward creating an innovative menu for Valentine's Day and Restaurant Week. Everything from sauces for the savory dishes, decadent desserts, and some of the best cocktails I'd ever had. Landing that consulting gig had been a huge opportunity, and it seemed like it could lead to more work in the coming months. If my luck held, it could snowball into a long-term contract—and a long-term paycheck. And once Fairbanks began to thrive, my business would hopefully ascend to the next level.

It was something to cling to when my personal life was basically a dumpster fire. And like everything else in the restaurant business, there were no guarantees. Fairbanks could find a fresh new consultant, and I'd be exactly where I was now . . . watching reality TV and waiting for the January doldrums to come to an end.

I was about to switch off *Bake Off* and search for something entirely nonfood related to keep me from dissolving into a puddle, when I was pulled from my fog by the sounds of a rustling at my door and a key in the lock. For a moment I thought it might be Jonathan and was more than a little relieved to hear Stephanie's voice in the entryway. *Time to get my key back from him.*

"Yeah, I'm here. Give me a minute to get set up." Stephanie angled the phone away from her mouth. "Get out your laptop and fire up FaceTime. It's Avery."

"Great to see you too. No, I didn't have plans for the evening. Would be thrilled if you could stop by. So glad you let yourself in. I don't regret giving you a key at all."

She rolled her eyes. "Glad we have that established. Your results are in. Chop-chop."

I blinked, having expected that the results would take at least a month, perhaps two, before they landed in my inbox. Then again, Avery's charms were . . . formidable. I motioned for Stephanie to join me at the kitchen table that served as the only real dining space in my tiny one-bedroom downtown apartment. I willed the less-than-speedy machine to hurry along and clicked through a pile of menus until Avery's face took over my laptop screen. She wore an evening dress and sparkling fake eyelashes. They would have been garish on anyone else, but she had the gravitas to pull them off. She was on her way to some posh fashion gala, one of many, but was unfazed by taking a call in her office in formal wear.

"The document should be in your inbox, totally secure," Avery said. "I had them send it directly to you so I wouldn't be tempted to peek."

"So you're going to just read over my shoulder remotely from New York?" My tone was dry.

"No, you can read it for yourself, but we'll be here for moral support." Stephanie nudged me with her elbow. "You shouldn't be alone for this. Avery and I planned it."

Of course they did. I exhaled. Really, I probably would have preferred to be alone to read it over and begin to process *whatever* the report contained. But they wanted to be here for me, and it wasn't something I should take for granted. Stephanie scooted her chair so she couldn't easily see my computer screen but was less than an arm's length away if I needed her.

I shoved the window for the video call off to one corner and proceeded to my email, where a complicated set of instructions logged me into a website with all sorts of medical data, lists of relatives, and ancestry reports all waiting for me to begin clicking. It was almost overwhelming in scope, and I could have been there for hours.

I started with the easiest. The medical reports were favorable. A slightly increased likelihood for glaucoma and a higher-than-average predisposition for restless leg syndrome didn't seem too bad a fate for my old age. No markers for various cancers, Alzheimer's, or any of the really nefarious conditions they tested for. I filled Avery and Stephanie in on those details, to which they seemed appropriately pleased, though their impatience for the juicier details was thinly veiled.

I then clicked over to the ancestry. Very Western European. I was very fair skinned and was not surprised to see the result, but I'd perhaps hoped for something a little more unexpected. A family line that traced back to some remote corner of the Middle East or Africa?

But no. "One hundred percent euro mutt," I declared to the girls.

"Not unexpected," Stephanie said. "You could get a sunburn in an indoor shopping mall in February."

I rolled my eyes in her direction. "Gee thanks. It shows mainly like Irish, Danish, and French ancestry with a small trace of Italian." That last bit *was* perhaps the most interesting. I could very well imagine that Mom and Avery had some Italian heritage, perhaps Dad too, though his surname was classically English.

"I'd have laid odds on Ireland with that hair," Avery mused. "And the rest makes sense too. You certainly cook and eat like a French or Italian woman. Some Danish bone structure too."

"I can see it." I nodded.

"Okay, how about the last tab?" Stephanie prodded.

My hands shook as I dragged my index finger over the track pad. I clicked on the final tab to see a list of names and how closely the genetic data believed we were related. It was still blank, and relief rushed through my veins. Over the years I'd considered the possibility of a whole other family out in the world, but the prospect of meeting them didn't hold much appeal for me. I didn't need to hunt down distant relatives in a desperate hope to kindle a relationship built on tenuous genetic bonds when my own family loved me more than they ever could.

I angled the laptop so Stephanie could see, a sign of trust. "Nothing at all."

Avery waved her hand. "They warned me that was likely. The database keeps growing and you're an early adopter. But the rest is interesting, isn't it? To know where your ancestors came from at least?"

I scanned the map that showed the countries in various shades of pink and red, based on how likely it was that my ancestors had originated there, with large swaths of the globe left gray. It did feel strange to see the small corners of the world that were . . . mine. In a manner of speaking anyway.

I shrugged. "I guess it feels like a few small pieces of the Veronica puzzle are coming together."

I had in my head a vision of a jigsaw puzzle jumbled in a box. You could only see bits and fragments of the picture; most were obscured or flipped over to the brown kraft paper backing. We'd just begun flipping the pieces and testing the fit of thousands of knobs and sockets of the intricate puzzle that formed my life. I hoped against hope that I'd like the image once we began to make sense of it.

"Well this certainly is nice," Mom said, placing the crisp white napkin across her lap.

"I'm glad you came down," I said. It had been months since Mom and Dad had made the trek down the mountain to see me, and she'd never made the trip solo before. But lately the unexpected wasn't the rarity it once had been.

"I just wanted to see your face. You're so good about calling, but it's not the same." She beamed across the table before scanning the menu. Her eyes flashed wide when she noticed the prices next to the entrées.

I leaned in, conspiratorially. "Don't worry, Fairbanks says it's on the house as a thank-you for the vanilla. And a veiled bribe for you to sell him more."

When Mom had said she was coming down to Denver for the day and wanted to get together for lunch, I'd immediately thought of taking her to 540 Blake so she could sample what Fairbanks and I had done with her handiwork. As the vanilla additions to the menu were doing so well, he was glad for the chance to play host.

Mom shook her head, a wry exasperation sacred unto mothers. "Well, of course I'll sell him more, for your sake. No bribes necessary."

I placed a finger to my lips and winked. "Not too loud or he won't comp the table."

Her eyes flitted back to the menu. "Fair point. Your father isn't a frugal man, not these days, but my heavens, this would cause even him to go pale."

I shot her a knowing look. Fairbanks was a hell of a chef, and his concept was solid, but he forgot he wasn't in New York anymore. Denver was growing younger, hipper, and a lot more expensive . . . but Manhattan we were not. I'd gently raised the issue with him, but he waved it off with a trite explanation that he didn't want to lose cachet by becoming "too accessible."

Mom's eyes took in the room. "Anyway, it does seem like a nice special-occasion place. I can imagine lovely rehearsal dinners here. And power lunches to boot."

"Definitely. It's got the white linen thing down." And it did have the feel of a place one would take an important client or a date one really wanted to impress. The ambiance was a little bland for my liking: The same minimalist décor and clean lines one saw at any high-end restaurant. There wasn't any creativity in the crisp white linens, the plain bone china with a gold band on the edges, or the art on the walls that might have come from any random furniture store. I knew what Fairbanks was doing. He was trying to minimize the distractions from his food. Given that his nouveau-industrial venture in New York had been a colossal failure that was still chuckled about in the inner circles of the restaurant world, it was probably best that he play it safe.

But my gut told me he was taking that impulse several steps too far. In trying to avoid his previous mistakes, he had taken the soul out of the place and boiled it in bleach.

Fairbanks himself emerged a few minutes later, bringing us each a glass of a light white wine meant to tantalize the palate and entice the appetite. He was a tall man, broad chested, with just the barest hint of silver at his temples. He greeted my mother like they were old friends, though they had only ever communicated through me.

Fairbanks pulled out the spare chair and spoke in low tones as if conveying a state secret. "I wonder if you ladies wouldn't let me prepare you something off book today? I've been playing with some new ideas Veronica and I've been tossing around, and I'd really love your feedback."

"No such thing as a free lunch, am I right?" I said to Mom, put upon, as if he were asking us to wash dishes instead of sampling whatever marvel he was concocting.

Fairbanks smiled, a sight I'd rarely witnessed, given how high tensions ran in his kitchen. "You know it, Stratton. Are you game?"

I crossed my arms in defiance. "Always, Fairbanks. Impress us."

He gave a mock salute and headed back to his kitchen

"Trust me, this will be good," I assured Mom. "But if there is something on the menu you really wanted to try, we can let him know."

"It'll be wonderful, darling, I'm sure." She had her hands laced in her lap, and I saw the telltale jiggle of her knee, which always bounced when she was nervous.

"Everything okay?" It was a stupid question, really. The DNA test had shaken the foundation of our family after more than a decade of my trying my best to keep everything stable by keeping the whole thing to myself. I reached a hand across the table. "You know a little cardboard box and a plastic tube of spit doesn't change anything, right?"

She squeezed my hand. "It does, Veronica. Whether we want it to or not. It doesn't change the things that really matter, but we can't pretend that having the whole thing out in the open won't take some adjusting."

"I suppose that's true." I knew it was asinine, but I felt the pricking in my gut, like a dozen tiny daggers whenever I'd indulged in the worry that my parents might think of me differently—love me less—if my status as an adoptee was no longer a secret.

"Your sister called us after the results came in. She didn't tell us much, to respect your privacy, but she, your father, and apparently Stephanie cooked up a scheme. One I want you to consider."

I took a fortifying sip of the wine, making a mental note to snap a photo of the label before we left. "Go on, then."

She exhaled slowly. "We want you to go to Europe, our treat."

I blinked. "Umm . . . Why?"

"So you can process everything, dear. This is not something small, no matter what you might tell yourself."

I leaned back in my seat. "But why do I have to go all the way to Europe to process what's happening here?" I gestured between the two of us. "It seems rather counterintuitive."

"Your father thinks you won't deal with things if you're at home.

You'll lose yourself in your work and sweep it all under the rug. You're just like him in that respect. We think taking some much-needed time off will maybe give you the headspace you need to deal with this. Or start dealing with it, anyway."

"I don't know, Mom. A week or two in Europe sounds fun, but I don't know if now's the right time."

She gave me the kind of pointed glance I hadn't seen since my teen years. "There never will be a right time. And it's a month, dear. Avery and Stephanie have it all sorted. Once I send them a text, the whole thing will be booked within a quarter of an hour. A week each in Ireland, France, Italy, and Denmark. Enough time to see the places properly."

I gasped. "A month? Mom, that's insane. I have work."

"You can answer emails from Ireland as well as you can from your studio. Your clients won't wither away without you for a few weeks. It will be a chance for you to see all the places your ancestors came from and get a change of scenery. It will be good for your soul, Veronica."

"This sounds so very much like Avery. Why were *you* selected as family emissary if it was their idea? Avery has never been one to share the credit for one of her ideas." Which was part of the reason she was already so successful at her job.

She exhaled slowly. "Because Avery, Stephanie, and even occasionally your father, are far too free with their powers of persuasion. I wanted to honestly give you the choice to go without their bulldozing you."

I scoffed. "You're not exactly being impartial, Mom."

She took a pull from her own glass of wine. "No, I'm not. I think it's a brilliant idea, really. But if you truly don't want to go, I won't force the issue. I don't think the others would extend you such courtesy."

I snorted a laugh. Were Avery left to her own devices, it would have been booked on Dad's Amex before she bothered to tell me where I was going. "You're right about that."

"I usually am, dear."

Just then, Fairbanks emerged with our appetizer: panko shrimp served with a vanilla-infused beurre blanc. I'd spent hours in the kitchen with him fiddling with the right ratio of vanilla extract to vinegar in the beurre blanc and the right consistency of the bread-crumbs for the shrimp coating. The shrimp were the best to be had and were pan-fried to perfection, but there was no denying that the creamy vanilla butter sauce with the earthy notes and arresting tang had stolen the show.

Fairbanks stood silently, but as stoic as he was, he couldn't keep the expectation from his face. *What do you think?* was all but etched on his forehead.

I decided to relieve him of his misery. "You used the Madagascar in bourbon for this . . . I told you."

"As much as it pains me to say it, you were right. The Tahitian in the rum was too sweet. The Mexican in the whiskey was too over-powering. You've got good instincts, Stratton."

I mused. "Use the Mexican in individual chocolate lava cakes at Valentine's and you won't have an empty seat in the house for the rest of the year."

"Like I said, good instincts." He hurried back to the kitchen, pre-sumably to prepare our main course.

I turned back to Mom, who was on her third shrimp, looking more pensive than the eating of crustaceans usually called for. "Don't you like it?"

"Darling girl, it's possibly the best thing I've eaten in my entire life."

She didn't speak with pride but rather remorse. She didn't voice the words, knowing that they'd just lead to a rehashing of an argument more than ten years standing. What was the point in consulting with other restaurants and playing food matchmaker when I could be running a kitchen of my own?

As though picking up a discarded dream after a decade was as simple as riding a bike.

Mom focused back on me, swallowing the lecture she so longed to give. And I loved her for it. "Listen, darling, just think about going, please? I don't know if it will even begin to help you sort through everything, but it will make me feel better knowing that you at least had some space to do it."

I forced down a deep breath. "I promise, Mom."

We continued the rest of the meal in amicable conversation, never really discussing how either of us was coping with the results from the little cardboard box and plastic vial of spit, but neither of us could summon the courage to ask. After all this time stifling my feelings, hiding them from her and Dad, to voice them now seemed contrary to my every instinct.

But nothing could ever go back to normal until I dealt with the maelstrom whirling in my head. And I wondered if just maybe Avery's scheme didn't have a bit of merit. But even if it didn't, as I looked across at the woman beaming with pride at the recipes I'd helped a master chef create, I knew I owed it to her to try.

Chapter 4

Week One: Ireland

E very website I'd researched listed January as one of the months best avoided in Ireland, and so far none of them were wrong. It was cold, bleak, and rainy, and the daylight hours were incredibly short this far north. Avery and Stephanie dove headlong into planning this trip, and no amount of thoughtful planning or color-coded itineraries could change the realities of the weather. But they were right that offseason travel would be far less disruptive to my work, and taking several weeks off in better weather would be next to impossible.

As I'd hauled my suitcase through the Denver airport the better part of a day before, I had resolved I wasn't going to sulk the whole time. I *was* excited to sample anything made with Irish cheese and butter. France and Italy had boatloads of culinary delights in store. I even held out hope for some unique finds in Denmark, which had a world-class restaurant scene. I'd resolved this would be a useful trek, if not an enjoyable holiday in the traditional sense.

If I was going to go on this madcap trip on Avery's and my parents' dimes, I would use it for the benefit of The Kitchen Muse so I could dazzle Fairbanks and the others on my return. I'd find new vendors, find new products, find new inspiration. *That* was my mission beyond whatever ancestral sentiment the family was hoping to evoke in me.

Had I planned the trip myself, I'd have given myself several weeks instead of a few days' worth of lead time. I would have read up on the places myself, researched where to go. I would have reached out to potential business contacts well in advance to potentially make the trip a more profitable one. But I would have to make the best contacts I could on the fly.

I barely had the chance to download a few travel apps on my phone and to peruse Stephanie's hyperdetailed itinerary. I hoped I wouldn't regret not purchasing paper guides and maps to lug around. I'd discovered that if there were two uncertainties in travel, they were the availability of reliable Wi-Fi and the dependability of the battery on my six-year-old smartphone when I needed them. But when Stephanie had come over to help me pack, I'd conceded that traditional guidebooks would have added more weight than I wanted to bother with. I'd simply have to hope my luck would hold out and I'd be able to navigate to where I needed to go.

Avery had sent an overnight express care package of clothes for the trip, and the sheer amount of merino wool layering pieces and waterproof outerwear was staggering. She insisted merino was lightweight and compact to be practical for packing—far less bulky than my usual winter wear in Denver—but still warm enough and water resistant to stand up to the January climes in the north. Of course she'd also thrown in a few brightly colored scarves and other fun accessories to lift the darker, muted tones of the merino. Winter climes were no excuse not to look one's best, after all.

My head was buzzing from jet lag, and I wanted nothing more than to take a nap, but I was hours away from my B and B on the outskirts of Westport on the opposite side of the country, and to nap at eight in the morning would have been disastrous for my internal clock. My train to Westport wasn't for another three hours, and I found myself in the heart of Dublin with time to kill and an over-whelming sense of gratitude that I'd heeded Avery's advice to travel with only a carry-on.

There wasn't much within a stone's throw of the train station aside from the Guinness Open Gate Brewery, which wasn't all that appealing in the early morning, so Stephanie's itinerary suggested I use the time to prowl around the pedestrian mall on Grafton Street. Most everything was still closed, but at least a few places should be showing signs of life.

I wasn't much of a shopper, much to Avery's consternation, but there were any number of good restaurants I could peek in on. A lot could be discerned from a glance through the windows and gleaned from the menus posted outside. Even if overshadowed by London and Paris, Dublin was regarded warmly in the restaurant world. It boasted a handful of Michelin-starred restaurants and was similar to Denver in that it was a Goldilocks city in terms of the restaurant scene—big enough to matter, small enough to stand a chance.

After perusing the restaurant fronts for an hour and filling my phone with a long list of notes, the cold was beginning to wear on me. There weren't any kitchenware stores, so I ducked inside a quirky-looking thrift shop called Objets Trouvés—"found objects"—in a building that was probably a hundred years older than the city of Denver. The façade was a stately green, but the sign was colorful and delightfully bohemian.

I'd taken to thrift shopping to save money while avoiding "fast fashion," but I really knew nothing about the art of thrifting. I wouldn't know the difference between a five-dollar Goodwill shirt that could be resold for two hundred dollars and one that was barely worth the cost of the price tag, but I did find the hunt for pieces that seemed well-made and flattering to be a fun exercise in small doses.

The selection in Dublin was different from back home, to be sure. Denver's thrift shops housed a collection of two- to five-year-old cast-off clothes from all the recognizable mid-level brands; this assortment was far more eclectic. I found myself wandering the racks and not knowing why. I perused outdated blazers, all manner of blouses, and an eclectic collection of handbags before happening onto the dresses in the back of the shop. There was everything from barely there sequined numbers that would have looked at home in Vegas to the most horrendous avocado-green jumpsuit that was something out of a seventies horror film.

I almost passed up the garment bag altogether, not wanting to bother with zippers to reveal the contents, but when my hand touched the hanger, I felt an unshakable tingling in the tips of my fingers. I unzipped the plastic sheath to reveal a flawless lace gown that almost literally stole my breath.

"Oh, that's a lovely thing, isn't it?" The shopkeeper had materialized out of nowhere at my elbow. "It's a pity to think it's been here so long. More than ten years now. I know it's daft, but I couldn't bear to bin it for the charity haul like so many places like this do after a few weeks."

"No," I agreed, gently running my fingers along the pristine lace.

She showed me the label at the neck of the gown. It was an old-fashioned embroidered script on the tag that made me think the dress was from the 1940s or even earlier and was far more yellowed with age than the dress itself. "Do you know Ordaithe? It was a fine house back in its day. They don't make dresses like this anymore."

I blinked. "The dress looks brand-new. Maybe the label was switched?"

She shook her head. "I did a bit of research, and this was a style they made shortly after the war when fine fabrics were easier to get your hands on and before the 1950s when shorter wedding gowns and fuller skirts became en vogue. The lass who brought it in had it restored and then backed out on the wedding. She pressed it into my hands and refused to take a penny for it. Poor dear was in a right state."

"Oh, that's too bad." I stroked my finger along the lace. It had to have cost a fortune when it was new, and I felt a twinge of sadness for the unhappy bride-to-be and the unwanted gown. Both deserved better.

"It just wasn't her time to be married and it wasn't her gown. It just happens that way sometimes. I do hope she finds what she was looking for eventually."

"Me too." I'd never met this woman, but I couldn't help but imagine she'd been in a low moment when she'd given up such a lovely gown.

I felt compelled to know how this saleswoman seemed to *know* after ten years that she hadn't found someone, but the question died on my tongue. She looked from me to the lace dress and back again, her expression pensive. But rather than pressing for a sale, she zipped up the bag.

The muscles in my neck loosened a bit . . . The last thing I wanted to do was try on a wedding dress so soon after a breakup. I wasn't sentimental about clothes, but even I wasn't immune to the mystique of a wedding dress.

"I'm guessing based on your accent and your suitcase, you're here on holiday from the States?"

I nodded. "Obvious, is it?"

She smiled warmly. "Well, yes. Though most of your country-men tend to come in the warmer months and travel in packs. You're rather cunning to come in the offseason."

"Cunning or supremely stupid?"

"Most assuredly cunning. I see you've got a decent coat and wel-lies on." I looked down at the waterproof winter coat and boots Avery had shipped out. The coat was sturdy and lined in merino wool against the cold but managed to be reasonably stylish in the process. The boots were, mercifully, not the usual death traps she favored. "Your skin isn't a violent shade of green like the Wicked Witch of the West. I don't think you need to worry about melting in the rain. Far better to see our fair island when she isn't overrun."

"You're probably right about that," I conceded half-heartedly. I wasn't as quick to discount the short daylight hours and colder tem-peratures as a travel deterrent.

"You need a trinket to commemorate your travels." The shop-keeper ushered me toward a case in the front. She removed a thick silver bangle with gilded edges that was patterned with intricate scroll-work and a filigreed disc in the center resembling a shield. "A warrior maiden's cuff, my dear girl. A reminder of your own strength."

She affixed the bangle on my wrist. I wasn't used to wearing bracelets, as they often got in the way in the kitchen, but the weight of the thing was pleasant on my wrist. It was the weight that gave me pause. That much silver had to be expensive. "How much?" I asked, ready to find the clasp and return it to her in a heartbeat.

"Five euro, dear. Consider the discount a welcome present." She patted my hand like an old family friend, and I felt like I was taking advantage of this kindly woman's misplaced benevolence.

"I couldn't possibly. That's far too generous."

"Nonsense, my dear. You wouldn't deny an old woman the pleasure of a small gesture of welcome to a guest in her country?" Her eyes, which I noticed then were a remarkable shade of blue, were pleading.

"Very well," I acquiesced. My eyes scanned the shop as I pulled out my wallet. My gaze settled on a small Santa figurine resembling the collection my parents displayed each year. Slenderer than his American counterpart, clad in green rather than red, but unmistakably Santa. He had a pine tree slung over his shoulder and a doll and a lyre clipped to his belt for the sleeping children. I was sure this was one Mom and Dad didn't have and would be pleased to add to their collection. "Only if you let me buy the little Santa there for double the price."

Her face broke into a smile as she heaved an insincere sigh. "You drive a hard bargain, miss, but so be it. Twenty euro for the lot and not a penny more."

I handed her the colorful bill, adorned with arched windows rather than a political figure, which she accepted. She wrapped up the small figurine in some tissue and placed it in a handled shopping bag.

She took me in with her intense blue eyes as handed me the bag. "I do believe you're going to have an extraordinary time while you're here with us, my dear. I hope you'll come see me again to tell me all about your adventures."

I exited the shop, pleased with the trinket I'd found for Mom and Dad but somewhat baffled by my interaction with the shopkeeper and a bit distracted by the bangle on my wrist. Why a shopkeeper would go out of her way to give an expensive piece of jewelry to a tourist when she was certain to see hundreds of us every year, I couldn't be sure. But I loved the idea of a token to remind me of my strength. With the upheavals of the past few weeks, such a trinket couldn't come amiss.

Chapter 5

The weight of the warrior's cuff on my wrist pulled at me like one of the many thoughts swirling in the typhoon inside my skull.

As the train from Dublin rumbled toward the ragged western coast of Ireland, I tried to clear my mind of the exchange with the shopkeeper and return to my research for The Kitchen Muse. Unfortunately, there was no market research to be done on a moving train beyond the meager options in the café car, but I could permit myself a few moments to brood and dream of a hot shower and a dram of Irish whiskey while thumbing through the Michelin app and other online food resources to scout out places to try. I was impressed by the number of acclaimed restaurants in the country, which I had to confess was never one I'd associated with great culinary prowess beyond cheese, butter, potatoes, and perhaps seafood on the coast.

Westport was home to just over six thousand inhabitants, so roughly the size of my parents' beloved Estes Park, and was the third largest city in County Mayo. Stephanie and Avery chose this for my base of operations in Ireland based on the map in the DNA report and the fact that it was, reportedly, a charming small coastal town with sweeping views of the Atlantic. Despite the gloomy skies, it wasn't the worst idea they'd had.

At midday, after three hours of whirring past green countryside, the train pulled into Westport, which was bustling enough in winter that it must have been teeming in summer. I got only the barest glimpse of the town as we pulled into the station, but the colorful shop fronts must have been designed to defy the bleak gray of midwinter. I hoped the vast quantities of wool Avery had sent would be enough to combat the frigid air. Denver was colder and certainly a lot snowier than the west of Ireland, but the damp air had a way of seeping into the bones, making you feel like you'd never again be properly warm.

Apart from the staff milling about, only one man waited at the train station, sitting with a curtain of newsprint between him and the world. The rest who descended from the train with me appeared to be locals who had gone to Dublin for shopping, amusement, or simply to give themselves a change of scenery to break up the postholiday monotony and headed straight to their own vehicles in the car park.

I wheeled my case to the waiting area, where I planned to inquire after a taxi or rideshare as the bed-and-breakfast appeared to be too far to walk. Why Stephanie and Avery had decided to book a place so far out of the way was beyond me.

"Are you Veronica Stratton?" The man cast aside his newspaper. His brogue was lyrical but not so thick that I felt like I was trying to parse a foreign language. "I considered making a sign like they do in your American movies, but to own the truth of it, even the thought of it made me feel like an arse."

I hesitated. Denver wasn't a big, scary city in the way New York or LA was, but it was urban enough that a person learned to be wary of strangers. But then my more rational side caught up with me. Only one reasonable scenario existed in which this stranger knew my name: He worked at the bed-and-breakfast and had my information from the reservation. It wasn't a stretch to think Avery had shared my arrival time with him. Heck, if she'd even given him a ballpark estimate of my arrival time, he could have easily guessed which train I'd be on.

"Yes?" I was annoyed at the hesitance in my voice but tried not to appear flustered. I assessed the man. Tall, dark curly hair under a woolen flat cap, broad shoulders, and gray-blue eyes. Not the freckled red-haired Irish stereotype that I was. He was definitely good-looking, but not intimidatingly so, and thankfully didn't appear particularly threatening. I gathered myself. "Are you with the bed-and-breakfast?"

"Right you are." He doffed his cap. Now *that* was a gesture out of a movie. "Niall Callahan at your service, Miss Stratton."

I extended my hand. "Do you always come to pick up guests from the train station?"

He took my suitcase and gestured for me to walk with him. "Oh, that wouldn't be possible in high season, but in January I was itching for something to do. And I was rather eager to meet the tourist who was either bold or foolish enough to come in winter. Have you any thoughts on which one it is?"

I chortled. "Both and neither. My best friend and my sister schemed this up. They thought it was perfect timing because it was the low season at my work. I don't think they took the time to think about why winter tends to be the low season in *most* places." I shivered for effect.

He smiled at that, stowing my case in the trunk of a well-used Hyundai SUV that was perhaps even older than my senior citizen of a Toyota. He opened the door and waved me to the seat that should have, from my American perspective, been reserved for the driver. He eased the car onto the street with confident ease, but it took a few seconds for my stomach not to flop at the cars being on the "wrong" side of the road.

"So a misguided Christmas gift, was it?" He chuckled. "Bit of a shame, really, as there is no grander place in summer, but it's a bit dreary for most folks in winter." He said "most folks" almost like an accusation. As if there was something wrong with them.

I angled to examine him better. "But not for you?"

He shrugged. "Oh, I like the warm same as any sane person, but there is something underappreciated about the broody winter sea at sunrise." His expression seemed far away, musing on something not meant for me.

"Well, it's easy enough to wake up in time for it, with sunrise being at nine in the morning and all." I didn't try to keep the sarcasm out of my voice.

He shot me a stern look. "Eight thirty this time of year. No need to exaggerate, missy. We have to pay our penance for the long days of summer sometime, don't we?"

"That sounds very Catholic." It reminded me of my Italian Catholic mother's old maxims that boiled down to everything in life having a cost or a price of some kind. I never liked the idea of life being commodified like that. Her directives about good works and community-mindedness sat better.

"Well, you're in the right place for it. It's ingrained in our DNA. Even nonbelievers can't scrub it all off in the wash."

My mood, which had been lightening as Niall drove us out of the town proper and into the rugged countryside, grew weighty again. "That expression is more apt than you realize."

"What do you mean?"

I paused. I barely knew this man, so he was hardly entitled to an accounting of my unfortunate Christmas debacle, but there seemed precious little to lose by confessing the truth about my trip to someone who I'd never see again when my week was up, so I gave him the bare-bones overview to get him up to speed.

"Visiting the land of your ancestors, then. We get a lot of that. It's fair to say that for more than a century, the biggest export out of County Mayo was her sons and daughters, so plenty of your countrymen have ties here. Welcome home."

I smiled at the notion of a country I'd never set foot in somehow being "home." "Who knows how long it's been since any relation of mine ever lived here. But it should be interesting to see."

"The odds are good that your family left with the Famine. My guess would be they sailed to Boston in the 1840s or '50s along with a quarter of the population."

In school I'd only learned vaguely about the Potato Famine and the subsequent wave of Irish immigration to America in the years that followed. I was compelled by the stories of suffering and overcoming adversity, but it was rarely more than a brief sidebar in classes.

"You're probably right. It's the most logical conclusion to arrive at with the sparse data I have. All the relatives listed on the ancestry site were third cousins or even more distant, but heaps of them had Irish names like Doyle, Murphy, and O'Malley."

Pensive, Niall drummed his fingers on the steering wheel. "So you haven't any special places with ancestral ties you want to see while you're here, I gather?"

I shook my head. "No. I could stumble over the birthplace of my great-grandmother to the ninth degree and never be the wiser."

"Well, I'll take it upon myself to ensure you get a good view of our fair country while you're here. I dub myself your tour guide for as long as you desire my services." He placed a hand on his heart as if taking a sacred oath.

"That is really gracious of you, but I don't want to take you away from your duties. My meddling sister and best friend came up with a multipage color-coded itinerary, and I'm sure I can manage."

"Nonsense. It's not unusual for the host at a bed-and-breakfast to be more attentive when the guest load is light. It would be my pleasure. And speaking of which, here is your home away from home for the next week: Blackthorn."

The breath caught in my throat as we pulled in front of what could only be described as a castle. Not the Disneyfied elegant sort with turrets and blonde princesses with pointed hats who lowered their hair for a gallant prince. No, this castle was an unadorned rectangular tower with skinny windows, a fortress on an unforgiving coastline. To see it felt like stepping back in time, and it was the closest sensation I'd ever had to falling in love.

Chapter 6

Y ou live here?" I asked, not caring that I sounded like an imbecile as I gaped at the ancient structure. I felt my annoyance with Avery and Stephanie dissipating. What they lacked in consideration for the practicalities of travel, they seemed determined to make up for with once-in-a-lifetime lodgings. It wasn't the worst outcome, though the lack of a rental car might prove a challenge.

"I do. In the caretaker's cottage in high season, but I take one of the rooms in the castle itself in low season. Winter is hard on these old buildings, and I like to be on-site in case something goes wrong. Catching a broken pipe within a few minutes or even an hour or two is a headache, but not catching it until the next day can be disastrous."

"I imagine so." I was more than a tad relieved to hear mention of indoor plumbing. Not all the castles in Ireland, even those used for bed-and-breakfasts, boasted such modern comforts. Some rugged tourists probably thought a sojourn in a medieval castle without heat or running water would be charming. Character building, even. And for a night or two—in summer—I might be game. But for a full week in winter? No. My character could remain weak and underdeveloped if that was the cost. "Have you lived here long?"

"My whole life." A note of pride rang in Niall's voice that made the corners of my lips turn upward. He loved his work. Caretaking couldn't be a glamorous job, but he clearly thought it was worth doing.

"Do you own the place?"

He shook his head. "No, it's rather an odd arrangement. The castle is owned by the county, and I'm paid a salary to maintain the place. It's allowed to be run as a bed-and-breakfast so it can pay for its own maintenance. Rather elegant solution, I think. My da was caretaker before me, and his father before him. And generations of Callahan men before them have worked in the castle in some capacity or another dating back centuries."

"That's quite the legacy."

"My granddad claimed my family has served this castle and the families who held it for over seven hundred years until it went vacant. They've been stewards ever since. Of course anything going back that far is hard to prove with certainty, but it seems more likely than not based on what I've parsed together from the castle archives."

I gave a low whistle. It was almost hard to fathom from my American perspective. Back home, any building approaching this vintage and significance, usually the remnants of native societies, was preserved as national monuments and historic parks. These castles were still being *used*. Perhaps not in the way they were designed for, but they were still homes—albeit temporary ones—for travelers and history buffs. And the Callahan family, it seemed.

"She's a beauty from the outside, but there's plenty to see indoors, so we might as well stop gawking or she'll take offense."

I giggled, but it didn't seem entirely like jest. It seemed perfectly logical to me that this massive edifice before me had feelings. A personality. A beating heart.

He carried my case into the Grand Hall. Replete with iron

sconces, a roaring fire in an immense fireplace, and sturdy furniture built to last centuries. And it had. Rugs made of animal hides made the space seem less austere and somehow closer to nature.

"It's incredible," I breathed.

"I still wonder when the sight of this place will grow old. I'm beginning to think it won't."

I couldn't tear my eyes from the place long enough to read his expression. "How could it?"

"Why don't we settle you into your room, and I'll rustle you up a hot meal, shall I?"

I imagined this giant bear of a man fumbling through the kitchen, cursing his way through preparing a meal, burning and cutting his fingers along the way.

"Oh, you don't have to go to any trouble. I'm sure I can find a pub." I paused. It would be a four-mile trek back into town, and I'd be hard-pressed to make it that far on airplane food and the sad train depot sandwich I'd hurriedly purchased in Dublin more than four hours ago. "Or maybe you just have something I can reheat?"

"Oh now, I see that look on your face. I'm a skilled hand in the kitchen. Let me show you upstairs."

The staircase to the second floor was impossibly narrow, and I was glad Niall was wrangling my case.

"Apparently people were a good deal narrower eight hundred years ago," I mused.

Niall chuckled. "In general, that has to be true. We have fast food to thank for that. But don't forget, castles weren't just passive fortresses; they were active weapons, and every inch was designed with that in mind. Narrow staircases gave the soldiers encamped here an important tactical advantage. Invaders would be forced to fight an uphill battle without the possibility of sneaking past the guards. A grand staircase out of Kensington Palace would have just been an invitation for trouble."

As I walked I wondered how many bloody encounters happened on these very steps. Living such a brutish life would have been unthinkable, but as I sneaked glances out the narrow windows at the wild landscape beyond, it wasn't hard to imagine a time when this didn't feel like the edge of the world.

"Here you are." Niall opened the door to what must have been the bedroom of the lord and lady of the house.

"Wow." I could only sputter a monosyllable as I took in the room. It was sparsely furnished with a bed, a nightstand, a wardrobe, and a small writing table, but each piece was heavy and imposing like the pieces in the Grand Hall. The four-poster bed alone looked like it weighed more than Niall's car. There were more pelts, and the blaze in the fireplace was prepared for my arrival.

"I take it you approve?" Something eager infused his voice. He wanted me to approve of the room. This castle. It was like an artist waiting for a critic to give her opinion on his chef d'oeuvre.

I was certain my eyes fairly bulked from my head. "How could I not? I've never seen a medieval castle before, let alone slept in one."

"Well then, you're in for a treat. Loo's down the hall, so you'll have to adjust to that small inconvenience, but it would have meant gutting the place to put a bathroom in every suite."

I examined my room more closely. "No, I like indoor plumbing as much as the next girl, but that would destroy the place. This isn't the Ritz or the Savoy."

He broke into a smile. "I'm glad you see that. I'll have a bite ready in about thirty minutes. Take your time."

I exhaled as the door clicked behind me. My cobalt suitcase looked garish in its modernity against the earthen tones in the room.

I unpacked as quickly as I could so I could stow it away and return the room to its rightful state.

I thought I saw a glimmer to the left of the fireplace, a flash of orange and green, but it passed so quickly I dismissed it as a play of the afternoon light against the lapping yellow flames in the massive stone hearth making mischief with my jet lag. I rubbed my eyes and fought against the pull of fatigue.

I ventured down to the bathroom, which I guessed had been installed sometime in the last hundred years and definitely appeared antique. It boasted a row of porcelain sinks and stall showers, reminiscent of an old boardinghouse. It was devoid of any sort of twenty-first-century luxury, but it would have been a marvel to anyone who'd lived in the castle when it was built. I thought of the indignities the lady of the house would have had to suffer, bathing down in the kitchens. Hauling hot water up the narrow stairs would have been a beastly task to ask often of the servants.

I placed my hand on one of the stones from the wall. Cold and unyielding. Ancient and immutable. It was hard to think that as lifeless as these stones were, they had witnessed centuries worth of living.

After half an hour, once I'd washed off the day of travel and changed into fresh clothes, I went downstairs and followed the scent to the kitchen where Niall had set the rough-hewn table with earthenware plates already loaded with a generous portion of soda bread and glasses brimming with amber liquid. My mouth gaped, unladylike, at the welcoming sight. Two matching bowls sat to his left at the stove, waiting for their contents.

"I told you I was a good cook. Serves you right for doubting a Callahan." He winked as he stirred the contents of an enameled Dutch oven.

"I won't be making that mistake again." I took in a deep whiff. Whatever he was making smelled more delectable than it had any right to. My stomach rumbled in hunger. "Beef stew?"

"No, no. This is a proper Irish stew with lamb. My grandmother's recipe." He ladled a helping into the bowls, placed one before each place at the table, and gestured for me to tuck in.

I took a spoonful and felt myself melting as it trickled down my throat. The lamb was tender, the broth seasoned to perfection. My eyes were closed, but I could hear him chuckling at me. "I'm glad you like it. It's gratifying to see a meal I created eaten and appreciated."

"No worries here," I said once I'd swallowed. "I'm a food matchmaker. A professional eater, in a sense."

"You have me intrigued, Miss Stratton. What exactly is a food matchmaker? I'm worried that I've missed my calling."

I finished another bite of stew and explained the ins and outs of my work as The Kitchen Muse, endeavoring to eat politely, despite my baser instincts that longed to lick the bowl clean and move on to devour the rest of the contents of the Dutch oven left simmering on the stove.

"That is fascinating." He'd been nodding with enthusiasm as I spoke. "I source all the ingredients I can from the estate here. And what I can't, I find from the nearby farms. My mother says I've gotten to the point I can tell which farm raised the cow a local cheddar came from."

"That's exactly the sort of thing I do. I can tell you which farms in Palisade have the best peaches each season. Who's got good rhubarb and whose millet crops are subpar. Even the best chefs in the world can't work their magic if the ingredients are shoddy."

"Amen to that. I've been trying to convince the powers that be to expand the food service here. There isn't a bed-and-breakfast in Ireland that doesn't serve a platter of dry scones, a bit of jam and clotted cream, and a pot of weak tea of a morning, but I want to host grand feasts here. Give people an idea of what a holiday meal might have been like in the times of yore. Food made with local ingredients, done well."

"Sounds like a sound concept to me. And there's no saying that you can't improve upon the techniques and give the guests an updated version of what they might have eaten when the castle was in its heyday instead of giving them a more museum-like experience. Bland mutton and the like might not be a huge sell. Could you really keep up with the castle and a more elaborate food service?"

"It's impossible to say until I've tried, but we could start off small and seasonal. A Christmas gala or an Easter luncheon for people in the surrounding area, and expand from there."

I could immediately imagine the place festooned with evergreens and long, scarred tables laden with food and fires blazing. Mulled wine, roasted pigs over the fire, and all the lush trimmings. "I love that."

"Your eyes glazed over as you pictured that. I'll take it as a good sign."

I imagined my face was in full Kitchen Muse consultant mode. "I think you're onto something. It would be a way to boost business during slow periods, which I assume would be a good thing?"

"Of course. We aren't suffering, but what businessman doesn't want a buffer to see him through lean times? And it would be a nice treat for the locals who never have much cause to visit the place, which is always a nice move for PR."

"PR is never a bad move, and there are plenty of lean times to be had in the hospitality business." I took another spoonful of the stew, which somehow tasted better with each bite. "Though in a perfect world, your skills with stew would shore up this estate for the rest of time."

"Well, bless you for that." He sat across from me and tucked into a bowl of his own. "And you're right enough about the fickle nature of this business. I've seen a lot of good restaurants come and go just in Westport. Dublin must be even worse."

I nodded. "Easier and harder at the same time. More potential clientele but fiercer competition. A two-hour wait to get into a flashy place with a big-name chef, while a better place with an up-and-comer with twice the talent and a million times the drive and creativity sits empty. I see it all the time in Denver."

"I imagine you do. Now what is it you want to see while you're here? It's my solemn duty to make sure your brief time in County Mayo becomes a pleasant memory to carry home without weighing down your carry-on."

I smiled, despite the corny language that seemed right out of a travel brochure. I wondered if that wasn't exactly where it came from. A glossy *Guide to the Charms of County Mayo* pamphlet that the locals joked about. "You don't have to go to any trouble. If there is a rental car agency in Westport, I might prevail upon you for a lift if it isn't too inconvenient."

He shook his head. "Nothing closer than Castlebar, especially in winter. I could take you there if you like. But I'm sincere in my offer to serve as your tour guide if you don't mind my company. You'll find the price is right—free with the cost of your lodgings—and you wouldn't have to fuss with adjusting to driving on the left."

I shuddered. "That is a very compelling argument. But I couldn't impose like that."

He waved his hand dismissively. "It will give me something to do, and I'd be grateful for it."

I paused. Did I really want to spend my week in Ireland tagging along after this man I'd only known hours? Certainly anyone with good intentions had more to occupy their time than shuttling me around. But everything *had* seemed sleepy, and there wasn't a town in the world that didn't cope with tourist cycles. He was probably vying for a huge tip when my week was up. Which wasn't necessarily unreasonable. If he was a decent guide, I could hand over whatever I might have paid for a rental car and gas.

"Are you sure?"

"Of course. There's nothing like seeing County Mayo with a native. And one that's on a first-name basis with every farmer in this county and most of the neighboring ones if you're on the lookout for ingredients for your fancy big-city chefs. Now have some soda bread before I collapse. Try it with the butter."

With a poorly concealed laugh, I ripped a hunk from the serving of bread and slathered it with butter from an earthenware crock as he'd instructed.

"No raisins. Well done," I said, approvingly. I wasn't an expert on Irish cuisine, but the introduction of raisins into soda bread was inauthentic and unwelcome in my book. Unwelcome in most things, really.

"You know of what you speak. And perish the thought of a Callahan doing such a thing." He held a hand over his heart. "If my gran found any of the children she'd helped see raised up adding raisins to her recipe, she'd come back from the great beyond to collect our hides."

"Sage woman." I inhaled before taking a bite, breathing in the scent with the flavors. There was something earthy and grassy in everything that seemed unlike any place I'd ever been. The crust was thick and crunchy, the fluffy white interior was still hot from the oven.

"The butter," I breathed. It was the creamiest—somehow the butteriest—butter I'd ever had. Of everything he'd served it caught my attention most. "This is truly incredible."

"I thank you kindly. Made it myself this morning."

"Let me guess. You probably learned the family method for making butter passed down for twelve generations and a three-hundred-year-old butter churn, and you've made magic. It's alchemy instead of butter."

"You're spot on about the method, but not about the butter churn. I retired it and bought a professional-grade stand mixer. Had a row with my ma about that one, but she let it go when I offered that she could come churn the butter for breakfast herself if she didn't like my 'dreadful modern ways.' And once she tasted my handiwork, that was the end of it. I'm not one for wantonly disregarding time-tested traditions, but the constant speed of the motor makes for a better consistency. And I'm the first to do anything with herb-infused butters and the like. She asked for a crock of my cinnamon butter for her Christmas gift."

"I source vanilla beans for my mother so she can make her own concoctions. I'm convinced her bourbon-and-Madagascar-vanilla-bean extract is more magic than food. Once you've had an angel food cake made with it, you'll never buy store-bought vanilla again."

"Lord in heaven, that sounds divine. Will you show me how it's done?" The eagerness in his eyes lightened my spirits. Finding someone just as devoted to food as I was didn't happen often.

I nodded resolutely. "Nothing simpler. Perhaps we can source ingredients when we're out? If you want to play tour guide, let's go. Show me what there is to see."

"Grab your coat, and I'll do better than that. I'll show you what there is to eat."

Chapter 7

Niall had us back on the road within fifteen minutes, and I found myself lost in the wild beauty of the coastal countryside. To imagine that my ancestors had possibly once lived here, and freely chosen to give it up, baffled me. The Rockies had an overabundance of beauty too, but perhaps I'd grown too used to the rugged peaks and lush valleys. The west of Ireland was a thing apart, so very different from any place I'd ever seen, and I couldn't peel my eyes from it.

"If you keep gathering wool like that, one of the sheep farmers is going to put you to work." Niall's baritone snapped me back to the present.

I chuckled. Did he have nieces and nephews that inspired the dad-like humor? Maybe he had children of his own. It struck me that I knew next to nothing about this man, and I had made more suppositions than actual discoveries about him. He was a devoted caretaker and a heck of a good cook, but beyond that, the rest was conjecture.

"Sorry, I guess I'm brooding."

"Well, you came to the right place. It's the national pastime. Likely why we have more than our share of writers."

"And heavy drinkers," I added.

"Ouch. But you're not wrong, I suppose. Brooding comes naturally over a pint. Which is, by the way, an experience you need to have."

I arched a brow. "Brooding over a pint?"

"More specifically, drinking a pint of Guinness or Smithwick's in a proper Irish pub. Brooding optional. Given that you're on holiday, you might consider taking a miss on that." He signaled and turned the car onto a narrow lane.

"Where are we going?" I saw nothing nearby but vast expanses of hilly fields.

"To show you the secret behind my alchemy, as you called it."

We pulled up to a farmhouse that looked new in comparison to Blackthorn, but I would have been shocked if the shell of it was less than a few hundred years old. The house appeared to be meticulously cared for, as was every inch of the grounds.

An older man walked from the house, his step sprightly for a man who seemed to be nearing his eighties. Niall opened the car door and escorted me over to the man.

"Veronica, I'd like you to meet Pat O'Brien, the best dairy farmer in County Mayo and, consequently, the known world. Pat, this is Miss Veronica Stratton, here on holiday from America and staying at Blackthorn."

"And here I thought you'd finally found yourself a bride. More's the pity." Pat extended a bony hand and seemed pleased that I matched his firm grip. "But why have you brought the lovely young lady to a dairy farm of all places? Surely she'd prefer to see the town or something more amusing than this." He gestured to the plot of land that represented his life's work.

"Oh, we'll get to that soon enough. But she's sampled the butter

I make for the guests and is enough of a food expert that I thought she'd enjoy learning a trick or two of mine."

Pat doffed his cap with a flourish. "If Niall Callahan thinks that highly of you, you're more than welcome here, Miss Stratton. I'm afraid my old knees aren't up to a full tour of the place so late in the day, but I can show you as far as the barn."

"That would be grand, Pat." Niall clapped him on the shoulder, and the pair led me to a barn not far from the house. I'd expected it to smell terribly, but each stall was pristine with a fresh bed of hay and a satisfied-looking cow watching our entry with vague interest. The small crew of field hands never seemed to stop moving.

"The cows are brought inside for the winter months," Niall explained. "Most of the year, they're free to graze in the fields. When the grass goes dormant for the year, they're brought here and fed until spring."

One of the cows lowed softly, almost like a greeting, and Pat reached out to scratch her between the ears. He cooed, "Oh yes, wee Daisy's a good girl," as she angled her head to receive scratches on a larger surface of her head.

The cow was so pleased with the attention, I couldn't help but giggle. "I don't know if she's a cow or a golden retriever."

"Oh, I'm not sure she's puzzled that out herself. I swear she'd crawl in my lap if given half a chance." Pat gave the cow's muzzle a scratch and she lowed again, expressing her appreciation.

"You won't see happier cows anywhere in the world," Niall said as Pat took his leave back to the house. We toured the rest of the barn, and the rest of the livestock seemed just as friendly.

"Pat seems like a gentle soul. You can tell he's nurtured these cows with more love and attention than most," I mused aloud.

He chuckled. "The cows dash over to greet him in the morning to be milked. It's quite a sight to behold. And I'd bet my last dime you can taste the difference in the milk. That's why I always buy milk and cream from him to make my butter. I wouldn't go anywhere else. I only hope the family carries on as well as he has done."

He showed me outside, and we walked along the expansive fields until they got too boggy from the winter rains. "You can't see it now, but in spring these hills are a riot of clover. That's the other secret. The cows have some of the most luscious grasses to eat in all of Ireland, and the little scamps know it."

I gazed out at the dormant fields. "It all makes sense to me. With a good diet and lots of affection, what isn't possible?"

Niall patted my shoulder. "That ought to be printed on bumper stickers and T-shirts. Sounds like a life motto to me."

I chortled. "It was more or less my mom's mantra."

I thought of my mother back in Estes Park and the state she'd been in when I left at Christmas. She felt so horrible about everything, and there was nothing I could say or do to convince her that I was going to be fine. That *we* were fine. Most of all, she expressed guilt about not telling me herself. I tried to assure her that I understood the situation was complicated and all, but there was no consoling her. I was glad we'd been able to share a meal together in Denver after she'd calmed down a bit, but I knew all the emotions were still there, bubbling just below the surface.

I had felt terrible for her, and the more I considered it, the more I felt pity for the fifteen-year-old me who'd pieced it together in sophomore biology class too. The girl who worried that if she confessed what she knew, her parents would love her less because they couldn't pretend she was their kid anymore. Intellectually, I knew it was hard for my parents. I realized now that they were bound by the NDA and would have faced legal hassles if they violated it. I knew, as a headstrong teenager I probably would have railed against the vague answers they would have been forced to give.

But part of me still wished they'd told me *something*.

Even more of me wished I'd been brave enough to raise the questions when I'd pieced it all together.

"You're brooding again, lass." Niall's voice called me back to the here and now. "Penny for your thoughts?"

"I'm not sure they're worth that much, even with inflation. Just thinking about home."

"Isn't the point of being on holiday to get away from home a bit?" He bumped me playfully with his elbow.

"Gah, you're right. This place is so beautiful. I should be more invested in the moment."

"I'm only teasing. Truly. Sometimes being away from home makes us see home troubles more clearly. Whenever I venture away from Blackthorn, I come up with solutions to her woes in a way I can't do when I'm home. Perspective can be a great gift."

"You're probably right. Thank you for bringing me here. I loved seeing this place."

"I knew you would. And it's just one of the many secrets I keep in Blackthorn's kitchens."

"I look forward to learning more of them," I said as he opened the car door for me.

"Oh, I've a feeling you and Blackthorn are going to get on famously."

Chapter 8

The castle seemed pleased at our return, and I scoffed inwardly at such a preposterous thought. Then again, if any buildings were entitled to have thoughts and feelings, it would have been ancient ones like these, which had seen the comings and goings of generations the way we watch minutes pass by on the clock.

Niall reheated some of the leftover stew shortly after we returned. It was, if anything, more flavorful the second go-round, but I found the room going in and out of focus.

"You're knackered, aren't you?" Niall said with a chuckle as I struggled to comprehend the questions he was asking.

I nodded. "I'm so sorry. It seems the travel has finally hit me all at once."

"As it's wont to do. Why don't you turn in early tonight so we can get an early start in the morning? You'll feel loads better. And don't worry about the odd sound that goes bump in the night. It's an old place and does a fair bit of wheezing and creaking like any old codger."

I yawned by way of response, unable to even ask what he had in mind for our sightseeing adventures. I spared a brief moment of regret for Stephanie's carefully planned itinerary but ignored it quickly as I focused on making it up the stairs in one piece.

The four-poster canopy with its thick blankets and rich linens was beyond enticing, and I was all too eager to fall into it. I forced myself through my evening routine. I could have easily fallen asleep in my thick wool leggings and fleece on top of the covers, but I would sleep far better with a clean face and brushed teeth. Of course the bathroom was down the hall, so I had to try to find my way around by memory in the soft glow of archaic electric lighting that wasn't able to fully conquer the vast darkness.

I abbreviated my nighttime ritual as much as I could, not wanting to fall asleep where I stood in the sterile bathroom. As I returned I was glad to be the only guest of the castle, knowing that I wouldn't run the risk of barging into anyone's room, but being alone in the ancient space was a level of solitude I wasn't used to. Back in my apartment, there were always soft rustlings of the neighbors even in the quietest hours. The silence here was more absolute. Still and contemplative in ways the New World hadn't yet achieved.

Grateful that Avery had thought to send slippers in her care package, I padded down the length of the cold stone corridor to my room. I cursed myself for not counting the number of door handles to my room. I guessed which door was mine and was relieved at the sight of my purse on the bedside chair when I tentatively peered inside. As I crossed the threshold the handle grew warm and the room began to spin . . .

The room was much the same as mine, but a torrent of rain beat against the windows. Thunder and lightning crashed with unbridled fury where moments ago the weather had been fine. I didn't see my purse any longer. Had I actually gone in the wrong door after all? But why would Niall have lit the fire for an empty room?

I turned to go find him but was greeted by the sight of an imperious-looking woman whose mane of red curls had been tamed, in violation of the laws of man and physics, into a towering mass of braids atop her head. She wore a determined expression like a general marching into battle, juxtaposed by a fine silk dress with billowing floor-length skirts she clenched in broad fists for ease of movement. Her resolute gaze penetrated me, and her stride showed no signs of stopping. I sidestepped out of her way, but her shoulder should have clipped mine at full force—

I felt nothing but a rustle of damp night air caress my skin.

She turned into the room I'd just opened, dropped her skirts, and placed her hands on her hips.

"Aoife Caitria Laoise MacWilliam, what was the meaning of that shameful spectacle you just put on at supper? How dare you speak to a member of the Tierney family in such a way? You know what that might do to your father's standing in the county."

I turned to see that the room, which previously had appeared empty, was indeed occupied by a young woman dressed much like the woman I assumed was her mother. Clearly dressed for important company . . . but appropriate for an era long passed. I wasn't enough of a historian to place when, but sometime in the nineteenth century was my best guess. I rubbed my eyes, but the mother and daughter still occupied the space. And where, just moments before, the room had been empty save for the furniture, it was now adorned with the trinkets of a young lady on the cusp of womanhood.

There were a few remnants of girlhood—a once much-loved doll that now lived on a shelf next to some equally worn wooden horses—but there was a vanity with a silver-plated brush, comb, and hand mirror set that had probably been enormously expensive, and little pots of what might have been various handcrafted face creams, which had to be the mark of a monied landowner.

What madness was this? Had I fallen asleep while brushing my teeth? I must have. And Niall would find me snoring in a heap on the bathroom floor and have a good laugh at my expense.

I rubbed my eyes, willing my brain to reboot . . . but the visions were still there. Clearly the jet lag was getting to me, but the women before me felt just as real as Niall had, just twenty minutes before, if a little hazy around the edges. They lived somewhere between dreams and reality, and I couldn't make sense of any of it.

The young woman, Aoife, turned to the older, fire dancing in her green eyes. "I speak this way because I won't allow you to poison my father's ear and marry me off to the most worthless man in all of Ireland just because you think it will serve your interests, Mairéad."

Mairéad, a given name. Not Mother. Perhaps an aunt or some other relative who felt she had authority over the younger woman. I should have left them to their argument and not violated their privacy, but I felt rooted to my spot. I didn't think I could turn away from the scene before me, even if I'd wanted to. I took some comfort in the fact that I was fairly certain they couldn't see me, given that Mairéad had passed right through me once before.

"You have been told to call me Mother countless times, child."

Impressively, Aoife didn't blast her temper in a fit of rage, but I could sense it rolling off her skin like a poisonous fog. "I have told *you* countless times, I will never do so as you are *not* my mother. You may wish to be called a duchess, but that won't confer the coronet on that empty head of yours. My father has explained to you countless times that I am under no obligation to call you any such thing."

Mairéad huffed so her nostrils flared and crimson rose in her cheeks. "You ungrateful little witch. You have no sense of duty or honor. You ought to do what you're told and be glad anyone has taken the time to think of your future. Do you *really* think you're deserving of such attentions?"

Aoife didn't hesitate. "Of course I am. I'm not some poor street urchin without a name or a shilling to call her own. I am just as deserving of my father's consideration as your children. If anything, more, as I am the oldest."

"Girls should be obedient to their parents. How dare you wield that nasty tongue of yours at me?"

Aoife crossed her arms over her chest. "Spare me. Seamus will get everything, by right of law. You'll see the son of your flesh take my father's place, just as you wanted. I don't see why you seem so intent on making my future miserable. Just let me be."

Mairéad scoffed but did not deny the accusation. "Because I won't have you in the way. I wish your father had seen reason and sent you to a convent. I've begged him time and again. But he's convinced your marriage will be of more use to us than your absence, so I'll have you married and out of this house before your next birthday or so help me, your father will be *made* to see reason and have you locked away with the nuns."

Aoife snorted in derision. "My father has never spoken about me that way in all his life, like a cow to be sold at auction, so stop spreading lies. He loved my mother and he promised her he would choose my husband with care."

"Your mother indeed," Mairéad spit on the floor. "Grace Bourke was a trollop and deserved the cancer that ate away at her evil core. And you're just like her. Oh, I knew your mother from the time she was a wean and she paraded about the village acting like the very queen of Sheba. Claiming she was descended from the great Gráinne Ní Mháille. As though being the whelp of a heathen pirate whore is anything to be proud of."

"Grow up, Mairéad. You just couldn't bear that she took attention from you. She was beautiful and you're plain. She was clever and you're dull. And you didn't even have the decency to wait until her body was cold to bewitch my father into believing you were anything like a fit replacement for her."

Mairéad, rather than taking offense, threw her head back and laughed. "Stupid chit, your mother may have been those things, but you know what I am that she is not? Alive. And mistress of this castle. And you had better get used to that truth, you dolt. I've finished playing games with a half-witted child. Mark my words, your father will be brought to heel."

She turned from the room with an audible swish of her skirt. Aoife waited until her stepmother had left the room, then buried her face in her hands. She'd made a show of bravery to Mairéad, but she was straining under the weight of the horrid woman's demands.

I wanted, more than anything, to rush over to Aoife and wrap my arms around her. To tell her to be strong and not to buckle under Mairéad's conniving, but part of me didn't want to risk breaking the spell. The word seemed apt. Whatever this was, the most reasonable explanation for it was magic.

A few moments later, heavy footsteps sounded down the hall, and a man with red hair and a beard streaked with white knocked. Aoife didn't respond, and he entered the room after a short pause. Moving with the confidence of the lord of the manor.

"That was quite a scene at dinner, daughter of mine," he said by way of greeting. His tone was wary. This was not the first time he'd been forced to play referee between his wife and daughter.

"Tell that cow to stop meddling." Aoife raised her head, staring at her father with startling bottle-green eyes, made all the more brilliant by the tears that threatened but never spilled.

"You can't speak about her that way. Her position demands respect." He sounded weary, as if this was a refrain he'd been forced to repeat scores of times before now.

"That bitch is *not* my mother." Aoife jumped to her feet. "I will not treat her as such."

Her father's eyes flashed dangerously. "I am aware of that, child. But she is my wife and the lady of this house and does not merit such abuse at your hand."

"So you think it perfectly well that she clumsily arrange for a marriage with that absolute boiled turnip of a man? Declan Tierney is a waste of man flesh and shoe leather, and you bloody well know it. Did she even tell you what foolishness she was concocting?"

His expression softened. "She did it under my orders, Aoife."

She blanched. "How could you? Did it even occur to you to warn me?"

"It did not, as I expect young ladies under my charge to obey orders. Though I see in retrospect some warning might have helped you to keep your tongue at bay. That said, I will not treat another outburst of this kind with any sort of indulgence, is that clear? I don't think you appreciate the tenuous situation we find ourselves in, daughter. The MacWilliam family is one of the few families of consequence who concern themselves with Irish interests. If families like ours and the Tierneys don't band together, we have no sway whatsoever."

Open-mouthed and aghast, she stared at her father. "Does that matter more than I do, Da?"

"Aoife, I've sheltered you far too much from this world we live in. The blight has seen our people dropping dead in the streets. If you don't believe me, I'll take you on a carriage ride to show you myself. Five minutes in a workhouse would show you just how ivory this tower is that you've been living in. You are one child. Your unhappiness is a small price to pay for some chance of getting some support from England."

"I'm not as blind as you think I am, Da. I simply don't think a handful of Irish lords has a chance to turn hearts of stone. They see men drop dead in the streets, children who've never owned a scrap of clothing, the miserable huts they're forced to live in. If that doesn't inspire them to charity, nothing will. Even if all the Gaelic families rose up, nothing would change. The English will never stop exporting our grain to line their own pockets. They don't care that our people are dying in the streets. And more, you must make peace with the truth that England will never cede any measure of self-governance for the Irish without a war. One that starving men can't win."

A flicker of despair crossed his face. "We have to try, Aoife. How could I live with myself if I don't?"

"And I am to be sacrificed on the altar of *your* conscience, Da? Declan Tierney is a fool. Worse, he's a brute. Would you really see me wed to such a man? His own dog cowers at the sight of him."

His expression softened. "*Mo stór*, he would not dare mistreat you. He knows the MacWilliam clan wouldn't stand for it."

"And if I don't see you for six months or a year at a time? How will you know I am in need of defense? Do you think a man like that will let me send letters freely? Every servant in his infernal keep will be under orders to surveil me every waking moment and while I sleep too. You don't think he has the means to keep you in the dark if he's mistreating me?"

He looked downcast at his feet, unable to meet his daughter's eyes.

"Tell me truly, Father. Would it even matter? If I showed up here with a blackened eye and an arm in a sling, how many days before you'd send me back for more of the same?"

He finally met her gaze. "Three. I wouldn't presume to keep you from your lord and master for any longer than that. This is to be your lot in life, and you will learn to endure it. You will learn to put others before yourself for once in your life." His words sounded like he was parroting Mairéad. He turned as if the matter were closed but craned his head back to look at her once more. "You will be wed to him within a fortnight."

"Mother would be ashamed of you." The fire in Aoife's eyes could have lit the very stone walls of the castle ablaze.

"Perhaps she would be, and I will answer for it in heaven. But here on earth, I have other considerations I must take into account with more immediacy than the wishes of my deceased wife. Someday, I pray you will be wise enough to understand."

Aoife's father left the room, but her eyes remained transfixed on the doorway, just to the right of where I stood peering in at her private world.

"I'm so sorry," I said, my voice just above a whisper. "That's grossly unfair."

If Aoife heard me, she made no sign of it. She took a glass pitcher from her vanity and threw it against the doorjamb. I jumped back, reflexively, and braced myself for the impact of the shards of porcelain. I opened my eyes to see my room returned to its regular state, my modern purse on the chair sticking out like weeds in a rose garden.

My heart was thumping against my rib cage. How would I sleep tonight?

And how crazy would people think I was if I ever dared to tell them what I saw?

Chapter 9

I was certain I wouldn't sleep that night after the vision . . . daydream . . . hallucination . . . whatever it was. But apparently my jet lag was more powerful than the bewilderment I felt at the events of the previous evening. As I readied myself for the day, I debated whether I'd tell Niall about Aoife and her predicament. It sounded insane, but I only had a week in Ireland, after all. Even if he thought I was nuts, no real harm could come of it. And the urge to share what I'd seen with someone was overwhelming.

Niall was a particularly promising candidate because he knew the castle, he knew the country, and he might have some insight as to what I saw. I rehearsed gentle ways of working the topic into conversation as I washed my face and applied some of the skincare samples Avery had included in my suitcase. I mused over the right wording to make myself sound nonchalant as I applied a light dusting of makeup from the small assortment of high-end travel-size cosmetics she'd also included. If I was going insane, at least my darling sister had called in the right favors so I wouldn't *look* like a harried, crazy woman.

That was comforting, I supposed.

I found Niall happily ensconced in the kitchen, brewing coffee with the efficient movements of a barista, and sought the right line from the options I'd hashed over in my head.

"So what are the chances this place is haunted?" It was . . . not one of the lines I'd rehearsed, and I certainly didn't sound nonchalant. But what it lacked in subtlety, it made up for in directness.

He threw his head back in a laugh that showed his full mouth of straight teeth. "This place is over seven hundred years old. If there weren't a few ghosts hanging about, it would be a sore disappointment, wouldn't it? Did something fall over in the middle of the night? A door slam unexpectedly?"

"It was a little more vivid than that." And, as calmly as I could manage, I relayed the scene with Mairéad and Aoife, and later Aoife and her father.

"You saw Riordan MacWilliam? He was the last of his clan. We Callahans had been in their employ for generations, and the stewardship passed to us after Riordan died."

My muscles slackened a bit as I realized he wasn't about to scoff at me and think I was going dotty. "So what I saw was real?"

"Well, it depends on how you define 'real,' but the way you describe it, they sound like real people whose history was tied to this castle. They were the last of the old guard to live at Blackthorn. They knew just how nice to play it with the Anglo-Irish, and it helped curry favor and relief during the Famine."

I pondered a moment. "Riordan had sons with Mairéad. How could he be the last of his clan?"

"They died as young men before they started families, according to what my father and his father told me. By the time it happened, Mairéad was no longer of an age to give him more children. The grief of it was too much for Riordan to bear."

"But what about Aoife? Did she have to marry Declan?"

"Nah. The lore is that she disappeared after a row with her father. Some say she died in the cold on the shores, and they can hear her wails on bitter-cold nights. Others say she hightailed it to America along with everyone else fleeing from the Famine. It's likely enough she could have disappeared in the crowd. She had trinkets to pawn and coin of her own."

"So you're an expert on local history as well as a castle keeper? That would sure stand out on a résumé."

"Oh, the former comes with the latter. More than half our guests are keen to know a bit of the history of the place when they visit. If they weren't, they'd find a chain hotel with a Jacuzzi tub."

"Good point. I hope Aoife did get away. I don't know who these people are, but Declan Tierney sounded like the worst sort of man. He would have been an awful husband to her."

Niall nodded. "There isn't much dispute on that. County legend has it that he had three wives and none of them lived to a happy, old age. He was a brute, just as Aoife described."

I found myself, inexplicably, envisioning a red-haired woman bundled in wool on the deck of a ship, her eyes fixed forever westward, away from the father and stepmother who would have so happily condemned her to an awful fate.

"She must have gone to Boston. I know it in my bones. She wouldn't have let them cow her."

"I think you're probably right, Miss Stratton. You saw yourself that her mother was said to be descended from the great Gráinne Ní Mháille, and that wasn't stock that bowed easily to expectations and duty. She would have had a sense of loyalty to herself as well as her family. And the more she felt betrayed by them, the more tenuous those bonds would have been."

"I wish I were better versed on my Irish history," I confessed. "I feel like I could know that name."

"You'd more likely have heard the English version of her name: Grace O'Malley. She was a chieftain, a pirate, and one hell of a woman. Probably the greatest figure ever to come out of County Mayo."

My eyes widened. "She sounds incredible."

Niall handed me a perfectly brewed cup of coffee. I melted as the caffeine made its way through my bloodstream and reached my soul.

"She was that. But too rebellious to be allowed to live on in the history books until recently. She divorced her husband and stole his castle at Rockfleet until they reconciled. She laid siege on her own son when he was being a traitorous git. Apparently she and the first Elizabeth over in England made quite an impression on each other when they met. Alas, Grace wasn't the sort of woman the Catholic Church, or the English, would have been keen to celebrate."

"Not likely," I said. "I have to believe Aoife was cut from the same cloth and found a way out of Ireland."

"I've not given it much thought. Perhaps less than I should, but I would suspect you're right. And I wouldn't be shocked if you aren't from that same bolt of fabric yourself."

I looked up from my plate. "What do you mean?"

"I don't think Aoife would have come to you without a reason. I think you have to figure out what it is on your own, but there *was* a reason for it."

"So you don't think I'm crazy?" My voice sounded small, even to me, and I rolled my eyes at how meek I sounded.

"No. Maybe if we were in a fifteen-year-old flat in Dublin, I'd look askance at you, but old, storied buildings like these don't follow the rules of the modern world, do they? I'm not a superstitious man. Skeptical even, but in my years here, I've had to become comfortable with things that logic can't explain. There are times I'd sleep better if I could come up with a rational explanation, but such is the cost of a life at Blackthorn."

"I can't tell if that's philosophy or poetry." The more of the omelet I ate and the longer I spent in Niall's reassuring presence, the more I felt grounded in the here and now, which was a relief.

"As with most things worth thinking about in life, it's a bit of both. But I wouldn't worry too much about what you saw. Buildings like these, they retain a bit of their pasts, the way bricks take the chill in winter. Echoes. There's too much history here for the place to let it go altogether." He dished up his own breakfast and looked just as contented with it as I felt.

Echo. I liked the term. It seemed the best descriptor for it. Not a dream, but not reality either. A sort of imitation of something that once had been.

His words made perfect sense. In some part of the more romantic reaches of my brain it *did* make sense. What mattered most, inexplicably, was that Niall didn't think I was nuts. Part of me wanted to take him in a hug for the simple act of not mocking me. Hot tears pricked at my eyes, and I forced myself to think of something— anything—else.

"I suppose you know where the chickens roost that gave the eggs and met the farmer who grew the chives, and so on." I pointed to my plate.

"Aye, that." His brogue thickened a bit. "The chickens are roosted in our own barn, I grew the chives myself, and the bacon is from a farm about three miles from here. I selected the pig myself."

"And the cheese?"

"From the market, I confess. I do love a good aged Gruyère, and I've convinced the local shopkeep to order in some good stuff. I enjoy Irish cheddar as much as the rest of my countrymen, but it's just a wee bit greasy in an omelet. Not *everything* has to come from the neighborhood, but I believe most of it should."

I raised my mug of strong black coffee and clinked it against his. "I'll drink to that. I think there's something special about making a cobbler from Palisade peaches and premium imported spices. Cinnamon from Sri Lanka still in stick form and whole nutmeg from Indonesia you have to grate into the mixing bowl so that they're perfectly fresh. It's truly incredible."

"No question. And now you have me craving a pudding first thing in the morning, you temptress. But we'll see to that. Are you up for another outing a bit later?"

"So where are you taking me?"

"Patience, my American friend. Haven't I earned your trust by now?" Mischief glinted in his voice rather than his eyes.

I paused to consider the question. It was just yesterday we'd met . . . but I couldn't deny that I *did* trust him. I couldn't be sure if that was me intuiting that he was a decent human, an instinct honed by generations of my foremothers' insights that had kept them alive over the millennia, at least long enough to procreate . . . or if it was just epic naivete. But regardless, I couldn't shake the feeling that, fundamentally, Niall was a top-shelf guy. I mean, the great Julia Child herself said, "People who love to eat are always the best people"—and by extension, I think she'd include those who love to cook. And that was Niall. He was one of the few people I'd met who wouldn't think my caring about where my chocolate was sourced from was some sort of PC affectation.

Niall understood how I felt about food—we understood each other—in a way I wasn't used to. Mom was the closest I'd ever come to that sort of a connection. She wasn't as avid about learning all the intricacies of it as I was, but she was willing to pay for quality ingredients for her shop. She also knew that ofttimes the familiar brands and suppliers were not always the last word in value, freshness, or flavor. It was something we could chat about and bond over.

Dad? Well, he knew that whatever magic Mom and I were working up in the kitchen wasn't to be argued with. He footed the grocery bill without a word of complaint and never questioned if it was really worth the time and expense of buying produce from the farmers' market instead of the big box store.

Jonathan had been another matter. In the beginning he viewed my foodie proclivities with a sort of "benevolent bemusement." Of course there was probably a correlation between good health and carefully selected ingredients, he would allow, but maybe not worth the serious time commitment I devoted to the pursuit. Later, that bemusement turned to something more like contempt.

It could have been my guilty conscience trying to justify my rejection, but I couldn't say it was all hindsight goggles. There was the huffing when I took too long at a market stall. Annoyance when I protested against canned or frozen vegetables when better fresh ones were to be had. Frustration when I refused to save money buying hyperpigmented ground beef from the sketchy meat section at the big box store.

For someone whose tastes were so bourgeois, it baffled me that he found my food habits irksome. And it niggled, deep in my soul, that he only found them annoying because it was *me*. I hadn't wanted to consider that for a long time. I repressed it. Dismissed it as familiarity breeding contempt or some such thing, and that we just needed a weekend apart. I rationalized that it was natural. The longer a relationship went on, the harder it became to ignore the little peeves that seemed insignificant in the bloom of early love. But my relationship with food? It wasn't a small foible like forgetting to rinse the sink or leaving piles of books around the house. It was my career. My passion. One of my core values.

I shook my head back to the present. "Of course I do. You've had plenty of opportunity to murder me and you haven't yet. So either you're safe or just playing a long game. Seems a waste of time to me."

He let out a full-bellied laugh. "I'm a patient man, Veronica, and there isn't all that much to do here in winter."

"I'll take my chances anyway . . . Your omelets are worth the risk."

Chapter 10

N iall had things to do around the castle—it still seemed crazy to say "castle" like it was a perfectly normal thing—so I was left to explore on my own that morning. It wasn't all that expansive a place as far as castles went. County Mayo had far grander castles, like Ashford, converted to five-star hotels that met even the most starry-eyed princess-crazed little girl's vision for a proper fairy-tale castle. But Blackthorn hadn't been expanded in later centuries to be a showpiece the way Ashford had been. It retained much of its original character: small, austere, and easier to defend from hostile clans looking to expand their territory and influence.

The castle's second floor housed five guest rooms and one larger room with a massive fireplace that had been converted into a library and a small gathering space for guests. I could imagine posh couples from Australia, Japan, Germany, and the US converging here with a cognac after dinner to discuss their adventures traveling to destinations both glamorous and obscure. The space was cozier than any other part of the castle, owing to the fire blazing in the hearth. I was surprised Niall took the time to light it, given that it was just the two of us in residence, but I was grateful for the gesture.

I walked along the expansive shelves of leather-bound tomes, reading the spines in hues of saddle brown, oxblood, and deepest black with gilt lettering. Some had to date back a century or two and were housed on higher shelves, likely so guests would be less tempted to take them from the shelves on a whim. Others were more recent reprints of the classics that could be handled with less delicacy. There were also a number of modern paperbacks that had been left behind by guests for others to enjoy. Many were popular mysteries, and there seemed to be a penchant for anything set in Ireland.

I smiled at the idea of pausing a trip to Ireland to immerse oneself in Ireland through fiction and admired the commitment. I loved the combination of the ancient and the recent housed in one space. A cacophony of shapes and colors that somehow managed to produce a symphony of words.

I grabbed a copy of a Maeve Binchy I'd started in high school and never finished when the ending was spoiled for me by a friend who had seen the movie adaptation. I was about to settle into the posh armchair when the familiar *ping* of my phone sounded and I felt the vibration in my rear pocket.

AVERY: Hey, sis. Everything okay? How's the B and B?

ME: Um . . . It's a freaking castle. What's not to like? Also, isn't it like 4 a.m. there? Shouldn't you be asleep?

AVERY: I'm getting ready for my 5 a.m. barre class.

ME: You. Are. Insane.

AVERY: You know what they say about early birds . . .

ME: Yeah, but I'd rather have a couple more hours of sleep than worms.

AVERY: Haha. So seriously, everything is okay? Mom is worried but didn't want to intrude on your trip.

I felt a tightness in my chest. Mom was an Olympic-level worrier. She'd taken the gold in every games since I was born . . . or shortly thereafter anyway. If she wasn't texting me, she was still bothered by what happened at Christmas. Which wasn't surprising—it was a pretty major family bombshell. But she was acting differently because of it. Treating me differently because I knew. Maybe it was easier for her to pretend I was hers when she thought I didn't know, but now that it was out in the open, maybe things between us would be different.

> ME: Yeah, it's fine. I mean it's January in Ireland, so it's cold, dreary, and dark . . . I wouldn't give up your day job to become a travel agent just yet.
> AVERY: Well there goes my Plan B 😉 . . . but are you at least seeing the sights? Bonding with your countrymen?

I chuckled. I considered telling her about my vision of Aoife the night before, but I had no idea how to broach the topic on text.

> ME: I got to see a dairy farm yesterday.
> AVERY: Ew. Why?
> ME: Because those cows make the milk that produces the best butter I've had in my entire life.
> AVERY: So very you. But eating tasty things is definitely a key part of being on vacation, so carry on. Just don't ruin those new boots stepping in a cow pie. They weren't cheap.

I admired the sturdy black boots she'd sent with the rest of my travel gear. They fit better than any pair of shoes I'd ever bought myself and were attractive despite being practical. Of course they were expensive. I didn't want to know how much this little guilt trip had cost her, but it was probably more money than I would have earned in many months. The cold, slimy tentacles of guilt started to slither their way around me, but I warded them off. I hadn't asked for this.

ME: Will do my best. They're great boots. The whole care package was perfect.

AVERY: Just looking out for you, big sis. Also? I have another surprise.

My stomach dropped. I'd reached my lifetime limit for surprises and had no desire for more. I started typing out a snarky comment but thought better of it.

ME: Oh gawd. What now?

AVERY: Nothing bad. Steph and I want to join you in Italy. My results came back too, and it's the one place you and I had in common. Apparently Mom and Dad both have a lot of ancestry there. And Stephanie wants to tag along for the shopping. We both managed to snag the vacation time and thought it would be fun.

I brightened. Having them tag along for a leg of the journey was a possibility I hadn't planned for, not that I'd had time to plan much of anything. But there were a lot worse prospects than tooling around Lombardy and eating our body weight in pasta, pizza, granita, and gelato with my best friend and kid sister.

ME: That sounds epic, actually. On the condition your collective diets will be on pause.

AVERY: Okay, but bear in mind, not all of us have the metabolism of a hummingbird and actually have to watch ourselves.

ME: Seriously, one week, no food guilt. Can you handle it? It's good for the soul.

AVERY: For you, yes. As long as we get to do some shopping too.

I chuckled out loud.

ME: Fair. If I ask you to indulge my vice, the least I can do is indulge yours.

AVERY: I am totally going to get you some new clothes while we're there. You can be my Barbie. The European stuff will fit you way better than it does me.

ME: Don't make me regret this before you even get here.

AVERY: You're excited. You just haven't admitted it to yourself yet.

ME: You can tell yourself that, Stinkerbell. Now don't you have a Zumba class or something?

AVERY: It's barre. Zumba is so 2010. I hope the rent is cheap under that rock where you've been living.

ME: Have fun, brat.

AVERY: 😜

AVERY: Be sure to text Mom.

I set my phone on the side table. Should I text my mother? Hmm . . . not right then, as a text at two fifteen in the morning would send her to the ER with chest pains, but in several hours when she'd had the chance to wake up and have some coffee. A good daughter would reach out and reassure her mother that all was well. I'd done so, even on my short escapades around the West. But I wanted *her* to reach out to *me*. I wanted to know that she wasn't using company manners with me all of a sudden.

Another part of me wanted to text Stephanie, but while she was the most energetic person in the entire northern hemisphere, even she wouldn't appreciate a *ding* in the middle of the night if it wasn't a life-or-death thing. And it wasn't. My concerns about my relationship with my mom would hold until after the sun rose in Denver.

And my concerns about my own mental well-being and the visions I'd had of Aoife could hold indefinitely. Steph was the hyperrational sort who would have a million very plausible, scientifically verifiable explanations for the vision I'd had. And I didn't want to hear any of them. I wanted to believe, if only for a little while longer, that what I'd seen was real. A glimmer of what had transpired here in earlier generations.

Echoes, as Niall had called them, of past events that still reverberated off the stone walls. Sorrows that permeated the curtains and tapestries like smoke from a devastating fire long since extinguished but whose traces still lingered in the air.

Niall hadn't called me crazy. He seemed to think my visions were somehow perfectly reasonable in the confines of this ancient castle. And for now, I'd cling to that.

Chapter 11

By late morning Niall collected me from the library for our excursion. I'd made the decision to text Mom when the hour was more reasonable in Estes. Maybe the best path back to normal would be pretending nothing had changed. Eventually we'd move past the awkward and reclaim something like we used to have, but that was more or less a variation on what I'd been doing for more than ten years now. We'd have to face the uncomfortable conversations at some point.

I pulled myself back to the present, with Niall, which was far more pleasant to contemplate. "So where to?" He seemed intent on keeping the outing a surprise, but I couldn't help but press out of curiosity.

He playfully tapped his fingers on the steering wheel. "I'm taking you to a corner of Ireland you might not expect. I want you to get a taste of something different."

I cocked my head. "I'm intrigued."

"Something tells me you'll enjoy this particular excursion." His lips curled into a feline grin, and I knew he was probably telling the truth, and that I'd end up well fed by the end of it. We chatted easily as his SUV zipped through the Irish countryside at terrifying speed despite the narrowness of the roads. Pauses in the conversation were rare and never awkward.

We approached a small town, not a picturesque coastal or river town like Westport, but more of an inland working-class town with modest, well-kept homes and a population that was in the midst of a workday like any other. The Main Street was lined with the expected sort of businesses: pharmacies, corner markets, and antique shops. There were a few typical Irish pubs that seemed to be the quaintest buildings the town had to offer. Chances were, they did a dependable trade and could afford a nice façade, regular paint, and little flower boxes for the windows, which were currently draped with evergreens until it grew warm enough for spring flowers.

"Ballyhaunis?" I deduced from the names of several businesses.

"Indeed, Miss Stratton. And I am going to take you for some of the best Polish and Pakistani food of your life."

I looked over at him. "Really? That seems an odd combination."

"Less odd than you think. You are standing in the town with the highest percentage of immigrants in all of Ireland. Your ancestors may have fled almost two hundred years ago, but it seems we've become a land of opportunity once again while our American cousins were busy making their livelihoods overseas. Pakistani, Indian, Polish, Portuguese—all come to work and to share their culture in the meantime."

"And their food," I mused.

"Right you are. It's generally the best gateway to any culture in my experience. Polish first, I think."

We crossed to a stone building, typical of the region, with Irish and Polish flags flying from the roof. The name in the window read *Alesky's*. Simple, avoiding the kitsch and cliché, which was often the first sign of a good restaurateur. The interior was cozy and uncluttered. A massive fireplace was the centerpiece and required little in the way of fuss to create an ambiance. The tables were bare wood, eschewing the formality of white linens, and it suited the place.

There wasn't a host, so Niall directed us to a table a bit off to the side, but in a central enough location that we could get a sense of the place's energy. A tall, blond waiter who appeared to be in his early twenties smiled in recognition when he saw Niall. The two shook hands with the warmth of long-lost friends.

"Veronica, I want you to meet a good mate of mine, Marek. His da, Alesky, is the chef, and Marek here runs the place along with his sister Zofia. Their mother, Maria, keeps them in line. I find any excuse I can to come get some of Alesky's pierogis and potato pancakes." Niall's eyes shifted to the waiter, and he gestured in my direction. "Marek, this is our charming guest from America."

Marek and I shook hands, his grip warm and self-assured. "Welcome, friend. I hope you came hungry." His accent was Irish, with only the barest hint of Polish, so his family either immigrated when he was young or he'd been born in Ireland and acquired the music of his parents' intonation from living and working together in such a tight-knit family.

"Always." I couldn't help but smile at the pride in his voice.

He handed us menus and whisked back to the kitchen to let us browse in peace. There were several kinds of pierogi, gołąbki—cabbage rolls—and pyzy—dumplings. In addition, there were more familiar options like burgers, chicken, and fries. A staggering variety of fries with any number of sauces and spices.

"The Irish do seem to like their chips." I gestured to the French fry section of the menu.

He rolled his eyes. "It's the equivalent of putting chicken nuggets and grilled cheese on the menu in America. Something to placate the picky eaters. Alesky couldn't bear to run a chippy, even if he probably makes more money from them than he does for the rest of his dishes."

"Profit margins for chips, especially the 'fancy' ones, are probably off the charts."

"We'll steer clear of those for now. Do you mind if I order?" There was something of a dare in his voice, but I was not the one to be intimidated by a culinary challenge.

"Please do. You know what Alesky does best."

Rather than wait for Marek to reappear, Niall stood and poked his head into the kitchen. Clearly these weren't just casual acquaintances of his. I couldn't make out the words, but they were met with approving sounds from the disembodied voices in the kitchen.

"You're in for a treat." Niall reclaimed his seat. "Alesky's been bored."

I smiled knowingly. "There is nothing like a bored chef with willing guests and a kitchen full of promise."

"No indeed. I wonder that you didn't go into the restaurant business as much as you love it."

"So unpredictable. So hard to compete in a crowded market. A lot of the great restaurants fold because the profit margins are too thin. Or worse—"

"They become chip shops."

"Precisely. One of the best chefs I ever met ended up tossing out his entire book—great Mediterranean food—and converting his place into a pizzeria. A really good one. Wood-fire ovens, authentic Italian recipes, extensive wine list and everything. He ended up closing after a few years because he grew disenchanted, offering people the world and having them order cheap beer and pies night after night with so many discordant toppings you can't taste the actual pizza. I'm pretty sure he went back to school for a degree in some tech field because he was so discouraged by having to compromise on his vision."

His face grew somber. "It'd be heartbreaking for sure. It's a shame when people don't know what they're missing out on."

I found my arms clutching over my chest. "Horses to water and all that. I just couldn't bear the idea of opening a restaurant and watching it die, you know? More than half of all restaurants go out that way."

He leaned back in his chair. "You don't strike me as the sort to let odds get in your way."

I stiffened just a bit, reflexively defensive. It wasn't the first time I'd heard this argument, and even if it had been a while, it wasn't any easier to defend my choices. And Niall didn't know me . . . not really. "Maybe I am indeed that sort. Especially when something so important is on the line."

He held up his hands in mock surrender. "Peace, Veronica. I was just curious. It just seems to me the field you've chosen isn't all that much easier. Niche food broker isn't exactly a recession-proof job."

"Maybe not, but it doesn't all ride on the fate of one restaurant or one farm. Sure, I have a fancy client on the hook who could be the making of my business, but if he doesn't come through, I'm not without options."

"Fair point, but when one restaurant suffers, it's often a trend."

"Don't I know it," I agreed. "But it's a way of being in the food business without keeping all my organic free-range nonantibiotic-laced eggs in one basket."

He tilted his head as if conceding the point but didn't seem truly convinced. "I think I came close to hitting a nerve." He looked at me, assessing how close to that nerve he was tap-dancing.

"Yeah." The heat rose in my cheeks as I realized how transparent I was—something I was usually careful to avoid. "I can't tell you the number of times I've heard, 'Why don't you just open your own restaurant?' in the past seven years or so. As if it's just that easy. Securing the loans to open a place is an Everest-level hurdle all by itself. Get into the logistics of finding a good location, getting permits, finding reliable staff, and it begins to seem impossible."

Niall crossed his arms. "It *is* that easy to do. You just have the sense to know it's not easy to do *well*."

"That's a distinction without a difference. Why do something if you can't do it well?" My father's words spilled out of my mouth and I almost smiled. Biology or no, I really was his kid.

"You can't do anything well if you're not willing to do it badly first. Isn't that how the expression goes?"

I was about to accuse him of sounding far too much like Avery or Stephanie for my own liking when Malek rescued me with an impressive platter of food. It was an assortment of everything on the menu plus a few off-book items. Every bit was fit for the cover of a glossy foodie magazine.

"Tuck in." There was genuine enthusiasm in his voice, and the question of my would-be restaurant was mercifully forgotten for the moment.

"For better Polish food, you'd have to go to Warsaw. Even then, the best of it probably doesn't outstrip it by much. Not enough to make the trip worthwhile."

"I wonder why they didn't stay in Poland so they could make proper Polish food in a town that would appreciate it." I mused aloud, not fully realizing I'd spoken my thoughts.

"For the same reason the Chinese came to America and morphed their own dishes into things like chop suey. Better opportunities for their kids, more prosperity. Your people left Ireland to chase a brighter future and now others are emigrating here to do the same."

I sat thoughtful a moment. The sensation of what I saw was creeping back into the crevasse of my memory. "I think Aoife would have liked that. She felt so trapped, but she *loved* her home."

Niall blinked. "The echo was that strong for you?"

"It wasn't just that I could see what was going on, like in a movie or a dream . . . I could feel her. Not read her thoughts exactly, but her emotions—as clearly as feeling rain on my face."

I bowed my head. How ridiculous that must've sounded. Maybe this was some sort of trauma response to the fallout from Avery's DNA kit. Maybe it was all an especially vivid dream, but I remembered too much to reject it as such. I wished I could.

"Your ties to Aoife and Blackthorn must run deep. And I think you're probably right . . . She'd be glad to see how Ireland has changed and grown, mostly for the better. Her father would think we've all gone soft, but I've never put too much stock in his opinions."

I felt my lungs expand enough to accommodate a proper breath. "You're talking like what I saw was completely normal. Like I haven't gone off the deep end."

"Because I don't think you have. I mean, maybe—but not because of Aoife. There is some connection between you, whether it's family ties or because she sees something of the kindred in you. I'm not sure it matters much which it is, but she chose to show herself to you."

"So have *you* seen her?"

He paused and my stomach fluttered. I wasn't sure which I wanted more: to know I wasn't alone in my visions or to cling to the idea that they were somehow unique and meant for me.

"I've been living in or at least adjacent to Blackthorn my whole life. I've seen whispers of the former residents. A wee prickle on the skin here and there. But never a real echo. My family has been there for generations, but somehow your roots go deeper."

"I don't see how. My sister and Stephanie chose the castle because it was the coolest-sounding vacation rental near where the DNA company said my ancestry was from. It's got to be a coincidence."

He shook his head. "That's the pragmatic American in you. Maybe this doesn't have to have a reasonable explanation. Maybe it's okay not knowing how, why, or even *if* what you saw was true."

That sort of thinking was so contrary to the hyperrationalism I'd grown up with that I had to pause to consider. "Maybe I should just roll with it, but that will take some getting used to."

"I'm sure you'll adjust in time. You just have to give the Old Country time to seep into your bones."

"You make it sound like gout." Neither of us could suppress a laugh.

"You wound me, Veronica."

Veronica. The way he said my name was imbued with more gravitas than I was accustomed to. I was "Vero" to so many people, the sound of my full name was almost foreign to me.

There was something in his face I couldn't read, and the sudden wing flutters in my midsection made it too uncomfortable to try.

I glanced down at the platter of rapidly disappearing dumplings, cabbage rolls, and other delights Alesky had prepared for us. "You weren't kidding about this food though. Totally worth the drive. How did you discover the place?"

It hardly seemed the sort of restaurant that would get the coverage in the culinary media and was far enough from Blackthorn that he wouldn't have stumbled across it by chance.

"Car trouble a few years back and a mate recommended a repair shop here. I had time to kill and found Alesky's. You can piece together the rest. I try to get back every month or two when I can and spread the word in Westport, but there aren't too many willing to come all the way out here, even if Alesky makes the best pierogi west of Krakow."

I could tell he cared about Alesky and his family. About the restaurant and their livelihood. And he was doing what he could to help them along. "You're a good friend, Niall."

"Bah, a fair neighbor when I can be is all. No more than that."

It was false modesty, but there wasn't much sense in arguing the point.

"I think we've had a fair sampling of Alesky's handiwork. Shall we get a move on, then?"

My eyes widened. We'd eaten so much I couldn't imagine packing away any more food, but he *had* warned me to be prepared with my appetite.

He tossed some bills on the table, stood, and reached a hand out to mine. I stood and took it, trying not to think about the warmth of his palm pressed against mine, and we walked back out into the biting winds of January.

Chapter 12

For the rest of the day, we sampled food in any number of villages between Ballyhaunis and Westport. He insisted I try a Pakistani chicken curry dish from one of the local shops before we headed out. It was less creamy than its Indian counterpart, at least the versions I'd tried in Denver, and I loved the blend of spices they used to draw out the flavor in the chicken.

We then drove back in the direction of Westport, taking a winding route along the craggy hillsides, stopping for smoked salmon in Knock, mussels in Claremorris, duck confit in Balla, coffee and porter cake in Castlebar. By the time the glistening lights of Westport came into view, dark was beginning to fall despite the early hour.

He pulled in front of a pub, and I groaned involuntarily. "No. I'm crying 'uncle.' No more food. You've found my limit, and that's saying something."

"No, no more food. But you can't leave Ireland without a pint in a proper pub, can you?"

"I suppose not." The sign read *Padraig O'Shea's* and appeared to be the very picture of a quaint Irish pub, exactly as Hollywood would have depicted it with scarred, heavy wooden tables and mismatched chairs, a cheerful hum of activity from patrons who were just off from their shifts for the day, and a crackling fire to brace us all against the fanged chill in the January air.

Niall directed us to a table tucked away in the back corner, away from the din of the bar but close to the warmth of the fire. A sturdy-looking waitress well into her forties greeted Niall by name and smiled politely to me when she took our order. I passed up the inky-black stout, despite it being the pride of Ireland. The thought of an entire pint of the heavy beer caused the discordant array of foods we'd consumed that day to roil my gut. I chose a local craft cider, aged in whiskey barrels for months instead. It wasn't light, but at least it lacked the oppressive creaminess of the stout. The golden-red liquid was cold and soothing, and I felt the muscle knots in my neck, which I didn't know I possessed, begin to unwind a bit further with each sip until I was sure my shoulders were resting a number of inches lower than they had been.

Niall raised his glass, filled with the traditional stout, and clinked it gently against mine. "To charming guests from America who know the difference between a mutton stew and a pork chop."

I chuckled. "I can drink to that."

"Do you come here very often?" Heat prickled at my cheeks as I recognized the clichéd undertones of the question just a beat too late. "Um, I mean, is this your regular pub, or do you visit a few? Is that considered bad form?"

He swallowed his grin, bless him. "Yes, this is my regular pub, and I admit to being a creature of habit. But no, it wouldn't offend O'Shea if I took my Friday pint at The Rusty Anchor or Jim Malloy's on occasion. There aren't any feuds between the pub owners, thank the stars, and they all know how important business is, especially in the offseason."

I nodded. January tended to be when restaurants folded in Denver, after they'd tabulated their December receipts. I always dreaded the emails of client restaurants letting me know they were liquidating stock and terminating leases. In those situations, I did my best to help the restaurateur recoup some money by seeking out buyers for their equipment and other assets. In turn, I helped their vendors, often my clients as well, to find new markers for their product to make up for the lost revenue. I was a shoulder to cry on when needed, and it was the most heartbreaking part of my job.

"What's this about Malloy's?" A tall man with a thatch of auburn-red curls took the seat on the other side of Niall.

"Just discussing the local haunts with our American guest." Niall gestured to me. "Veronica, I have the unfortunate duty of introducing you to my best mate and the biggest lout in all of Ireland, Ciaran Walsh."

Ciaran rolled his mischievous brown eyes. "Some friend you are, Callahan." He extended his hand to me, his grip firm. "So you're taking advantage of our fine January weather for some sightseeing in Ireland?"

The corners of my lips turned up in a smile. "I'll take drizzle and cold over tourists."

Ciaran's head tilted. "I can't say I disagree with you." He turned to Niall. "She's not half bad, this one. Better than most of the lot you play host to."

Niall raised his glass in my direction. "I hate to admit it, but you have a point. Our Miss Stratton is far more pleasant than the common tourist."

Ciaran's eyes locked with Niall's for a moment. The silent communication possible between those closely acquainted for decades. I felt like I was intruding on a conversation in a foreign language I didn't speak, and I looked away.

"So what plans do you have for your stay? A lot of the tours and sites aren't open this time of year."

I opened my mouth to answer, but Niall responded for me. "I've been showing her around the less visited parts of our fair county. And I thought to bring her to meet the family for tea tomorrow afternoon. My mother just sent a text to invite us."

Ciaran's eyebrows raised, but he didn't comment. Clearly it wasn't something he did with most of his guests, who would be busy with ferry rides and horseback tours when the weather was fair.

Niall's eyes met mine. "If you'd like to, of course."

I cleared my throat. "Oh, sure. I mean . . . I'd love to. I'm sure they're amazing."

"Kinder people you'll never meet," Ciaran vouched. "But I don't think you'll have to wait that long to introduce her to Caitlin. She was at the bar ten minutes ago."

Niall heaved a theatrical sigh. "I apologize in advance for the antics of my younger sister."

I snorted a laugh. "No need. I have one of those. I know how much of a pain they can be."

"Lucky for Niall I'm delightful." A woman with a thick crop of red hair and skin so pale she looked to be made of porcelain seemed to materialize out of the mist and took the final seat at our table without further preamble. She was as mischievous as a pixie freed from her cage and twice as cunning.

"Speak of the devil," Niall muttered. He introduced us with a tone of mock annoyance that betrayed he actually adored his younger sibling. It wasn't unlike the tone I took when Avery was in earshot. He introduced us and we exchanged the usual niceties.

Caitlin assumed a relaxed pose, but her dark eyes were laser-focused on me. She had a gift for steering the conversation—

usually in ways that allowed her to ask me probing questions without sounding like the bad cop in an interrogation. The men had no idea what she was doing, but she knew I was fully aware that she was masterfully handling the flow of conversation. But because I was willing to play along and answer her questions, I met with her preliminary approval. Why I, as a very temporary visitor to the area, would need it, I wasn't sure, but I supposed it was better to have it than not.

It didn't take her long to home in on the question she'd been maneuvering toward. "So you're traveling alone, then? No special fella to come along?"

I went to take another sip of my cider to stall my answer, only to find I'd downed my first pint already. As if reading my thoughts, the waitress appeared with another round for the table and a motherly pat for Niall's shoulder. By the time she'd replaced our drinks and cleared away the empty glasses, I hoped Caitlin would have forgotten her query, but she peered at me with expectant eyes as soon as the waitress walked away. Little sisters really *were* a pain.

"As Facebook says, 'it's complicated.'" It was a glib nonanswer, but I didn't think I needed to provide a full rundown of my breakup just then.

"It's also none of your business, Cait." Niall said, his expression growing somber, which she promptly ignored.

She fixed me with her pointed stare. "If you don't know if you have a fella, the answer is no."

I knocked back more of the cider. I'd been in Caitlin's company for less than half an hour, and she'd already managed to find my vulnerable underbelly. She was far too perceptive for her own good.

"A breakup a couple months back. Nothing all that earth-shattering." I shrugged in a vain attempt at nonchalance.

"Best to get past it and move on to better things, don't you think?" Her tone wasn't insistent or pressing, but more matter-of-fact.

"My god, Caitlin. Can you keep from meddling in other people's lives for the space of one evening?" Niall shot her a warning look to which she seemed impervious, like raindrops on a yellow slicker coat.

"What? She's a guest in Westport. I won't have too many more opportunities for meddling, will I? I have to provide my valuable services while I can."

"Like I said, my apologies for this." Niall rubbed his eyes, both in consternation and amusement.

"If only she'd focus this energy toward climate change or the national debt, she'd be an international hero." Despite the words, Ciaran fairly beamed at his best friend's younger sister. Admiring her for the force of nature she was.

"Oh, I'll get to that when I've run out of more amusing pursuits. Plenty of time for all that serious stuff when I'm old and boring."

Niall chuckled at her. She glanced down at her watch and downed the last of her drink.

"Shoot. I've gotta run. Seamus is picking me up for dinner and a movie. Do bring this one back to the house tomorrow. I like her better than most of the lot you cavort with."

"Off with you, and behave yourself, brat." Niall leaned over to kiss her forehead before she popped out of her seat like a human jack-in-the-box.

Niall shook his head. "She's a whirling dervish that one."

Just like Hurricane Avery. I remembered Dad's remark at Christmas. Caitlin wasn't elegant or statuesque like Avery, but they both seemed to have harnessed the energy of the sun somehow and not let me in on their secret. Stephanie too. I was the moon to their sun, seemingly built only to reflect the light of others.

Ciaran's eyes tracked her to the doorway. I sensed he wasn't happy to see her go, nor did he seem pleased that she was going out with this Seamus fellow. Such was small-town life, however. And while Denver felt a bit impersonal at times, I wondered if I'd find the limited social circles stifling or charming after a few months.

I felt a buzz in my pocket and instinctively reached for my phone, imagining Mom had finally broken her radio silence. Instead, it was Stephanie. Niall and Ciaran had fallen into conversation about football, a subject about which I knew nothing, so I didn't feel too bad about firing off a few texts.

> STEPHANIE: Having fun?
> ME: In a pub as we speak.
> STEPHANIE: Good for you. Do you have a fresh round?

I felt a flitter in my gut. She had news that required booze. I had most of my second cider left, which was plenty, as I made a point to keep my alcohol consumption in check.

> ME: More or less. Why?
> STEPHANIE: I was out to dinner last night. Fairbanks' place. I saw Jonathan. With another woman.

The flitter dissipated as quickly as it arrived.

> ME: I'm sure it's a colleague. They go out to talk shop all the time.
> STEPHANIE: Not this time, hon.

She sent a picture, which took longer than usual to load given the less-than-optimal signal in the bar. When it finally popped up, sitting at Fairbanks' best table was a man who was unmistakably Jonathan with an attractive, dark-haired woman in a tight Kelly-green dress that clung in all the right places. She was alluring but was classy enough not to stoop to something as cliché as a red dress. Perfect for Jonathan who bemoaned my adherence to the code of Colorado casual attire, where The North Face and Patagonia were considered formal wear.

He had pleaded with me to wear more dresses and skirts, and I resisted. Despite having a number of dresses and fashion-forward pieces from Avery in my wardrobe . . . I let them linger in the back of the closet. His arm was around her, and they were just an inch or two away from kissing.

ME: Oh.

STEPHANIE: I debated about telling you now or when I saw you in Italy, but if it were me, I'd want to know sooner rather than later. Don't hate me.

ME: Never. You're not the jerk here.

Who was? Jonathan? Maybe. He had just broken up with me a couple of months before . . . Did I mean so little to him? But we *were* broken up and I had no claims to him anymore. Maybe the jerk was me for not being a better partner to Jonathan when we were together. But all the same, a few months of mourning the four-year relationship would have been a nice gesture on his part.

STEPHANIE: Don't let this ruin Ireland for you. Promise me. He isn't worth it.

ME: I'll be fine. Promise.

Niall, having noticed my head buried in my phone, turned to me. "Everything okay back home?"

I scrolled up in the text chain to see the picture of the beautiful woman in green who seemed to have ensnared Jonathan. She was beautiful in ways I would never be. Sophisticated and worldly in ways I could never claim. They were a good match, and I hoped I'd be a big enough person—someday—to wish them well if things worked out for them.

But today was not that day.

"What do you all say to another round, gents? On me." It was answer enough to the query.

"I knew I liked this one," Ciaran pronounced, waving over the waitress.

Niall didn't smile. He shot me a glance of concern I chose to ignore.

I might tell him later, but for tonight I wanted nothing more than to chase my sorrows to the bottom of a cider glass.

Chapter 13

Y ou're a genius, you know that?" I tried to keep my words from slurring as Niall pulled the car up to the entrance of Blackthorn.

"Because I insisted you eat chips once you started in on your third pint?" He was wiser than I and stopped at two, asking the waitress to switch him over to club soda with a twist of lime. A trick I used at parties all the time myself.

"Exactly. You all make amazing French fries here."

"Let it never be said the Irish don't know their way around a potato. You'll be even gladder that I talked you out of the curry ones if tomorrow morning goes as I suspect it will for you."

"Like I said. Genius."

He met me at the car door, ready to assist me out, but I didn't struggle as much with my footing as he expected me to.

"I'm really fine," I protested, as he gently took hold of my elbow. "Like not okay to drive, but I can walk."

"I'd rather stay close until you're up the stairs. I don't care to test out the castle's insurance policy." He stayed close by my side, and I loved the feel of the warmth of him on my hip as we walked.

True to his word, he stayed with me until we'd made the climb up the stairs, and I was grateful I didn't do anything to make his presence necessary.

We paused at the door to my room. "Thank you. You're a proper gentleman." I kissed his cheek in thanks, and his hand rose reflexively to the spot where my lips had been. "It's okay, I wasn't wearing lipstick."

He chuckled. "I wasn't worried about that."

"What were you worried about, then?" The four pints of cider hadn't completely dismantled my filter, but they'd done a great job at lowering it.

"You just went through a breakup . . ."

"Oh, big news on that front. Apparently he's upgraded already." I pulled the phone from my pocket, opened my text app, and found the photo Stephanie had sent. "See? She's beautiful and they look so happy."

Niall glanced at the phone for a moment before he handed it back. "He's a fool, Veronica. You're well rid of him."

"It's my fault." I rested my head against his chest, glad to have its solid warmth to lean on. "I could have tried harder."

"So could he. But he didn't. You deserve better." His arms circled around me, and I let myself melt into his embrace.

"You're wonderful." I should have been embarrassed by my lack of inhibition, but in that moment, I couldn't bring myself to care.

"As are you, *mo stór*. Let's get you to bed."

I pulled my head back and widened my eyes in surprise. I wanted to say something, but the words were a lump of cement in my throat.

A feline smile tugged at his lips. "You dubbed me a proper gentleman not three minutes ago, remember? A gentleman doesn't take advantage of ladies who've had more cider than is wise."

Relief and disappointment tugged in almost equal measure, but I followed as he opened the door to my room, and he ushered me to the bed. He pulled back the covers and urged me to sit. He deftly pulled off my boots and tucked me under the heavy blankets.

"Thank you." The words were groggy, but I kept a grip on his hand. "You didn't have to be so nice, but you were."

He stroked the side of my face with his free hand. "You deserve nothing less."

My eyes met his and I saw an irresistible tenderness there. "I wish—" I struggled with the words I was too timid to speak. *I wish I hadn't drunk like a barfly so he wouldn't object to kissing me.* In my current state I couldn't think of any less stupid way to put it.

"I know. I do too. But not like this, *mo chroí.*" His voice was a wisp of down as he spoke. "I won't have you regretting your time here."

Even in my hazy state, I knew he was right. "I'm glad my sister found this place for me. Found you."

He sat on the edge of the bed, lowered his lips to my forehead, and pressed them gently against my skin. Tenderly. Reverently. I fought the urge to run my fingers through his thick black hair and ask him to kiss me properly, but I chose to linger in the sweetness of what he offered me. My heartbeat quickened and I willed time to stand still so I could live in this moment.

His voice rasped when he raised his lips away. "Sleep well, lovely." He stood and let his finger lazily trace the side of my face one last time. "I'm going to sleep in the room next door in case you need me."

"Thanks." I watched with bleary eyes until the door shut behind him.

I awoke at some ungodly hour the next morning as the sun was struggling to crest over the horizon. My head wasn't too thick from drink, though heaven knew why I'd been spared the well-deserved discomfort of a hangover. I said silent thanks that I hadn't had need of the red plastic sand pail Niall had apparently left on the bedside table in the middle of the night.

Had he checked on me? I normally would have been horrified at the thought of a man I barely knew coming into the room while I slept, but this didn't bother me in the least. He'd been worried about me. He'd nurtured me. I felt a sting in my throat as I considered the gleaming red bucket, even as I knew the gesture wasn't entirely selfless on his part.

I found myself drawn to the fresh air, so I threw on some fresh clothes and headed out for a ramble on the grounds. I'd heard no sign of Niall in the castle, so I wandered toward the outbuildings. He might be gathering up some eggs for more of his amazing omelets.

A short jaunt later, and I was standing in the barn on the castle grounds. A haze enveloped me, much as it had the other night. One moment I could see the barn, a utilitarian space mostly devoted to chickens and tools. At once it transformed into a thriving, active part of the estate. The horses were brushed to gleaming and the tack was polished and supple, ready to ride in a moment's notice should the lord of the manor or any of the family require it.

Aoife, looking resolved, strode into the barn with a confidence I envied to my marrow. The sort I longed to feel at least once in my life.

A groom emerged, as if from the ether. He was of middling height, but his profession had chiseled the muscle into him. His hair was under a cap but was a deep brown that glinted red in the beams of sunlight that streaked the barn through its high, narrow windows. "Will you be riding today, milady? I'll saddle Bradaigh straightaway."

"I came to talk to you, Tadgh. Not to ride." Aoife stood, arms akimbo like she expected something else from the groom. "And you can dispense with the 'milady' nonsense. I thought we were long past all that."

He paused, his hazel eyes locked on her green ones for just a moment before he broke his gaze and turned back to the massive black saddle he was polishing. Judging from the embossed seal, it belonged to Aoife's father and merited special attention. "I'm afraid I've too much work to stop and chat, milady. Perhaps another time."

"There won't be another time. I've taken my mother's best jewels from my trousseau—the ones that cow didn't get her hands on anyway—and I'm going to America."

Tadgh froze with the polish rag still in his hands. "I heard your father was going to announce your match soon."

"The two events aren't unrelated." She tried to keep her tone measured but wasn't entirely successful.

"You don't like him then?"

"Catching on, are you?" She threw her hands in the air and huffed. "He's the worst sort of horse's arse. No offense to your charges."

"I thought once your father introduced you to some fancy man, you'd be off planning your wedding."

"Do you really think I'm that fickle, Tadgh Callahan? Do you think I'd trade a decent man like you for a louse like Declan Tierney? Do you think the time we spent together means nothing to me? The long rides out in the countryside? The quiet moments by the stream where none can see us?" Her voice was both feral and pleading.

I half expected her to grow claws and fangs to eviscerate Tadgh for the insult to her integrity. But she approached him and placed her hand on his arm. It was a forward gesture for an unmarried woman in these times and felt more significant than if she'd embraced him.

He looked down at her hand with ill-disguised longing. "I didn't figure you'd have much choice." He raised his eyes and returned to the saddle.

Her voice softened. "There is always choice. It may not always be the choices we hoped for, but there is always choice, Tadgh."

"Maybe for fine ladies, but not for apprentice stable hands like me." The defeat in his tone laced the barn air like a freezing fog.

She put a hand on each of his biceps and forced him to face her. The pleading in her eyes was potent, but she didn't allow her voice to waver. "Come to America with me, Tadgh. The famine is eating away at the soul of this country, and I don't want to stand by idly and watch."

"And what will happen to my family, Aoife? My da can't find work enough to put food on the table. Ma's expecting another wean by Christmas. My brothers and sisters are half starved. If it weren't for my wages and the food you're able to sneak from your father's kitchen, there'd be no 'half' about it."

"Convince them all to come. I plan to leverage my mother's family for my dowry before I leave the county. She left it in trust to them when she fell ill. I thought it odd at the time, but now it makes sense. She knew Da might well fall in with a harpy, and so he's done. Just think, Mairéad will be furious, and we'll be able to gloat about it from Boston. We'll be able to provide for all of them far better in America than we can here."

"Da was stubborn before, but he's been obstinate since he fell from the castle rafters. He'd rather be hanged than leave Ireland."

"If he gets caught in my father's henhouse again, the MacWilliam men just might arrange it, no matter how long your family has been in service to mine. It's lucky I happened on them and fed Father's men a line of malarkey to get them to unhand him."

Tadgh flung aside his saddle brush with a clatter. "Da is foolish and thinking of his own empty belly rather than sparing any concern for damaging my prospects here. He can't get it through his addled brain that if I don't stay on here, the rest of the family will suffer for it. Especially since he isn't fit to work anymore."

Aoife softened a bit and leaned closer to him. "Can't you at least try? I know your father hasn't been right since the accident, but can't you or your mother persuade him? It would mean a new life for all of you."

Tadgh shook his head slowly. "It's of no use."

She placed a hand on his to still his deft movements with the bridle. "I matter so little to you, then? You won't even ask them?"

He finally dared to meet her eyes. "It's no use wasting breath on it. I promise you the answer wouldn't change if I begged. The old man won't budge."

"So we strap him to the bow of the ship like a Viking maiden. We won't be able to hear his protests from the cabins."

He looked like he wanted to smile but wasn't able. "I'm sorry, Aoife. Ma won't defy him, even now that he's not in his right mind. She's of the old sort who won't contradict a word he has to say. Especially in front of any of his children."

The color drained from her face as the fire rose in her eyes. "Fine, Tadgh Callahan. You stay and watch as this green rock crumbles to dust. I won't give up on my own future so easily. Saddle my horse. And if you ever felt anything like love for me, you won't tell them where I've gone. A lady has no call to disclose her comings and goings with a stable hand, so they should well believe I didn't burden you with the truth."

Wordlessly, Tadgh complied. Within moments, she rode off down the path toward town, presumably to make her way to Cork where she could buy her passage to Boston. She didn't spare a backward glance as her fine bay mare cantered down the road. And she never heard the sound of Tadgh's weeping for his lost love.

Chapter 14

I walked back to the castle, the scene with Aoife and Tadgh swimming in my brain. I wanted to weep for the couple, so desperately in love, but so unjustly separated by the cruel hand of family and circumstances. I didn't know how, but I could *feel* Aoife's searing pain. Tadgh resigned himself to a life of monotony and duty, too easily in her view, because he couldn't defy his injured father. I sensed his longing as well. Had he thought he had a prayer of convincing his father, he'd have stood beside Aoife as the ship left his beloved Ireland in its wake.

And Tadgh's last name was Callahan, like Niall's. It was a common enough name, but I knew the shared surname was no coincidence. Niall had said his family had been part of this castle's history for ages. Looking back five or six generations would have been rather recent history for a place of this vintage. I'd seen Niall's great-to-some-degree-grandfather, I was sure. But what, then, was Aoife's connection to me?

Back in the castle, the glorious perfume of coffee and sizzling bacon wafted from the kitchen, so I didn't bother searching for Niall in one of the guest rooms. I followed the scent like one of the cartoon characters from my youth, floating toward the wafting steam of a cooling pie.

"Mmm . . . coffee," I said by way of greeting, claiming the stool at the counter across from the stove.

"How's the head?" he asked, his voice a few decibels lower than usual, prepared for the worst.

"Fine." And it was, amazingly, true. Perhaps escaping to the fresh air had helped to stave off the worst of it. I imbibed frequently in my line of work, but never all that much, as a matter of principle. Too much alcohol dulled the palate, and I couldn't afford to be off. So the fact that I managed to wake without a hangover after four pints of cider was rather remarkable.

He was both appalled and vaguely impressed that I'd emerged from my bender none the worse for wear. "What sorcery have you been meddling in? It is simply indecent for a person to drink like you did and not have the courtesy of a proper headache to show for it."

I shrugged. "I have no idea. I've never really overindulged before. I was a boring teen and young adult."

He gave a noncommittal grunt. "If a person has to get pissed to have a good time, they're usually fairly boring in my book."

I chuckled. "Good point. I'm sure Mother Nature is just giving me one free pass on the whole hangover experience. I'm sure I wouldn't be as lucky the next time. But I don't plan on there being one."

"All the better. Do you remember much?"

I accepted an empty plate from him with a grateful smile. "Everything, I'm pretty sure. I don't think I was quite as poorly as you imagined. We'd had enough food to stave off a disaster."

"In either case, I should apologize. I was a bit forward last night."

I wrinkled my brow. "You just kissed my forehead, right? And put the little bucket by the bed?"

Red tinged his cheeks. "Yes. It's silly, but I came in while you were sleeping to make sure you were still breathing. And I'm sorry about the bucket. We do have tourists who overindulge at the pub, and it can be a bit of a mess, so I have a supply of them handy."

I shuddered at the thought of him dealing with those buckets on busy mornings. "Smart of you. But what do you have to apologize for? Being kind to me?"

His shoulders seemed to lower a bit. "I'm glad I didn't overstep the mark then."

"Not at all. You took care of me when I needed you. I hope I'd do the same. You were a good friend to me last night."

"Since we're skating perilously close to that topic, I meant what I said. You're better off without that Jonathan fool."

"Thank you for saying so." I reached over and placed my hand on his. Our eyes met, and I couldn't hold his gaze for more than a few seconds.

He served up fried eggs and bacon along with thick slices of toast and slid in the spot next to me at the counter. The food was simple but executed perfectly.

"So we could tour along the coast today if you'd like. Or I can let you be if you prefer." His eyes were focused on the skillet as he ate his own breakfast.

"I thought you were going to take me to meet your parents." I felt a sinking sensation in my core. Did he not want to introduce me to them anymore? Had I embarrassed him so thoroughly last night?

"I wasn't sure you were really interested. I mean, they're lovely people and all, but do you really want to spend a few of your precious holiday hours with a couple of stodgy pensioners? Don't tell them I call them that, even if it's true."

I laughed. "If I were the manipulative sort, I'd blackmail you with that. But yes, I do want to meet them." Anticipation fluttered in my gut as Niall considered this. Meeting his parents shouldn't have been a big deal. In three more days I'd be off to France and likely would never see these people again. But logical or not, I *wanted* to meet them.

He pushed his egg a few inches with the tines of his fork. "All right then, but don't say I didn't warn you. And Caitlin will be there, so brace yourself for another typhoon."

I smiled. "I'll bring my rain slicker."

It was less than a ten-minute drive to his parents' house from the castle. It seemed even once they were freed from their responsibilities to Blackthorn, they couldn't bear to be separated from it by too many miles. Their cottage, overgrown with ivy and wild roses contrasted with perfectly manicured hedgerows, looked like something out of a Tolkien novel, fit for hobbits rather than ordinary people.

His parents walked out to greet us as Niall pulled his car into the drive. His mother's hair was dark like Niall's, while his father's was a deep red like Caitlin's. She followed her parents outside, a small container of chocolate ice cream in one hand and a spoon in the other. She trailed us in as we exited the car.

"Caitlin has been telling us all about our American visitor." Mrs. Callahan kissed her son on the cheek and extended a hand to me. "Come in, come in, dears." I was immediately bidden to call them Liam and Molly, as they said they weren't the sort to abide formality.

"Don't believe half of what the wee brat says," Niall declared, hanging his coat on a rack in the entryway and extending a hand to take mine. He shot me a wink as he whisked me into the sitting room. "She's a nice lady no matter what Caitlin may have led you to believe."

"Oh shame on you, Niall Thomas Callahan. Your sister had nothing but nice things to say about our guest."

"I figured that wasn't interesting enough a tale for Caitlin and she'd have to throw in a bank robbery or ties to the mafia to make it a tale worth telling," Niall countered.

"I'd have gotten there if you'd taken much longer to get here." Caitlin flopped dramatically on the couch, ice cream still in hand. Niall's mother had prepared tea and a platter of finger foods, but Caitlin seemed interested only in her ice cream.

"It's rather early in the morning for a pint, isn't it? Beer, ice cream, or otherwise." Niall's tone was joking, but there was an undercurrent of genuine concern.

"Seamus Finnegan is an arse," she declared, implying no further elaboration was necessary. She took a generous spoonful of ice cream for emphasis.

Niall leaned back on his spot on the sofa, exhaling with an almost-audible roll of the eyes. "I told you that six months ago. Had you listened to your older brother, it would have spared you some heartache and Da his favorite dessert."

She stuck out her tongue in response. I sensed Niall wasn't particularly sad to see Seamus on the outs with his sister, and I was certain Ciaran wouldn't be saddened by the news.

"Enough foolishness." Molly shook her head despairingly at the antics of her children. "I'm interested in our guest. How does Blackthorn suit you, dear?"

I beamed. "It's wonderful. It's the sort of place I never thought I'd get to see outside of the movies."

Caitlin scoffed as if I spoke a heresy. "Crazy that. I spent my whole girlhood dreaming of life on the beach in California while rattling about that place and you come all the way here instead of having the good sense to hop over a few states and find a beach chair and a straw hat."

I laughed. "Southern California in January is in the mid-sixties—maybe eighteen Celsius? Hardly beach weather."

"Well, the Caribbean is still closer than here, isn't it? I still think you're daft. But, you know, welcome to the Emerald Isle and all that."

"Such a warm greeting." Liam scoffed good-naturedly. "Pay her no mind. None of the rest of us do when she gets in a strop."

"That's enough teasing. Caitlin is entitled to her mood today," Mrs. Callahan warned, but it was clear she shared some of her husband's exasperation. She turned to me. "I'm so glad you've taken to Blackthorn. It's a beautiful, storied place."

Caitlin chimed in. "But you're off to France soon, yeah? Paris?" Her eyes glistened a bit at the mention of the city.

I shook my head. "No, Beynac-et-Cazenac. It's a small town on the Dordogne."

She mumbled under her breath and took another bite of her ice cream. "It's a shame your people didn't come from *interesting* places, really. Paris, London, Madrid. Even Dublin would be better than here."

Niall rolled his eyes again. He seemed perfectly content with his life in Westport, but clearly the small-town charms had long since lost any hold on Caitlin. "People find different things amusing, sister dear."

"That's a load of pickled codswallop, and you know it. Everyone wants excitement and adventure if they're honest with themselves. It's just that some people are more comfortable being bored than others. You, *brother dear*, happen to be the Irish gold medalist in that sport."

Niall tossed a pillow at his sister, which vividly called to my mind Christmas Eve with Avery. "Watch it, brat. And don't take your sour mood out on me."

"Maybe I wouldn't if you weren't wasting yourself here," she rebutted.

"I won't have this conversation with you again, Cait." Niall lost all glimmer of humor in his tone.

Caitlin clenched her teeth, and her eyes shot daggers at him. "It's never been much of a conversation, has it? At least not for me."

"Enough." Molly gave Caitlin a look that would have caused greater women than she to cower. "I don't mind making allowances for a sour mood when you've had an upset, but I won't have you berating your brother when he had nothing to do with your troubles."

"Fine. I won't spoil your tea any longer." She stood, anger still sparking from her like a downed live wire. Her gaze turned to me. "I do hope you'll enjoy your time here, Veronica. Even if you must spend part of your holiday with this prat." She grabbed the ice cream carton and turned to make for the stairs that presumably led to her bedroom.

"I'm sorry, dear." Molly spoke to me, but her eyes were on the stairs where her daughter had been moments ago. "It's a long-standing family drama, you see."

I glanced to Niall, who remained impassive, then turned to Molly, doing what I could to play nonchalant. "What family doesn't have those?"

"It seems a family would be dreadfully dull without them." Liam seemed more relaxed with Caitlin off in her room. Tension between those two had roots far deeper than the episode today.

"Perhaps it was a bad time to come." Niall leaned forward and rubbed his temples, exhausted from the encounter.

"No indeed. I'm glad you brought Veronica here to meet us." Molly refilled my teacup, then patted my hand. "A guest in the offseason is quite a treat. Especially one who seems to appreciate Blackthorn as much as we do."

"It *is* lovely. Niall is a marvelous caretaker." I hoped the praise would help improve the mood of the room.

Liam gave a not-entirely-joking harrumph. "He's young and has a lot to learn yet, but he'll get there."

Niall turned to me, conspiratorially. "Da doesn't like my plans for extending the meal service at Blackthorn."

Liam's eyes flashed toward Niall. "What's been done for hundreds of years will do well enough for now. Blackthorn doesn't need you to meddle in how she's run, lad. I don't want to see the place turned into a theme park for tourists. No offense, dear."

"Saints above, Da. It's a hotel now, not a cathedral. I'm talking about hosting grand dinners as the MacWilliams used to do two hundred years ago. I'm not putting in a waterslide and a souvenir stand, for heaven's sake."

"You listen, lad. We've not had any vacancy at Blackthorn during high season in thirty years. Why change what isn't broken?"

"I'm the caretaker now; it's for me to decide, isn't it? I've told you a dozen times; you will leave the running of Blackthorn to me, or you'll come back and take over the whole thing yourself. I'll not deal in half measures with you, good sir."

Molly slapped her hand down on the table with a decisive *thunk* that caused both men to sit straighter. "Right now, you two are going to shut your fool mouths before Veronica learns the truth about what a pair of idiots you are." Molly's was a tone not to be trifled with, but both men continued to share withering looks when they thought she wasn't paying attention.

Niall avoided his father's gaze and turned to his mother. "Speaking of Blackthorn, it seems the ghost of Aoife MacWilliam has taken a liking to Veronica. Paid her quite a visit, it seems." Niall looked intent, keen to see what his parents' reactions might be, then cast a glance back to me. "Her history is a special favorite of Ma's."

He spoke as if the echo were as common as a visit from the postman, and his family seemed none too concerned for my sanity, either, which was oddly reassuring.

Molly shook her head. "The poor lass. Such a sad story. No one knows whatever happened to her or why she left. I always felt her presence there when Liam and I were caretakers." She spoke sadly, as if recounting a family tragedy. And in a way, for her, it was.

"She was in love with the stable hand Tadgh Callahan," I ventured. "She wanted him to flee to America and he wouldn't go, so she left without him."

Niall opened his eyes wide, wordlessly questioning.

"I saw another echo. In the stables this morning." I wasn't sure at what point they'd find me ridiculous, but I hadn't found that line yet.

"I wonder why he didn't go with her. She had means and was, according to lore, quite a beauty. I suspect she had a bevy of suitors who would have been happy to spirit away with her." Molly spoke as if Aoife were an old friend, and I supposed to her she was.

"It was the Famine, and he was worried for his family." I didn't know why I felt compelled to explain things on behalf of people who were, at best, dead and buried for more than a hundred years and, at worst, figments of my overactive imagination.

"Well, for my sake and that of our children, I'm glad he decided to stay put," Liam chided. "Had old Great-to-some-degree-Grandda gone off with her, the lot of us wouldn't be here."

"True that. Heartbreak aside, sometimes things happen as they must," Molly mused.

Liam looked thoughtful as he rocked in his chair. "In all my years as caretaker, I've never heard of Aoife making such a vivid appearance to a guest. It's usually more of a faint whisper." He used the same word Niall had. As though the sounds, the experiences the place witnessed, still reverberated from the walls.

"Likely because most of the Americans don't have the same connection to the region as Veronica has." Niall's expression was serious as we told his family about my DNA test and the reason for my trip. Of course we had no way to know if his hunch was right, but I warmed at the idea of a link between Niall's ancestors and my own.

"I'd not be surprised if you have some MacWilliam or Bourke blood in you, even if it's a wee bit diluted over the past few generations. You feel like a familiar soul, if you don't mind me saying so," Liam said.

"Of course not. There is something *comfortable* about the place. Something that feels like home." It sounded batty after only a few days in the county, but saying so in front of the Callahans didn't feel all that embarrassing. If anyone would understand a connection to Blackthorn, it was them.

Molly noticed the bangle on my wrist, and I angled the bracelet so she could better examine it. I explained about the odd exchange with the thrift shop woman in Dublin.

Molly nodded as I spoke, her lips pursed in thought. "If you'll indulge the ramblings of an old woman, I suspect you were brought to Blackthorn for a reason. I hope you'll come back to see us from time to time." She squeezed my hand and offered me a warm smile. The invitation was a sincere one.

Warmth kindled in my chest at Molly's kindness. "I'd like that too."

"I'm glad to hear that, dear. Now I best go see to young Caitie before she sulks her way through County Mayo's entire supply of fudge ripple ice cream."

Liam's gaze followed his wife as she ascended the stairs, and he rolled his eyes. "She'll be embarrassed in a few hours when she's had the chance to see reason."

Frowning, Niall turned to his father. "I don't know, Da. She's well and truly unhappy."

"She'll find her way, lad. Don't you fret. Now you've wasted enough of the lovely Veronica's holiday. Why don't you two young things go off and do something amusing?"

When she returned, we bid goodbye to Molly and Liam with hugs and kisses on the cheeks, and it reminded me of how my own parents had the gift of making new acquaintances feel like family. Even business-minded Dad morphed into a teddy bear when there were guests in his home. As we piled into Niall's car, I slipped my phone from my pocket and sent my mother a quick text:

ME: Hey, Mom. All is great here. Love you! Let's come here together sometime.

Chapter 15

D o you mind if we go back to Blackthorn for a bit? Cait and Da have put me in a mood. I'll be a far more charming tour guide after I've worked off a little steam." Niall's eyes were fixed on the road, and he was forcing himself to take even, measured breaths.

Something about the exchange with Caitlin was eating away at him, a years-long feud boiling under the surface that an outsider like me wouldn't be privy to. They had gone from typical sibling bickering to something closer to genuine resentment with what seemed like minimal provocation.

Avery was prone to her moods too, especially when she'd faced romantic disappointment like Caitlin had, but we'd never thrown daggers quite like they did. And there was clearly a long-standing disagreement between Niall and Liam and their disparate visions for Blackthorn. Stepping in to these years-old feuds felt like starting a good novel a third of the way in. It was engrossing but lacked some necessary context.

"Of course." I considered asking him what was going on between his sister and him, but the query was better left for later, when he'd had time to decompress . . . or perhaps not at all. It wasn't my family matter to involve myself in, but I couldn't help but wonder what was behind the feud, given that they seemed to genuinely care for one another.

We rode in silence back to Blackthorn, and Niall immediately went off to the grounds in search of useful occupation. While the library fire and a good book were appealing, I wandered to the kitchen. It was Niall's domain, but I thought preparing lunch might be a short relief from his duty as caretaker and tour guide and a small way to thank him for all he'd done while I was visiting. I barely knew him, but I was pretty certain he wouldn't consider my commandeering his kitchen for one meal too grave an intrusion.

The kitchen, outfitted in professional-grade no-frills appliances, could have served as a culinary school textbook model for how to organize a kitchen for peak efficiency. I didn't have to waste time hunting down ingredients because it was obvious where they belonged. We'd had a pretty ample tea at the Callahans', so I had time for simmering and to let flavors bloom. When I was alone, I usually just tossed a salad or had a cup of yogurt, and Jonathan never seemed to care much when I made a fuss, so I stuck with basic steak-and-potato dishes when he'd come over. The only times I had the occasion to really cook was when I was able to coax my parents out of the mountains, which was a rare occurrence.

I lost myself in a haze of oregano, basil, and thyme, grown in the Blackthorn greenhouse and dried for winter. I had a marinara simmering before long and let the aroma of the herbs seep into my pores. I made a simple pasta dough, then availed myself of the sausage we'd bought from the Polish market in Ballyhaunis, along with some cheese and egg, and began to make a filling for ravioli. It was a comforting dish—and filling. Things I thought Niall could use in that moment.

Just as the ravioli had come to a boil, Niall emerged in the kitchen, his nose sniffing comically. "I swear I could smell this all the way from across the grounds. What magic have you concocted?"

I presented him with a heaping plateful, the tendrils of steam rising toward the kitchen ceiling with the grace of a ballet dancer. "Sausage ravioli and marinara. I hope you don't mind my barging in on your private sanctuary."

"I'll leave in a fit of pique more often if this is what I come back to." He winked as he sat at the kitchen counter. I held my breath as he took his first bite. This was the hardest part of cooking for someone, especially someone who knew his way around a kitchen. I was always afraid I'd missed the mark, no matter how scrupulous I was about tasting as I went along.

"Veronica Stratton—I wish I knew your middle name—this is a marvel."

I chuckled and dished up my own portion. "It's Louise. I trust you not to middle-name me in vain."

"I wouldn't dare insult a woman who can cook like this. I consider myself a fair hand in the kitchen, and you've outclassed me by a mile." He punctuated his words with another bite of ravioli.

"I wouldn't say that. I've probably put on five pounds in the few days you've been cooking for me."

He made an exaggerated show of looking me up and down. "Well, if you have, it suits you."

We ate in companionable silence for a few moments before I worked up the courage to address the Caitlin-shaped elephant in the room. "Caitlin seems to be taking her breakup hard." The words sounded stupid as I voiced them, but there was no graceful way to broach the topic.

"No, not really. Seamus was just a diversion for her. I don't think she really fancied him. The truth is, she's mad at me."

"But why? What did you do?"

"She always dreamed of living in Dublin and being part of a more vibrant sphere. It's hard to imagine wanting something more vibrant than Westport in offseason, I know. But my parents are old-fashioned to a fault. Probably comes with being late into the world of parenthood paired with four decades of being the caretaker of an eight-hundred-year-old castle. They wouldn't let her move to Dublin without me."

"And you didn't want to go," I supplied.

He sighed. "We had it all planned. I was going to start at the university, and she'd come after she graduated. We'd share a flat, and I'd be there to look after her. But Da had a heart attack my last year in high school, and he needed my help to care for this place. It was just going to be temporary. We'd start courses locally and revisit our plan in a year or two, but two years slips into ten mighty fast. She never forgave me for staying."

"Wow. And they haven't relented all this time? Isn't she twenty-six or so?" There had never been a question about my going to school in Boulder, or even Avery going to design school on the opposite end of the country.

"I know it has to be hard for an independent American like you to understand. They've always felt protective of Caitlin. They worried, and let it be said, not without probable cause, that she'd have got herself into trouble in the big city if she didn't have someone looking out for her. In my parents' time, girls lived at home until they were married. She may have a rebellious streak in her, but she doesn't have it in her heart to defy them. And the employment opportunities here aren't such that she's got a tremendous amount of savings to be fully independent, either."

I felt a prickle of indignation. "Maybe so, but she should have been allowed to make her own mistakes so she can learn from them. It would be up to you all to help her out of trouble or not, but forcing her to stay seems unreasonable and cruel."

"I don't disagree with you. And while it was maybe prudent not to let her move there alone at eighteen, she's a grown woman now. I've tried to persuade them to let her go until I'm blue in the face. My father can be a stubborn man, and Ma likes having all her chicks nearby. She can't understand why Cait wants to leave."

"You got most of it right, brother, but you've left out a few key details."

Caitlin entered the kitchen, having been quiet enough that she'd surprised us both.

"I really don't feel like fighting, Cait. I've had enough for one day."

"Fair enough. So have I. I came to apologize, especially to Veronica. Ma is mortified and begged me to come patch things up. She said she didn't want our guest thinking she'd raised two hooligans, even if it is the truth."

Niall barked a laugh. "That's Ma all right." His face grew somber again.

Caitlin sniffed the air and her eyes twinkled. "Since I didn't come to fight, do you think I can have a plate of whatever it is you're eating? I could do with something that isn't ice cream."

Niall rolled his eyes, but I rose to fix her a plate. She refused the third stool, preferring to stand in the corner by Niall. "Consider it a peace offering and a great sacrifice. I was looking forward to seconds. Maybe thirds."

Caitlin helped herself to a bite. "I'd give you the mickey, but this stuff is incredible, Ronnie. I like you fine, but you need to go back to America before I gain ten stone."

It was my turn to laugh, but I was pleased with the compliment as she ate heartily. I'd not been called Ronnie since I was a preteen, but it sounded natural and friendly coming from Caitlin.

Niall twirled his fork a moment and met her eyes. "I'll regret asking this, but what do you claim I left out of my explanation to Veronica about our . . . spat?"

She glared at him as if it were as obvious as the sun rising in the east. "That I've begged you to leave a million times, not just for my sake, but for yours too."

He looked back down at his plate. "It was always going to end here, Cait. I'm following in the footsteps of countless generations of men in our family. I was born to be the caretaker of Blackthorn."

She sighed dramatically. "Oh for the love . . . You sound like a medieval knight who's sworn fealty to his lord. You're living in the twenty-first century, for Pete's sake."

Niall pinched the bridge of his nose, trying to rein in his temper. "I won't be the Callahan to drop the torch."

"What torch, you daft fool? You're not beholden to anyone." Realizing her tone had become too confrontational, she lowered her voice. "Listen, if I thought you really and truly wanted to spend your life as a ruddy innkeeper, I'd not have a word to say about it. But I don't think you do. Not really."

Niall's color had returned, and his expression softened by a degree or two. "I've been the caretaker for a decade now. I haven't been brooding or snappish, have I? We haven't drudged up this old hatchet in several years, so why now?"

"You may not be unhappy, but you aren't *happy* either. Seamus acting a fool and sneaking around with Nora Doyle was just a reminder of how small and bleak this place is. You have brains and talent. You could have done so much more."

"But I've done all I wanted," Niall said more gently.

Caitlin looked more serious than I'd ever seen her as she placed her fork down on her plate. "I know you believe that, Niall, and I'm truly not trying to be a prat . . . but I don't think you have. I think your dreams are bigger than Blackthorn. And I mean this sincerely—it would kill me to see you at Da's age filled with regret. My motives may not have been entirely selfless, but I truly don't want that for you."

Niall stood and wrapped Caitlin in his arms. "I know, Caitie Rose. I know."

He didn't try to persuade her that she was wrong about him and his choices but let her cry out her frustration and her grief for time lost on his shoulder.

At length she pulled away, wiped her tears, and turned to me. "And now you must think I'm a proper dolt."

"Not at all. I think every single one of your feelings is justified. But, of course, I'm lucky enough to come from a family where daughters aren't kept on such short leashes." She reached for my hand, and I squeezed hers in return.

"Thank you for that," she said. "I know they love me to the moon, but their ideas are, well . . ."

"Well-meaning but old-fashioned?" Niall supplied.

She nodded. "That's as apt a description as I can come up with."

"I'll try to work on them again," Niall promised.

"I'd appreciate that, brother dear." She turned to me again. "I'm only sorry you're here such a short while. If my fool brother is going to spend his life here, you at least brighten up this gloomy dump."

The heat rose in my cheeks at the compliment, and I was grateful Niall didn't bring attention to it. He also didn't rebuke her for the insult to Blackthorn. He understood it as the symbol of the forces that kept her from finding her path out of Westport.

"It's a shame indeed," Niall said, his tone lighter. "We'll only have a few days left to persuade her to cook more ravioli."

Caitlin laughed. "Typical Callahan man, as motivated by food as a gun dog."

Playfully, he ruffled her hair. "Guilty as charged."

"All right then, I've made my peace and eaten your food. I should be off." She gave me a side squeeze and kissed her brother on the cheek. She bounded toward the kitchen door but turned back before passing through it. "If you had an ounce of imagination, you'd go to France with her, you know. It'd do you some good to see something outside the county for once."

She ducked out without waiting for his reply.

Chapter 16

Over the next few days in Ireland, Niall took me farther afield from County Mayo on our daily jaunts. The advantage to visiting a country slightly smaller than the state of Indiana was that one could experience an awful lot of it over the course of a week. There was no corner of the country that was an uncomfortably far drive from my perspective as an American living in the West who had been raised on ten-hours-a-day-in-the-car road trips, and Niall seemed fond of driving, so he was glad to follow the winding roads from one end of the country to the other.

I wasn't sure if he was a skilled enough tour guide to have purposefully selected the most charming routes from town to town, or if Ireland simply was that picturesque, but I found myself able to relax in his company without obsessing over plans for The Kitchen Muse or trying to piece together my visions of Aoife. There hadn't been another, and I was both glad to be free of them and longing to know what had happened to her.

For the first time in ages, I was able to just *be*, and it was glorious. We talked endlessly of cooking and travel, books and cinema, and I felt entirely at ease in our moments of silence too.

The one subject we didn't broach was Caitlin's suggestion for Niall to accompany me to France. I loved the idea, to be honest. I wasn't the sort of person who loathed to be by myself—quite the contrary—but to be in the country largely considered the food capital of the world with a like-minded companion sounded far more enjoyable than taking the trip alone. Niall had brought Ireland to life for me, and discovering France together could be an incredible adventure. But no matter how close I tap-danced toward the topic, I couldn't bring myself to ask.

So, as we went ambling out on the rugged shore in County Kerry, or went for a sumptuous gastro-tour of Kinsale—the foodie capital of Ireland—I kept my mind on the here and now. Enjoying Niall's presence in my life as a temporary pleasure. Hadn't it been said that some people who were meant to come into our lives for a short while had the biggest impact? Perhaps Niall was that for me.

Two days before I was scheduled to leave, we spent most of the day in Kilkenny, visiting the Medieval Mile Museum, and we were just finishing our grand tour of their famed castle. The region was breathtaking, and I was ever so glad Niall had brought me here. But as we made our way back to the car park, and back to Blackthorn for the night, I couldn't keep my mind from wandering. I was supposed to leave for France, and while it was the stop I was most excited about in many ways, I was dreading the departure. And wrestling with everything that implied. It was silly to think we'd be able to continue any sort of real relationship, no matter how strong a connection we might feel.

What was more, I didn't want to cheapen the memory of our week together with insincere promises of exchanging texts or emails. Sure, we'd manage it for a few weeks. Perhaps a few months, even. But by the time high season hit at Blackthorn, he'd be consumed with catering to his guests. And I, hopefully, would have clinched a contract with Fairbanks and would be busy as well.

No, there would be more dignity in letting the friendship end when I stepped on the plane in Dublin, moving on to the next leg of the trip, and the next chapter of my life, on my own.

"You're far away, Miss Stratton." Niall nudged me as his car exited onto the street. "Care to tell me what's on your mind?"

I shook myself. "Sorry, daydreaming again. A bad habit of mine I ought to break while in one of the most gorgeous places on earth."

Niall kept his eyes on the road, but I could see a glimmer of concern in them. "I find that sometimes sharing your thoughts helps ease the burden. I promise I won't offer advice unless you want it."

I weighed his offer but only briefly. Of all the people I could discuss this with, he wasn't the one I'd want to start with. How would I even start? *I think you're great, but I'd rather not talk to you again after I leave because I will feel awful for weeks when you inevitably stop emailing?*

"It's okay. Just mulling over the same old stuff, really. Nowhere near coming to any good conclusions, either. I'd do better to enjoy myself in the present moment." I hoped my tone came off as nonchalant, but that was never my strong suit.

He reached over and squeezed my hand, then dropped it almost as quickly. "I've no doubt your future will be a bright one, Veronica. With your skills in the kitchen and the good brain you've got in your head, you'll pave a path for yourself wherever it is you want to go."

Good. Let him think it was business troubles. Easy to explain and far less personal than the truth.

"I hope you're right. I know I've got some talent and all. To borrow your metaphor, it feels like I have all the paving stones I need to make a path most anywhere I want, but I have to decide how to lay it all out, and most importantly, where that path should lead."

"You've taken my trite metaphor and done well with it. You *are*

Irish, aren't you? But let us set aside the philosophy for one day. We've one more stop before we head back for the night."

He pulled me across the street and into a shop with *Kilkenny Handwrought Silver* emblazoned on a small wooden sign. I arched a questioning brow.

"I wanted to give you a keepsake from Ireland, if I might be so bold. I was hoping to find a necklace to compliment the lovely bangle you acquired in Dublin. I thought the matching set might look a treat."

The displays ranged from simple pendants to the elaborate. Some plain, others encrusted in fine jewels. While some would be affordable pieces for the cash-strapped tourists, others had to be staggeringly expensive.

"Oh, I'm really not a jewelry person." I rubbed a hand over the bangle I'd yet to remove since Dublin. "Not all that big on keep-sakes really."

While the latter wasn't entirely true, I was the kid who mused way too long over what keepsake to lug home from every national park gift shop my parents could be persuaded to let me enter when I was a kid. I'd grown more cautious with my money as an adult and business owner.

"Be that as it may, I'd like to offer you a small token. You've brightened my dull January, Miss Stratton, and I'd like you to have a small remembrance of it. As a friend."

I began to protest, but he held up a hand. "It's a small thing that will give me pleasure. Consider it payment for my time as your tour guide."

"That seems incredibly backward. Shouldn't I be giving *you* a gift in that case?"

"Your graciously accepting a small offering is gift enough. Now show me what strikes your fancy."

I shook my head. "No way. This is a gift, and the recipient shouldn't have anything to do with the choosing of it." I'd either insult him by choosing the cheapest item in the case or embarrass myself by inadvertently choosing something too dear.

"A compromise: I'll make a suggestion or two and you'll give me your honest opinion." He reached out a hand. "Have we an accord?"

I sighed. "Very well."

He took his time scanning the rows of glass cases, finally lingering over the selection of medallions that were wrought with filigree and various designs of ancient origin. He pointed to a slightly larger one, the size of a fifty-cent piece, toward the back. It was a lovely pattern with a large Celtic cross with a few gold accents to highlight the silverwork. It was a perfect complement to the bracelet.

"That seems like it might suit? I'm no expert on these matters, but to my eyes it would look as nice with a T-shirt as it would a fancy dress."

"It is lovely, but it's not necessary," I stammered.

Before the words were out of my mouth, he'd summoned over a clerk and asked her to remove it from the case. He clasped it on my neck while the clerk fetched a mirror so I could admire the piece. It sat at the perfect spot on my breastbone and reflected the light beautifully.

"I've always liked that style," the clerk commented. "Small enough to be tasteful but large enough to be worth noticing."

Niall produced his wallet. "She'll wear it from the shop if it isn't a bother."

Before I could object, the woman was processing his credit card and handing me the green leatherette gift case it came with. I shouldn't have paid attention to the total but was glad when it wasn't exorbitant. Regardless, it was still more than he should have spent.

Back on the street, he stopped to admire the medallion in the daylight. "Not nearly as lovely as the recipient, but it will have to suffice. Thank you for being gracious enough to accept it."

A trace of melancholy lingered in his eyes. He was sad I was leaving too. I'd been a fun distraction from the January gloom at the very least.

The heat, maddeningly, rose to my cheeks. I should have simply said thank you. Or even expounded on my gratitude for the attentions he'd paid me that week. Instead, I blurted, "Caitlin was right. You should come to France."

He turned to meet my gaze. "Beg pardon?"

"Come with me. Caitlin says you never take time off. We'll have fun wandering the markets and dreaming up menus. At least think about it."

My mind raced to Tadgh, who wanted so desperately to follow his love to America but was bound by honor and duty to his family. Despite the one and three-quarters centuries that separated them, Niall wasn't all that different.

"Do you really want me to?" It was his turn to stammer.

"I do." I sounded more resolute than I expected. "It could be fun. I've had a lovely week traveling with you."

I let out a shaky breath, hoping he understood what I'd truly meant: I wasn't quite ready to say goodbye.

He brushed a tendril of hair from my face. "I have as well, Miss Stratton. And Blackthorn will tolerate my absence for a week. For a place so old, my comings and goings are but the scurrying of ants."

"Really?" I hadn't expected such a quick acceptance, and my pulse raced as we stood on the sidewalk, oblivious to passersby.

"As my sister is so fond of saying, 'Why not?' I've been stuck in the same place for a long while, and a bit of wandering might do me some good."

Chapter 17

Week Two: France

JANUARY 22

BEYNAC-ET-CAZENAC, DORDOGNE, FRANCE

Night had fallen on the village, but the ample moon and antique streetlamps illuminated our path as we navigated the narrow streets in our rental car. The medieval buildings of Beynac-et-Cazenac were uniform in their humorless beige-and-brown stones but found joy in the vines that had made their purchase on the façade and the flower boxes that would host a bevy of color when the seasons obliged.

We were both wilted with exhaustion, having spent the last thirteen hours in transit. The trip from Westport entailed a three-hour drive to Dublin, two flights, a train, and a rental car to reach the little village in Dordogne—an ordeal I hadn't been fully prepared for.

Avery had reserved an entire five-hundred-year-old cottage, as the offseason rates were reasonable, so it saved the trouble of altering the accommodations to include Niall. Avery had alerted our host to the addition of another guest, and to her credit, she hadn't pelted me with questions. Just an "atta girl" and a winky emoji that elicited an eye roll from me she probably could have seen all the way in New York.

Niall had volunteered to drive since he was far more accustomed to maneuvering around the narrow, serpentine streets than I was. Both of us sagged in relief to find the cottage and a minuscule parking spot that barely accommodated the compact Peugeot. The instructions Avery gave on how to get the key were a bit cryptic, but a note on the door directed us to the bookshop three doors down.

Niall made a grunt of disapproval. Greeting guests personally was a point of pride, and he invariably showed guests to their rooms and made sure they had what they needed before he left them to their own devices. He strove to find the balance between attentive service and intrusiveness.

Blearily, we stumbled down the road to the address on the sign. It was a building made from the same stone as all the others, with deep maroon shutters to defy the insistent beigeness of it all. Not a garish shade of violet or vermilion, but a deep burgundy that skated the lines between staid and splashy. The sign read *Fermé*, but the light was on, and a woman sat in a plush chair in the corner in a shell-pink dressing gown, a long gray braid draped over her shoulder and a book open on her lap. Her head tilted back and her mouth was slightly agape in sleep, and I felt a pang of remorse knowing she'd tried to stay awake waiting for us. In slumber she looked shrunken and frail like a dried leaf in autumn.

Niall rapped gently on the store window until she was roused from her chair. She wiped the sleep from her eyes and padded across the shop floor, then unlocked the door and ushered us inside.

The bookstore was a cheerful jumble of tomes, mostly used, with a small table of recent releases at the front. The centerpiece of the room was a massive fireplace framed in intricately carved wood. The scent of the smoldering fire and book dust hung in the air laced with a faint twinge of vanilla. Green velvet armchairs, deep and lush, flanked the fireplace, inviting guests to peruse the books in comfort. It was in one of these the elderly woman had been napping.

"Forgive me for falling asleep on duty. You must be the charming American couple coming to claim the keys to the cottage, *oui?*"

I glanced over to Niall, trying to assess if I ought to correct the American part or the couple part first. He just shook his head, his meaning evident: *If you try to explain anything, she'll ask a million questions, and it will just delay our access to a hot meal and warm beds.* I turned to her and smiled. "Yes, thank you."

"How lovely. I am Madame DuChâtel. I do hope you'll enjoy your stay. It's not the most exciting time of year, but you'll get to enjoy our little village in peace and quiet." She walked slowly to a massive wooden desk and fiddled with the drawer until it finally tugged open. She rummaged through its contents, ostensibly searching for the keys to the cottage, but seemed to be coming up empty.

"I'm sure we'll have a delightful time. We'll be excited to explore in the morning. Quite the long day of travel, you know." My eyes were pleading silently for her to find the key so we could fall into bed.

"Oh yes, you must be simply done in, poor dears." Her acknowledgment didn't seem to inspire any haste in movement, and I could feel Niall groan inwardly, impatient as I was to get some rest.

"Exhausted, yes." I let the desperation seep slightly into my voice, hoping it might hurry her along.

She clucked her tongue in sympathy, still rummaging in the drawer. At long last she held up a key, held it up to the dim light of the bare light bulb that hung from the ceiling, and placed it back in the drawer, shaking her head. "My daughter Sylvie has taken over all this from me, and she doesn't manage things quite like I used to. Since it's so quiet this month, she asked me to take the reins again while she's on holiday in the Canary Islands. She needed some sun. I don't blame her, but I couldn't bear to travel so far these days."

Niall rubbed his eyes and forced a smile as she continued her digging, and I felt the room coming in and out of focus as fatigue enveloped me. After a few moments I cleared my throat. "Can we help?"

"No, no, they— Oh that's right. She left them in the envelope on her kitchen counter upstairs. This old brain isn't what it once was. I won't be a moment."

She began to teeter her way across the room, each step shuffling slowly toward the staircase, but I intercepted her before she got more than a few steps.

"I'd be happy to grab them for you if you tell me where they are. I'd hate for you to have to take an extra trip up the stairs."

She turned back and smiled gratefully. "I hate to ask it of you, but my old knees would be grateful. I keep a room on this level, behind the shop, so I don't have to bother with them anymore and can leave Sylvie to have her peace and quiet upstairs. The kitchen is to the left at the top of the stairs. There should be an envelope in plain sight on the counter."

"Not a problem at all." I walked quickly, though my urge to dash for the keys was tempered by my fatigue. I got the very strong feeling that the apartment upstairs had been Madame DuChâtel's home for many decades, even if she'd resigned herself to the rooms downstairs in her old age.

I stopped in my tracks at the sound of a low disembodied growl. The creature wasn't imminently menacing, but his cold expression told me he could quickly become so if trifled with. I turned into the kitchen where an enormous cat with a resplendent long gray fur coat sat on the counter next to the coveted envelope. The fur on his head and legs was shorter and darker, like black velvet, which gave him the appearance of a black cat wearing a gray fur coat, perhaps fashioned from the fur of another cat who had wronged him. The snarl died in his throat, and he stared at me for a long moment, then blinked slowly. A sign of trust.

I reached hesitantly for the envelope. "I feel like I need to answer a riddle for you before I take the key, but I hope you don't mind if we skip the formalities this time."

He didn't move to bite or swat my hand. Just offered a questioning meow. Emboldened, I moved to stroke the fur on his head, and he permitted my touch, apparently accepting my intrusion on his evening.

"You've quite the gatekeeper upstairs," I said, once I'd returned to Madame DuChâtel and Niall, holding the envelope up in triumph.

"I hope Maximillien didn't bother you. He isn't often fond of strangers. I ought to have warned you."

"Not at all. He's magnificent. The perfect bookstore cat."

She blinked, bemused as if I'd said I'd found him driving away in her car. "He rarely ventures down here when we have guests. Hisses and yowls at them when he does. Grumpiest old man of a cat I've ever encountered in my eighty-odd years. He rarely allows me to pet him, never mind that I've fed the little ingrate every meal he's had these past ten years."

My eyes widened, but I decided not to tell her he'd allowed me to pet him, worried it would wound her feelings.

"Now, my dears, you must come back to see me when you've had a rest. I've lived here my whole life, and I can tell you where to go and what to see. And if there is anything amiss, my telephone number is next to the phone in the cottage." She held the door open for us and waved us from the shop.

"I think Madame DuChâtel is as old as the cobblestones," Niall whispered as we walked up the dark, narrow street back to the cottage. "I hope everything is as it should be. I'd hate to think how long it would take her to fetch towels."

I giggled. "We'll manage. Sweet old thing. We should visit her again before we go. She probably gets lonesome with her daughter gone."

Niall tentatively wrapped an arm around me. "You're a kind soul, Veronica Stratton."

I loved how familiar, how comforting, his touch was. I leaned into the embrace just a bit. "I do try. And I've a soft spot for bookstores."

He smiled. "Especially the cozy kind with cats?"

"Especially those, though I think Maximillien fancies himself a guard cat rather than a lap cat." We reached the door to the cottage, and mercifully the keys Sylvie had placed in the envelope worked in the lock while Niall fetched our bags.

The door swung open to reveal a cottage that had been lovingly restored and gently brought up to date. The furniture was understated, chosen to blend in so the scarred wooden floors and the rough stone walls could speak for themselves. They called it a cottage, but it was what I thought of as a town house: narrow and two stories. The main level had the kitchen, living area, and a primary bedroom suite. The top floor had another, larger bedroom suite and a quaint little sitting area, which Niall offered to me and I accepted without complaint.

"Whoever is up first has to get pastries and coffee from the corner bakery, Miss Stratton. I may be a gentleman, but I'm all about equal opportunity when it comes to being wakened gently with coffee and *pain au chocolat*."

"It's a deal. And if you're up first, I prefer brioche with jam or Nutella."

"It takes all kinds, I suppose." He leaned in and brushed a kiss on my cheek, lingering a heartbeat longer than was decorous.

I smiled as I shut the door behind me. Closing my eyes, I rested my back against the wall and absently let my hand rise to my cheek.

When I went to open my eyes once more, the room became a whirlwind of color . . .

Chapter 18

I braced myself for the scene that was about to unfold before me. Though I'd experienced this twice with Aoife, my brain tried to rationalize what was happening, but no plausible explanations fit. Whatever was happening, I was meant to bear witness and do my part to parse it out later. The bedroom was much like it was now, even if the furnishings weren't as modern and the linens weren't a bleached white, but rather a hand-stitched quilt in a riot of colors. A young woman with flowing blonde waves sat on the edge of the bed, weeping with a sheet of paper trembling in her hands.

"Are you all right?" It was daft to ask, but I couldn't stop the reflex. I knew she couldn't hear me. She was like Aoife—an echo, a memory of the lives these walls had witnessed over the centuries.

A couple, presumably the young woman's parents, entered the room. My stomach constricted, hoping they were kinder than Aoife's father and stepmother.

The woman paused at the sight of her daughter. "Oh, Imogène . . ." Her voice caught with emotion, which only caused Imogène's shoulders to shake with more violent sobs.

"Is it Lucien?" The man spoke in low tones suited for church. Suited for a funeral.

Imogène nodded, her head still buried in her hands. "One of his comrades in arms wrote me. It was Lucien's dying request that I get word before the list of the fallen . . ." A wail escaped from the depths of her. Primal, instinctual, like a wounded animal.

The woman crossed to the bed, sat next to Imogène, and wrapped an arm around her. She pressed a kiss against her forehead.

The man began to fume. "These damned wars. The blasted royals using our sons like chess pieces to be used and discarded." He emitted a low growl and started to pace the room.

The woman looked up toward her husband. "Guillaume, I don't think that is helpful at the moment, *mon cher*."

"I suppose not, Martine, but it's all maddening. What did we have a revolution for if not to depose these petty tyrants constantly carving up the land like greedy children with a cake? To put an end to wars that steal our boys from us and leave us poorer than when we entered them? I wish you could explain it to me, because I certainly can't understand it."

Martine turned her gaze to him, pleading. "You speak the truth, but I think now is the time for sympathy."

Guillaume's face softened by a few degrees. "Imogène, my darling girl. You have your cry. Lucien loved you well enough that he deserves it. I hope you'll forgive me if my heart gives in to rage for a while yet. I'll do my best to keep it in check."

Imogène gazed up at her father, giving me the first clear view of her lovely, tearstained face, her blue eyes brightened by the evidence of her grief. Her voice trembled so I could barely make out her words. "You cared for him too, Papa. Grieve as you must."

Martine brushed a stray lock of hair from her daughter's face. "We all did, *chérie*. And I understand you both. It is a tragedy and an outrage that he was taken from us so many years before his time."

Guillaume railed again. "Outrage is right. I've heard the Prussians will be at the gates of Paris within a week. What sort of leadership is that, I ask you? Another Napoleon dragging us into a war we cannot win."

Martine clucked her tongue, echoing her husband's disapproval. "It's a disgrace."

Imogène seemed to stiffen for a moment before another torrent of sobs broke from her chest. "I begged him not to go when he was drafted. To pay one of the poor farm boys to take his place. We could have found the money with his mother's help."

Guillaume bowed his head, shaking it slowly. "No, our Lucien was too honorable to send someone in his place, *ma chère*. That is the way of the dukes and marquesses to keep their sons from harm. Cowardly. Hypocritical. That wasn't who Lucien was raised to be."

"It may be hard to hear, but your father is right. Lucien never could have lived with himself if he'd bought his way out of the draft." Martine moved to tighten her embrace, but Imogène brushed her arm away.

"He couldn't have lived with himself? Now he won't live at all. I'd have taken a guilt-riddled fiancé over a dead one in the space of a blink." Her words were a low, feral rumble.

Guillaume held up a hand to stop her. "You have every right to be furious. But Lucien wouldn't have allowed some poor farm boy to die in his place. He would want you to be proud of that."

"I'm sorry if I can't be proud that he died for nothing." Imogène jumped to her feet and crumpled the letter that had informed her of her beloved's death into a ball and threw it in the fire, her hands shaking with rage.

"No, but eventually you can be proud that he died *well*. I hope in time it will give you comfort." Martine rose also but refrained from going to her daughter, whose pain was beyond the gift of her mother's comforts.

"I know you mean well, but I will never find comfort in Lucien's death, Maman. I will bear the scars of it forever."

"Oh my darling . . . I know it seems that way now, but you *will* heal from this. Perhaps imperfectly, but you will have a life again. You will love again, in time."

"No, Maman." Imogène bowed her head, her eyes directed down to her midsection. "No one will have me. I am expecting Lucien's baby."

Martine gasped. Mouth agape, Guillaume stared at his daughter. It was he who broke the silence. "What were you thinking, Imogène? You are the brightest girl in the Aquitaine. I didn't think you capable of such foolishness."

She walked over to the window to look outside, but the village was covered in the inky cloak of a moonless night. "We couldn't bear to wait until he returned. These wars are always interminable. We knew it was imprudent, but we wanted a memory to keep us warm on the long nights alone."

"You gave yourselves a lovely memory at the cost of your reputation. Your future. And it's not Lucien who will bear the shame." Martine's arms were crossed over her midsection, gripping her waist as if it was the only way to keep from dissolving on the floor.

"We were engaged, Maman. We would have been married by now had it not been for the war. We wanted to have it done before he left, but the priest wouldn't marry us before the banns could be read. He claimed it would violate church law and he refused to do so."

"How far gone are you, then? Two months?" Martine asked.

Imogène lowered her head. "I just realized this morning my basket of rags hadn't been touched since two weeks before Lucien left."

Martine buried her face in her hands for a moment, then examined her daughter with eyes that suddenly seemed ten years older. She let out a mournful sigh. "You've got time before the quickening, then. Have you felt it move?"

Imogène shook her head. "I would guess that's another month or two away yet."

"Perhaps things will sort themselves. It happens often as not."

"You speak as if you *want* me to lose what little I have left of Lucien." Imogène spat her accusation. Her eyes were no longer wet but flashing blue pools of fury.

"If you were married, there would be no shame in having the child of a fallen soldier. There would be honor in that. But this child, no matter how much you want him, will be branded a bastard, and you a harlot with him."

"The town will understand better than you think," Guillaume said to his wife. "Lucien isn't the first of our sons to be taken, and he won't be the last. She isn't the first sweetheart left behind in the family way."

"I have no doubt they'll have sympathy. For a while. But when the rest of the boys come home—God willing—their mothers won't have them near Imogène. They don't want to see their sons saddled with soiled goods, and another man's child to feed and raise up on top of that."

Imogène looked at her mother with hollow eyes. "You make me sound like a bolt of linen dropped in the mud."

Martine didn't flinch. "Fine silk from the Orient that could have fetched a king's ransom. Fine enough that you'd caught the eye of the only son of our wealthiest merchant. Now spoiled beyond salvation."

Guillaume set a hand on Martine's shoulder. "That's enough, wife."

"I don't speak to be cruel. I speak so that we may face the future with open eyes. Imogène will have a rough road ahead, and I don't see any utility in pretending otherwise. The sooner we accept it, the more time we will have to plan." Her tone was earnest but unyielding. It had been her chief duty to protect her daughter from this exact scenario, and she'd failed.

Guillaume ran his fingers through his graying hair. "All may not be lost. We could send Imogène to a convent some distance from here. We can say she went to stay with a relative for a time. The village had too many memories of Lucien, and she needed to escape them until her heart had a chance to mend."

Martine took up Guillaume's habit of pacing for a few moments, considering. At length she turned to him. "That might work. Even if people suspect, they may be willing to overlook the indiscretion if we try to be discreet. It's the appearance of the thing that matters."

"So that's what my child is to you? An indiscretion?" Imogène stared at her mother, incredulous and trembling. Fear, rage, despair fairly crackled in the air.

"My only concern is for the child's future and your own. The child can be given to a good family who cannot bear children. He will be cared for. And you will have another chance to be a respected wife and mother, not just an object of pity."

"How can you be sure the sisters will place the child with a loving family? They'd happily rid themselves of any charge to a willing buyer. Do you honestly think they much care what sort of homes these children go to?"

Martine blanched. "A newborn babe will stand a better chance than a child."

Guillaume interjected, "I can send out inquiries myself to find a family for the little one. The sisters can just work to facilitate the adoption."

"You can't send letters out all over the country, husband. People will find out and all of this will be for naught."

"I can be discreet, woman. Imogène's concerns are not without merit. I'll find the right family myself so she can be at ease." He shot his wife a warning look that was plain: *Agree to this or she will never set foot in the convent.*

She sighed. "You may be right. But discreet, mind you."

He placed a hand on his wife's shoulder. "I'll scour my contacts in Lille, Bayeux, Lyon . . . outside of the region."

"Well, it seems like you have it all planned, don't you?" Imogène crossed her arms over her chest. "You're sending me off to some godforsaken nunnery to give birth alone and selling your only grandchild off to strangers in some far-flung city where I will never be able to see my baby again?"

"That's how it must be, *ma chère*. I hope you can see that."

Imogène crossed the room and took a shawl from the back of the chair at her writing desk and wrapped it around her shoulders.

"Where do you think you're going?" Martine asked. "It's the middle of the night. You'll catch your death."

"It's August, Maman. I'll be fine. I'm going to console Lucien's mother. She'll have received an official letter from the army this night. She has just lost her son."

Martine grabbed her by the arm. "You mustn't tell her about the baby. Every person who knows is a danger to your future."

"She is a good woman, Maman. She wouldn't want to see me ruined. For Lucien's sake, if nothing else."

Martine blanched. "Even so, you cannot risk a servant overhearing or a passerby on the street."

Guillaume again placed a hand on Martine's shoulder to still her words. "You won't be doing her a kindness, daughter. Knowing her son left behind a child to face the world as a fatherless bastard will only add to her grief."

Martine latched onto this. "Precisely. You mustn't go at all. To see you will be too painful. Lucien wouldn't have wanted it."

Guillaume sighed in exasperation. She was overplaying her hand. "No, she must go. Tonight. It is only natural and right for the fiancée of a fallen soldier to go pay respects to his maman and share in her grief. If she doesn't go, it will reflect poorly on her."

Martine stiffened. "Very well. If you put it like that, she must go. But not a word about the child. Our plan depends upon complete secrecy. Is that understood?"

Imogène straightened her spine. "I understand you perfectly, Maman."

She exited the bedroom door, her footsteps sounding on the stairs. The heavy front door creaked as she exited onto the street below into the dark of night.

Chapter 19

How I managed to sleep that night, I wasn't entirely sure, but I did rest soundly. It wasn't until the sun made a half-hearted attempt to crest over the horizon that I woke and the memory of Imogène and her torment flooded back to me. They rippled over me like licking flames of fresh grief, and I had to sit up to force air into my lungs.

I ached for her. The agony of losing her love. The fear and dread she must have borne in her heart at the prospect of bringing their baby into the world alone. How excruciating it would have been to feel that her only option was to give her child to others to raise as their own. My heart thumped a melody of anguish, my stomach churned, my throat burned with bile at the tragedy and injustice of it all. And as well-meaning as Imogène's parents were, they were steamrolling her into giving up the last vestige of her love for Lucien. Their baby.

And I could empathize with that. Avery and Stephanie had, despite my mother's attempts to give me a measure of agency, steamrolled me into coming on this very trip, and while I was grateful, I'd have preferred if the decision had been mine. The same went for the pressure to open my own restaurant. And I got the sense that

Niall felt like he'd been put in the same position when it came to Blackthorn.

I sat on the edge of the bed, trying to regulate my breath, agonizing that I could do no more for Imogène than I could for Aoife. I was grieving for women who had long since been dead, but they were only slightly less real to me than Niall or Avery. There was no logic in any of it, but I couldn't ignore their pain any more than I could my own.

Remembering the bargain I'd made the night before, and knowing the pastries would be at their peak in the first hour after opening, I threw on some clothes, left a note for Niall, who would be happy I'd made good on my promise, and grabbed the market basket by the door that had been left for visitors' use.

My phone informed me there was a patisserie-boulangerie of questionable quality a few streets away, and one with much higher reviews less than a fifteen-minute walk away on the outer perimeter of the village. I was glad for a walk to soothe my nerves and clear away my cobwebs before I had to try and be a pleasant travel companion to Niall. The directions on my phone's mapping software were straightforward, so I was able to pocket my phone and take in the village as it gently rose to greet the day.

A woman with a starched apron, severe bun, and flawless makeup was sweeping the patio of the café that was equipped with outdoor heaters to welcome guests on all but the coldest of days. A few homes were beginning to show signs of movement, but most remained dark, the occupants choosing to enjoy another hour or two of sleep on a gloomy winter's morning.

I was not the first customer at the bakery when I arrived shortly after it opened at seven thirty, nor had I expected to be. I'd assumed that the truly dedicated locals would be waiting as the shop opened to get their bread and pastries when they were fresh from the oven. Two gray-haired women and a stooped older gentleman who eyed me with surprise were waiting in line. They could easily deduce I was a tourist, as it was a village of only five hundred people.

I'd broken the norms of my kind by not keeping tourist hours. They expected travelers to drag themselves in at ten fifteen, hoping for the last scraps of coffee and carbohydrates. I gave the other patrons a polite nod, trying to avoid the stereotype of the overly friendly American, and they seemed to forgive me for the slight breach of tourist etiquette.

I was grateful they couldn't see my thoughts as the images from the night before ran through my brain. To them I was like any other customer, scanning the glass case with the beautifully arranged pastries, preparing to make my order when it was my turn at the counter, but I replayed the scene with Imogène and her parents in a continuous loop, spliced in with the visions I'd had of Aoife a few days ago, comparing their plights.

Both women had lost the men they loved, either to war or circumstance.

Even if the plan they concocted was cruel, Imogène's parents had meant well.

Aoife's parents were happy to use her as a social and political pawn at the cost of her well-being.

Lucien had sacrificed his life rather than dishonor himself by paying someone to take his conscription orders.

Tadgh had sacrificed the woman he loved to protect his family from starvation in the Famine, and his family stayed rooted to the castle ever since.

Aoife had refused to yield to duty and sought her refuge in America.

But what of Imogène? Would she obey her parents and go to the convent? Would she bring herself to give her child away and start her life anew, as though Lucien and the baby had never existed?

I wanted to know. It felt like the cliffhanger at the end of a season of a well-crafted TV show, and I was craving resolution that wouldn't come for months.

But in this case, I couldn't be sure it would come at all. I couldn't control these visions, these echoes. I certainly wouldn't have welcomed them if I'd been given a voice in it.

Because the questions these visions raised in me were ones I wasn't equipped to face. I'd lost Jonathan, and it hurt. But the secondhand whispers of the agony these long-dead women felt for their lost loves were orders of magnitude more than the grief I'd felt when Jonathan made his exit. Grief that was already waning faster than I'd expected, considering the duration of our relationship.

I forced myself from the reverie when the last patron ahead of me had been served. At once I was famished, so I loaded the market basket, not just with the previously agreed upon coffee, pain au chocolat, and brioche, but also a wider selection of croissants, profiteroles, and golden-hued buns. I added a robust *pain de campagne*, a denser, heartier version of a baguette, for good measure, hoping the cottage had some jam and butter on hand. It was more than the typical French person might have for breakfast, but I thought we might be grateful for any surplus later in the day. I tried to focus on clearing my head on the way back, but my thoughts wandered despite myself.

At the cottage I carefully set one of the paper coffee cups on the sidewalk as I fiddled with the key and let myself back in, grateful not to scald myself with the steaming brew in the process. I heard the sounds of Niall stirring in the bedroom as I busied myself by artfully arranging the pastries on a small platter I found in one of the cupboards, and poured the coffee in the little ceramic bowls the French seemed to favor at breakfast.

Niall emerged from his room, the sleep still in his eyes and his thick hair tousled. He wore his flannel pajama pants and a white T-shirt, and warmth infused me at the intimacy of seeing him disheveled. He wrapped an arm around me in greeting, and I accepted the embrace without giving in to the temptation of melting into it entirely.

His eyes widened at the display of pastries. "Hungry, are we?"

"I got carried away, but you know, when in France . . ."

"Eat all the French pastries. Not a bad idea." He pulled out his chair and transferred a few pastries and a length of baguette to his plate. I took a healthy swig of my coffee before following suit.

"You couldn't sleep." It wasn't a question.

"Fine until dawn, but then I woke up and couldn't get back to sleep. Hence the bakery raid."

"And you sought the cure for insomnia in carbohydrates." He gestured to the platter.

I shrugged. "I find they're usually as good an answer as any. And I supported the local economy in the process. Win-win."

He set down his half-eaten pain au chocolat and stared at me intently. "What's bothering you, Miss Stratton?"

I leaned back in my chair, my brioche and *chausson aux pommes*— apple turnover—untouched. I exhaled slowly, trying to let my agitation and confusion out with my oxygen before I spoke. "I had another vision. I'm pretty sure I'm losing it."

"Aoife again? It's a bit far from home for her to wander, I'd think."

"No. Someone new . . . Her name is Imogène." I related what I'd seen to him, every detail as fresh as if I'd just witnessed it minutes ago.

He leaned back in his chair as he absorbed the words. "You don't feel poorly in any way, do you?"

"No, fine, really. Aside from the sudden bout of visitations from the great beyond . . ."

"I think you've been through quite a lot, and this may be your mind showing you things you need to see. Or it may be that these old places have taken a liking to you and shown you some of their secrets. But I don't think it's cause for concern yet."

"I wish I could understand it. I wish I could make sense of why it's happening . . . I'm a natural skeptic. I'm not the sort to listen to ghost stories. I don't read horoscopes except for laughs. If someone told me they were seeing these things, I'd be the first to research the best psychiatric care within fifty miles and give them my recommendations."

Niall chuckled. "Maybe that's the reason these visions came to you. Perhaps you need to lose a smidgeon of that skepticism."

I returned a smile. "It's served me well up till now."

"I think what you need is something more quantifiable to satisfy that logical, rational brain of yours."

"What did you have in mind?" I asked, finally able to tear into the edge of my brioche.

"To start I think we should find our favorite local bookseller this afternoon and ask her for some reading on the history of this fair village."

"This afternoon?" I glanced down at my watch. It was only a quarter past eight in the morning.

"We have plans this morning, which will be revealed in due course." He arched a brow comically high, which elicited a laugh from me.

"I'm game."

"One of the things I like about you. So after our morning excursion, you can lose yourself in history books to your heart's content."

I glanced back up to the bedroom where I'd slept. "I hope she can dig up something."

"Well, when the history books don't turn up anything, we take the logical next step . . . ghost stories."

Chapter 20

D o we really have to leave the village today? We've barely seen it." I stared at the red compact car with low-grade contempt. I sounded like a whiny teenager, but the previous day's travels from Ireland had been exhausting enough that I would have been happy just to stay in Beynac and wander the little maze of streets for a few hours and relax in the cottage with the rest of the bakery haul and a book.

"This is a one-day-only opportunity. If we miss it, we won't have another chance this trip. Trust me, you won't be sorry."

I took my spot in the passenger seat with an overly dramatic sigh, and Niall slid behind the wheel, giving me a comforting pat on the knee before he started the engine. "Less than an hour, and you'll be glad we did it. I promise."

He'd not given me reason to doubt before now, so I tried to let go of the angst I'd been carrying all morning. The muted colors of January did nothing to dull the beauty of the Aquitaine morning, and the conversation flowed freely as Niall confidently maneuvered the car along the winding two-lane highways.

We arrived at the outskirts of a larger town and left the car behind. Niall grabbed the market basket from the back seat, which I hadn't even seen him stow, and he offered me his hand as we walked toward the center of town. His fingers interlocked with mine, like two halves of a whole.

He led us to the town square that was lined with market stalls filled to brimming with all manner of produce, meat, fish, and artisanal foods. The booths were teeming with customers keenly assessing the ripeness of the produce and the freshness of the meat. The chilly January air didn't deter the loyal crowds in search of the best ingredients for their meals. "Welcome to Périgueux, Mademoiselle Stratton . . . home of one of the finest gourmet markets in France and, consequently, the world. I thought you'd like the opportunity to do some, well, market research. All puns intended. I didn't figure you'd mind mixing business and pleasure."

I squeezed his hand. "Absolutely not, especially when my business *is* pleasure. Food should never be just about fuel. It should delight all the senses when it can."

"I can agree with that. So show me the market through the eyes of a food matchmaker. What are you looking for?"

I found the muscles that had knotted in my neck start to loosen as I got out of my own head and into business mode. "The best plan is not to have a plan at all. Go and see who's growing what. What's growing well. Who's come up with a creative new bottled sauce or spice blend. It may dictate where I source my tomatoes for that season or whether I steer my clients away from a bad year for snow peas."

"So what if your clients have their hearts set on, let's say, raspberries for a recipe they're famous for and you can't find any worth having?"

"I try to encourage restaurateurs to have constantly evolving menus so that precise thing doesn't happen. I have a client who makes a strawberry mousse charlotte russe, and I won't eat it nine months out of the year because they use frozen berries in the offseason."

He grimaced, as if the idea were a blasphemy in the face of the bountiful produce that surrounded us. "And they won't listen."

"No. It's always best in June when they can get berries from Colorado farms too. If it were my restaurant, I'd literally only ever serve it when the berries were local and in their prime. I've tried to get them to experiment using different fruits so it can be an all-year dish with seasonal variations, but they're worried their loyal patrons will be disappointed not to see "Strawberry Charlotte" front and center on the dessert menu. I've said those same patrons will come weekly when it *is* on book so they can get their fill. And there will be a subset of their patrons who think the strawberry is fine but have always wished they'd offer cherry in the late summer or apple cinnamon in the fall. And all the most decadent flavors, like choco-late mocha, for winter."

"It's a shame they don't listen."

"Yep. And their Yelp reviews on the Strawberry Charlotte dip in the winter and spike in the summer. Plenty of 'it's just not as good as the last time I went in, but not bad' sort of reviews. They think people can't taste the difference between fresh and frozen, but they can—even if they don't know *why* it's different. I can't tell you the amount of data I've shown them to back it up."

I stopped by a booth with locally scavenged truffles, the famed Périgord black, in small cloth-lined wicker baskets. The prices were high enough to make my eyes pop from their sockets yet more reasonable than those we imported to the States. Despite the con-straints of my budget, their earthy aroma of rich leather, cocoa, and autumn leaves beckoned, and I found myself at the booth with the other patrons who were agonizing over buying a few ounces of truffles to add to their evening pasta.

Niall peered over my shoulder. "This is one of the few weeks when the truffle vendors show up, and it was one of the reasons I wanted to come. Curious things, truffles. Good flavor, but I never quite understood the obsession."

"I've been truffle hunting in Oregon. One of the weirdest experiences of my life. It's a cult. But it's a flavor like no other, if you know what you're doing." I longed to pick up one of the samples, to smell it and feel it in my fingers, but I feared such behavior from someone who didn't intend to purchase would probably get me thrown out of the Périgueux market in perpetuity.

"And I imagine you do. Given an unlimited budget, which truffle would you choose and what would you use it for?" The question was asked with the same note of dreaminess that one imbued the question, *what would you do if you won the lottery?* Though given the prices, it was just a variation on the same question.

I stared at the array of baskets and felt my culinary muse flex her interwoven fingers as she readied herself for the creative exercise. I discreetly gestured to a particularly fine specimen of black winter truffle. It wasn't overly large, but it had the rich black-purple color and the characteristic coating of bumps. A cross-section would reveal a vast network of white veins creating intricate pathways that nourished the truffle in life and were conduits of flavor in harvest.

"That lovely one, just there. I'd find the best marbled filet mignon in the region, aged and tender, broiled to medium rare in cast iron. I'd top the steak with fresh butter infused with black truffle oil. And that beautiful fresh truffle there? I'd just barely warm it in a skillet to release the flavors before arranging it on top of the whole thing. I'd pair it with duchesse potatoes and sautéed Brussels sprouts. To drink, I'd go for a low-acid red to avoid undermining the truffle. Maybe a Châteauneuf-du-Pape or a Côtes du Rhône if the vintage is right." Niall's eyes locked with mine and I realized I'd been prattling. "Um, sorry. I got carried away."

"I swear by all I hold dear, I've never heard anything more incredible in my whole life. We have a decent kitchen at our disposal at the cottage, so let's make the most of it. I promise to be a worthy and obedient sous-chef."

I snickered. "The idea of you following orders with a 'Yes, Chef" or 'No, Chef' sounds fun at least."

He set a hand on my shoulder. "I'm perfectly serious. We are surrounded by some of the most incredible ingredients in all of France in this very square. Let's see what you can do with them."

It was a challenge, and one I wouldn't shrink from. "Very well then, are you willing to mortgage Blackthorn for a few ounces of truffle?"

"If I must, but I don't think we'll need to." He gestured to the vendor, who approached us with a warm smile. To my surprise Niall spoke to him in better-than-respectable accented French, far better than my own. Apparently Irish schools took foreign language learning more seriously than my American one had done. And I had to think living within a reasonable distance of France had been a boon as well.

The vendor gestured for me to pick up any truffles I was interested in so I might sample their aroma. They were organized by the area in the region where they'd been scavenged, separated into small clusters that had been harvested on the same excursion. I held to my nose a few samples, all wonderfully aromatic and excavated at the perfect moment of maturity, then went for the particular truffle that had caught my eye earlier. The scent was deeper, somehow, conveying notes of toasted chestnut and browned butter with a slight hint of garlic.

"Yep, this one," I said to Niall.

The vendor gave an approving nod. "Excellent choice. One of

my better finds this year." He took one of the smaller morsels from the same basket and cut off two-paper thin slices. Niall and I each placed a slice on our tongue and took in the flavors as it dissolved. Sheer bliss as the chestnut and browned butter morphed into an earthy cocoa as they faded away.

Niall reached for his wallet. "We'll have the one the lady wants, then. And don't tempt me further or I'll buy the whole blasted basketful and have to rely on my mother's invitations for supper for the next six months if I want to eat again."

At this, the vendor cracked a genuine smile. He weighed the truffle, wrapped it in cloth, and accepted Niall's payment in bright-colored euros. A hefty sum but less than a quarter of what I'd seen restaurateurs in Denver pay for lesser specimens.

"I'll get the filet," I promised as we thanked the truffle vendor and continued on to the rest of the market. "That was very generous of you."

He waved his hand. "Only if you insist. My pay might not be princely, but I've no rent to pay and few bills to chip away at it. It'll be a treat to see you really let your hair down in the kitchen. The ravioli you made still haunts my dreams, but I'm eager to see what you can do with more time and the culinary world at your fingertips."

I felt a tingling sensation on my scalp, the sort that always accompanied inspiration. "It's been a long time since I really let loose in the kitchen. I'm usually haunting everyone else's, so I don't bother so much with my own."

He took my hand in his. "A capital shame that, but we'll put it to rights soon. You've the heart of a chef, Veronica."

"A cook at any rate. And that's good enough."

Niall looked like he wanted to protest but seemingly thought better of it.

We wandered from stall to stall, buying what we'd need for the meal, especially lingering over the butcher's stall to select the best filets the vendor had to offer. We found Brussels sprouts still on the stalk, artisanal truffle oil, sumptuous potatoes that met with Niall's stringent standards, and even a booth selling plump vanilla pods I could use to infuse the cream for dessert. I spoke to several of the stall keepers about unique products my clients might like and collected some business cards.

As we walked along, if Niall's hand wasn't in mine, it would find its way to the small of my back or my shoulder. It was something Jonathan had never done, being averse to even minimal public displays of affection. The only time he made an exception was when we were at a work event, and he offered me his arm like I was a trophy wife. Or a casual arm drape around the shoulders if I ran into a male client who was under the age of sixty when we were out together.

Whether the purpose was making himself look good at work or giving other men a subtle hint to keep away, the message was clear: *She's mine.*

It wasn't the same with Niall. The gesture meant *I'm here, and I'm glad you are too.*

For the briefest of moments, my chest was a band of fire as regret crushed down on me. Niall had shown me how I wanted a relationship to feel. He'd given me a glimpse into the easy rapport and the small joys of complementary interests.

But his life was rooted in Blackthorn.

Mine in Denver with my family and my bourgeoning business.

The more I considered the impossibility of it, the more I wanted to dash back to the car in tears. But I wouldn't give in to the impulse and ruin what little time we had together. I pushed against the band of ice constricting around my chest and forced myself to breathe.

Chapter 21

The bookshop welcomed us with the tinkling of the bell over the door, the crackle of the fireplace, and the sweet twinge of burning cedar. It truly was a glorious little nook of the world with mismatched shelves and jumbles of books in every little cranny. It was the sort of place where I'd gladly spend hours perusing the stacks and thumbing through more tomes than I'd be able to read in a lifetime. The only shops that intrigued me to that extent were kitchenware shops. Preferably with the same warm, jumbled vibe and an eclectic mix of antiques and shiny new gadgets.

The old woman's face lit up as she saw us, probably the first customers she'd had that day. Perhaps longer. I wasn't sure how a shop like this could afford to keep its lights on, but I had to assume the building had been in the family for generations, which would have lowered their costs significantly. "Ah, you've come back to see me. What a treat. Make yourselves at home, dears."

Madame DuChâtel padded to the back room, leaving Niall and me to browse. A shaky breath escaped my lungs. "I don't know what to ask her without sounding like a madwoman."

He placed a hand on my shoulder. "You weren't nervous about confiding in me."

I tilted my head. "I was. More than you know. And you weren't quite the stranger Madame DuChâtel is." *Not even then.* I left the words unspoken, but he heard them all the same. His gaze warmed.

"You don't need to explain everything to her. Just that you're curious about local lore. The history of the house. You don't have to confide more than you feel comfortable sharing."

He was right. I could ask about Imogène without betraying why I was curious. Certainly I wouldn't be the first American to become fascinated with the history of the place. My breathing became deeper, more measured, as I perused the shelves. Dusty tomes on the history of the Aquitaine and all the conflicts that had scarred the verdant valleys here. Novels of every imaginable provenance and vintage. A section of cookbooks that could have occupied the rest of my stay in the Dordogne. Niall, too, scanned the shelves, occasionally taking a volume to examine more closely.

Ten minutes later, Madame DuChâtel emerged from the back room with a silver tray laden with a coffee service and a plate of French galettes—a lovely buttery cookie that paired marvelously with a hot beverage.

"You didn't need to bother with all this." I helped her with the heavy tray.

"You wouldn't deny an old woman the pleasure of playing hostess, would you? It's been far too long since I've had visitors."

"Of course not," Niall said. "But it's kind of you all the same."

She gave a resigned sigh. "It's not what it should be. I used to be rather handy in the kitchen, but I haven't the spunk for it often anymore. Store-bought cookies instead of homemade tarts are my lot now. But it's a small price to pay for the privilege of growing older."

She gestured to the chaise, but I insisted on helping her serve the coffee.

I handed Niall a cup, then Madame DuChâtel, before I filled my own. "A wise philosophy. Too many think 'growing old gracefully' is about hair dye and avoiding wrinkles."

She shook her head. "That misses the mark by a mile, I agree. Do tell me, is everything as it should be at the cottage? Have you everything you need?"

"We couldn't ask for anything better. It really is an enchanting place." My stomach lurched at my choice of words, but I tried to remain impassive.

"It must have a fascinating history," Niall added. "After five hundred or so years, it must have more than its share of stories."

It was several hundred years younger than Blackthorn, but he spoke with the sort of reverence for the cottage's antiquity that a caretaker like Madame DuChâtel would appreciate. Likely extending the courtesy he hoped to receive from his own guests.

"Oh yes. I couldn't start to calculate all the generations that have lived and died there. It's been in my family for over 150 years, and we're considered the new custodians. It was in the Bonneau family for several centuries. Quite possibly since it was built."

I felt a tingling sensation in my fingertips. *Follow this thread.* "How did it come to be in your family?"

"It seems that the Bonneau family lost their only daughter. They moved away to be with a branch of the family in Provence to forget their grief. A sad story, given the length of their family connection here, but with no family to pass the cottage on to, I wonder if they didn't prefer to leave it behind so they wouldn't spend their golden years reminded that their family legacy was at an end."

"That *is* sad. Do the records say what happened to her?" I leaned forward in my seat, my coffee and cookies forgotten.

She set down her coffee cup and folded her fingers. "I assumed for many years that she succumbed to some sort of illness. It was so common in those days. But I have never been able to find records to prove anything. I always thought it odd that she wasn't buried in the cemetery here with her parents and generations of her family, but I can do no more than speculate what the cause for that might be."

I thought about reaching for my coffee cup out of politeness, but my hands were shaking too much to attempt it without incident. Just then Maximillien padded down the steps and crossed the room to where we were gathered by the fire. He sat for a moment, appraising me, then hopped into my lap with an impressively agile leap for such a large cat.

"Hello, friend. I'm glad to see you too." He circled in my lap twice before he settled down, emitting a constant low purr I could feel through to my bones.

"My God in heaven, I've seen everything now. I've never seen that hell beast of a cat sit on anyone's lap, let alone purr. He tolerates the occasional pet on the head or near the base of his tail from Sylvie or me, but he's a terror to anyone else who tries."

"Perhaps Veronica here is a cat whisperer and never told us?" Niall suggested.

"This cat wandered into this shop ten years ago as the scruffiest, scrawniest-looking kitten you've ever seen and refused to leave. He claimed this as his home and has been acting like its guardian ever since. That he's taken a liking to her is a remarkable thing indeed."

"Perhaps he feels a kindred spirit?" Niall suggested.

I swallowed my courage, gently stroking between Maximillien's ears. "Was the daughter they lost named Imogène?"

Madame DuChâtel blinked a few times. "How could you know this? Have you been researching our history for a book of some kind? Surely there was no trace of her in the cottage."

"More than you realize. I . . . dreamed about her last night. Vividly." I didn't try to persuade her that I was, in fact, wide awake when I'd seen Imogène. I didn't go into the depths of the pain she'd felt, the shame her parents had inflicted on her. The least I could do was protect a sliver of her privacy.

"This is a remarkable thing. Clearly, you are of Beynac, my dear girl. I'd believe that just from the cat's behavior, never mind the dreams. Imogène Bonneau was the last of her family."

I hoped Imogène wouldn't mind my divulging more of her story. "No, she was pregnant with her sweetheart Lucien's baby. They were to be married, but he was killed in the war."

Her eyes widened. "Indeed, my dear. Lucien DuChâtel was killed in the Prussian War in 1870 near Sedan."

My mouth gaped for a moment before I could find my words. "DuChâtel?"

She nodded solemnly. "Yes, my great-great-uncle was killed in the war when he was just nineteen years old. His brother, my ancestor, was too young to be conscripted—and selfishly I thank the stars for it. There was mention in the family records that Lucien had an understanding with a young woman here in the village, but it never mentioned who. Imogène would have been as likely a candidate as any."

"Her parents wanted to send her to a convent to have the baby. She was heartbroken about it." I tried to keep my tone neutral, but I couldn't erase entirely the pain she'd felt. That I had felt for her. With her.

"Ah, that is how it was done in those days. People aren't quite so fussy about these things now. I wouldn't call myself a 'modern woman,' but I think it's better when people don't judge others so harshly for their decisions." She looked down at her hands, lost in thought. "People can be cruel. I'd like to think that little by little the world is becoming a kinder place. At least in some respects."

I wondered what memories were being triggered just then, but I couldn't bring myself to pry. "I hope you're right about that. Imogène did insist on going to visit Lucien's mother before she would allow them to send her away. She refused to go along with the plan if they denied her that chance."

"That would be Coralie DuChâtel, née Joubert. My great-to-the-third-degree grandmother," Madame DuChâtel mused. "According to village lore she was a skilled apothecary and respected in the village. It seems she was regarded with some suspicion because she never remarried despite being young enough to be interesting to suitors when her husband passed. I suspect some were jealous of her ability to support herself and her children comfortably without a man's interference."

A cloud passed over Niall's face. "It would have been the same in Ireland. Perhaps worse." Was he thinking about Caitlin? I knew he'd texted her a few times, sending her pictures of the market and the village. She'd seemed unimpressed with any town smaller than Paris, but I think she would have happily come along if she'd not worried about being a third wheel.

For a moment I imagined what it might be like if I *did* try to keep up communications with her and with Niall. Maybe she and Niall could come to Denver before tourist season picked up. It was strange to think of Niall out of the context of this strange adventure and in the context of my everyday life. Denver might be just enough excitement for Caitlin. But it would just be a tease. A reminder of a delicious idea that could never be brought to fruition.

Madame DuChâtel rose and wandered about her stacks a few moments before she handed me a battered old tome. Careful not to disturb Maximillien who dozed contentedly on my lap, I opened the text, able to parse it, if only poorly, owing to my French courses in high school and college.

"The History of Beynac-et-Cazenac?" I looked at her quizzically

"It is a fairly definitive book, but of little interest to anyone who does not live here. It's a gift, my dear. I hope you find something of interest to you in its pages."

Chapter 22

Later that afternoon, I began the process of infusing the farm-fresh butter with the truffle oil and the cream with the vanilla pods so the flavors would have time to mature. Niall lounged contentedly in the living room with a travel guide a previous guest had left behind. We wouldn't be hungry for hours, and I was glad to have plenty of time to coax out flavors and to indulge that culinary muse, whom I could visualize shaking the dust off her apron and picking the cobwebs out of her hair.

How long had it been since I cooked a meal that called for real creativity and stretched my skills? Two years? Three? My shoulders relaxed, and I gave in to the magic of the kitchen. Chopping, trimming, sprinkling herbs and spices. It was a choreographed dance, and I lost myself in the music of simmering sauces and sizzling oil. Time was irrelevant, and so were the rest of my troubles. My young business, Jonathan's antics, rebuilding trust with my parents . . . While I let the muse have me, none of it really mattered.

I puréed and piped the duchesse potatoes into perfect swirls, and they browned in the lower oven. The Brussels sprouts were a vibrant green as I sautéed them in a bit of bacon fat. The wine was uncorked, letting the tannins mellow. I'd seared the steaks and placed them in cast iron in the upper oven at a low temperature to cook slowly.

I had the infused truffle butter at the ready, and there was nothing left but to prepare the truffle. I sliced it paper thin and warmed the slices one at a time for just a few seconds, reserving four slices for later use.

I was almost sad when my futzing about the kitchen came to an end. Like Christmas morning, the buildup to the event was almost more fun than the moment itself. I called Niall in from the living room, and his eyes nearly fell from their sockets.

"You're no woman, Veronica Stratton. You're a kitchen witch through and through."

"I must have forgotten to give you my business card. I, sir, am a kitchen *muse*. Giving inspiration to great chefs and letting them create masterpieces for the masses. I just happened to use that inspiration for my own benefit tonight."

For once the stars aligned and I happened to have a card in my wallet, which was still residing in the ample pockets of the utilitarian-yet-sleek travel pants Avery had sent me.

Niall examined the card, navy blue embossed with gold stars, with *The Kitchen Muse* in a whimsical font and the rest of my contact information in a more readable style. Straight out of the twentieth century, but I still found them useful.

"I stand corrected, but this meal is still incredible."

He pocketed the card and took his seat, and I placed the platter with the steaks before him. I spooned on the infused butter and arranged the slices of truffle decoratively before he took his portion. We helped ourselves to the lot of it. The duchesse potatoes were perfectly browned pinwheels of cheesy, buttery purée that had been piped onto parchment and baked in the oven until a crisp shell had formed. A labor of love but worth the extra effort.

For one of the first times ever, I snapped Instagram-worthy photos of the dishes in various stages of completion and decided I'd send them to Fairbanks with a breezy note expressing how nice it would be to chat when I got back. It was more direct than I was used to, but the cooking adrenaline had me feeling bold.

A breath caught in my throat as Niall took a bite of his filet. His eyes closed, shutting off one sense to heighten the others.

"This is an utter marvel, Veronica. I've never met your equal in the kitchen. You've outstripped me by an order of magnitude."

"I disagree. Your omelets are far better than mine. And your bread skills probably outdo my own too. We just have different talents."

Niall took another bite, looking pensive as he chewed. "Perhaps. I've always enjoyed the precision of baking. Not a wide margin for error."

I cut into my own filet and took in the swirling flavors of the earthy truffle with the tender meat, each lifting the other. I lost myself in the sensation so thoroughly, I had to fight my way back to the present to rejoin my conversation with Niall. "Maybe that's it. Cooking provides a bit more scope for the imagination while baking requires focus and balance."

He cocked his head in contemplation. "Right. The creativity with baking is in finding the flavors and coming up with a way to shoe-horn them into a workable recipe. I enjoy the challenge of it."

The tingling in my scalp returned as I considered his words. It was rare that I got to speak with someone who viewed the process from a similar light, and it was exhilarating in a way I didn't have the vocabulary to describe. "I get that. Finding a way to introduce fresh cherries into a cake recipe that's already liquid heavy. It's like a battle of the wills to make it work. Given the elevation in Denver, I'm surprised more of our bakers don't end up in the psych ward."

Niall chuckled as he started in on his potatoes. "One advantage to Ireland: It's far easier to get dough to rise properly at sea level."

"No doubt." I took a sip of the young Châteauneuf-du-Pape and sighed with delight. Seeing my reaction, Niall followed suit.

"A lovely choice, this." He held the glass up to observe the golden hue of the kitchen lights playing off the velvety purple-red wine.

I took another sip and allowed it to linger on my tongue. "Isn't it? Just the right notes of black cherry and a spicy finish. I thought it would pair well without competing with the truffle."

He took a sniff at his glass. "I don't think you could have done better. Let me guess, sommelier school too?"

"No, just on-the-job training. Châteauneuf is a special one. It's a blend, which I don't usually love, but in this case, the varietals tend to cancel out the harshest characteristics of the others. The blend works together to create something greater than the sum of its parts."

"Sounds a lot like people," Niall mused. "They can bring out the best in one another."

I paused, considering. "If it's the right combination. In some cases one varietal will completely dominate the other. In other cases the flavors are a discordant mess. Finding the right blend is tricky."

"So . . . *exactly* like people, then?"

"More or less," I finally agreed.

"You were born to do this," Niall said after a pause. "It's not just the cooking. Anyone with patience and a brain can make a decent filet. It's knowing how the flavors pair together and how to tie them all together into a cohesive meal."

"Loads of practice, I suppose."

"No, it's skill and talent, Veronica. Honed and developed to be sure, but the seeds of it were in you all along. You should be running your own kitchen."

I felt the blood slowly draining from my face. Like everyone else, he spoke as if opening a restaurant were as small an undertaking as, say, picking up tennis. He was trying to urge me into taking a life path, just as others had done for Aoife and Imogène, and I further bristled at the idea. I sought a reply, but a feeble "um, thanks," was the best I could muster.

"I'm sorry. It isn't my place to say such things. I just marvel that you haven't tried, is all," he pressed gently.

I cleared my throat. "Enough about me. What about you? What is it that *you* would have done if your dad hadn't fallen ill and you hadn't been needed at Blackthorn? What was the plan in Dublin—college?"

He took another bite of the potatoes, a subtle technique to buy him a few more moments to ponder. "Pastry school. Da had wanted me to go off and study hotel management so I could do right by Blackthorn, but I was sure it would be dull and I wanted no part of it. But all the plans went out the window, so all our arguments were for naught."

"So you dreamed of opening your own bakery? You fancied getting up at three in the morning to make bread and cakes?"

"I don't know. I guess I figured I'd improve and expand the menu at the castle and maybe sell to some of the restaurants in Westport. The kitchen at the castle is as well-equipped as any commercial kitchen in Mayo, and it seemed a good way to shore up our finances if the castle had a bad year."

He was due a bit of prodding after the dose he had given me. "Very pragmatic, but is that the whole and unvarnished version of what you wanted to do with your life?"

He took another sip of wine before meeting my gaze. "I always expected to become caretaker of Blackthorn, but I dreamed of a couple decades off on my own first. Having a café in Dublin where, in the morning, folks could come get pastries and a good cup of coffee that weren't mass produced. A sandwich on fresh-baked bread with ingredients you could pronounce. Not the grandest of ambitions, I know, but it would have been a fun interim project before I went back to Westport for good."

"It's a shame you didn't have that opportunity. Your devotion to Blackthorn and your family is wonderful, but it didn't leave you with a lot of breathing room for yourself."

"No, I suppose it didn't. Caitlin always likens it to the crown prince ascending the throne. And as you might expect, she's no sort of monarchist and speaks of it with the same disdain."

I laughed, well able to imagine Caitlin on a tirade. "How does she make that connection?"

"Well, the crown prince spends a fair amount of time waiting for his turn, yes? But in the interim he goes to university and lives a bit, you know? Now consider our neighbors to the east. The poor sod had to wait almost three-quarters of a century to get his chance, but his mam was hauled into the job in her midtwenties . . . like I was. He probably feels like he got shortchanged, but she had an awfully long time to wear the crown. Her neck was bound to get sore from the weight of it."

"I see Caitlin's point. You don't want to spend your life in the waiting room. You wanted the chance to make your mark on Blackthorn and run it as you saw fit, but you didn't expect to jump in so early."

"Right. A life is meant to have seasons, and I seem to have jumped to the autumn of mine with only the barest hint of summer, if that makes any sense at all."

"It makes a *lot* of sense. You've had some choices taken from you, and it's natural to harbor a bit of resentment."

Niall set down his knife and fork, pausing before he spoke again. "What about you, Veronica? You've had all the choices in the world, and you refuse to make the leap of faith to do what you really want to."

"I never said I wanted to open a restaurant. Just because someone enjoys something doesn't mean they want to make a living from it. A person may love acting and enjoy doing regional theater, but they'd be miserable if their hobby became their profession and they lost their escape from the tedium of daily life. It might be the same for me."

"Veronica Stratton, that is a load of malarkey, and you know it. You've said yourself you don't even cook all that often these days. You've been telling yourself excuses to protect yourself from failing. It's not like the profession you've chosen for yourself is some ultrapractical field. You're not a doctor or a primary schoolteacher. You're in the restaurant business without really *being* in the restaurant business."

I gripped the edge of the table to keep my hands from shaking. I'd heard variations of this from every member of my family a dozen times over. I wanted to cast it back at him, to refute his words with the eloquence of an Ivy League debate captain, but I couldn't. I leaned back in my chair, exhaling slowly and staring at the wall, searching for a proper response, but I found no answers in the mottled beige plaster.

He let out a low groan. "God above, I shouldn't have pressed the matter. After you made this glorious meal for us and all. I am a proper horse's arse."

I took a sip from my wineglass, not meeting his gaze. "No, don't worry about it. I just don't understand why everyone just assumes that running a restaurant is my burning desire. Like everyone knows me better than I know myself."

"I suppose that's fair. It's presumptuous of me to push. Forgive me?"

I waved a hand dismissively. "There's nothing to forgive, Niall. Let's just drop it for tonight."

"Agreed. I don't want to spoil the evening more than I have. And God knows I've had my share of my family making presumptions about what's best for me and my career. And for added drama, my sister and my father have diametrically opposed ideas for the course of my life, and my poor mam is caught in the middle."

I softened. "That has to be extra hard. At least my friends and family all have a unified front to turn me into Chef Veronica."

"A unified front is harder to defend against. I'm not sure you haven't got the worse bargain there."

"Maybe so. I know they care, but it *is* maddening to be surrounded by people who are entirely convinced they know what's best for you."

"And I'm truly sorry to be one of them. I'll do better."

He laid his hand on mine, and my chest constricted as if caught in a vise. I couldn't remember ever having such a visceral reaction to Jonathan, and it just added to the list of reasons I should have known better than to let the relationship drag on as long as it had. But *why* in creation did I have to feel this way about a man who lived half a world away from Denver? I wanted to take my free hand and run it through his thick hair. I wanted it as profoundly as I wanted my next breath, but to do so would only lead to more heartache.

"Dessert," I said abruptly. "If you're not too stuffed. We can wait until you've had time to digest first if you want."

"No, I'm sure you've crafted it to fit with the meal. Let's have it now."

I bounded to the refrigerator, feeling reinvigorated at the prospect of showing off my creation. I'd been flummoxed as to how to create a capstone that would live up to such a meal. I decided simplicity should reign and opted for a classic crème brûlée I'd baked before I began the rest of the meal and chilled it while we ate. Only in France would a vacation rental come complete with a set of ramekins for the custard and a kitchen blowtorch for the topping. I sprinkled on a layer of coarse sugar and fired up the blowtorch to create the signature layer of crisp caramel on top of the fluffy vanilla custard.

I'd decided to take a twist on the traditional crème brûlée and added a light garnish of truffle pearls I'd purchased with the truffle oil. They were like small beads of caviar that burst in the mouth with an explosion of truffle flavor. I added the last two slices of truffle atop the dessert and presented it to Niall.

"Truffle in a pudding?" he asked. "Bold of you."

"It's an experiment, but I think it will work. Just trust me."

Slowly, almost reverently, he took his spoon and cracked through the garnish and caramel into the custard below. He made sure to get a bit of everything in one bite. Like an experienced food critic, he took his time to take in the flavors and give it an honest try.

His eyes locked with mine, but he said nothing.

"Is it that bad? We can scrape off the truffle bits. The custard should be fine on its own."

"Take a bite as it is," he said at length.

I obliged, feeling the satisfying crack of the caramel as my spoon pierced through. I carefully took a bit of everything in one spoonful as Niall had done, hoping I hadn't embarrassed myself too thoroughly. The earthy umami of the truffle, the intense burst of flavor from the truffle pearls, the sweet creaminess of the custard, and the bittersweetness of the toasted caramel didn't war for attention in my mouth, but they worked together as harmoniously as woodwinds, brass, and strings to form a symphony of flavor.

I set my spoon down as I let the flavors come to rest on my tongue. "Wow."

"You can say that again. It's incredible."

I took up my spoon again, hoping the next bite would live up to the first. If anything, the flavors grew more complex as they had time to bloom.

"I think your muse has been held captive for a bit too long. She gave you this as a reminder to let her out a bit more often."

"Maybe you're right. I *should* cook more. If only for friends and family. It would be a good outlet. And good for market research for my clients."

Niall opened his mouth to speak but closed it again. Dutifully swallowing back his arguments as he'd promised he would. But even unspoken, they permeated the air, heavy and acrid like traces of scorched sugar.

We finished the crème brûlée and decided to brave the cold January air for a walk to help us digest the rich food.

He took my hand in his like it was the most natural thing in the world, and I reveled in the feeling of his fingers interlaced with mine. We wandered without direction, just enjoying the quaint village houses bathed in moonlight and the soft glow of streetlights.

"I hope you aren't mad at me for overstepping. I just hate to see your talent go unappreciated."

"People *do* appreciate it. I just choose to use it in an unconventional way. I get to have my fingers in dozens of pies. I don't have to choose if I want my restaurant to serve Italian food or French food . . . or if I want to specialize in something more niche like Colorado wild game. Bison steaks, elk sausage, and all that."

Niall stared off at the starry horizon. "There is a lot of fun in what you do, I'm sure. I just hope in thirty years' time you won't come to regret your decision. I'd hate to see you look back and wonder what might have been."

I took in his chiseled profile. "What about you and your café? Do you think you'll look back with regret when you're seventy and wish you'd done it when you'd had the chance?"

"I think the person who can look back on life without some measure of regret is either blessed with never having to make hard decisions, or else they resigned themselves to always making the easy ones. I'm sure I'll have a twinge of sorrow for the café that never was, but I don't think it's a regret that will haunt me like some."

I was on the point of asking him what regrets would be that serious, but it was far too nosy a query. Though the question went unasked, he could sense it on the tip of my tongue. "There aren't too many regrets in my life, but not doing this would be the worst of them."

He dipped his head and kissed me, hesitating just a moment before his lips met mine in a silent plea for permission. I felt myself melt against his hard chest as his breath mingled with mine and his fingers threaded into my hair, pulling me closer. I didn't care that we were on a public street where anyone could see. The only thing that mattered was Niall, and how I'd longed for this moment since he tucked me into bed back at Blackthorn. How desperately I'd wished, for just a few beats of my heart, that he wasn't raised to be such a gentleman.

But he was, and I couldn't deny that it was one of the many reasons I'd grown to care for him. And I couldn't deny those feelings any longer. I lost myself in the warmth of his arms, his heady cologne of sandalwood and pine, and allowed myself—just this once—to linger in something beautiful.

Chapter 23

Our embracing continued after we returned to the cottage, our affections simmering slowly in front of the crackling fire. We sat on the couch, and I ignored everything that wasn't the feel of his lips on mine or his arms around me. I could have lived in that moment forever and been grateful for it, but I eventually disentangled myself with a reluctant groan. If I allowed things to progress further, no matter how much I might want them to, my heart would pay the ultimate price. Niall made no attempt to dissuade me from going up to my room alone. He didn't seek the invitation he wanted so keenly, because I couldn't offer it freely.

I changed into my nightgown and stared at the door, half hoping he would knock and ask for one last good-night kiss. How tempted I would be to invite him in and see where the night might lead. But he would not tempt me because he wouldn't want me simply to give in to him. It had to be my choice, and I would have to be enthusiastic about it when the time came.

If it ever came at all—which wasn't all that likely.

He would go back to Blackthorn and I to Denver, and our worlds would probably never collide in any meaningful way again.

Of course I'd love to have Caitlin and him come to visit. Of course I'd long to go back to Blackthorn and the halls that felt so much like home. But those would be little remembrances of a lovely couple of weeks. He might come to see me once, then I him . . . but would we be able to rekindle the spark we'd just shared? Would it feel hollow and forced or lose its luster when subjected to the harsh light of reality? We might have a few fun interludes, but then as time marched on, communication would fizzle and die. Wasn't that how long-distance relationships worked?

I tried to distract myself from the ache in my core by reading from the tome Madame DuChâtel had given me. I didn't try to wade through the early pages that listed all manner of census data and miscellany that didn't pertain to Imogène. After some digging, I found a vague reference to her, saying only that her family left the village after the death of her beloved. There was an interesting section on Coralie DuChâtel, the regionally famous apothecary who had loyal patrons all over Aquitaine, Occitanie, and beyond who would travel to her for their remedies. But nothing about what became of Imogène or her child.

It was perhaps an hour before my eyes began to droop and I set the book on the bedside table so I wouldn't risk dropping it and damaging the brittle binding. I glanced at my phone to check the time, to see that a message had popped up in the time I'd been reading.

JONATHAN: Are you doing okay? I thought I'd check in. I hadn't seen anything from you in a while.

I resisted the urge to hurl my phone but didn't want to wake Niall who was likely already asleep.

ME: I was supposed to keep sending texts after we
broke up?

JONATHAN: I guess not. I went by your place, and you
weren't there . . . I'd just hoped to clear the air between us. I can come meet you if you're out and about.
Take you to dinner or whatever.

I checked the time, as I had originally planned to do. It was past
one in the morning here and shortly after five in the evening there.
He'd swung by my place unannounced on the way home from the
office and thought I might drop everything to join him? Some light
sarcasm would be the right approach.

ME: It would be an awfully long way to come for dinner.

JONATHAN: ???

ME: I'm in France.

JONATHAN: Wow. How did you manage that?

I gritted my teeth. It was his little code for *can you really afford
that?* Finances first, foremost, and always with him. And he saw
all nonbusiness travel as an extravagance, no matter how frugal the
arrangements. If we'd ever come to Europe for vacation, he'd have
been counting every euro and heaving indulgent sighs with every
mundane purchase, like we'd have been able to forgo the cost of
food and gas at home somehow.

ME: Avery and my parents are footing the bill, if you
must know. Not that it's any of your business.

JONATHAN: I don't think I deserve that. I've been el-
bows deep in the finances of your business for the

past three years. I know you can't afford to gallivant
around in France on your own dime.

ME: You may have been in the past, but my finances are
no longer a concern of yours.

JONATHAN: I honestly don't think I've done anything to
merit your anger. I'd hoped we'd be able to be adult
about things.

I sat up in bed, and the effort it took not to growl at my phone like
an angry dog was nothing less than Herculean. But I would not re-
sort to anything so unseemly. I would do the mature thing and send
him the photo my best friend had taken surreptitiously of him with
his date. Let the photo speak the thousand words for me.

JONATHAN: Where did you get that?

I paused to consider my reply. I could see no reason to circumvent
the truth.

ME: My best friend saw you. Having a grand time it
would seem.

The three dots appeared and disappeared as he typed and discarded several attempts at a message.

JONATHAN: It was one date.

ME: Six weeks after you ended our relationship of four
years out of the blue?

JONATHAN: Was it really out of the blue, though?
We'd been having the same struggles for months and

months. I can't believe you didn't see it coming. Or initiate it yourself.

I typed out a snarky response, which I promptly deleted. As much as a diatribe would have been cathartic, it would *not* have been productive.

ME: It **was** unexpected. I'd hoped we'd eventually find some solution, but you never seemed invested in doing more than just complaining about the issue.

JONATHAN: Well, I'm talking now. Doesn't that count for something?

Ah, sarcasm with a hint of passive aggression. His specialty. I thought about volleying back, but it wouldn't come to any good outcome. It was definitely past time for a postmortem on our relationship, and it was better to seek out some level of closure so we could both move on. I took a measured breath and texted back.

ME: But why bother? My schedule won't change. Yours won't. Our problems won't go away.

JONATHAN: I've been thinking . . . It was silly of me to be so bent out of shape about temporary inconveniences. Once we have kids, it'll be a nonissue.

I blinked, uncomprehending. We'd only discussed kids in the most hypothetical terms. We were both open to parenting and only wanted two kids at most. It was just discussion enough to know we were compatible in that arena.

ME: How do you figure? That will mean even more
complicated scheduling issues.

JONATHAN: Well, you won't want to work after that,
right?

ME: Whatever gave you that idea?

JONATHAN: I thought deep down it would be what you
wanted.

His talent for assumptions was impressive in scope. My mind
wandered to Imogène and how passionately she'd loved Lucien.
How desperate she was to keep hold of her one tie to him after he'd
died. I thought of Aoife having to leave Tadgh behind. No part of
me believed they'd have ever been so blind to the desires of the person they claimed to love best in the world.

ME: If you thought that, you haven't been paying attention to me. At all. My career is important to me and I
don't plan on sacrificing it.

JONATHAN: I thought your feelings would change when
kids were realistically in the picture.

ME: So you thought you knew better than me what *I*
wanted.

JONATHAN: Listen . . . fine. I screwed up. I'm sorry. I
want the chance to make it up to you.

I blinked at my phone and rubbed my eyes. Surely it was just my
travel-weary state and the food coma playing tricks on me. There
was no way Jonathan really and truly wanted to make up. No. I had
to be misinterpreting.

> ME: So you want us to make amends so we can part as
> friends? I'd like that.

And I'd typed the truth. Four years was a long time to devote to a relationship, and I liked the idea of parting on the best possible terms. I didn't envision us catching brunch and a matinee anytime soon, but I liked the idea of waving cordially to each other if we crossed paths near the Sixteenth Street Mall or in the lobby of the Performing Arts Center. It seemed like the adult thing to do.

> JONATHAN: No, I mean I'd like to give us another
> chance. I want to try and do better. I hope you do too.

My hands shook as I read his text. This was the least likely message I ever expected to receive. A Google alert that an alien invasion was imminent might have shocked me less. And what did it mean that I'd have almost welcomed the little green men over his message? Because, this? This required an answer, and I wasn't about to give him the one he wanted.

> ME: Are you serious?
> JONATHAN: I usually am.

True words. He rarely had patience for frivolity. He said what he meant and meant what he said . . . and expected the same from everyone around him.

> ME: I don't think so. Clearly we want different things.
> JONATHAN: Listen, we've both invested a lot in this, and
> I hate to throw it all away.

That was the financier I knew: worried about the investment of his time, the only resource, he'd always touted, that was more valuable than money. I stopped myself from making a reference to the sunk cost fallacy and how just because a person spent a lot of time making a mistake didn't mean they should stick with it. But I held back.

> ME: This is really a lot to take in, and it's late here. I need some time and I'll get back to you.
>
> JONATHAN: Fair. I shouldn't have expected an answer right away.

Read: He absolutely *had* expected an immediate answer and was disappointed not to get it, but he was trying to be adult about it. Brownie points for trying, I guessed. His three dots popped back up again before I could think of sending anything worth the international data usage.

> JONATHAN: When do you get back from France? I can get you from DIA. We can grab dinner and reassess then if you want.
>
> ME: A little over two weeks yet.
>
> JONATHAN: Wow, that's quite the extended trip. Are you sure your business can handle your being gone so long? I know it's the down season, but still.

He was always skeptical of my work. And it hit me: He was always worrying the joy out of the small wins. A new client? Well, better not neglect the ones you have. A great new vendor? Hopefully their prices won't cause the restaurant clients to run too close to the margins. It. Was. Exhausting. I shouldn't have been surprised at his assumption about me giving up work, really. Jonathan made plenty of money, after all, and I was sure to have a whole bevy of things to occupy my time. Hosting dinners to impress his colleagues and clients. Being active in the Denver charity scene to put an extra shine on the Jonathan Phillips brand. And, of course, a pair of little Phillipses to carry on the name and legacy. I evened my breath and thought out a measured response.

> ME: It's not all sightseeing. I'm making some good contacts here. Hoping to impress the clients I have and woo some new ones, as always. You wouldn't believe the truffle market we went to.
>
> JONATHAN: I'm sure it was all kinds of fun for you. Right up your alley. But if you want to look into changing your flight, I'd spring for the difference and the fees.

His impatience was another charming quality of his. He didn't want to wait two weeks or more to mend things now that he had the idea in his head.

> ME: Avery and Steph are coming over next week to meet up in Italy. Then I'll be off to Copenhagen.
>
> JONATHAN: Wow. That's . . . quite the trek. Sounds exhausting.
>
> ME: It's actually been amazing. I wish you could see it.

I paused before hitting Send and deleted the last sentence. Jonathan and Caitlin had one thing in common: Both of them would have hated the quiet, sleepy towns where this trip had taken me.

Right now, we were smack in the middle of France's "empty diagonal," a large swath of the country whose youth fled to the cities for jobs and amenities, leaving these ancient villages and towns to simply age out and die. Places like Beynac managed to hang on due to the wine and foodie tourism draw of Bordeaux and Périgord. It was a haven for the gastro-tourists like Niall and myself, but it would have been deadly dull to either Caitlin or Jonathan. But while Caitlin would have made the best of things and just been happy to leave Westport behind for a week, Jonathan would have groused at every turn. I could not, in good faith, wish that he was here.

ME: I'm really enjoying myself.

That, at least, was the truth.

JONATHAN: That's good. Let me know when you fly in, and we'll meet up.
ME: I don't think so, but thanks for the offer.

I set the phone aside and forced myself to breathe. It wasn't a kind answer, and nothing like the one he wanted, but it was the best I had to offer and better than he deserved.

Chapter 24

The siren song of coffee lured me from my sleep the following morning. Niall had won the honor of fetching breakfast that morning, and I wasn't surprised he'd beaten me to the task. I didn't need a NASA-grade fitness tracker to tell me I'd slept like crap. Jonathan's texts were swirling in my brain, and I had no idea how to react to them. Did I message him my return flight info so he could get me from the airport? Did I play it cool and wait for him to text again? Or . . . did I tell him to go pound sand?

All the options had their merits, but I was in no headspace to consider them with any sort of coherent thought before the caffeine had the opportunity to enter my bloodstream.

Niall had procured another assortment of pastries, more reasonable than the quantity I'd purchased, but by no means lacking.

"A blessing on your house," I said by way of greeting. My tone sounded something akin to Lurch from *The Addams Family*, and I helped myself to a glass of tap water to help rehydrate from the abysmal night's sleep.

"And good morning to you, sleepyhead. It's already half past eight. You're usually an early riser." He placed a mug brimming full of coffee before me, having figured out the coffeemaker that I hadn't wanted to bother with on our first morning. I muttered another blessing and took a sip of the deep-black nectar.

"I usually am. Terrible sleep. Not Imogène this time though."

His brow furrowed in concern. "Something you want to talk about?"

I shook my head. "Nah. It's personal stuff. Denver stuff. I don't want to drag down your vacation with it."

"I happen to care about your 'personal stuff.' Even the 'Denver stuff.'" He put a hand on mine, and my breath grew shallow.

I had to be more guarded with my feelings if I wanted my heart to remain intact. I didn't pull my hand back, but I focused my eyes on my plate. "I appreciate it. I really do. I just—" Words failed me as I scanned my brain to articulate everything spinning all at once.

"Let me guess: it's to do with the breakup?"

I nodded. "Yeah, he texted in the middle of the night. I couldn't sleep as it was, and his texts didn't help. He had no idea I was here."

Niall stared into the contents of his coffee cup for a few long moments. "So he wanted to have a bit of a postmortem on things? I've had one or two of those chats myself. If it doesn't end with me wearing a pint of Smithwick's down my front, I usually call it a win. "

I fidgeted with the handle of my coffee mug. "Not really. He actually wanted to pick me up from the airport and talk things over."

"Closure and all that?"

"He wants to talk about maybe trying again." I exhaled now that the words were out there. This was exactly the conversation I didn't want to have with Niall, but I was a bit relieved to have it all in the open.

"And do you want to?" His tone was impassive, but his face was less successful at the endeavor.

"No. He's absolutely the wrong man for me—the conversation last night proved that. I just feel stupid for wasting four years of my life with someone who obviously never understood me and never cared to."

"That would sting, yes, but better four years than forty, no?"

"I know in time I'll agree with that, but for right now, I just need to be angry." I picked at my croissant for a moment, searching for some insights in the flaky pastry but finding none.

"Fair enough. He's a right dolt and deserving of your wrath, I'd say."

I shoved the pastry away. "It's not him I'm angry with. Not entirely. I'm mad at myself for not seeing who he was."

"I know we've only known each other for a short while, but I've truly never felt about a woman the way I do about you. You're at a crossroads in your life right now, and that's unsettling. But the grand part about a crossroads is that you have the opportunity to make some choices."

"If only having the opportunity to choose and the moments we have good choices at our disposal lined up neatly, life would be a much easier place. It's easy to say 'go west' or 'go east,' but I put everything into my business and I want to see it through. Not to mention the financial aspect. I can't just decide to go and reinvent myself anywhere."

"Maybe not *anywhere*, but you have Blackthorn as an option. Me. We'd have a grand time turning Westport into a sleeper foodie haven. First Blackthorn, then the rest of the town. You'd have a ball."

I couldn't bring myself to meet his gaze. It would have been too hard to remain steadfast. "Niall, I've known you two weeks. It's crazy to think this way. Sure, it might be fun, but what if it all goes south?"

"What if Blackthorn is swept away in a hurricane? What if a bovine plague wipes out the cows and Ireland's butter and cheese export dries up altogether? What if the euro crashes and we end up in another financial crisis? You can ask those questions until the end of time, Veronica. But what if—just hear me out on this—none of that happens? What if it all turns out and we build a beautiful future together and we all live happily ever after?"

"You're speaking in fairy tales, Niall. That doesn't happen in real life."

"Speaking in fairy tales is a risk of being born in the land of leprechauns, and I won't apologize for it. But you bet your life it does happen. I refuse to believe we live in a world where happily ever after doesn't happen. Sure, it's not wrapped up pretty in a bow. And it takes a bloody lot of work to keep it up. Every day you have to wake up and choose to make that a reality over and over again. And some days you won't want to. You'll want to roll over in bed and push the snooze button on it all. And that's when you've got to get up, fry yourself some eggs, and try even harder than you did the day before. But happily ever after *is* possible, if you want it badly enough."

Tears welled up, but I refused to let Niall see them fall. Of course a man who had grown up in a literal castle would believe in fairy tales. For him bold knights, elegant ladies of the manor, and lowly serfs weren't abstract concepts. They were all part of the history of the building where he'd taken his first steps. He knew the history was far more brutal than the children's stories would ever dare to intimate. But there was still a tinge of the romantic and the fantastical in such a place.

I left the cottage and wandered alone for what might have been hours, rambling down every cobblestone street and dirt path in the place, hoping to outrun the dread in my gut. The dread that I was making a huge mistake even taking Jonathan's texts. That I was a fool to think The Kitchen Muse was anything more than a cover for my own cowardice.

That Niall was right about everything, and I was making a huge mistake.

Living in Ireland with Niall *could* be an incredible life. But I would have to be bold enough to make that choice.

Chapter 25

I wandered the winding cobblestone streets of Beynac for some time, pondering my conversation with Niall and the flurry of texts with Jonathan. Trying to convince myself that I hadn't been creating an elaborate web of self-deception to keep myself from failing professionally. The more I pondered, the less I liked the conclusions I came to.

Eventually I found my way to the bookstore. The door was unlocked, but Madame DuChâtel was nowhere to be found. I thumbed through the titles of the old books. I settled in the posh chair next to the fire with one of the cookbooks. After a few moments, Maximillien padded down the steps and hopped into my lap, purring contentedly.

Less than a quarter of an hour later, the bookstore swirled until it was replaced with a sort of apothecary shop. Rather than books, the shelves were filled with labeled bottles of liquid in a muted rainbow of colors, jars with dried ingredients that went beyond the limits of my vocabulary's ability to describe, and innumerable empty vials for the finished concoctions. Scales, mortars and pestles, and thick books containing the precise measures for all their medicines took up residence on a massive worktable.

The bell, which sounded identical to the one Madame DuChâtel used—perhaps the very same one—sounded as Imogène entered the antique pharmacy. A woman who appeared to be in her late forties emerged from a back room, summoned by the gentle tinkling. Her face was red and streaked with fresh tears. The unending tears of a mother who should never be forced to bury her child. She pulled aside the veil of her grief just long enough to recognize that her guest wasn't a common customer. She rushed to Imogène and took her in her arms like she would have her own daughter.

"Oh, my darling girl. You've heard the terrible news."

Imogène mumbled something like "yes" in her would-be mother-in-law's embrace. "I'm so sorry, Coralie. It was never meant to be like this." Imogène's words were drowned in sobs, but her meaning was plain enough to the only other woman who could have claimed to love Lucien as well as she did.

"No. You two were meant to grow old together. You were meant to take over the shop and have a happy, prosperous life together with a gaggle of children underfoot for me to spoil in my dotage."

At this, Imogène burst into a fresh torrent of tears. She released her agony on Coralie's shoulder, allowing the older woman to cradle and soothe her with even more patience than her own mother had shown.

"It's a tragedy, Imogène, but Lucien wouldn't want you to fall apart. He'd want you to go on living for his sake."

Imogène gently pulled away. "It's not just that, Coralie."

The older woman studied Imogène's face, and the light of recognition shone in her eyes. She placed a hand on Imogène's abdomen. "Two months gone?"

Imogène nodded. "I'm so sorry. We just—"

Coralie held up a hand to silence her. "You owe me no explanation for giving my son a happy memory to take with him, my girl. You will find no judgment here."

Imogène's shoulders sagged in relief. "My parents want to send me to a nunnery. As soon as it can be arranged. They expect me to give the baby to strangers."

Coralie blanched. "That would be a cruelty to you." She began to pace the floor, rubbing her temples methodically. "Lucien wouldn't want to see you ruined, nor would he want you to live through the agony of being parted from your child under such circumstances. I could make you a tincture . . . It's early enough that it might still work, though I cannot promise there won't be consequences to your health later on. Other women have been made barren by it."

Imogène wrapped her arms protectively around her middle. "I couldn't bear it, Coralie. I can't bear to do anything to what little is left of Lucien. I loved him—love him still—and I want the chance to love his child. I know it's reckless. I know I'll be shunned, but I just can't."

Coralie took Imogène in her arms a second time. "The choice should be yours. I only wish the world were a kinder place than it is. For both of your sakes."

Imogène returned her embrace. "It's all so brutally unfair, but there is nothing for me to do except to accept my lot as it is. Will you let me work here to earn my keep? I've been training with you, and you know I will continue to learn under you. My parents will cast me out if I refuse to go."

Coralie's face fell. "Dearest, I would, but the church would see my doors shuttered if I allowed it. They are suspicious enough of me in a man's profession. They only permit it because I never let anyone think I am anything less than a respectable widow."

Imogène exhaled, as if the last hope were leaving her body.

"Darling, I am so sorry. They would love nothing more than to have a reason to close me down. If that happened, I'd have no means to support my other children. Not to mention the customers who depend on me."

Imogène just bowed her head meekly. Given the offer she'd made Imogène, I suspected Coralie was a far more sympathetic apothecary, in particular to her female clients, than most. She would be willing to ease the pain of childbirth, while other apothecaries would hold the line that women were meant to suffer in childbed to atone for the sin of Eve. She would be willing to ease the discomfort of a woman's monthly cycles when it would be beneath the notice of other practitioners. And when a woman's health or dignity was on the line, she could be persuaded to take extreme measures if they were called for. She would have been indispensable to the people of Beynac, especially to the women who needed her gentle guidance.

Imogène seemed to compose herself. "Of course. I wasn't thinking. I couldn't ask that of you. It was thoughtless of me."

"I have been training you as my replacement. It was the most natural idea in the world. I only wish I could oblige you. It was the fondest wish of my heart to pass this on to you and to Lucien. You would have taken my place in Beynac to protect the women from the abuses they are too often called upon to endure."

"But you cannot risk your livelihood or the well-being of your patrons. I understand."

Coralie held Imogène, one hand on each bicep, bracing her for an uncertain future. Her chin suddenly jutted up in a defiant angle. "I would gladly continue your training and live to see you take over this place when I grow old. To know Beynac was in good hands. I'd give the world to have you stay here as my own daughter. But if I can't do that, perhaps I *can* give you the world."

Imogène cocked her head. "Whatever do you mean?"

"I'm going to give you money. And more importantly, I've given you training. You can sail for America and put your knowledge to use there. I daresay they'll be more tolerant of a woman in this profession than our own people."

"I—I couldn't—"

"Of course you can. You'll go to the New World as a broken-hearted young widow searching for a fresh start with her new babe. You can claim the papers concerning your marriage and Lucien's death were lost in a fire or some such thing. Left behind in the Old World and beyond recovery. No one will have any reason to question your story. And you'll have the money I'd set aside to give you and Lucien as a wedding gift."

Imogène clapped a hand to her mouth for a moment. "You would do that?"

She took Imogène's hands in hers. "The money was for you and Lucien to start your life together. Since my son is gone, it is only fitting you and his child should have it."

"Do you really think it might work?"

"I do. And Lucien's baby can be raised by his doting mother, not some stranger. I know that's what he would have wanted." At this moment a massive cat jumped on the apothecary table, meowing inquisitively.

I would have thought it was Maximillien himself if the gray portion of this echo-cat's fur weren't a few shades lighter, approaching silver. Neither woman shooed him from the work area, and Imogène absentmindedly stroked the fur between his ears.

A few silent tears made tracks down her face. Not the racking sobs from before, but quiet tears of desperation. "I'm scared. Scared to go so far. Scared to have this baby alone. How am I to know what to do?" The cat approached Imogène, then pawed at her elbow to demand affection, which she readily gave, and offered her reassurance in turn. And it seemed the cat's antics had their desired effect. "Yes, Horace. You're a very good boy."

Coralie looked at the pair mournfully. "I wish I could send your guardian with you, but I doubt they'd allow it. I'll have to put up with him pining for you for weeks. But never mind that; you are a smart and capable young woman, Imogène. I have every faith you'll find your path. And I can send a letter of introduction for you to my cousin Giselle in Philadelphia. She'll be able to help get you on your feet."

"Why would she do such a thing for me?"

"Because my mother taught her all she knows, and she understands that she owes this family a debt of gratitude. The DuChâtel men are steadfast, but there is no equal to the Joubert women for their loyalty to friends—and most especially, their family. You are one of us because you carry one of our own in your womb. She will welcome you as a daughter because she knows that to do any less would be a dishonor to her name."

"Coralie, I don't know what to say . . ."

"Tell me you'll go. Tomorrow night. Don't bother packing clothes. Put anything you truly can't live without in a small satchel. Bring nothing more than what you can sneak away without raising suspicion, and meet me here tomorrow after supper. I'll have travel papers and everything you need packed and ready for you and will devise a plan to get you to Bordeaux and the port. We can't risk you staying much longer than that. Heaven knows your mother is probably hovering at your father's shoulder as he writes letters to every nunnery in France this very night to secure a place for you."

Imogène slowly began to pace, seeming to consider Coralie's

words. It would be the solution to so many of her problems, but it would mean abandoning every aspect of the life she'd known. A hand floated absently to her midsection, still flat and lithe, but which would become round and plump with new life. For this child she would have to make that sacrifice. She screwed a determined expression on her face to mask the uneasy grimace that keenly wished to take up residence there.

"I'll go to Philadelphia if you think your cousin will welcome me. If you think there will be a future for the baby and for me there."

"Nothing is promised, my dearest, but I know your chances there will be far greater than anything that awaits you here. I would not send you or my grandchild there if I didn't believe it to be true."

Imogène took Coralie in her arms one last time, gave the magnificent cat a farewell, and slipped back out into the inky night to quietly prepare for her escape.

As soon as the door shut, Coralie hauled out a trunk and began to fill it with whatever clothes and necessities she could spare and a healthy supply of funds for Imogène to take with her to the New World. Her hands shook with apprehension, but her face was lined with resolve. She could not save her son, but she could give his love and their child a chance at a better life.

Later that night, after I'd taken the time to digest the scene from the bookshop, Niall and I had a quiet dinner of simple pasta. While we ate, I relayed the events that unfolded in the bookshop. He seemed as relieved as I was that Imogène had found an escape that hadn't cost Coralie her livelihood or the women of the village access to her services.

"I wish I understood why I'm seeing these things," I finally said. "And I honestly wish it would stop. I have enough of my own life to fill my head without worrying about these women too."

"They may be trying to tell you something, Veronica. Obviously they have some connection or affinity with you, and they want you to know what happened to them."

"At other times in my life, I might have thought being visited by Aoife and Imogène was next-level cool. Right now, I'd enjoy some peace."

"Those times weren't the season in your life when you needed to see them. I'd stop worrying about your mental health so much and just listen to what they have to say. What meaning this has for you and your future."

I set my fork aside. "You're probably right. And for what it's worth, I'm really sorry about earlier. It's just been . . . a lot."

"And you have me acting like a sod, pushing an idea—a life—you're just not ready for. I was being selfish."

"Offering me a life in a castle doing fun cookery things with you? Doesn't sound all that selfish, really."

"It is, more than you know. Caitlin isn't entirely wrong . . . Blackthorn is a heavy mantle to wear, and it can be dreadfully isolating at times. Having you with me would make it all infinitely more supportable."

I reached my hand toward his. "And more than part of me is tempted to just chuck my life and do it, despite it being entirely crazy."

"It *is* crazy. And given all you're dealing with, it was wrong for me to push the idea on you, no matter how much nicer my life would be for having you in it."

I willed the word "yes" to spring from my lips, but it simply stuck there, as if affixed with superglue. I hated the idea of him alone and miserable in that place, doing a job that wasn't meant to be his for another twenty years or more.

"Remember, I'm not the only one with the ability to choose. Blackthorn may be your birthright, but it doesn't have to be a curse. We've both been told by people what we should or even *must* do, but the choices really are ours to make."

He squeezed my hand. "I'll try to keep that in mind. And since I won't be continuing my misguided attempts to persuade you to be my chatelaine, I hope we can move past it and enjoy our last days together as friends."

"Friends," I agreed. And as precious as friendship was to me, the word still felt hollow on my lips.

Chapter 26

I woke up on our final day in Beynac with a feeling of dread. No visions of Imogène that night, for which I was grateful, but the prospect of bidding Niall goodbye was enough to rob me of my sleep. Shortly after six in the morning, I gave up on trying to catch another sleep cycle, sat up, and instinctively reached for my phone.

In my business inbox there was a message from Fairbanks.

> Hey Veronica,
>
> Those photos are amazing. Glad you had the chance to visit the truffle market—it's incredible, isn't it? I had no idea you were so talented in the kitchen in addition to knowing how to source ingredients better than anyone in the American West. I should have suspected as much. We definitely need to catch up. Shoot me a text (personal cell below) when you get back and we'll set up a time to discuss some opportunities for you at the restaurant. I have a few ideas in mind.
>
> —E. Fairbanks

P.S. If you don't make me the truffle crème brûlée, the
deal is off. 😉

I read the message a few times over. This was a job offer, I was
sure. A long-term consulting contract. Perhaps with an exclusivity
clause that would mean he'd have to pay me handsomely. Perhaps
even a job in his kitchen.

I pushed the images of me in a chic 540 Blake double-breasted
black chef's coat with *Chef Stratton* embroidered on the left side,
directly over my heart, out of my head. It was a delicious fantasy,
but I didn't have the credentials he'd require to put me on staff in
that capacity. Everyone in the back of house who outranked the
dishwashers had the words *Escoffier, Culinary Institute of America,*
or *Le Cordon Bleu* in their CVs.

But it seemed like there was something waiting for my career in
Denver, something worthwhile in my chosen field. The Kitchen
Muse ran closer to the margins than I would have liked more often than not, but this could change everything. Still, I would be
working for Edward Fairbanks rather than for myself. I did enjoy
being out on my own, and being under Fairbanks would certainly
be an adjustment, but it could mean gaining a lot of valuable
experience.

I mulled over the email as I dressed and descended the stairs.
Niall, surprisingly, was already up and doing something miraculous
with eggs, looking as sleep-deprived as I felt.

"Good morning, sunshine," he said, his tone not matching the
brightness of his words.

"I think we're the only two people in the world who get up before
dawn while on vacation." I accepted a proffered cup of coffee with
a grateful smile.

"The curse of being an innkeeper. Your body gets so used to rising with the chickens, it's hard to break the cycle. And there's nothing like the early morning hours for a good brood, as my countrymen and your ancestors would attest to. Add to that an early flight back to Dublin, and here we are."

I felt an intrusive pang in my gut. He'd have to leave within a couple of hours to get to Bordeaux so he wouldn't miss his flight home. He'd take the rental car back, and I had the choice of going early with him or taking the midday train into Bordeaux later.

"Indulging in your national pastime?" The question was glib, but I hated the thought of him mired in a bog of unpleasant thoughts.

"A bit," he confessed. "This being the last day of our holiday and all. I'll miss spending time with you, Veronica, and I won't deny it."

"I'll miss you too." I couldn't bring myself to say more. That I wished this leg of the vacation didn't have to end. That I wished things could be different for us. But it would only lead to more heartache for the both of us.

We ate our breakfast despite our lack of appetites. During the meal I filled the pregnant silence by telling Niall about the email from Fairbanks.

"That's grand, truly," he said, between half-hearted bites of omelet. "It sounds like it will be a marvelous opportunity for you."

His tone was guarded, and I couldn't help but prod. "I sense a *but* lurking in there somewhere."

He set down his fork. "You don't need Fairbanks, Veronica. You just need your own kitchen. But if this opportunity excites you, I won't be the one to naysay it. I'm sure he's a brilliant chef with all sorts of fancy letters after his name, and you'll learn loads from him."

"I'm sure I will," I managed to reply. "Even if I wanted my own kitchen, doesn't it make sense to gain some experience under a master chef like Fairbanks?"

"Maybe so, love. But don't sell your own skills short."

Heat rose in my cheeks at the endearment, which was as meaningful as "dearie" in Irish but still caused a twang of something like regret to pierce my heart. "You've already got more theoretical and practical knowledge than many successful restaurateurs had when they got their start. You have what it takes to make a real mark on the industry. And I'm not just saying this because of the truffle crème brûlée."

I arched a questioning brow.

"Fine, fine. Not *entirely* because of the crème brûlée. Only in part. But you're a rare talent. Don't dismiss that talent out of misplaced humility."

"On one condition," I said. "You promise to do the same. Your dreams deserve their fair share too. Blackthorn has stood and thrived for hundreds of years before you and will outlast us all. I think she is part of your destiny but not all of it."

He stared down at his hands. "I'll try, but it seems like the ship has sailed in so many respects. I can't be the one to let the place fall into ruin."

"It won't. You're smart enough to find a solution."

He remained silent for a while until finally looking up at me. "I'd like to think I'm a smart man, but not always. I'm about to ask you for something monumentally daft."

"Anything," I said. And I meant it. On the precipice of parting, there wasn't anything I wouldn't have done to make him a bit happier.

"A goodbye kiss. Please. I thought the memory of the other night might be enough, but I confess I'm greedy when it comes to you."

He rose and offered me a hand. This wasn't going to be a chaste kiss goodbye at the threshold. We settled on the sofa, where I let his lips explore mine until I wasn't sure where I ended and he began. I wanted mothing more than to continue this embrace for the rest of time, but our minutes together were becoming ever fewer.

When, at length, he pulled away, both of our faces were wet with tears. "Love, I know you don't want to make promises we can't keep, but can't we at least manage a few texts and emails? I'd rather have you just a bit longer, even if it fades away over time."

I nodded. I wasn't equal to speech, but I couldn't deny either of us that small pleasure.

He pulled me in close and tucked my head under his chin. I could feel a few more tears drip down onto my head. "*Mo stór*, I have to be going. Come with me to the airport so we have just a bit longer together?"

I swallowed hard and rushed to gather my things. I didn't know what the Irish words meant, but I could guess well enough that knowing would only make the parting more difficult. Niall held my hand all the way to Bordeaux and until his flight home was called. I watched until he disappeared down the Jetway, completely unfazed by the tears rolling down my cheeks as I found my own gate. I had a week in Italy with two of my favorite people in the world in store, yet it took all the reserve I had not to find a ticket agent to get me on the next flight into Dublin. But I couldn't abandon Avery and Stephanie like that. Not even for the whispers of a beautiful dream that crumbled under the impossible weight of the waking world.

Chapter 27

Week Three: Italy

As the plane from Bordeaux landed in Milan, the lurching in my stomach had little to do with the descent of the aircraft. Niall was on his way back to Westport, likely with half a day left in his journey, and I felt an emptiness that, over the past couple of hours, I'd come to resent. I knew better than to develop feelings for a relationship fling, so the heartache I felt now would be a good penance for my stupidity.

Shrieks greeted me as I walked off the Jetway and into the terminal. Avery and Stephanie, a bit travel worn yet chic, bounced up and down when they saw me, and threw their arms around me before dragging me to the rental car counter.

"Remind me why you rented a place three hours out of Milan?" Stephanie shot an annoyed glance at Avery as she accepted the keys to the Fiat that would be ours for the week.

"First of all, don't exaggerate. It's an hour and twenty minutes at most. And second, because it's where Veronica's DNA records said she was from." Avery was smug as she punctuated the sentence with a beep from the car fob, letting us know which compact car was ours. "And don't worry. We'll come back to do some shopping. I'd be fired if I went to Milan and didn't come back with a suitcase full of gorgeousness."

"Thank God," Stephanie muttered as we shoved our bags in the minuscule trunk, and Avery and Stephanie endeavored to shove their tall frames in the car that was definitely not designed for American body types. "I love you both, but a week of living like the farmer in the dell is a lot to ask, even for the pair of you."

Avery, the most accomplished big-city driver, was on driving detail. I gestured that Stephanie should take the front passenger seat since she was far taller than I. For once I was glad I'd never quite cracked five-foot-four and wouldn't have to be miserable for the drive to the farmhouse outside the village of Piozzano, which Avery had secured for us.

"Small towns aren't all that bad," I finally protested once we were settled in the car.

"Well, it seems your ancestors were fond of them," Avery quipped.

Stephanie snorted. "And the one thing they have in common is that they left."

I summoned a smile but didn't comment. They had no way of knowing the circumstances that led to their decisions to leave. If Aoife and Imogène were indeed my foremothers or had some other connection to me, it wasn't mere boredom that had driven them from their homes. No one picked up and left a life just because she was bored. Not back then when it meant leaving everything and everyone she ever knew with little chance of ever seeing them again.

Avery's eyes flicked to the rearview mirror. "I feel bad sending you on a trip where you're missing the highlights like Dublin and Paris. At the time, I thought you'd want to see the actual towns that popped up on your report, but I've been worried that I made a mistake. I hope you've managed to have some fun."

My eyes took in the swirling city streets, so different from the antique cobblestones in Aquitaine. "Oh definitely. I mean, I can't see myself spending months in a village like Beynac or anything, but I'm glad I saw it. The cottage you found was perfect, by the way."

Avery and Stephanie seemed to be having a silent conversation in the front seat until Avery broke the silence as she turned onto the highway that led out of the city.

"We hoped you'd haul the sexy Irish castle keeper with you. We have plenty of room. He'd have been welcome."

I stifled a grimace. "As the job description implies, he had to get back to keeping the castle. He doesn't have a lot of time for extended holidays."

Stephanie exchanged a glance with Avery. "As much fun as it would have been to give him the third degree, I'm glad you came solo. I want to spend time with *you*, not the rebound fling."

I sat up straighter in the back seat. "He is *not* a rebound fling; he's a friend. A good one. And Jonathan . . . Well, he's an idiot."

Stephanie craned her neck around from the passenger seat to meet my eyes. "That photo I sent you about two weeks ago was pretty sound proof of that. Do you have other evidence to further support this?"

I prattled off a summary of my last text exchange with Jonathan. By the end of it both of them looked ready to throttle him.

I ducked my head. "I was monumentally stupid to ever think he was a good person, wasn't I?"

Avery glanced back at me in the rearview mirror. "Listen, Vero. I know you're the big sister, but you're not doing this again."

"What do you mean?"

She exchanged a glance with Steph. "Browbeating yourself for someone else's mistakes. Someone else's selfishness. I've seen you do this a lot over the past few years, and the only one who deserves your low opinion is him. Not you."

"I don't browbeat myself."

Another shared glance between Avery and Stephanie, and I couldn't help but feel a bit excluded. They'd always been friendly, but they seemed to have bonded further over my life implosion. And that was great. Few people could say that their best friend and little sister got along so well, but I didn't love this new third-wheel experience.

This time Stephanie spoke. "It's sort of your specialty. But the good news is, you can cut it out immediately and feel a million times better. Now repeat after me: Jonathan Phillips is a massive jerk and is beneath my notice."

I obliged.

Avery gave an approving click of the tongue. "Attagirl You've been through some crap, and you need us to be your support squad."

"That's nice, I suppose." My voice sounded flatter than I'd realized.

"Come on, now. When the tables have been turned, you've said way worse things about our exes who deserved it far less than that moron." Stephanie craned her head to give me a wink. "But enough of the trash talk about undeserving men. We're here to have a stellar girls' week."

"I'm glad. It seems like forever since I got to hang with either of you for more than just a couple hours without a crisis."

"Being an adult is *so* overrated at times," Avery said. "The lack of slumber parties is a serious drag."

Stephanie rolled her eyes. "I don't know. Being able to drive, buy alcohol, and vote are decent trade-offs."

Avery scoffed. "Taxes? Bills? Accountability? Having every waking minute spoken for? I don't think it's quite as good of a deal as you think it is."

Stephanie shot me a pointed look in the rearview mirror. There it was, their chief personality divergence and sometimes bone of contention. The extra two years Stephanie had on Avery sometimes felt like fifteen. Stephanie was doggedly independent, while Avery had no compunction about leaning on Mom and Dad for help as she established herself. And it wasn't like she was mooching without holding up her end of the bargain. She was working her tail off, and Mom and Dad, in their wisdom, considered her a worthy investment.

Stephanie, on the other hand, hadn't taken a dime from her widowed mother from the moment she got her first work-study job on the CU Boulder campus. Not because her mother was struggling financially, but because she'd been determined to find success without having to give anyone else credit. There were times I worried that this level of independence wasn't entirely healthy, but to suggest she could lean on people for support from time to time was akin to suggesting she was incompetent—at least in her view. And in the grand scheme of things, I fell closer to Stephanie's philosophy than Avery's, which partly explained why we'd ended up so close.

The rest of the ride was filled with bright chatter—mostly between Stephanie and Avery—but I didn't mind the opportunity to look out at the countryside that passed by in a blur, thanks to Avery's lead foot. They talked about their high-profile jobs, their vibrant dating lives, and all their big-city exploits, taking breaks to ask me about my adventures the past two weeks. I found my answers more terse than usual. Neither of them were foodies, though both didn't mind checking out the latest hot restaurants just to "be in the know." I doubted very much they wanted to hear about the truffle market in Périgueux or the amazing Polish food in Ballyhaunis. I didn't feel right opening up to them about whatever it was Niall and I had shared. And telling them about Aoife and Imogène? That was something I just wasn't ready to share with my nearest and dearest yet.

But as we drove through the small town of Piozzano and then pulled into the driveway of the farmhouse, I felt my pulse slow back to its usual state of relaxation. I could breathe more deeply and didn't mind that my own little world was so different from theirs. The farmhouse was expansive and rambling and full of light in a way that neither Blackthorn nor the cottage in Beynac could ever pretend to be. The main structure had to be at least two hundred years old but had clearly been expanded and extensively remodeled in the subsequent decades. It lacked the aura of history that the other two vacation rentals had possessed in abundance, but it felt warm and welcoming, despite the brisk January air.

Niall would have loved it, but I pushed that thought away. He was on his way back to his life in Westport, and I had two weeks of travel still ahead. I would not waste them by wishing away my present moment and losing myself in a frivolous dream.

Chapter 28

S tephanie stepped into the living room of the farmhouse, scanning the space with an assessing eye. "Okay, this isn't half bad, Ave. I'll grant you that. Aside from being out in the boonies, its only deficit is the lack of room service." Stephanie was usually The Ritz-Carlton/Four Seasons/The Plaza Hotel sort of traveler, but the recently renovated farmhouse was undeniably gorgeous. The furniture was modern and minimalist without being too spartan, and the floor-to-ceiling windows let in expansive views of rambling farmland and vineyards. It had clearly once been a country home for a wealthy family, meticulously maintained over the generations.

"Isn't that why I'm here?" I chided. "I'll cook for us. Real Italian food."

Stephanie shot me a questioning glance. "Seriously, Vero. Do you really want to cook on vacation?"

"Sure. I mean, we can definitely find restaurants and takeout too. But I don't mind at all." I understood why Stephanie was dubious about my offer. She'd come to the conclusion that I considered it a chore, akin to laundry and scrubbing toilets. And to be fair? A lot of people felt the same. I just wasn't one of them. "Why don't we go classic? I can make pizza. From scratch. Maybe tiramisu to go with?"

"That sounds labor intensive," Avery said, clearly concerned about getting roped into KP.

I waved my hand. "I'll manage it all. Get yourselves settled and I'll find a grocery."

Avery insisted I get my choice of bedroom, as there were four to choose from. I selected one on the second floor that was somewhat smaller than the others but with an oversize bed and expansive views of the vineyard off in the distance. Avery chose the sprawling primary bedroom on the main level and Stephanie the one next to mine. The fourth would be reserved as office space if either of them had to take a Zoom meeting for work that couldn't be put off for a week.

The farmhouse was located almost equidistant between two small towns: Piozzano and Rezzanello, and a quick search on my phone directed me to an open grocery only seven minutes away, and thankfully Avery had put my name on the rental car as well so I didn't have to haul the jet-lagged pair of them to the market. I left them with promises to purchase high-quality wine and chocolate, since calories were no longer being counted, and I only fumbled for a few moments getting the hang of the rental car, which was mercifully not a stick shift.

The market I found was a small one. It made even a modest grocery store in the US look enormous, but it *smelled* like food instead of the industrial-cleaning-agent smell of an American chain store. The mélange of fruits, vegetables, meat, and fresh bread wafted to my nose as soon as I entered the shop, and I let it soak in for just a moment before I began to shop in earnest. Apart from its diminutive size, the grocery store held fewer processed foods than its American counterpart. Naturally, there were boxed pasta and cookies, but very few of the neon-colored kid-centric foods that contained more chemicals than nutrition. I loved the idea of being a parent here and not having to worry that the "Mommy, may I have——?" item would be laced with Red No. 40 and preservatives that were barely a molecule away from antifreeze. And unlike the natural grocery stores in the US, the total bill wouldn't equal a month's pay.

I got the basics I'd need for the dough, the promised top-shelf wine and makings for tiramisu, as well as coffee and some staples for breakfast. I decided to make three pizzas: a vegetarian option with artichoke hearts and a resplendently green spinach, a meat option with artisanal sausage and mushrooms, and a classic Margherita with tomato sauce, a generous blanket of mozzarella cheese, and leaves of fresh basil. We could mix and match as we liked, and leftovers would reheat beautifully.

As a concession to vacation, I found a respectable-enough jarred sauce rather than taking the time to whip up a marinara from scratch. To do it right would take all day, and if I rushed it for dinner that night, the results would be on par with the store-bought sauce at best. The dough would take time enough, so I tossed the makings for a modest charcuterie board in the cart as well. And as I reached the checkout, I felt revivified. Most of my Coloradan counterparts went into the mountains to hike, bike, or ski to recharge. Apparently being in a decent grocery store was my way of getting back to nature.

Advisable or not, Avery and Stephanie decided to indulge in a nap to assuage their jet lag, so I set about making the pizza dough and leaving it to rise in the warming drawer below the oven that looked so new I checked to make sure the protective film wasn't still affixed to the front. The kitchen had every modern convenience and was laid out with the sort of efficiency that came from a contractor who had designed a thousand kitchens and had settled on the design that yielded the fewest complaints. It was a pleasant enough place to cook. It was less cramped than the cottage in Beynac and had even a few more bells and whistles than Niall's commercial kitchen at Blackthorn, but it was less welcoming somehow.

Both of the previous kitchens had been renovated multiple times in the course of their existence, but this one felt like the house had somehow not cared for the changes. It missed the original cast-iron stove and massive sink that had washed everything from dishes to vegetables to newborn babies. It missed the massive scarred wooden worktable where thousands of loaves of bread had been expertly kneaded. It missed having a family that gathered in this space every night to share a meal and family conversation. Such a thought was obviously daft—a house *missing* the love and continuity of a family—but I seemed prone to those lately.

I cleared my head and put together the layers of tiramisu—ladyfinger cookies dipped in cold espresso and rum, mascarpone cheese blended with whipped cream and sugar, and a top layer of grated chocolate—so it could chill long enough to solidify before dinner. Then I arranged meat, cheese, and crackers on a cutting board and focused my thoughts on the here and now. I made no special effort to keep down the noise, knowing that Avery and Stephanie's internal clocks would be royally screwed up if they were allowed to sleep much longer. But I wasn't about to face their wrath by waking them up directly. Once the charcuterie was in place, I poured the wine into three glasses. Apparently the faint sound of the cork was enough to rouse them from their slumber, and they each gratefully accepted a glass with the same veneration as their morning coffee.

Stephanie sniffed before taking a sip. "Not bad, Stratton. Good to see you're not losing your touch on vacation."

I assumed an imperious expression that I hoped was comical. "We're in the heart of Italian wine country and I've just come from Bordeaux. I'd have to actively beat my touch off with a stick to lose it here."

Avery, true to form, had taken a deep draught from her glass without paying any mind to the bouquet or observing any of the wine-related niceties. "More likely she's met every vintner between here and the Atlantic Ocean and has a whole suitcase full of business cards to lug back home."

I thought of the tidy stack I'd acquired in the Beynac area but didn't concede the point. If any one of those contacts helped bolster The Kitchen Muse, it'd be well worth hauling them home.

"She'd have done the same in Ireland too if they made wine there. Wait, they do, don't they?" Stephanie eyed me with short-of-wary suspicion.

I laughed. "Technically, yes, I believe there are a few commercial vineyards in Ireland, and the wine's not half bad. But the cider? Life altering."

"You're supposed to be on vacation, Vero," Avery scolded. "I hope you haven't spent the *whole* time working."

Stephanie spoke up on my behalf as she polished off a cracker and some particularly nice sheep cheese. "She'd relax less if she wasn't low-key working, Ave. I know this one, and forcing her to shut all the open browser tabs in her brain would just cause her to blue screen."

Avery gave Stephanie an intense stare. "I had no idea you were such a nerd. Well done." She turned back to me. "To follow *that*"— she made a dramatic gesture Stephanie-ward—"um . . . metaphor, we hoped you'd come here for a reboot."

"And so I have. It's been great and I can't thank you enough for all of this." I went around to the other side of the kitchen island where she and Stephanie sat and gave her a one-armed side hug. "I thought you were crazy at first, planning this spur-of-the-moment offseason trip, but everything has been sort of . . . perfect, really."

Avery sat straighter in her barstool. "Of course it has. Project management is my thing. Fashion isn't just about pretty fabrics and trips to Fashion Week. Logistics, baby."

Stephanie raised a glass to her, and I followed suit. "To logistics," Stephanie proclaimed.

"To girls' week," Avery echoed.

We had a sip of our Chianti, and I turned my attention to getting the pizzas formed and ready to bake while we talked.

After a while Avery looked a bit distant and almost squirming in her seat, which was not typical for someone who, if not perfectly comfortable in her own skin, was pretty dang confident in it most of the time. I gave her a hard look after I placed one of the pizzas in the oven. "Spill it, twerp. Something's bothering you."

She rolled her eyes. "Says you."

"I've known you since the day you were born, and I can smell your BS from a mile away. Dish or I'll text Mom that you're being weird."

Avery huffed and took another sip from her wineglass. "I just hate that we're not related, you know, biologically."

I went over and pulled her into my arms. She didn't break down into sobs, but there were a few muffled gulps against my shoulder. I pressed my lips to the top of her head. "I was a jerk not to ask how you felt about this, but if it's any consolation, I didn't ask because it didn't even occur to me that it would change anything between us."

She lifted her head off my shoulder and wiped a few errant tears.

"Thanks, sis. I mean, I know this is happening to you more than anyone, but it really *is* happening to the whole family too."

Stephanie leaned over and squeezed Avery's shoulder in solidarity.

"It is," I acknowledged. "And I'm sure it's a lot for all of us to process, even if Mom and Dad have known for almost twenty-seven years."

"Are you mad at them?" Avery asked.

I glanced away, searching for the right words. "I wish they'd been the ones to tell me years ago. I know there were NDAs and they just sort of wanted to pretend the adoption part didn't matter. That we were a family like any other, but the truth is . . . we aren't. And that's fine. Everything I am I owe to Mom and Dad, and I'll always be grateful. I just wish they'd trusted me—us—with the truth."

"That's fair," Avery said. "And for what it's worth, they feel terrible about it."

I sighed. "They don't need to."

Avery shifted uncomfortably some more, and I gave her my infamous side-eye. *You weren't finished so fess up, little sister.*

"So you've been busy traveling. I know you've been dealing with a lot . . . so I've been keeping tabs on your DNA site for you while you've been away."

I ran my finger along the rim of my wineglass. "That's nice, but did something change? Did they find some Estonian ancestry somewhere in the strands or something? And by the way, I am *not* going to Estonia in January, so don't even think about it. Denmark will be bad enough."

"They found cousins," she blurted. "The company's new, so it takes a while for all the data to come in. You have mostly third and even further removed cousins, but they seem legit from some very modest cyberstalking. I didn't think you'd mind a little sleuthing on such distant family members."

I took the barstool between Avery and Stephanie but slid my wineglass a few inches farther away from me rather than drinking from it. I didn't trust my hands not to shake.

"Wow," I managed to finally mutter. Stephanie placed a hand on my back and rubbed gently.

Avery rubbed her eyes, looking more than just travel weary. "You don't have to meet them or anything. But I wanted you to know. FamilyRoots finally released their app, and you can keep tabs on it all yourself now."

"Good to know." I took a few breaths, digesting that there were, existing somewhere in the world, people who shared some actual DNA with me, even if it was just 1 to 5 percent. It was a connection. "I mean, seeking out distant relatives is kinda weird, but I wouldn't mind seeing their names. Maybe knowing where they settled . . . It could be interesting."

Avery laced her fingers, her knuckles growing white. "They're bound to find more, Vero. Maybe closer ones. Just promise me you won't drop us for them?"

"Of course not, you turd." I wrapped an arm around her and pressed my lips to her temple.

I was doing my job. Being the big sister and comforting Avery in her time of need. But inside? My head was spinning. There was a very real possibility that I had half brothers and sisters out there. Who knew, maybe full siblings? I had no idea why my birth mother had made the decision she had. I didn't know if my birth father had been involved in that or if he even knew I existed.

Did I want to know them? Aside from medical history—which the DNA test had been helpful with—there wasn't a *practical* reason for it. It felt like opening up a tremendous can of worms . . . and there would be no cramming them back inside once the lid was off.

But I couldn't think of that right now. It was too big, too much. I downed the last of my wine and stood. "I know exactly what this situation needs, ladies. Pizza. Let's eat."

Chapter 29

We ate pizza and drank Chianti until the wee hours of the morning. And it was better than great. It felt like a high school slumber party again, but with better food. The wine was a nice improvement too. And definitely useful given the heavy topics we ventured toward early in the evening. I had to admit, I wasn't sorry when the conversation grew lighter as the evening wore on. I knew, in my heart of hearts, that I'd have to make some decisions about how to move forward with the information Avery's Christmas gift had dumped in my lap, but I wasn't even sure how to start processing it.

The girls eventually had to give in to their jet lag, and I hoped the wine would help quiet my mind well enough so I'd be able to sleep as well. Steph and Avery deserved more than a zombie travel companion, and given my track record over the past couple of weeks, it was even odds as to whether sleep would come.

I ascended the stairs to my little room, grateful for the fatigue I felt settling into my bones. I was at the point of curling up under the starched white down comforter when the plastered walls of the farmhouse and the modern furniture gave way to rough-hewn furniture and worn curtains and linens.

Again.

My hands trembled as I waited for the scene to come into focus, wondering what new people would come to me. What pain they would be suffering.

Because that was the common denominator between Aoife and Imogène. They had experienced such pain that the only option that seemed tenable was to leave everything behind. They shared a desperation I hoped I would never know for myself, and I couldn't help but brace for the heartache the echoes might show me.

A woman, perhaps middle-aged, paced the floor, letter in hand. A younger woman, practically the mirror image of the elder, lay on a small sofa, hands over her ears. I had to assume they were mother and daughter given how much they looked alike. They were statuesque like Avery, and similarly had glossy black hair, large intelligent eyes, and flawless olive skin I couldn't help but envy. Their dresses were crafted of fine fabrics—the mother in a deep crimson, the daughter in a light blue. The waistlines were high—regency style, right out of a Jane Austen movie adaptation, so I hazarded a guess that this was roughly in that era. The 1820s perhaps?

The mother placed a hand on her daughter's shoulder. "I know, *cara*. It's never pleasant when your father comes to visit, but we must make him feel welcome."

A low moan escaped the young woman's lips. The news of her father's arrival wasn't just unwelcome, it was a source of acute dread.

"Please, Donatella. Your father will only stay a short while. We need more time and must keep him happy until then, or it may all be for nothing. You remember the last time he got into a temper, don't you?"

Another groan, this one quieter, and somehow more pleading.

"Darling, it's only for a couple of hours at most. No matter his intentions, his work lures him back to the city, praise be. I know how awful it is for you, but it won't be long."

A forceful knock sounded at the front door. The sounds of a maid scurrying to answer, followed by the sound of a man barking indistinct instructions came from the foyer. A diminutive man, given to fat in his middle, barged inside without waiting for a reply. He wore a fine suit of clothes, befitting a wealthy merchant or even a lesser noble, and walked with a confident swagger I could sense he hadn't earned. Everything about his attire seemed too new, everything about his manner overly varnished. I felt the hairs at the nape of my neck stand on edge, perceiving he was not a kindly sort of man.

The man threw his head back in exasperation at the sight of the young woman, presumably his daughter, on the sofa. He turned to his wife. "Another fit of pique is it?"

She straightened to her full height but took care not to tower over her husband. "She's been well for weeks here in the solace of the countryside and my family home. The news of your sudden arrival simply gave her a bit of shock. A bit more warning might have been warranted."

"I sent a messenger an hour ahead. Am I supposed to wait for an invitation chiseled in stone like the commandments to visit my own home? My own wife and child?"

The woman bristled but appeared to swallow back her words that, from the expression on her face, would have been laced with acid. I got the feeling this was an old argument rehashed many times over.

The mother steadied herself. "Of course you are welcome in my home whenever you wish to grace us with your presence, Giacomo. But your messenger was delayed, and we had almost no time to prepare to receive you properly. You must forgive us if your welcome isn't what you hoped."

His expression softened by a fraction of a degree. "It's of no consequence, Carlotta. I've come to collect you both to come back to town. It's high time you both returned. People are beginning to talk. I've asked your maid to have the staff gather your essentials. Anything else can be brought later."

Carlotta retained a calm mien, but her rage fairly glistened beneath the thin veneer of serenity. "You didn't seek to ask me first? Give us time to prepare?"

The color rose in his cheeks. "I don't ask you, wife. I give orders. Whatever ideas your family may have put in your head, I am the head of this family, and my wishes are to be obeyed."

Try though she might, the anger that gripped at Carlotta's soul with its talons and fangs finally belied its presence in the form of blazing hatred in her eyes. "You would do well to remember what your life was like before my blessed father took a liking to you, before you treat his daughter like a willful servant boy in need of a lashing." The unspoken words hung heavy in the air: *You would be nothing without me. Tread lightly.*

He grunted in frustration. "Dammit woman, she's the prettiest girl in all of Milan, and we must leverage that before the bloom has gone off the rose. She's already twenty, for heaven's sake."

Carlotta scowled. "Be that as it may, the town isn't good for her. The noise, the smells, the crowds. It's overwhelming to her. Not to mention the unrest against the Austrians. If you want her to receive suitors, better to do it here where she's at ease."

"The Austrians will quell the rabble-rousers before long." Giacomo shook his head and crossed to the sideboard to pour himself a measure of thick red liquid. Some sort of fortified wine like a port perhaps. "But more to the point, no suitor worth having will want to venture this far to call on a prospective bride. The sort of man I have in mind will want a wife who can be a social asset to him in the city. She'll be a charming bride for one of the Austrian officials if she'll just come to her senses."

Carlotta's expression was unyielding. "Austrian dignitary or not, if a suitor isn't willing to ride two hours on easy roads to meet our daughter, he's not a suitor worth having. You have seen the fits of melancholia that plague her in town. She simply isn't fit for the role you envision for her. Better you find her a quiet country squire with a large estate where she can find peace."

"*Fits of melancholia* indeed. I won't see her chance to make a great match squandered by marrying her off to some nobody in a backwater. I would be remiss as a father. How can I possibly be expected to fulfill my duties and see her well-married if I cannot make arrangements?"

Carlotta's expression turned hard. "I believe your chief duty, husband, is to love your daughter. Your daughter as she is, not as you wish her to be."

He scoffed. "You speak like a simpleton. You know full well that she must be married well to have any sort of a future. All this comes from you coddling her, you know."

Daggers shot from Carlotta's eyes and she met him toe to toe. "I don't coddle her; I love her. You would understand the difference if you had some semblance of a feeling heart in you. I've told you countless times she needs to see a doctor about these spells."

Giacomo took one step forward, and a wave of fear washed over the room that I could feel in the pit of my stomach, even if the emotions weren't my own. This was a dangerous man, and Carlotta knew it from firsthand experience. "We cannot risk taking her to be seen for such an affliction, and you well know it. If word got out, no man worth having would take her."

Carlotta sighed. "So we tell everyone she was going for her hay fever or a stubborn cold she couldn't shake off. No one will be the wiser."

He set down his glass with an audible *clink* against the wood. "These things always have a way of spreading. Indiscreet nurses. Doctors who jabber too much over their wine. Nosy neighbors who put two and two together. And it's not like you'll be taking her to the corner physician. All it would take is her being seen walking up the steps to the wrong office and all her prospects would disappear."

"So we go to Florence or Rome. Perhaps Paris or Vienna if you want to be even more discreet. The Austrians you're so enamored of take extended foreign holidays at every possible occasion. It would lend us cachet, don't you think?"

Giacomo sighed. "As much as I wish we could claim such status, we are not on the same level as they. If we take any sort of prolonged holiday, we will simply cease to exist in the eyes of their kind. Your absence in town these many months hasn't helped matters."

Carlotta's voice lowered. "Would it really be so terrible to remain in the station we were born to? Your father was the most respected jeweler and goldsmith in Milan, and you've turned his business into an empire. You don't need the approval of barons and counts. They have done nothing to deserve their status, but you've earned the admiration of everyone in this city on your merits. You're *above* their notice, not below it."

Carlotta spoke with the passion of true belief. She had loved this man once and found him worthy, but sadly he had not done himself the same kindness.

"If only the world worked the way you see it through those naive eyes of yours. It wouldn't matter if I amassed a fortune to rival the Hapsburgs, I would still be seen as a tradesman and a merchant. A talented one, yes. But a common tradesman all the same. It's not enough to have my jewels glittering about all the finest ballrooms. I want to be welcomed in them."

"Is entrée into ballrooms truly your biggest concern? Don't you want to see our daughter happy? She needs a quiet life in the country, not the maelstrom of city life and society."

"Happy at what cost, Carlotta? Wasting her beauty and her opportunity to make the match of the decade? To be the envy of all Milan?"

Carlotta's jaw clenched as she fought to temper her rage. "Those are your ambitions, husband. Not hers. To foist them on her is a cruelty and you know it. I believe she can be helped. We can research treatments and facilities together, and I'll take her on my own with Filipe, Eduardo, or whichever one of the footmen you can spare. You can stay in Milan and look after our interests and tell all of society that your wife and daughter are off on a decadent tour all over the continent, but you simply couldn't bear to be away from the city for so long. I'll have some new clothes made in Paris to lend credence to the story, and if you spin the tale properly, you'll be the most talked about man in Lombardy."

"Yes, and I shudder to think what they'll be saying. Now get that girl in the carriage in the next fifteen minutes, ready to head back home, or I'll take a strap to her backside. Maybe that will wake her up." He turned on the ball of his foot without a backward glance and slammed the door so hard the walls shook.

For a fleeting moment Carlotta buried her head in her hands. Her shoulders racked with silent sobs, but just as quickly, she straightened her spine, stood, and knelt beside her daughter.

"Cara, I need you to get dressed. You can sleep all day tomorrow. I promise to get you help, but you must not make your father angry before I can do it. Vincente and I are working on a plan, but it will take time. You remember Vincente the solicitor?"

Donatella sat up. "Yes. He's going to help us?"

"Yes, but making inquiries to the doctors is taking time, dearest. We can't leave without a sound plan."

Donatella buried her face in her hands for a few moments but then looked at her mother with a pained expression. Like her mother, she was the very picture of Italianate beauty, but the deep pools of her eyes were haunted. She suffered in a time when such afflictions were either dismissed as caprice or, worse, punished as wanton disregard for the established order. She was still young, but her life had already seen more than enough misery.

"I must go?" Her voice was a raspy husk.

"Yes, cara. I'm afraid it's for the best. We can't have your father in a state again. It will only make things harder for both of us as we bide our time."

Donatella's eyes locked on the door he'd exited moments before. "I hate him, Mamma."

Carlotta's shoulders sagged. "You aren't alone in that, dearest."

"You . . . hate him too?" Donatella asked with wide eyes.

"There's a reason we live here and not in Milan, cara. Beyond your need for tranquil surroundings." Grief suffused her voice. I supposed she was mourning the loss of her most vibrant years living with an overbearing lout of a man.

"Then why did you marry him?" Donatella stood so her mother could help her to the carriage where Giacomo waited.

Carlotta held her daughter's lovely face in her hands for a moment. "I was blind to many of his faults at first, as any seventeen-year-old girl would be. But I've grown wiser. My father urged the match because he was such a promising young jeweler. Mamma saw him for what he was, but she wasn't able to dissuade my father. He thought that I, and my family's money, might help him grow to greater things. And that I did . . . but I created a monster in the process."

"Me," Donatella mumbled.

Carlotta took her daughter by the upper arms. "Donatella Regina Maria Del Vecchio Valenti, I never meant you. Your father and his unholy ambition. That's truly the evil bubbling below the surface. I never confessed this to you before because you are from his seed, and I didn't want *you* to think any less of yourself."

Donatella turned to her mother with pained eyes. "But I am broken, Mamma. I am no use to him. So I am less than dirt in his eyes."

Carlotta crooked a finger under her daughter's chin to force her to meet her eyes. "You listen to me, daughter. We do not concern ourselves with the opinions of those who think little of us. Their bitter thoughts are none of our affair. And that especially includes your oafish father."

Carlotta wrapped her daughter in a velvet cloak of rich cobalt blue, which lifted her color and reflected the light so she appeared to glow like an apparition from heaven. Her eyes were heavy and glazed as she dissociated from the reality in front of her and the one that awaited her.

Carlotta gave her daughter one appraising look. "Your father was right about one thing, cara. You *are* the most beautiful girl on the continent."

Donatella's eyes seemed to snap back into focus. "Thank you, Mamma." Her voice was stronger, and she stood taller.

"Just do what you can to quell your father's anger, dearest. I promise I've got a plan to get us out. We must bide our time until I can set it into motion."

Chapter 30

Despite the visions, sleep had been kind. When I emerged from my room, I felt less weary than Avery and Stephanie likely would. Chances were, they'd struggle with jet lag for at least another day or two, which was a shame as their trip was only a week. I soothed my nerves by setting out breakfast. It seemed the French and Italians had similar philosophies regarding the first meal of the day: usually strong coffee with a pastry or bread with butter and jam.

Stephanie was the first to emerge from her room, grunting thanks for the steaming cup of coffee I placed before her. Her eyes widened at the array of food, but she helped herself to a portion of rustic bread and gave it a liberal slathering of lemon curd.

"Like you said, vacation calories don't count," she mumbled when the coffee had finally released enough caffeine into her system.

"You're learning." I lifted my own coffee mug in a mock toast and helped myself to some of the breakfast assortment as well.

"How you doing?" she asked at length. "Tell me without the family emissary in earshot."

"Fine, I guess. Just trying to focus on the trip and enjoy myself." For a moment I considered telling her about the visions I'd been having. The dreams, echoes, whatever they were. There was no denying that something was happening now—it had happened in all three countries I'd visited—and I worried it was just proof that I was cracking up. I couldn't be sure she'd buy into the idea as Niall did that memories could leave behind traces. Perhaps she would think I'd had a long-overdue meltdown and refer me to her shrink. Or worse, she'd downplay them as simple dreams whose meanings weren't nearly as significant as I made them out to be.

Just dreams, nothing more.

And I couldn't accept that either.

Stephanie gave me an assessing look. "Listen, Vero. I love you more than literally anyone on the planet, but you are the reigning queen of pretending things are fine when they aren't. Are you ready for some hard truth?"

I nodded, though I was anything *but* ready for it. Especially before I'd downed my first cup of coffee.

"You have the world's most understanding parents. When you suspected you were adopted, you could have said something. They wouldn't have been able to tell you everything, but you would have spared yourself a good twelve years of uncertainty if you'd spoken up."

I stared into the dark abyss of my coffee cup, wishing the right words would somehow magically appear in the little bubbles that formed on the surface. Alas, they did not.

"I don't know how I feel, Steph. But you're right. Whatever these feelings are, they aren't in the same ballpark as fine."

"Progress. I'll take it."

"Thanks, I guess?"

"Hey, real friends don't accept 'fine' for an answer when it's clearly a load of bull. A lesser friend would nod and go along with it because it's easier."

I couldn't argue the point. And more to the fact, she was here. Thousands of miles from her home and her work . . . for me. That it meant a week in a charming farmhouse in the Italian countryside didn't diminish that it was still a lovely gesture.

"Just promise me you won't bottle things up, okay? Talk to people—even if it isn't me—and work through it. You'll have a breakdown sooner or later if you repress all this."

I felt a pang in my gut, but I didn't want to keep it from her anymore. "Maybe I already am?"

Stephanie held up a hand and crossed over to the stove, where the large moka pot sat simmering, and poured another cup. "Sorry, this sounds like second-cup stuff."

And I loved that about her. She could make me laugh even when I was about to unload on her in a way that might change the way she thought about me forever. And not in a good way. I launched into a description of what I'd seen at each place. I tried to sound as casual as I could about it—to be open to the possibility that it was all some sort of manifestation of my subconscious. If she was glib, I'd roll with it. Laugh it off as travel exhaustion or whatever. But all the same, I didn't want her to.

When I finished, complete with a recap of everything I'd seen the night before with Carlotta, Giacomo, and Donatella, I tried not to act like I was awaiting judgment after a trial. Though, if I were completely honest with myself, that's exactly how it felt.

"So . . . that's a lot to unpack. How are you doing with that?"

I shrugged. "I mean, I have no idea if it means anything at all. When I was in Ireland, Niall didn't seem to think it was a big deal.

The castle was so old that weird stuff is sort of expected. I guess I just brushed it off like Niall and his family did as being par for the course with an eight-hundred-year-old castle. But when it happened in France, and now here . . . I have to admit I'm rattled."

Pensive, Stephanie took another sip of her coffee.

"You think I'm nuts, don't you?" I blurted the words, just wanting her to get on with it.

"Always have, always will. But maybe not for this."

I blinked.

"First of all, even if this is your subconscious playing tricks on you, it may be an experience you need to have to cope with"—she gestured broadly—"everything. And that's fine. Also, this is a whole crap ton of very specific details. Names, places, approximate dates. These are concrete details we can research."

"Who are you and what have you done with my best friend?" I went over to the stove and blocked the path to the coffeepot. "No more coffee until you confess."

Stephanie cringed in mock horror. "That is a poor way to suss out a pod person. Coffee is a core value that transcends the barriers of all civilized species."

I stepped aside. "It is you."

She scowled. "What did you expect? That I'd point and laugh at my best friend going through a hard time?"

Maybe a little? "I was vaguely concerned that you might excuse yourself to go phone Bedlam to reserve me a bunk."

"First of all, I'm pretty sure Bedlam has been a museum for about a hundred years. Second of all, you're my best friend. I'd get you a suite."

I barked a laugh despite myself. "You really are a great pal, you know that?"

"Only the best for you." She took another pause. "Do you really think so little of me? To mock you when you're down?"

And now that I saw it from her perspective, I felt like a proper horse's hind end.

"I'm sorry. You're just one of the most overanalytical people I know, and I figured that you'd try to rationalize out of existence everything I saw. To my credit, both these women exist in the historical record—or at least the local lore of their towns."

"And you don't want to let it go. I get it. And yes, I'm the seeing-is-believing sort, but I know the human brain is complex in ways we don't understand. And just because we don't understand something doesn't make it false. I don't understand quantum physics, but I can accept that it's a real science."

I wrapped an arm around her. "Thanks for that, Steph."

"Tonight, let's fire up my laptop and start researching the names of the people from your . . . dreams. Let's see if we can't flip the script and rationalize these folks *into* existence."

I shivered, thinking about the possibilities we might uncover. "That sounds like a great idea."

"What's a great idea?" Avery mumbled, padding into the kitchen. She was rumpled and bleary-eyed to a degree I hadn't seen her since high school.

"Getting you a cup of coffee." I shot a pleading glance at Stephanie. *We can tell her later. Just not now.*

She offered a sleepy smile. "I always knew I liked you. You're my very favorite sister."

"Convenient that I'm the only one you've got. That makes me your least favorite as well."

Avery raised a brow. "I only dwell on the one you deserve at any given time. So watch it; it can and often does shift from one to the other alarmingly fast."

I laughed. "So what do you all think we should do today? Vineyard tours may be hard because it's offseason, but I'm sure we can find something fun."

"Different plan altogether. We're not doing market research for your job—we're going to do some for mine."

Stephanie brightened and I groaned inwardly. "What do you mean?"

"Milan is the fashion capital of the world, sister dear. And we're going shopping."

She and Avery shared a conspiratorial wink, and I felt a slight twinge of dread as I was going to be pushed to the brink of my retail comfort zone.

The road back to Milan was far less charming when we were driving away from the farmhouse instead of to it. I would have much preferred staying out in the countryside and finding local haunts in the small towns, but this leg of the trip wasn't just about me. Avery and Stephanie would love to mill about the shops and spend obscene amounts of money on clothes, shoes, and handbags. And their jobs called for it. Stephanie's job was public-facing and she had to be polished. Chic Italian clothes would give her a material advantage in her work. Avery was *in* the fashion world, so her clothes always had to be on point.

But me? I spent most of my time driving out to farms and in commercial kitchens. Stilettos and suits would get me laughed out of my job. Sure, I had to come off as professional when I met with clients, but that usually meant crisp, dark jeans, a cute button-down shirt, and functional shoes that didn't look too orthotic, most often from a thrift shop.

But it would be fine. I'm sure I could find ways to amuse myself while they tried on a metric ton of silk, rayon, wool, and cotton, all dyed to the "in" colors of the season and cut and sewn into garments that conformed to arbitrary beauty standards.

"You aren't going to run away and find the kitchen stores, by the way." Avery shot me a pointed look in the rearview mirror. "It's one day. You can tolerate it."

I heaved a sigh. "As long as we have a real lunch. I will not be subjected to another day of shopping fueled with nothing but your stale purse granola." I thought back to a memorable occasion when Avery had dragged me to the Cherry Creek Mall one summer while she was in design school. She claimed she only needed one outfit, and we ended up on a six-hour expedition that led to the cargo area of my SUV being stuffed full to bursting. She couldn't bear to stop long enough even to grab a salad at the food court.

Stephanie, who hadn't been along but who heard the story several times, chimed in. "Seconded. Hungry shopping is the worst. I get mad and think all the clothes look bad."

I patted her shoulder, grateful for the solidarity.

Avery gave a put-upon sigh. "Duly noted; make sure to feed and water shopping companions at regular intervals. But no three-hour lunches please. Our time *is* limited."

Emboldened, I replied, "Fine, but if I *do* want to stop in a kitchen shop, you can deal with it for twenty minutes. Milan isn't *just* the fashion capital of the world."

I saw Avery's expression grow solemn in the rearview mirror. "Very well. Never let it be said I don't compromise."

I rolled my eyes but was glad for our peace treaty.

It was still early enough that the parking structure near the famed Corso Vittorio Emanuele II, which stretched from the Piazza del Duomo to the Piazza San Babila and was home to some of the best shopping in the known universe, wasn't full. And despite my reservations, the place took my breath away. It was a pedestrian mall, but with a soaring domed glass roof and brightly colored mosaic-tile floors that wouldn't have been out of place in a cathedral.

"You know what the best part is, ladies? We're here for the winter sales. Seventy percent off Versace? Yes, please." Avery was beaming. She was Charlie in the moment Wonka handed over the keys to the chocolate factory. She was ready to burst through the ceiling without the help of the glass elevator . . . and I felt most of my annoyance at being dragged shopping dissipate. Most of it.

"Lead the way, Queen of Capitalism. You two chart a course and I'll be here to tell you that no, your butt does not look too big in those jeans, skirt, shoes . . . whatever. I'm your one-woman fashion hype squad for the day."

Avery, who was already moving with the flow of foot traffic, glanced back over her shoulder at me. "Oh no, you're not getting out of things that easily. I'm armed with Dad's Amex Platinum with strict instructions to buy you a new wardrobe. Go ahead, say you're excited."

This time Stephanie and I exchanged a look, and I was glad to know Avery hadn't taken a complete monopoly on silent conversation with my best friend.

"It really isn't necessary—"

Avery whirled around. "The heck it isn't. I know I'm a fashion snob, but even *Mom* has been tempted to hold an intervention over your wardrobe."

"I don't live in your world, Avery. I don't need fancy designer stuff. I'd never wear it in my line of work."

"You underestimate me, sister. Did I send you on this trip with Jimmy Choos or Louboutins?"

"I don't know what those words mean." I shot her a pointed glare. I *did* know those brands, thanks to Anne Hathaway movies, but I delighted in feigning ignorance about the fashion industry at times to get a rise out of Avery.

She quickly scanned the growing crowd like a thief might troll for nosy police. "Oh my god, don't say stuff like that too loud here or you'll get us banned from the city. They're fancy high heels, okay?"

I snorted at the horror on her face. "Okay, okay, the clothes you sent me were great."

"Right. Forget the crazy runway image in your head. That's the spectacle. The first tenet of anyone in fashion worth their salt is to dress people for the lives they have, not for Fashion Week. The clothes I chose for you were comfortable, well-tailored, and ethically made from fabrics that won't disintegrate after the fourth washing like the stuff you get curbside with your grocery order because you can't even be bothered to try it on."

"First of all, how dare you? I don't buy groceries at any place that also sells clothing if I can help it. Aside from Pepperidge Farm cookies, because nostalgia is a thing. Also, I thrift."

Stephanie placed a hand on my arm. "Vero, she's right. An update will help you come across as way more professional."

Avery summoned her best pleading expression. "Let us do this for you."

"Wouldn't it be simpler to do this back home?" I protested.

"It wouldn't be nearly as fun, and the sales wouldn't be as good.

Now please have fun with this." Avery's voice took on a hint of the whiny twang from our teen years.

I heaved a sigh. "Fine, but don't go overboard. And please, nothing flashy that I'll never wear despite what you think. I feel bad enough spending Dad's money without buying clothes that will molder in a closet."

Stephanie shot me a death glare: *You've made your point, don't spoil her fun.*

I nodded. I was grateful, but I felt bad enough about the expense of the trip as it was. But the grumpier I was, the more miserable this would be for all of us.

For the next four hours Stephanie and Avery treated me like their very own life-size Barbie doll and dragged me from shop to shop, trying on everything from nice wool dress slacks to thick T-shirts and everything in between. Shoes, underpinnings, and jackets. I even enjoyed the wide array of leather bags, without the garish designer labels, and let the girls help me select a few: a larger one that could carry my laptop and a couple of smaller ones for daily use. And even I couldn't argue with the butter-soft cashmere sweaters on steep discount. Avery picked a deep forest green and a lovely heather gray for me, and I swiftly added a rich navy, a bright lavender, and a deep chocolate brown before she got to the front of the line.

Her blue eyes widened. "There might be hope for you yet."

"Hey, even I know a bargain when I see one. And it's sweater weather six months of the year in Denver." Ireland, too, but I forced the image of Niall's face from my thoughts.

"So are cashmere pajamas a thing?" One of my fingers absently stroked the sleeve of one of the soft sweaters as we waited for the clerk.

"Oh my gawd, I *am* going to convert you after all." Avery wrapped an arm around me. "You'll be a fashionista yet."

"Hardly, but maybe a low-key hedonist. I've never felt anything so soft."

"One of us, one of us," Stephanie chanted softly, shooting me a wink.

Avery pulled us away from the line of shoppers back to the area where we'd found the sweaters. There was, a bit farther back, an entire rack of cashmere pajamas in a rainbow of colors. I chose soft pastels for these, sage green and periwinkle blue, hoping the restful colors might help with sleep. I clutched them to my chest, feeling like a child who'd won a giant teddy bear at a carnival. The only difference was that these were softer than any plushie from the fairgrounds.

She motioned for me to hand over the pajamas, but I hugged them to my chest. "I'm going to get these. It's too decadent to ask it of Dad. And I want to take them with me."

Rather than lugging our purchases with us, exhausting ourselves, and tempting pickpockets, Avery had been arranging for our loot to be shipped back to our respective homes. Apparently it was common practice here in the shopping mecca, and the clerks all anticipated Avery rattling off our addresses as soon as the credit card cleared. But I had room in my case for these and wanted to put them to use.

If Avery thought it was an odd request, she didn't say anything. Tonight, before Stephanie went into sleuth mode on the Internet, I'd fill her in. As hard as it was to share it, it wouldn't be fair for her to be kept in the dark. And heaven knew she was trying her best to do right by me as a sister. Way beyond what was called for.

As we exited the shop, my new pajamas in tow in a shopping bag nicer than any purse I'd owned prior to that morning, I wrapped an arm around Avery. "You're pretty amazing, you know that, Stinkerbell?"

Avery's eyes actually welled up a bit, but she swallowed back the threatening tears. "For that, we can stop and have lunch."

"If that's what it takes, I think you're amazing too," Stephanie interjected. "Let's eat."

I pulled out my phone and pulled up the Michelin restaurant guide. Milan really was an embarrassment of riches on the restaurant scene, so we let proximity dictate, searching for the *Bib Gourmand* designation—cheap but good—rather than pricey places with star ratings. There was a highly regarded café half a block away that would have plenty of decent lunch options with outdoor heaters plugged in so we could enjoy watching the modest low-season crowds milling about. We were grateful to let our throbbing feet rest, sipping on Sanpellegrino as we waited for our meals to arrive. They'd opted for salads, Avery's with chicken and Stephanie's with salmon, while I'd ordered a lunch portion of pasta puttanesca.

Even Avery, champion shopper, leaned back in her seat, spent from the morning's exertions. She looked over at me from her slumped position. "I'm proud of you, by the way."

I raised a brow. "Whatever for?"

"You just invested in yourself. Not your business, not something that would benefit Jonathan or one of the family where you happen to benefit as a side note—you."

I cocked my head. "The pajamas?"

"Yep. I don't know the last time you did something that was for your benefit alone like that. Wait . . . It was the time you bought yourself those emerald earrings with your babysitting money."

I flipped back my hair to expose the tiny emerald studs set in gold. They weren't particularly high-quality emeralds, but they were real. I'd seen them in a shop window when I was out with Mom at the mall when I was maybe fourteen, and I was determined I'd save up enough to buy them on my own. It had taken three months of babysitting along with the birthday money I'd squirreled away. When I had the cash on hand, Mom had taken me to buy them. More than that, she'd made a day of it. She'd bought me a green dress and some cute shoes and then taken me out to a nice lunch. I'd felt impossibly grown-up and had loved every minute of it. I'd worn those earrings almost every day since and had promised myself that if anything ever happened to them, I'd buy another pair with better stones even if it meant scrimping for months.

Avery glanced at my ears. "Yes, those. I wondered why, after such a promising start, you stopped doing nice things for yourself. Those are still lovely, by the way. You have a better eye for the classics than you give yourself credit for."

Stephanie chimed in. "I hope it means that you're going to do that sort of thing more often. You deserve to pamper yourself sometimes. I don't mean you need to waste your money, but for goodness' sake, splurge on yourself every once in a while."

"I'll do better," I promised. "But when it comes to clothes, I'll be relying on your expert opinion."

Avery seemed mollified. "Good. And I'll start sending you sample pieces when the right ones come along, since I have a better idea now of what you really like."

A chirp peeped from my bag and I rummaged out my phone. My heart fluttered and I'd hoped the banner on my phone's lock screen had Niall's name displayed. Instead, Dad's name flashed on the screen. It was still ridiculously early in Denver, but Dad had retained his early-to-bed-early-to-rise habits even in retirement. I smiled at his contact photo, one of us at a family barbecue a few years back with him making bunny ears behind my head. I excused myself and opened the messenger app.

> DAD: Hope you three are having a great time. I know Italy will never be the same after this. I'm glad I had the chance to take your mother at least once before you all made landfall.

I smiled at my dad's corny sense of humor, which had been more reliable than the rising and setting of the sun my whole life.

> ME: No permanent damage done. Except maybe to your account balances. I'm trying to keep Avery in check.
> DAD: No stopping at the Ferrari dealership, but otherwise, don't you dare. You girls have fun. It's what I worked so hard for all those years.

I felt a stinging in the corner of my eyes.

> ME: Avery has basically replaced my entire wardrobe. And, Dad? I don't hate it.
> DAD: Best news I've heard all day, kiddo. My only request is that you come up to Estes to show off some of your pieces to your mom and me before too long.
> ME: It's a deal.

I passed on Dad's love to Avery and Stephanie, and we headed to the Via Montenapoleone and the Via della Spiga for the brand names and high-end stuff that Steph and Avery were more interested in. I gave them honest feedback on their choices and watched them spend spectacular sums of money for the sort of work clothes fancier than anything I'd ever dream of wearing but that would be amazing for their posh offices. They looked fabulous in everything, and their enjoyment was infectious. I was glad to be out of the shopping limelight, but it gave me plenty of time to mull over what Avery had said.

I might have told myself countless times that learning I was adopted was "no big deal," but clearly it had been. And I'd have a lot of work ahead to square myself with that truth.

Chapter 31

S o basically, you've been visited by the ghosts of Christmas Past, Present, and Future, Vrbo edition?" Avery did her best to act nonchalant, but her grip on her glass of Chianti was rather tight. She had eaten an extra helping of the reheated pizza, so I knew she was rattled.

"Mostly just Christmas Past. Except not Christmas at all. And the ghosts are showing me their own lives, not mine."

"Their lives are the prequel to yours, I'm fairly certain." Stephanie's face was illuminated by the glow of her laptop screen. She was typing furiously and never took her eyes away from the web page she was hunting on.

"So you think these are my foremothers?" I still hadn't fully wrapped my head around the idea that Stephanie was buying into all this but was grateful she wasn't overly concerned with my mental state.

"I've been mulling this over since this morning and I think it's possible. I'm pretty sure all these visits are showing you the moment they decided to leave for America. It's the pivotal decision that led to *you* being a possibility. If Aoife had stayed and married either Tadgh or the man her father wanted, or if Imogène had given the baby up for adoption like *her* parents wanted, you wouldn't have been born. I'm guessing there is a similar story for Carlotta and Donatella too. There are a million decisions they could have made that would have resulted in a different outcome, but that decision was the biggest one."

I squeezed Stephanie's shoulder in wordless thanks.

"So what are you searching for exactly?" Avery's face had grown serious, and the slight furrow in her brow betrayed her worry.

"I'm searching in immigration archives for all the names we know from Vero's visions, but it's not easy because a lot of these were pre–Ellis Island, so no real paperwork was required. The best we can work with are ship manifests. From what I can tell, ship captains had to hand over passenger lists back as early as 1820. That might be enough."

I dipped my finger in my wineglass and rubbed it along the rim of the glass, which emitted a low humming sound. "I wouldn't be surprised if Aoife and Imogène used fake names. They wouldn't have wanted to be detected."

"Two steps ahead of you. Imogène DuChâtel, a young widow aged twenty-two, was on board a ship in late August 1870, arriving in early September in the port of Philadelphia. She used Lucien's surname."

"I'd bet a nickel that Coralie sent her with a copy of Lucien's death records and had a marriage license forged so there wouldn't be questions about the baby's legitimacy when he or she was born. It would make sense for Imogène to use his name. And no one probably would have had cause to doubt her, so they wouldn't have gone to the trouble of writing to the authorities in Beynac to verify that the marriage license was genuine and waiting months for a reply."

Coralie was a woman who'd thought of everything, and she

would have done everything in her power to keep Imogène and the baby safe.

"I wouldn't bet against you on that. And Philadelphia kept better records than most ports, so that'll work in our favor."

Avery shifted position. "But what are you going to do? You've proven that Imogène was likely a real person, but that doesn't tie her to Veronica."

"That's where your list of cousins comes in. I'm going to try to trace Imogène's ancestry down until we find someone on that list. Barring that, I'll start tracing the cousins back up the line. If I hit a dead end, I'll start with the Irish and Italian sides of the family."

"How on earth did you learn how to do all this? Did you sneak off to PI school when no one was looking?" I was impressed, not only with her research skills but with her dogged focus on the task at hand. It was rare that I got to see her in work mode, and I could easily see why she was such a hot commodity in her industry.

"PR involves more sleuthing than you think. And my grandma was into genealogy stuff too. She asked for my help using 'that Google thing' and I delivered."

"Thank heavens for digital natives helping their boomer grandmas. You're a genius, Steph." Avery leaned over Stephanie's shoulder, scanning the rows of digitized script that was more than 150 years old.

"No doubt," she quipped.

Her hands were a blur as she typed and scrolled through the archives, occasionally pausing to scribble notes on the notepad she'd found in the kitchen of the vacation rental, and her face was as serious as I'd ever seen it.

My hands shook as Stephanie became further immersed in her search. I would have given anything for an occupation for my hands and my mind to distract me from what she might uncover. Did I even *want* her to find my family? Clearly, whoever my birth parents were, they had their reasons for placing me up for adoption. There was a better than zero chance that my showing up out of nowhere could damage people's lives.

Perhaps my parents were with new partners and they hadn't confided in them about me, and I'd cause irreparable harm to their relationships. Perhaps I had young half siblings who believed their parents were perfect and my intrusion would shatter that innocent worldview forever. On the flip side of things, with an NDA in place, I also ran the real risk of encountering legal troubles, which was decidedly *not* on my to-do list.

But this didn't have to be about my living relatives. There would be something meaningful in knowing that I truly was linked to these women from my visions. If nothing else, I'd feel a little more sane knowing they had not come out of thin air. I didn't have to know my present-day family to be able to connect with my ancestors. That could remain between us.

Avery met my eyes. "You doing okay?"

"Fine, I guess. I'm just processing it all."

She leaned over and squeezed my hand. "You know I'll love you forever, right? Even if your family turns out to be a pack of ax murderers."

I squeezed her hand back. "Gee thanks. Somehow I'm not worried about that. More worried I might come from a long line of delusional women who had to tread carefully not to get burned at the stake."

Stephanie looked up from her screen, her face illuminated with the electric glow of the archives reflecting back in the stylish black-rimmed glasses she wore for computer work. "That's like a 100 percent certainty, Vero . . . You're too sassy to come from a line of well-behaved women."

I thought of Coralie, who had to tread so carefully just to be allowed to run her business in Beynac, and smiled. I didn't mind being related to that sort of outcast at all. "Fair enough. I can live with that. Hopefully just willful women and not actually dangerous."

"In the era these women came from? There's no distinction between the two." Stephanie spoke, but her eyes were already locked back on the screen.

Avery turned solemn. "For what it's worth, I can totally see you as a descendant of an Irish pirate queen. It suits you."

I chuckled. "Thanks, I think."

Stephanie glanced up. "I'm not going back that far, you guys. You can do that on your own time if you want. But it would appear that one Lauren Elizabeth Martin of White Plains, New York, who seems to be your closest cousin on the DNA results, is an indirect descendent of Imogène DuChâtel of Bordeaux, France. Which means you very well could be a *direct* descendant—a great-to-some-degree-granddaughter."

I exhaled. Both relieved and unsettled in myself. "You're sure?"

Stephanie leaned back in her chair, stretching after her long stint at the laptop. "I mean, DNA tests aren't 100 percent accurate, and records from the nineteenth century are far from infallible, but I'd say, given the circumstances, it's more likely than not. I don't want to give in to confirmation bias, but this all seems too much to be a coincidence."

"Wow, I'm not quite sure what to say. Thank you for digging, Steph."

Stephanie's brow furrowed. "I can keep hunting for the other lines if you want. Ireland and Italy?"

"No, we've invested enough vacation time on this. I can look into this back at home later."

Stephanie slowly closed the lid of her laptop. "I can help you back in Denver. I'll have more resources and contacts there to help anyway. We'll fill in your family tree back to the Dark Ages."

I poured us each a glass of wine. "I don't think that will be necessary. But your skills are both impressive and terrifying."

Stephanie lit up in a mischievous grin. "My favorite self-descriptors. Thank you."

"Are you going to reach out?" Avery asked.

I shook my head. "No, I don't think so."

"You're not even a bit curious?" Stephanie asked. "I sure would be."

"Not really. They have their lives and I have mine. Does it feel good to know there are other people out in the world who share some genes in common with me? Sure. But I don't want to upturn anyone's life to satisfy my own curiosity."

Avery took a sip of her wine. "You're far more selfless than I am. I'd be banging on doors, trying to get answers."

I smiled at the image of Avery, so beguiling that she'd go in with guns blazing and likely end up with an invitation to Thanksgiving dinner. That just wasn't me.

"Lucky for you, your parentage is pretty darn certain. Hospital switchings are rare nowadays. Not to mention all the photographic evidence. There's a photo of Mom in a hospital bed holding you minutes after you were born." The absence of a similar photo for me had been one of my first clues about the circumstances surrounding my own birth. I'd been brave enough to ask about it once, and Dad had made a flimsy excuse about dead camera batteries or some such thing. Even then it struck me as odd, because Dad was the most overprepared person in existence and was the sort to have raided Costco for batteries to ensure he wouldn't miss photographing the birth of his first child. Now I knew they hadn't been allowed to, or else they'd have risked the adoption falling through and potentially devastating legal hassles. That knowledge *did* help quite a bit.

It was a small thing—my parents had taken thousands of pictures in my first years of life—but it always stung that there were none until they brought me home.

But I wish my father had seen that question for what it was: an invitation to tell me some portion of the truth.

Chapter 32

A few hours later the girls went to bed, and I found myself restless. I couldn't abide another night of tossing and turning, so I abandoned my bed as soon as it became clear sleep wouldn't come. I wandered down to the living area in search of a novel in English or even the notepad Stephanie had been using so I could attempt to "download" all the thoughts out of my brain and onto paper in hopes it might allow me enough peace to sleep. I found the notepad and a pen and settled on the sofa.

I'd only written a few sentences when the room began to swirl. The living room morphed into a cheerless parlor as it came into focus. The modern furniture gave way to the elegant trappings of a fine country estate. It was spring now, instead of winter, and the women were dressed in featherlight silks instead of rich velvet. Giacomo, now even broader around the middle, wore a black tailcoat with matching black trousers. The effect was comically penguinesque, but there was nothing funny about the miserable little man.

"As brilliant a performance as ever I could have hoped for," Giacomo boomed jovially as he bounded into the parlor, unbuttoning his waistcoat to allow his bulk its freedom. "I didn't think she had it in her."

Donatella collapsed in an armchair on the opposite side of the room from her father, ignoring his fleeting glare of disapproval. These evenings left her drained, and I could feel the last shreds of her energy seeping into the floorboards.

"I wouldn't doubt if Von Hügel asks for your hand within the fortnight. What a triumph, eh?" Giacomo helped himself to some grappa from the sideboard and took his place by the roaring fire that had been tended by a maid or footman in their absence.

"She has definitely earned her retreat to the country," Carlotta said, her tone dry. It was a reminder of a bargain made, I was sure. I could all too clearly see Carlotta bargaining with her husband: one ball, one week in the country. Anything to keep Donatella's nerves from fraying to their snapping point.

He grunted into his glass. "But a brief one, mind you. Von Hügel will want to see her again soon. Better to keep her fresh in his mind."

Carlotta looked to Donatella, whose gaze was fixed nowhere in particular. She had shut herself out of the world completely after so much stimulation. "What will happen if—or more likely when—she has a spell of melancholia after she is married?"

Giacomo waved dismissively. "I'm convinced within myself that marriage is the cure for all that ails her. She'll be so busy as a pillar of society, she won't have a moment to think of herself. And when the children come along, that will be doubly true."

Carlotta, who remained standing by the sideboard, perhaps considering a measure of grappa for herself, steadied herself against it as if summoning strength from the sturdy oak. "Husband, if I thought that were true, I'd have seen her married off three years ago. What do you think Von Hügel will do when she has a spell?"

"Beat it out of her with a strap, if the boy has any sense," Giacomo grumbled.

"Did it work for you when you tried?" Carlotta challenged. She was more resolved now, and it suited her. Some pieces of her plan must have fallen into place. "Is she any worse since I forbade it?"

Giacomo rose from his comfortable armchair by the fire and got so close to Carlotta I could smell the rank odor of rancid liquor and rotting teeth rolling from his mouth like a putrid fog. "Do not trifle with my anger, woman."

The corners of her lips turned up in a small feline smile. "And what of mine? Shall I get my solicitor involved in the matter?"

Giacomo's eyes flashed hot with fury. "What have I told you about casting that man and your family's trickery in my face?"

She stood her ground, and I could now see she towered over him by several inches, but she always made an effort to disguise it for the sake of his fragile ego. She leaned in closer, her voice dropping, low and deadly. "I'm not casting anything in your face, Giacomo. I am simply reminding you of what can be done to you if you raise a hand to me or my daughter ever again."

"Such an arrangement ought not to have been legal." Giacomo turned away from Carlotta, heading back to the center of the room to pace like an overfed caged circus bear. "Imagine a man not having sovereignty over his household. A wife with her own money and property to do with as she wishes. It's an affront against the natural order. I ought to have control over my family as is my God-given right."

Her lips pulled back in a sneer. "You've taken to religion? That's a change."

"I warn you, Carlotta, you may hold the purse strings to this home through your lout of a solicitor, but I won't tolerate more insubordination from you. A man can only abide so much."

Carlotta's eyes flashed in a warning. "My mother didn't want me to be at the mercy of a brute. She had the measure of you better than I did at seventeen. I've given thanks above for her foresight ever since."

Giacomo waved a hand in the air as if batting her words away. "Donatella will marry Von Hügel if—more likely when—he asks for her hand. The law is on my side on this, and I will hear no more prattle from you."

Carlotta glowered. "He will have her institutionalized, Giacomo. Thrown in a cell with a horde of lunatics to wither and die."

"What should it matter to us, as long as she's married well first? She will belong to the Von Hügels and they can do with her whatever they see fit to do. It will be no concern of ours."

"Do you really think we'll be invited to their fine dinners when they learn we knowingly saddled their innocent young son with a woman in need of serious medical care? Will that endear you to the top circles in society when that news spreads?"

"It needn't spread at all. We'll join them in lamenting her unexpected and sudden bout of illness. You'll do your best to keep her in line until he gets an heir and a spare off her."

"How will I do such a thing from separate houses? Or have you deluded yourself into thinking Von Hügel would somehow be delighted to live with his mother-in-law?"

Giacomo shot her a disgusted sneer. "You're supposed to be so clever. You'll find a way to keep it quiet long enough. Our future will be secure."

"It already is, husband. We have all the money we need, lavish homes, and every comfort a person could want."

"I don't want anyone to look down on me, woman. No one. And if getting a foothold in society means marrying her off to Von Hügel, the crown prince, or Father Christmas, I'll do it."

Carlotta very calmly grabbed one of the fine crystal tumblers on the sideboard and threw it at the wall, narrowly missing his head. "No, you won't, Giacomo. I won't let you sell my only child to the highest bidder to be used as a brood mare."

"You'll do as you're told, or I swear I'll *find* a way to make you suffer, woman. No matter what idiocy your family contrived to keep the Del Vecchio money out of my hands." His voice was a low growl, but Carlotta didn't flinch.

"You've had plenty of it in your hands and wasted most of it. You don't scare me anymore, Giacomo. I'm putting an end to this foolishness now and taking Donatella to America for help. My solicitor has it all arranged for us. He cares about Donatella's future, and he's been researching doctors and care facilities for months that might be able to help her. And if she can't be helped, she can at least be comfortable without you dragging her to endless dinners she can't stand. He told me just this week he's arranged everything."

Giacomo bridged the gap between them. "I am not going to America, you manipulative cow. I have worked too hard to give up on everything just because you've spoiled our only child and weren't enough of a woman to bear more children."

"No, *you* aren't going to America. Donatella and I are going with Vincente. You may keep the town house, but I'm taking every red cent of my family money so you don't squander more of it in this silly scheme of yours to ooze your way into the upper crust. You'll have to get back to your workshop and make your own way."

"You will not, woman. I forbid it," he growled.

She pretended not to have heard him. "Most of those posh fools you admire so much think you're ridiculous, by the way. I hear them laughing about you."

It was the worst possible thing she could have said. Giacomo went to raise his hand to Carlotta, but Donatella had crossed the room without anyone noticing her. She was a statuesque woman like her mother and was able to twist his arm behind his back until he whimpered in pain.

"Do. Not. Touch. My. Mother," Carlotta snarled.

"How dare you, you demented little—" His words were cut short as she twisted his arm tighter.

"You will not touch my mother ever again, you filthy cretin."

He grimaced as she tightened her grip. "You disobedient shrew, let me go." He thrashed wildly, but she managed to keep him pinned.

"No. I want you to die knowing your wife and child will never spare you another thought. It's the fate you deserve. Get out of this house or you'll have to figure out how to make jewels with a broken arm, you worthless son of a bitch."

Carlotta was perfectly calm, gazing upon her daughter with satisfaction. "Donatella, darling, mind your language. He isn't worth demeaning yourself." She strode across the room and pulled the bell with the same nonchalance as if she were ordering coffee for guests.

A few moments later, a footman—tall and broad shouldered—appeared. He was slightly out of breath from rushing from his room in the attic, probably not expecting he'd be needed again that evening.

Carlotta smiled. He was just the footman she'd been hoping for. "Ah, Niccolo. Very good. You will see Signore Valenti has all his belongings packed and see him back to his quarters in Milan. And you will ask Francesco and Matteo to ensure he doesn't enter the premises again."

"Very good, Signora Valenti." He bowed to his mistress.

"I shall be reverting to my maiden name, Niccolo. Inform the staff I am to be called Signora Del Vecchio from now on."

Chapter 33

I awoke on the living room sofa, feeling better rested than I expected. It seemed my body was learning to compensate for all the disruptions to my sleep and I had energy enough to take on the day, but I fervently hoped I'd be free of the visions and reclaim my life and my sleep soon. I'd slept without dreams, but now that I was awake, the scene from the previous night's visit replayed over and over. I gave up the pretense of sleep and headed to the village in search of breakfast.

On the drive, I pushed the visions from my mind and considered how much I'd come to love my time here. I'd been traveling for well over two weeks, and yet it didn't feel like I'd done more than scratch the surface of all the things I'd wanted to see. I'd have liked to go to Provence to visit Saurraut's, the famous antique kitchenware emporium that had taken the foodie world by storm. I'd have liked the time to take some cooking classes in Tuscany. I'd have liked to walk along the Mediterranean in summer.

There were a great many things I would have liked to do, but time was running short, and with the current situation in my bank account, it didn't seem all that feasible anytime soon unless Avery and Dad teamed up again. And I wasn't sure it was an offer I could allow myself to accept a second time. Maybe the memories I made on the trip would be all the more precious for being from an experience that would remain unique. But I hated the thought of years elapsing before I was able to return.

I felt some of Carlotta's resolve wash over me, and I knew it was time to stop hiding.

When I arrived in the village, I was glad to see that while most everything was yet to open, a lone bakery emitted a warm glow onto the streets. While the choices weren't as expansive as those in France, they were expertly crafted with fine ingredients, using techniques passed down for generations. The marmalade-filled *cornetti* were a close approximation to croissants and would be a welcome addition to breakfast, and I added a few *sfogliatelle*, an impossibly flaky creation that seemed to be an amalgamation of butter and divine intervention, and a few small *bombolini*—a sort of light doughnut filled with chocolate that looked too good to pass up. I managed the transaction in my halting Italian, but the woman smiled indulgently at my feeble attempts and even put in a few almond biscotti as a gift we could enjoy with an afternoon coffee.

The girls were awake when I returned, thrilled that I'd come armed with coffee and carbs. "Remind me to go on vacation with you more often," Stephanie said as she polished off her second pastry. "You're better than room service at The Savoy."

I scoffed. "Amateurs. I'm fit to cook under Ducasse at Le Meurice, and you know it. Fetching pastries from a bakery? Child's play."

Stephanie set down her coffee with a hard *click* on the counter. "I do. So why the hell *aren't* you, Stratton? The Kitchen Muse schtick? It's clever, sure. But you're hiding behind it. I know you enjoy helping source cool ingredients and you love consulting, but why are you so set on being an assistant fry cook in your own life when you should be the executive chef? If you had your own kitchen, you could *still* do all that jazz and charge a heck of a lot more for it because you've got the kitchen rep to back it up."

I held up my hands. "Don't hold back, Steph."

"I have been. For six years now. More. And it was a huge mistake to play along with you. You'd have a culinary school diploma and be a lot further along in your career by now if I'd been a better friend and given you the boot in the arse you needed."

Avery finally met my gaze. "She's right. I'm just as guilty. Mom and Dad have been so incredibly supportive of me and my work . . . and they feel terrible you feel like you can't ask for the same level of support."

"But I don't need it," I protested. "I'm not living in New York. I don't have expenses like yours."

"Do you know how happy Mom and Dad would be if we *were* both in New York? You killing it in the restaurant biz, me slaying in fashion? They'd be so tickled; they'd probably get us a penthouse to share. Just think, I'd make people pretty clothes and you feed them so much great food they don't fit, and then they'd need more clothes. Seems like the bulletproof business model to me."

Steph exhaled, a bit exasperated. "What I think your twerp of a sister is saying is that they'd have been happy to see you do the whole 'go big or go home' thing Avery's got going on, and they'd have been proud to pony up to make it happen."

"When was the last time you accepted a hand up? From anyone, including me?"

"Apples and oranges. My field pays better off the bat and doesn't require living in New York. But don't deflect, lady. This is about you. I'm doing my thing. Avery's doing hers . . . You need to own up to what you really want and go for it before life passes you by. No one wants that for you. Maybe it's your own kitchen, maybe not. But we can't even start to help you until you figure some stuff out first."

I finally tore into a pastry of my own. "I do. The Kitchen Muse is a sound concept, but maybe I am just too scared to give the restaurant biz a real shot."

Avery crossed over to me and enveloped me in her arms. "I'm glad you're warming up to that idea. I do think you have what it takes to make it."

I returned her embrace. "You're exceedingly annoying when you're right, d'you know that?"

She beamed. "It's one of the many gifts of being a little sister. I'll show you the handbook sometime."

Stephanie's tone was more solemn. "You have us for three more days at your complete disposal to be your sounding boards, shoulder to cry on . . . whatever you need. But use the time, Vero. We may not have been what you needed in the past, but we're here now."

Chapter 34

The hugs at the airport lingered longer than usual as Avery boarded her flight to New York.

"Promise me you'll come to New York soon. Please?" Her eyes were pleading as she joined the queue to board.

"I'll try. Honest." I couldn't bring myself to promise outright, but I would do better to make an effort. There were fare sales to New York often enough that I could find a way to economize a few hundred dollars.

Avery turned to Stephanie. "I'm trusting you to hold her to that. Bonus points if you tag along."

Stephanie chuckled and took Avery in for a hug. "It's a deal. Especially if an outing to Bloomingdale's is on the agenda."

"Always," Avery promised.

"The culinary capital of North America and you all are worried about clothes. Typical."

The two exchanged knowing glances, and Avery was soon sauntering down the Jetway and back to the bustle of the city she loved.

"Coffee?" I asked. Stephanie's flight to Denver wasn't for another hour, and she was never one to balk at a second cup in the morning. My flight to Copenhagen was half an hour after that, so I had time to kill as well.

"Always," she replied, echoing Avery's last comment.

We found a little coffee shop near her gate and settled in with our cappuccino, which we managed to order just a few minutes before it would have been gauche to order a coffee with milk of any sort. Italians took their coffee seriously and we wanted to honor that even in the airport where all manner of caffeine-related sins would have been forgiven.

Stephanie set me with a hard glance from across the table. "So how are you really doing?"

I took a fortifying sip of my cappuccino. "It's been a lot. But I really appreciate all your research. It makes me feel a little less nuts, you know?"

"I get it. And I want to keep digging when I get home. I think your subconscious wants you to learn more about your family than you realize."

I shrugged. "She's been working overtime the last couple of weeks, that's for sure."

"Can I tell you something? As your best friend?"

"Always," I said, eliciting an eye roll from Stephanie.

"I think that despite"—she gestured broadly—"everything, Europe has been good for you. There's a glow and a confidence about you I've not seen in a long time. Since high school to be precise."

"Travel is good for the soul. You're just seeing the magic of an American who has taken three weeks off from work. You see how relaxed the Italians seem, even here in a bustling city like Milan? It's the five weeks of annual paid vacation talking."

Stephanie snorted. "You're not wrong, but I don't think you're seeing the full picture. You've started to connect with your birth family, even if your methods are a little unorthodox. And I think the experience will end up being a positive one for you. It's opening your eyes to new possibilities about your past, and I hope it will do the same for your future."

"Why do I sense you're about to go tough love on me again?"

She pinched the bridge of her nose, searching for words. "No, not really that. I want to level with you and tell you something you've not been able to admit to yourself: you're not happy. Not in your career, not in your relationship with Jonathan, not with a lot of things. And it's not too late for you to change things. You're in your mid-twenties . . . Nothing has to be set in stone yet, nor should it be."

I wasn't sure which part of that to tackle first, so in typical me fashion, I deflected. "This is rich advice coming from the woman with her entire life figured out."

"Hardly. I have the job thing well in hand, maybe. But I have a lot of other stuff to figure out. I won't pretend otherwise. I like the trajectory of my life, sure. But I don't think you can say that. Sorry to be blunt."

It was a defining characteristic of her personality, but it didn't make it sting any less. "I love my work," I said, my defensive hackles raised, even if I knew she meant well.

"You love food. You love sourcing ingredients. You love the restaurant scene. But I don't think you love being on the periphery of it. The Vero I knew in high school wanted to be a Michelin-star chef, not mentoring them. At least not in lieu of running your own kitchen."

I scoffed. "I grew up. I realized what a slog it would have been to make a name in Denver, let alone beyond it. The Gordon Ramsays and Jamie Olivers of the world are rare. Most of us become Lou, the disenchanted restaurateur who now works as a line cook at Applebee's."

"That is the jaded and cynical talk of an old lady who's given up on finding joy in life. And if you were fifty or sixty years old and had given it an honest shot and failed, I'd live with it. But what I can't live with is you not even giving yourself the chance to succeed. The idea of 'making it' terrifies you, and you used to be the most ambitious out of all of us."

I laughed. "Please, you were designing ad campaigns for the student council candidates since middle school. You carried a briefcase starting in junior year."

"So I could keep up with you, Vero. I saw your eyes fixed on the prize, and I didn't want to be left behind. Avery too, if you haven't noticed. Your parents bought you a chef's coat with your name embroidered on it when you were in eighth grade. The briefcase was my feeble attempt to look like I had a plan as solid as yours."

I remembered the white jacket with *Chef Stratton* emblazoned in green thread on the right side. It was a real, honest-to-goodness professional chef's coat my mother had personalized. I'd loved the thing for years but left it behind in the depths of my childhood bedroom when I'd moved away to college.

But at the memory of Stephanie and her cordovan leather attaché case with her initials emblazoned in brass, I scoffed. "You can't be serious. You two have always been the most-likely-to-succeed types. Not me."

"No, they were far more specific with your yearbook superlative, weren't they?"

I sighed. "Most likely to be the next Julia Child."

"Exactly. We all saw it. And I bet every single kid from our high school would be shocked that you hadn't scurried right along to the Cordon Bleu or the Escoffier School. Or some private academy none of us have heard of that's even more prestigious. And the real shame of it is that you still could."

I turned my attention to my coffee. "I don't see how."

She gave an exasperated groan. "I assume there is an application process like any other educational establishment. Perhaps an audition of some kind, or whatever you'd call it in the cooking world."

"Practical examination."

"See, you know the jargon already. You'd get in anywhere with kitchen chops like yours, probably on scholarship. And if not, there are student loans if you won't accept help from your folks. It's a grand American tradition to go into unhealthy amounts of debt for an education. It'll help you feel connected to your fellow man."

I snorted. "You're a poor saleswoman on this, Steph. Hate to say it."

"I kid because I think you'd shut down if I were any more serious."

The truth hit like a sucker punch to the gut, impossible to ignore. "Listen, I know you mean well, but in case you haven't noticed, my life is kinda upside down. It seems like maybe not the best time to be starting an expensive new venture like culinary school."

"It couldn't be a better time. If your life wasn't upside down, you wouldn't need to change it. Why not summon some of Aoife's, Imogène's, or Carlotta's grit and take charge of your own future? They'd be proud of you."

She'd been listening. And she hadn't thought I was insane . . . and I found myself unable to come up with any reasonable arguments against her claims. I was spared the need to respond by the loud-speaker announcing the boarding of her flight. I walked her to her gate and embraced her as she joined the long queue.

"Just think about it, okay? You don't have to decide this minute. Just keep your mind open to it. And, Vero? You have always deserved better than what you've allowed yourself to accept. Please remember that."

I didn't have time to react before she turned and whisked off to the agent scanning boarding passes. I watched until it was her turn to disappear down the Jetway, relieved I was able to keep my tears at bay. She was probably right about everything, but it was just so much to consider all at once. I felt the overwhelming urge to text my mom, but it was four in the morning. She kept baker's hours, to be sure, but she took advantage of the quiet months to catch up on her sleep.

Boarding for my two-hour flight to Copenhagen would be announced before too long, so I tracked down my gate and camped in one of the seats in the mostly empty gate area. It seemed Denmark wasn't too popular a destination in January, and I wasn't horribly shocked to find that the plane was a smaller commuter-style aircraft that would be at maybe a third of its capacity.

It occurred to me that, apart from the flight to Dublin from Denver and the quick hop to Milan from Bordeaux, I'd not been alone on my travels. First Niall, then the girls had been my companions since this insane trek began. So as I sat alone for the final leg of this trip, the solitude felt oppressive. I enjoyed my own company well enough, but having the support of two people whom I'd loved almost my whole life, and another who had become increasingly important to me, had been more comforting than I'd realized.

I slipped my phone from my pocket and snapped a picture of the sign over the gate that read *Copenhagen* and sent it to Niall with the caption: Off to Denmark! Hope all is well at the castle.

Breezy and friendly. I'd considered adding Wish you were here to the end of it but erased the clichéd words before I hit Send. Clichéd or not, it was the truth—probably for both of us—and better left unsaid. To let him think I cared for him more than as a friend when neither of us would be able to act on those feelings was just hurtful to both of us.

When my turn came to enter the jet bridge and board the small aircraft, I didn't enjoy the feeling of isolation that washed over me, but wasn't it better to get used to the sensation?

Chapter 35

Week Four: Denmark

NYHAVN DISTRICT, COPENHAGEN

Though it wasn't even close to peak season, the streets of Copenhagen were far from empty, and I felt glad for the day I'd spent with the girls in Milan as a reminder of city life after my long absence from Denver. After the time spent in the country outside of Westport and the rambling cobblestone streets of Beynac-et-Cazenac, I'd grown comfortable with the solitude. The sensation of people milling about was enough to give me a vague feeling of vertigo.

Of all the countries Avery had scheduled me to visit on this trip, Denmark was the one I was least familiar with and the one I had the most reservations about. I didn't speak the language at all, which was disconcerting even if most of the people in the capital spoke English better than I did. I'd never yearned to visit Denmark as I had the other countries. But as the metro from the airport let me out at the city square, the charm of the colorful merchant city was undeniable.

The vacation rental Avery had secured for me was an apartment above a restaurant in Nyhavn. The building's façade was a vibrant shade of cornflower blue, and the rest of the buildings refused to be shown up. Kelly green, brick red, and sunflower yellow all did their best to ward off the gloom of winter. Given the temperatures that fought to stay above freezing and the sun setting at four in the afternoon, I better understood the Danish affinity for bold colors. Somehow, it did make everything seem a little less cold and bleak.

The apartment was large, especially by European standards, and tastefully decorated in a style that wasn't too spartan, nor too frilly. The undefinable Danish word *hygge* came to mind. Mom had read several books on the topic a few years ago, not that she needed any help making her home feel cozy and welcoming. She'd also mastered the art of finding the joy in food, friends, and family and dragged Dad along for the ride, especially now that he was retired. And I realized for the eleventy billionth time what a good match they were. Mom could show Dad how to slow down—and he desperately needed the lesson. And on the flip side, Dad was able to guide Mom with her business so she could turn a profit without working herself into the ground to do it.

Was that why I'd gravitated to Jonathan? I saw something resembling Dad's business acumen and worldliness and thought he would complement me as Dad did Mom? The difference was that Dad was so head over heels in love with Mom, he'd have mortgaged the heavens to make her dreams come true. They were so lucky to have found each other. Had their relationship set too high of a benchmark for my own? How could Jonathan have hoped to compete with that standard?

I let myself into the rental with the code Avery had sent via text. The airy apartment had high ceilings and massive glass doors that opened up to what was by all accounts a lovely balcony. Well, it would be lovely in summer with a nice Danish and coffee, even if unthinkably uncomfortable in winter.

I would have been happy to crawl into bed, take a nap, and remind myself that being alone had some true joys—like blissfully undisturbed sleep—but it would have been bad for my body clock to nap in the midafternoon.

I grabbed my day bag and headed back onto the street. The rain was light and insistent but not to the point where going out of doors was wholly unpleasant. And of course Avery had packed for every eventuality, espousing the mantra, "There is no bad weather, only bad clothes."

I wandered in the area near Nyhavn, which was supposedly one of the trendiest parts of town. In better weather it might have been enchanting, with more people milling about by the waterside and dining at outdoor café tables, but the cold had driven even the hardiest of locals to dine inside. And I understood how they felt. January was traditionally colder than December, which meant the rain transitioned to snow, but apparently the weather hadn't gotten the memo to update its calendar. I'd take a light to medium snow over any sort of rain any day of the week, but that was likely the Denverite in me talking. Snow could be brushed off, while rain penetrated everything and seemed impossible to escape.

Another reason moving to Ireland would have been a terrible idea. The bogs and the rain would have driven me mad. No matter how pleasant the fire and how warm the kitchens. No matter how lovely Niall was. I'd still have to deal with months of soggy gloom.

And even in my head it was the silliest of excuses. Would the rain really have mattered if I'd decided to uproot myself and move to Ireland? Hardly. At least not at first. But the time might have come when the charms of Blackthorn, and Niall himself, would cease to be enough to distract me from the unending drizzle.

But as Niall had once said, Blackthorn might get swept up by a hurricane one day too. And I hated how much my heart lifted with every text and email he'd sent. I'd promised to be a faithful respondent, and I would honor that pledge, but I was convinced my proposed clean break would have been easier on us both.

I wandered into a small bodega-style grocery. Having some coffee and a few snacks for the vacation rental might be wise. While I was usually consumed with inspiration in such a spot, I found the perfectly ordered rows of packaged foods, the immaculate meat counter, and the vibrant produce almost annoying in their perfection. I quickly decided on what appeared to be some basic wheat crackers, digestive biscuits with chocolate, and some decent coffee. Bland, dependable, and absolutely uninspired.

I wandered another hour and did my best to lose myself in the city's charm. I perused restaurants, scanning menus and taking note of interesting fare or unique ambiance. I picked up a few trinkets for the family and even a soft sage-green pashmina for myself. I treated myself to coffee and a slice of Danish *brunsviger*—a hearty yeast cake with a lovely butter and brown sugar topping, but even baked goods failed to materially improve my mood. Perhaps it was the loneliness of traveling alone, but I didn't think so. My job had me traveling all over the American West sourcing ingredients, and I was perfectly content on my own. But this time the lack of company meant I'd have to face my demons without distraction.

And it was all I could do not to find a dark spot and hole away from them until they retreated into the shadows. But no matter how long I cowered, they would be waiting for me. And these were the sort of beasties who grew fangs when left too long to fester.

The irony that I felt shrouded in a wet blanket of depression in what so many news outlets dubbed "one of the happiest countries in the world" was not lost on me. But wasn't it true that happiness was so much more dependent on the people in our lives than on where we were? I thought of all the times Dad had said when we were kids that he'd rather live in the gutter with us than in a mansion by himself. I'd thought it hyperbolic at the time, but as an adult I realized it was more or less the unvarnished truth.

And I was lucky to have four people in my life—Mom, Dad, Avery, and Stephanie—who were on my "gutter list." Many people didn't have as much. But it was clear to me, as the chilling rain intensified and I looped back toward the vacation rental, Jonathan wasn't on that list anymore. What was more striking, the more I considered it, was that I was fairly certain I'd never been on his. Not really. I held the "girlfriend" slot, but it was because of the position I held in his life, not who I was as a person, that made me important to him.

And acknowledging that I *deserved* an unconditional place on his list was a leap forward. For so long, since that lonely day we learned about genetic traits in biology, I'd allowed myself to believe that because I *hadn't* been on my birth parents' gutter list, I didn't believe I belonged on anyone's list at all. And that wasn't true. It was taking me a long time to own that, but I'd get there fully in time.

The rain had become torrential by this point and closer to sleet than actual rain. By the time I reached the rental, I was soaked through and ready to curl up for several months, sodden clothes and all, but I forced myself out of the layers of wet cotton and wool and into the hot shower before eating a handful of crackers. I begged my Danish foremother, whoever she was, to give me a pass that night. I crawled into the plush bed and hoped I'd find answers somewhere in the goose down.

Chapter 36

Frigid rain still poured outside the following day, and I had no desire to leave the vacation rental to explore more of Copenhagen that day. It wasn't even sunrise yet, and I cursed my travel-weary body for not letting me get proper sleep. I lay firmly entrenched in the covers and would remain there until hunger or the call of nature forced me from them.

I thought about reaching my arm out from under the blanket to grab my phone to research the Danish equivalent of DoorDash, but even that seemed like more effort than I was able to muster. And I wasn't eager to find out if the best breakfast offerings to be had were a smorgasbord comprised of a dozen kinds of pickled fish. As adventurous an eater as I was, breakfast was the meal for which I sought out the familiar.

After a quarter of an hour of indecision, I felt resolve begin to rise in my core, slow but sure. I gathered the courage to see if there was some sort of coffee shop with pastries close enough that I could walk to without getting entirely soaked.

When the screen came into focus I saw a new email alert from the FamilyRoots app Avery had installed on my phone.

Dear Ms. Stratton,

Congratulations! You have new DNA relatives. Click here to view details. Thank you for trusting our service to keep you connected with your loved ones.

Your friends at FamilyRoots

I clicked the link, expecting to find another batch of third to distant cousins as we'd stumbled across in Italy. Instead, there was a solitary entry under *Close Relatives*—the space reserved for first-degree relatives: parents, siblings, and children.

Tara Murray: Your Mother

The room fell out of focus. The metallic tinge of bile filled my mouth, cruel and biting. I couldn't be sure how long I sat there fighting to regain control of myself. Every breath was a conscious effort, and none too easy. It was several minutes before it registered that I had an unread entry in the in-app messaging service.

Dear Veronica, (I love the name your parents chose for you, by the way)

I hope this message is not an unwelcome intrusion in your life. If it is, please delete this and don't give it a second thought. You owe me nothing—not even a small sliver of your time if you don't wish to give it. If you're still reading, please know a day hasn't gone by when I haven't thought of you and wished that things could have been different. For a few very specific reasons, I haven't been able to contact you before now, but I have, with every fiber of my being, wished I could have long before now. If this were in the pre-digital era, I'd have a wastepaper bin full of discarded drafts. Thankfully, for the sake of the trees, I've just been reducing the life of my Delete key. Some things simply deserve an explanation face-to-face, no matter how ineloquent they might be. While you owe me nothing, I owe you that explanation and far more. I'm happy to arrange to meet up in New York, where I currently live. Or, if you prefer, I can come to you.

I know there is a good chance I will never hear from you, but I want you to know I wish you so very well.

Sincerely,

—Tara Murray

I read and reread the message several dozen times. It raised more questions than it answered, but she wasn't wrong in thinking that this was heavy stuff to get out in a letter. I didn't envy her the task of writing it. I couldn't say I'd never pictured my birth mother before—always red-haired and middling height like me—but this was the first time I'd felt real compassion for her. Reading between the lines, she'd not wanted to give me up and she'd wanted to find me. That was what every adopted kid dreamed of, right? A slightly more grown-up version of "they never meant to give me up in the first place" from the songs in *Annie* where all the orphanage girls dreamed of being rescued from the clutches of Mrs. Hannigan.

But I never expected a red-haired woman to appear on the doorstep in tears, calling me her baby and begging to atone for her years of absence. I'd only really wanted to be my parents' biological kid. But there was no amount of wishful thinking that could change the fact that I'd come to them by means of this other woman, who seemed to be a decent sort of human, from what I could parse from one short message.

I needed to talk to someone. Not Mom and Dad, but family. I checked the time on my phone, and it was still ridiculously early in the morning, which meant there was a chance Avery might be awake if she didn't have a sunrise barre class or something.

There was no harm in texting. If she was asleep, she'd have her phone on Do Not Disturb and wouldn't be roused. Given her fast-paced lifestyle, her ability to sleep hard and fast was one of her more useful superpowers.

ME: Hey, are you up?

Three blinking dots flashed immediately.

AVERY: Yeah. It's only 9 p.m. in LA.
ME: Oh, good . . . I didn't know you were there.
AVERY: Yeah. Last-minute trip to the garment district this morning. They put me up in a swanky hotel and I'm about to go soak my aching feet in the pool. I walked miles today.
ME: In inappropriate shoes, no doubt. But it sounds like your idea of a great time.
AVERY: Oh absolutely. I learned tons today and I'm here for the rest of the week. Usually they send senior staff for these buying expeditions, but they decided I was ready.
ME: That sounds like a big deal!
AVERY: Yep, appears I'm in line for a promotion. Will be able to give Dad's Amex a bit of a break.

I smiled despite myself.

> ME: You should still use it every so often so they don't cancel his account. 😊
>
> AVERY: Hahaha. The chef has become a comic. Why are you texting me at 6 a.m.? Unless you're nursing a hangover or something equally scandalous, that's far too early to be awake on vacation.
>
> ME: Fitful sleep. And when I woke up there was a message from my birth mother on FamilyRoots . . .

No dots appeared, but Avery's profile photo appeared large across my screen with an incoming call notification. I punched the green button.

"You couldn't lead with the birth mom thing? Why did you let me prattle on about LA?" Avery said by way of greeting.

"I mean, the news will keep and I'm always excited to hear about your life."

"So what do you know?" Avery pressed.

"Her name is Tara Murray and she lives in New York. She sent a message in the app. Didn't give a ton of details, but she did offer me the chance to meet up."

"So . . . are you going to?"

I shrugged. "I haven't even processed everything. I just needed to talk to someone and you were the first person I thought of."

She swallowed hard. "That means a lot, Vero."

I ignored the stinging at my eyes. "It's true. You're the best sister a girl could ask for."

She cleared her throat, pressing on just like Dad always did. "Whatever you want to do, I'll support you. If you want to meet her in New York, I can go with you. A united front and all that. I could even come back early from LA if you want." Her voice grew a bit raspy, but she was able to keep her emotions in check.

"No, no, no. This is a big shot for you, and you're not gonna blow it for this. I don't have to meet this person tomorrow, if at all. It can absolutely wait."

She heaved a sigh. "Okay, but I mean it when I say *whatever* you need, don't hesitate to ask. I'll be upset if you don't."

I held up a hand in a mock salute. "Scout's honor. I mostly just wanted to tell someone. And I'm not ready to get into this with Mom and Dad. Can you hold off on telling them anything? This feels like face-to-face stuff."

"Definitely. As much as I enjoy being a font of family information, which is rare given that I live a couple thousand miles away from you all, that show is all yours, Ronnie."

And with those words, I realized that, in a different way, Avery, too, had her moments of isolation from the family. She'd had to choose a coastal city to make her career feasible, while I was an easy drive from the family nest. It was her choice, certainly, but it had to have been a hard one given how close she was to all of us.

"So . . . how is Copenhagen?" Avery ventured after a few beats. She might as well have announced, "This is me changing the subject away from your birth mom until you bring it up again. See how respectful of your boundaries I am?"

And I wished I could have told her I found Copenhagen charming, because I'm sure it was. I wished I could have brought myself to offer some platitude, but it was beyond me. "It's a beautiful city from what I've seen, but the weather is gross, and I'd rather eat sawdust than venture outside today."

I heard a grunt from the other side of the line. "Of course it sucks. You're holed up in a vacation rental instead of enjoying yourself. I was an idiot for pushing you into this trip in winter—especially Copenhagen—and I'm sorry."

"It's fine, really. Maybe I'll find an English bookshop and hole up with a few novels. It's not quite the same as reading on the beach, but it could be restful."

"It seems a waste. Do you want me to change your ticket so you can go home? We can try the Denmark thing again in better weather."

"I don't know . . . I'm kinda not ready to face my own empty apartment yet. Yes, I'm in one as we speak, but it's not *my* empty apartment, ya know?"

"I get it. Why don't you go hang out in mine then? Chill on your own for a bit, and I'll be back in three days, and we can do some touristy stuff. Broadway shows and restaurants. I'll see what strings I can pull to get us into Le Bernardin or Daniel even. Make a real sisterly weekend out of it."

I paused. When I thought of all the places I could go, Denver, Estes, Blackthorn, or . . . anywhere else, New York might not have been the place I would have chosen first, but the invitation was the most appealing prospect before me. I'd never been to New York, and I'd always been curious about Avery's life outside of Colorado.

"Would it cost a fortune?" I braced myself for some staggering change fee she'd wave her hand at as if it were couch change.

"Not at all. I booked flexible tickets all the way, sis. It won't be a problem at all. I'll tell my super to let you in and give you my spare key, and you can crawl around the city to your heart's content or grab some novels at the Strand and order delivery if you really want to stay in. A mix of all of those things would be healthy. Whatever you want. And for the weekend, you can leave the planning to me. Nothing taxing, but a nice little itinerary for structure."

She knew me. I always preferred to have *something* on the docket rather than making all the plans on the fly. "That would be amazing. You can show me all your favorite places."

"You bet. It will be so fun you'll eventually forgive me for single-handedly upending your whole life."

"Avery, you didn't. Honest. You had nothing to do with Jonathan. And you certainly didn't mean to hurt anyone with the DNA kits."

"No. I really didn't. I made Mom and Dad do theirs too, by the way. Mom's Italian with a bit of French. Dad's Italian and English, just as we expected. And I'm the blend."

"You got the best of them. Brains, beauty, charm . . . the whole package deal."

"I wish you saw yourself through the same lens of kindness as you see me," she replied. "You've always been so hard on yourself."

"I'm trying to do better about it. Confronting everything has maybe sent me off in the right direction at least. And I have you and Steph to thank for that."

"I'm glad to hear it, sister. I've always only wanted the best for you."

"I know it. So go ahead and change the ticket. Whenever you can get me there that won't cost a huge upcharge."

"On it." I could hear clicking in the background to confirm she was, in fact, already in the process of changing my ticket despite it being ridiculously early in the morning.

"I can get you on the nonstop at 1:00 p.m. your time, *today*, at no charge since it's a same day change and we're more than four hours out. Is that too soon?"

I giggled. "No, I think I can manage to get cleaned up and to the airport in the next seven hours. Thank you for doing this."

"It's the least I can do. Can I ask you a question that is officially none of my business?"

"I'm pretty sure that was your minor in college, so yes, I think you're capable of that."

She exhaled slowly. "Do you think you're going to reach out to your birth mom while you're in New York?"

I peered out the window where the rain still pelted, but it seemed to be lessening as the gloom of night slowly gave way to morning.

I tried to keep my voice neutral. "It would be my opportunity, wouldn't it?"

"It would. You've been waiting for answers for a long time. This Tara person can give them to you better than anyone. You don't have to forge a lifelong bond with her or anything, but you could meet with her as a favor to yourself."

I took a long pause. "You may be right, Ave. I'm not sure if I'm up for it just yet."

"Completely fair, sister. But promise me you'll at least consider it. You deserve to know your own story."

"I promise."

I confirmed with Avery that I had the updated ticket in my email and all was in order, and she assured me she'd get everything set to access her condo when I reached the city. She even promised me an email with suggestions for getting from the airport and tips for navigating the city from a local's perspective by the time I landed.

Leaving Copenhagen so soon felt bittersweet. It was a shame that I wouldn't get to know and love the place as I had the craggy shores of Westport, the winding cobblestone streets of Beynac, and the lush hills of the Italian countryside. But I was in no sort of headspace to give the gorgeous city a fair shot. It was time to head back to familiar soil and get back to piecing together the next chapter of my life.

I saw a glimmer of a tall blonde woman in a corner of the room as I wheeled my suitcase from the bedroom into the living room. Unlike Aoife, Imogène, and Carlotta, she didn't seem all that keen to tell me her story. I felt a warmth embrace me as this woman, whoever she was, let me know I was welcome to return when I was ready.

Chapter 37

UPPER WEST SIDE, MANHATTAN

I arrived at Avery's condo a little before eight in the evening—and my body clock had absolutely no idea what to do with that information. I dragged myself from the lobby of her building on the Upper West Side to her fourth-floor walk-up. As tired as I was, I couldn't help but want to explore Avery's private lair I'd never had the chance to see. It was, as one might expect for a young professional living in Manhattan, cramped, but not markedly more so than my own apartment in Denver. Despite the limitations in size, Avery had made use of every inch of space to be both functional and beautiful. Because of my parents' help, she was able to live alone in a one-bedroom condo instead of a dingy studio or crammed in with three roommates. It was a huge advantage to her career to have a restful space of her own, and I was glad she had it.

The walls were adorned in vintage clothing posters, tastefully matted and framed. The furniture was sleek and minimalist, with a few cozy blankets and throw pillows to soften the vibe. It was almost exactly as I would have pictured a space she'd designed all her own. The wall of family pictures, both portraits and candid shots, were a touching addition I hadn't expected. There were several of her and me on various childhood vacations and a few of me alone, which surprised me the most.

One that caught my eye in particular was of me when I was a freshman in high school, wearing the chef's jacket Mom had made for me, standing in front of a massive cake and platters of appetizers I'd made for a cousin's bridal shower. They hadn't trusted a fourteen-year-old with the wedding cake, of course, but I'd begged to cater the shower. The assortment of canapés had been devoured, and the three-tiered lemon cake filled with fresh lemon curd and sliced berries and frosted in ivory buttercream with intricately piped scrollwork had been the talk of her shower. I'd spent weeks practicing my piping and perfecting the buttercream. It was the recipe my mother still used in her shop, and even now I was chuffed when I thought of that. When the bride pulled me aside at the reception and whispered that she wished she'd had me make the wedding cake instead of the professional she'd hired, it was the sort of compliment a kid remembers for a lifetime.

And it hit me that this was how Avery saw me. The budding chef with all the promise in the world who just changed the course of her life on a whim. It was how Mom, Dad, and Stephanie saw me too. I guessed they were trying to reconcile the version of me who seemed ironclad set on a career track for years, only to veer off on an unexpected trajectory.

I thought about the email from Fairbanks. It would be a path toward shoring up The Kitchen Muse for a more lucrative future, but maybe everyone was right about this particular aspect of my life: I was hiding behind the genius of other chefs to avoid failing on my own. Every rationalization I'd made about the perils of the restaurant world, while true, were nothing more than thinly veiled justifications for me not to take a risk on my own talent.

And I *was* talented.

It had been a long time since I'd acknowledged it, but it was true. And if I was ever going to take the plunge and go out on my own, I'd have to find the confidence of the girl in that photo who had outbaked the professionals.

I changed into the decadent cashmere pajamas I'd purchased in Milan and padded into Avery's small bedroom. It was large enough for a queen-size bed and a pair of nightstands, but without much wiggle room to spare. Her linens were top-notch, and the room was the perfect temperature for sleep, but despite my utter exhaustion, I couldn't slow my brain down long enough to doze off.

I'd have to make a decision about Fairbanks, and soon. But that wasn't even the most pressing issue. I was in the same city as my birth mother. I'd have six days in New York, three of them Avery-free, and I'd have to decide if I was equal to meeting with this woman.

I pulled her message back up on my phone.

Tara.

It smacked of a name that peaked in the late seventies. So the timing made sense. I was born in the late nineties, so signs would indicate she'd been fairly young when I was born. I'd expected as much—an older, established woman wouldn't have had a reason to give me up. And her surname was Irish, which would have pleased Niall.

I felt a pang at his memory and forced it aside.

I read and reread her message a dozen times or more as sleep eluded me. And I began to think that Avery was onto something here. Tara was the only person who could answer the questions that

I couldn't deny had been lingering in the back of my brain for years. Tara herself said I owed her nothing, but I did owe myself the peace of mind that answers might bring.

I didn't know how many times I rolled over a potential message in my brain, but I finally found the resolve to press the Reply button at the bottom of her message.

> Hello Tara,
>
> I'm glad you reached out. As it happens, I am in New York for the next few days. I know it's short notice, but I'd like to meet up if your offer still stands.
> —Veronica

I honestly wasn't sure what I wanted her to say when she responded. *If* she responded. She was just as entitled to cold feet about this meeting as I was, I had to admit. Whatever she might not be entitled to, I couldn't begrudge her a good case of nerves. As I lay in Avery's bed, wishing sleep would lap over me like gently cresting waves, I genuinely hoped the meeting would happen and that I'd come away from it with a few more answers than I went in with. Or perhaps new and compelling questions beyond the most obvious of them: Why?

Perhaps a quarter of an hour later an alert from the app flashed across my screen. Tara wasn't going to ghost me just yet, it seemed.

> Hi Veronica,
>
> I am grateful you responded. Could I take you to dinner tomorrow? I'd be happy to clear anything off my schedule if that doesn't work. Just propose an alternative and I'll be there.
> —Tara

Chapter 38

"A re you going to be okay?" Avery said over my cell as the cab pulled in front of the restaurant. "I wish I were there with you."

I appreciated the sentiment but feared her presence would have only served to further heighten my anxiety. "Yeah, definitely. If things get awkward I'll text you and beeline to the coffee shop you recommended and wait a bit before heading home in a cab."

Like any good sister, she was going to have her phone at the ready, poised to act if anything went awry even from three thousand miles away. We had backup plans and contingencies enough to make Stephanie proud. And if things went *disastrously* wrong, she had friends prepped to be able to rescue me within a quarter of an hour. I ended the call.

The restaurant Tara chose wasn't a particularly posh restaurant. Of course I'd googled immediately when she'd suggested a place and was happy to see it wasn't going to be a quiet white-tablecloth sort of establishment. Reviews claimed it served solid Mediterranean fare and had a good reputation. It wasn't necessarily a serious foodie's first pick, but not one they'd snub either, so we might have some common ground.

I sent Avery a hug emoji before sliding out of the cab and onto the busy sidewalk. I caught my reflection in the restaurant window, and I was impressed by Avery's handiwork. She had an outfit messengered from her contacts to her apartment two hours after I'd told her about the dinner meeting. She selected well-made pieces that played up all my best attributes and downplayed my flaws. There was nothing fussy about the chocolate-brown, wide-legged wool pants or the coordinating overcoat she'd chosen, and the emerald-green, soft angora sweater was definitely a luxury I could learn to live with. The low-heeled, brown leather ankle boots were comfortable enough I couldn't gripe, and they finished off the outfit nicely. I looked put together enough to meet my birth mother, even if I didn't feel it.

And that was a start.

At a table in the corner sat a petite red-haired woman who appeared to be in her mid to late forties. Her resemblance to me was nothing short of uncanny. She stood when she saw me, just as certain of who I was.

She was quaking a bit as I approached her table.

"Th-thanks for coming. I wasn't sure you would." She stammered her words but gestured for me to sit, then reclaimed her own chair.

"I can't say I didn't consider bailing, but I didn't know when I might ever get the chance to meet you again, so . . ."

"I don't blame you. I've been a bit of a mess for two days since our DNA matched. I honestly never thought I'd get to lay eyes on you after I gave you to your parents."

Your parents. That's how she saw them, and I suppose it made it easier for her. I was glad she acknowledged that they were the ones who had earned the title.

I reached for the carafe of water on the table, trying to keep my hands from shaking. "I don't know where to start."

"Our first thing in common," she said, clearly trying to keep the mood light. "I suppose the first thing I ought to say is that I'm sorry I couldn't keep you."

I found I couldn't meet her gaze. Logically I could think of a million reasons why a mother would have to put her child up for adoption. Poverty being the first of those. But the woman who sat across from me was wearing a well-tailored suit, fashion-forward and probably from a designer Avery would have been able to recognize without a glimpse at the tag. Her hands were perfectly manicured, and her hair was in a sleek bob annoyingly similar to my own but probably maintained at ten times the cost. She wasn't poor.

My hands began to tremble in earnest, and I couldn't focus on the words leaving her mouth. Maybe she had been twenty-six years ago. Maybe there was a different explanation altogether. She must have had her reasons, but right then I was in no state to hear them.

"I—I need to go." I stood abruptly and grabbed my bag. I felt myself trembling from head to foot and felt every bit a fool. "This was a mistake; I should never have agreed to this. I'm sorry."

I left Tara, open-mouthed and blinking at her table. And perhaps I should have felt bad about it, but it wasn't until I exited onto the sidewalk in front of the restaurant that I was able to take a proper breath.

I gave myself two minutes for my heartbeat to stabilize and texted Avery:

ME: On my way to the coffee shop . . .

I wandered awhile after I'd hidden away in the predesignated coffee shop and indulged in comfort food: grilled cheese, fries, and the best chocolate cheesecake of my entire life. I'd kept up a steady stream of texts to Avery, who reassured me both that I was perfectly normal in my flight response and probably safe enough to go about the rest of my evening once my meal was over.

I'd considered taking in a show, but that was already on the docket for the weekend. A movie seemed like a waste of time in the city. I decided just to put a few miles on the new boots and take in the sights of the city as it tumbled into night.

I walked until my feet ached, and when a light drizzle grew more insistent, I decided it was time to call a cab and head back to Avery's condo. Rather than getting myself soaked on the sidewalk, I ducked into the lobby of an apartment building to pull up the e-hail app Avery had instructed me to install when I'd arrived. Before I was able to pull my phone from my purse, I realized this had to be one of the premier addresses in the city. A bronze placard read The Mercury. I'd never heard of it, and I guessed it was because the residents were the "quiet money" sort that liked to keep their affairs private. The lobby was a marble showpiece to make an Astor turn emerald with envy and a throwback to the Gilded Age that engraved those families indelibly into the New York annals of history. I began to worry the doorman would chew me out for venturing in when I wasn't a resident or a guest of one, but apparently some unobtrusive taxi hailing during a rainstorm wasn't enough to raise his ire.

As I was waiting for the app to load—likely strained from a zillion other New Yorkers trying to hail cabs—I saw the profile of a young woman in smart business attire nod to the doorman as she strode to the elevator. The woman was slight and red-haired like I was. Tara.

But when I tried to focus my eyes on her, I realized she bore the same glimmering quality of the echoes I'd seen on my travels. Tara wasn't wearing the same clothes she'd worn to our failed dinner, and she appeared quite a bit younger—a few years my junior even.

She turned her head, and unlike the rest of the apparitions, she beckoned for me to follow her. I glanced to the doorman, who didn't seem to register my existence. Perhaps *I* was invisible too, and I hoped that I hadn't been the victim of a car accident and was now on my way up the elevator to the pearly gates or whatever lay beyond. As I slid into the elevator just before the doors closed, this echo version of Tara pressed a finger to her lips and kept her eyes on the doors.

The woman produced a key, turned it in the control panel, and pressed the now-illuminated button for the top-floor penthouse. It was just as well she couldn't hear me, because I wouldn't have been able to resist asking myself questions. How on earth was she able to afford rent in a building that had a penthouse at all, let alone live in the penthouse itself at that age? If she could have afforded such luxury, certainly she could have afforded some diapers and Gerber. I stilled those thoughts, giving this echo Tara the chance to show what she wanted me to see without a prejudiced heart.

The elevator reached the top floor with a *ding*, and Tara exhaled as she stepped out onto the thick carpet into the hallway. She rapped three times on the apartment door until heavy footsteps sounded.

The man who opened the door, handsome and tall and who appeared to be in his sixties but was incredibly well-maintained, blanched at the sight of her.

"Tara, you can't come here unannounced. We have our code for a reason. My wife is coming in from Connecticut tonight to spend the weekend in the city."

"I know. She had me arrange her train tickets, remember? She had me book a later one so she could stay with your grandson while your daughter-in-law took your granddaughter to a checkup earlier this afternoon. She won't be in for another two hours yet."

His color lifted with the corners of his lips. His blue eyes grew steely with intensity. "In that case, come in, kitten. Stay awhile."

He gestured for her to enter, and I hurried to slip in before he closed the door behind him.

She stood in the middle of an expansive living room, lavish but tasteful, decorated with minimalist lines but softened with buttery-rich upholstery and drapes in shades of ivory and bright navy with the occasional splash of burgundy for an added visual *pop*. And this wasn't the work of a talented interior designer. Every piece had been painstakingly curated by his wife.

The man approached Tara, wrapping his arms around her from behind.

"God, you always smell so good, baby. I'm glad you decided to surprise me. It'd be a shame to miss the opportunity if she's going to be late . . ."

She stiffened at his touch. "I didn't come for that. Not tonight."

"But you want to, don't you?" He continued kissing the side of her neck down to her collarbone. "You enjoy our time together, don't you?"

She turned so she was facing him. She opened her mouth to speak, but his mouth covered hers before she could utter a word. She didn't melt against his frame but seemed to wait for him to come up for air before she gently pushed back.

"Let's go to the bedroom." He groaned as she took a step back.

She shook her head. "I'm pregnant, Wally."

He took two steps back from her like she'd sucker punched him in the jaw. He even wobbled his head as if trying to bring the room into focus.

"How?" he muttered at last.

"Do you need me to explain it? Birth control isn't perfect. Mistakes happen."

"God. I was careless and stupid. But this was bound to happen to me eventually." He sagged onto a nearby sofa and buried his head in his hands.

She looked downcast at the implications of his words. From his reaction, I sensed Tara was one in a long line of interns, and she'd been the first to be unlucky. Or at least the first to tell him she was. She cleared her throat. "I don't mean to be a snit about this, but it's happening to me too. Arguably even more to me if we want to be precise."

He finally turned his eyes upward. His expression was soft, and he patted the sofa cushion next to where he sat. "Of course. I don't mean to be unfeeling. I was just overwhelmed for a moment. It's a lot to take in."

She crossed to join him. She took his proffered hand in hers and rested her head against his shoulder. "It is. I'm still in shock."

"How long have you known? Are you *sure?*"

"I realized I was late this morning. I took a test during my lunch break. Two blue lines."

He rested his head against the back of the sofa. "It's still early, then?"

Tara folded her hands. "Yes. I'm only a few days late. But paired with a bit of nausea . . . I was worried. And apparently for good reason."

"Smart girl. The sooner we know, the more time we have to plan." She sat up straighter. "Plan?"

"Naturally. Whatever you decide, a plan will have to be made."

"I decide?"

"Of course you. Your body, your choice. Isn't that the slogan these days? I won't decide for you, but I will do what I can to facilitate your choice."

Her tone grew serious. "Elaborate."

"If you decide to end the pregnancy, I'll make arrangements myself and make sure everything is handled discreetly for both our sakes, and that you are comfortable and given world-class care."

"I'm not sure I could——"

He patted her knee with a twinge of reluctance. "I didn't think so. If you prefer to find a family for the child, it will be a bit more complicated but not impossible. You'd probably be able to take courses in the fall, but I'd need to find you a suitable situation for the spring. Somewhere neither of us is known. Out west, probably." He shuddered as if he was vaguely repulsed by anything west of the Hudson River.

Tara looked at him expectantly, as if willing a third option to tumble from his lips.

"I'm sorry, kitten, but keeping the child isn't a viable option. I stand to risk too much if word got out. It's not like in Hollywood where an illegitimate child doesn't even merit a mention on the scandal sheets. Being in nonprofit is like being a politician. Reputation is everything."

She paled. "I understand that. I just can't imagine handing off our baby to strangers. I don't know if I have it in me."

"Tara, you're going to make a wonderful mother someday. To another child. Because you're strong enough to make the right decision for *this* child and make sure he or she is cared for by two loving parents who will do right by the little one. I can't be a father to this child. Considering the inheritance complications for my son and the future of the foundation alone just took two years off my life in the space of a few seconds."

He was trying to keep the tone jovial, but his eyes were as serious as any seasoned contract lawyer who was trying to manage a tricky negotiation.

"I wouldn't expose you."

"Not at first. But what about when the child is old enough to start asking questions? And think, how will you provide for the child without a degree in hand?"

"If the baby comes in early April, I'd be able to study right until the baby is due and take incompletes. I could finish my final papers over the summer."

"And what about your scholarship? How will the committee feel about an unwed mother receiving their funds? The twenty-first century may be upon us, but not everyone is as enlightened as you might think."

"They don't need to know. I'll wear baggy clothes and make excuses."

"These things always get out. And if there is a mark on your record with these people, it will make gaining employment in the nonprofit sector more than a little . . . challenging. But if you allow me to quietly intervene, you'll find your scholarship will allow you a semester's deferral. A year if you wish. And perhaps additional opportunities will arise for a graduate program or assistance finding a job with another firm. Both, if you want. Anything might be possible with a few simple phone calls."

There it was. The veiled threat. If she went along with his plan and kept quiet, he'd use his influence to make her future bright. If she didn't, there would be no job in any major nonprofit, maybe ever. No scholarship. Perhaps no degree at all.

In the space of a few minutes, he'd entrenched the ball so firmly in his own court, there would be no retrieving it.

Quiet tears streamed down Tara's face as she absorbed his offer.

"I know this is unfair, Tara. But you've learned the first rule of nonprofit. Never put yourself at the mercy of someone with far more influence than you have. It rarely comes to good outcomes."

"A sad lesson to learn from a man who purports to wield his influence for the common good."

"Ah, to see the world through such innocent eyes. I'm sorry to be the one to jade you."

"Are you really?" Tara's eyes flashed in anger. "It seemed to me you rather enjoyed it."

A mischievous grin tickled at his lips. "I certainly did enjoy showing you the ways of the world in a few respects, even if this result isn't what I'd have hoped for."

"So if I go out west in the spring . . ."

"I'll manage everything. And find the best possible family for the child."

"I'll want to meet them myself," Tara pressed.

"I'm not sure that's wise. It would make you easier to identify. And if they associate you with the foundation . . ."

"Would you rather take your chances with a grateful adoptive family blabbing, or me going to the *Times*? You may have more influence than I do, but people are happy to believe a naive young intern who was taken advantage of by a slimy CEO three times her age. Even with all your influence and money, you won't come through it unscathed. Your wife and family will know, and your reputation will be sullied."

"My, my. You are a quick study, aren't you? If my own neck weren't at stake here, I'd be prodigiously proud of you. Very well, you can meet the family if you insist. But be forewarned, there will be so many nondisclosure agreements, your fingers will bleed from signing them all."

"I'll run the risk." She extended a hand to him as if their negotiations had come to an end. "I'll go west after Christmas, but if you pull anything to harm me or the baby, I will make sure all of New York knows what you are. If anything mysterious happens to my scholarship, if my review from my internship is anything less than glowing, or if I have the slightest inkling you've blackballed me, I will eviscerate you. And that goes triple if I think you've done anything nefarious with the baby's placement."

"You are a marvelous creature, aren't you? I feel like a modern-day Henry Higgins face-to-face with Eliza Doolittle in her moment of triumph, but with sex, manipulation, and threats rather than grammar and comportment." He checked his watch. "We might have time for a quick lesson before my wife arrives. And we wouldn't have to bother with precautions."

Tara removed her hands from his. "As tempting as that sounds, I think your tutelage has taken me as far as your abilities will allow."

"Now, kitten, there's no need to show your claws."

"Isn't there? You've made it clear we're adversaries, not allies. I won't let your next lesson be about letting my guard down."

"And this is usually how these lovely trysts end. The young lady a little wiser and a little sadder. But I'm no monster, my dear. I'll ensure you have the best of care, and the child too."

"I hope for all our sakes you make good on that promise, Wally. I don't want to have to make good on mine."

Tara—rather this version of her—left the apartment with a self-assurance I admired in a barely twentysomething who was facing off with a much older, far more powerful man. I followed her down to the lobby, where she disappeared with a shimmer into the inky black of night.

Chapter 39

I spotted Tara in the restaurant before she spotted me. She sat in the corner once again and seemed even more nervous than she had on our first encounter. She stood when I approached and extended her hand as she'd done before. Formal and guarded. And I couldn't blame her.

I responded by opening my arms for a hug. She hesitated a moment before stepping into the embrace, but once we locked arms around each other, we both lingered there a long moment. She smelled of jasmine-verbena perfume with the softest hint of sandalwood. The scent seemed eerily familiar, though I couldn't identify it at a department store counter to spare my life.

"I was surprised you wanted to see me again," she said at length.

We took our places at the table, and I steadied myself with a deep breath.

"I'm surprised you came, to be honest. I didn't really deserve more of your time."

"Veronica, you're a smart and competent young woman. And, in my eyes, the only innocent party in this mess. You have the right to a reaction. And I never fooled myself into thinking that it wouldn't be a strong one."

I looked down at my hands. "That's true enough, but I was out of line. You weren't left with a lot of great choices."

"That was definitely the case, but you had no way of knowing that. I can see why, from your perspective, I wasn't owed any allowances."

"I was wrong to be so harsh with you. You were young, broke, and put in a bad position. You did the best for me that you could under the circumstances. You acted more selflessly than a lot of women might have."

She glanced down at her empty place setting before meeting my eyes. "I wouldn't say I was selfless. For years I hated myself because I felt like I acted to save my own neck instead of fighting to keep you."

"But my birth father was right. Without his support, which he never would have given willingly, how could you have supported us? Just because you made the choice that didn't destroy your own future doesn't mean it wasn't the best one for me too. He made sure to make the decision a no-brainer for you."

Her eyes widened and her lips parted momentarily in surprise. "How could you possibly know about any of this? I didn't tell you who he was, and he passed away ten years ago. And there's no way his family would have talked to you."

"They didn't have to."

I did my best to, matter-of-factly, relate what I'd seen in the apartment lobby the night before. I'd had to explain this so many times now, I'd become less awkward about it. Not that I found the visions any less strange. I'd just had time to make friends with the idea to some extent.

She was a bit pale when I finished my summary, but I expected as much. "What building was it?"

"The Mercury. I went into the lobby to escape the rain and hail a cab."

She exhaled slowly, a memory clouding her face. "That's where your birth father lived."

"I figured it had to be. Whatever this phenomenon is, it seems to be linked to location."

"I spent more time there than I should have. His wife is still there from what I hear. Obviously I do whatever I can to stay out of her circles, but it's hard to do so entirely in nonprofit. Her grandson is running the company now, and it seems like he's doing a decent job for such a young CEO. He seems eager to prove he's worthy on his own merit and all that."

"Makes sense. Do you think they know?"

Tara shrugged. "He claimed they didn't the last time I saw him, almost twenty years ago. But his wife was—is—a keenly observant woman. I can't imagine she didn't figure it out from financial records for my medical receipts and all the birth-related expenses. If not when he was alive, surely after he died."

"He seemed like a heartless goon. It was awful to force you to give birth without any support system at all."

"It wasn't as dreadful as you might think. It wasn't like some horrible home for unwed mothers from the 1950s. He sent me to a facility that was more like a day spa than anything else. He wasn't a total monster, though I liked to think of him that way for a long time. But he's part of you, so I won't disparage him."

The phrase made me think of Carlotta avoiding bad-mouthing Donatella's father, and the similarities made my stomach roil.

"It's fine. I don't mind, really."

Tara gave a full-throated laugh. "Thanks for understanding. I hope you understand . . . If I hadn't gone along with his scheme, he'd have found a way to keep me from finishing my degree and blackball me from every nonprofit from here to Honolulu. If I'd kept you, I wouldn't have been able to feed you. I was a scholarship kid and my parents barely had two nickels to rub together. I didn't want that life for you."

"I get that. And I do appreciate it. My parents are incredible, and my childhood was amazing. For what it's worth, I think you made the right decision."

"I knew I did, even back then." She took a steadying breath. "I only got to hold you one time. And it was because your dad whisked your mom into the hallway to give you and me a few moments alone together before they got to take you home. I couldn't bring myself to ask for it, but he just knew."

"That sounds like Dad. He's able to read situations like that. Sort of unnerving at times, but he's a great husband to my mom. And a fabulous dad."

Tara smiled. "I always believed they'd be amazing parents, but seeing how kind a person you are to someone you have every right to take issue with proves it. I wouldn't have blamed you if you'd come in here and thrown a glass of wine in my face."

I took the glass of wine from in front of my place setting and took in the bouquet and a small sip. "Bold of you to order a red if that's what you were expecting. But it *is* a pretty decent Spanish Tempranillo. Seems a waste to toss it."

She arched a brow in approval. "Beronia. One of my favorites. You have a good nose."

I raised a glass to her. "It's my job to know a Tempranillo from a Cab from a Shiraz."

"You're a sommelier? How swanky."

"Not quite. More of a kitchen muse." I went into a description of how I was able to cobble together a living.

"That sounds fascinating. I bet you'd make a killing here in New York. I can't imagine a restaurateur who wouldn't want a savvy consultant on their side."

"You'd think so, but no. There is so much kitchen talent in this town, I'd end up as white noise. I don't have the fancy certifications and diplomas to impress anyone here. It's a lot easier to get a foothold in a place like Denver. And thanks to Michelin, the restaurant scene there is growing, so that makes it a fun challenge."

"I see what you mean. Is there a reason you didn't go to culinary school? If it's a matter of money . . ."

I shook my head. Taking money from her was even less appealing than taking money from my parents. "Nothing like that. And honestly, I've been asking myself that question a lot lately." I took another sip of the wine, grateful it was there and fortifying. "So why now? Why did you start searching for me?"

"Simple. The NDA Wally made us sign was set to expire ten years after his death, and he passed ten years ago right around Christmas. I counted down the days to start my search in the back of my head from the moment I saw his obit in the *Times*. I doubt the NDA would have been enforceable after his death, but the family could have made things difficult for us all. I also figured your teen years would have been the absolute worst time for me to upend your life."

My breath caught. "Maybe so. That was about when I pieced it together in sophomore biology. It didn't take an A student to understand that the odds of two brunette parents with dark eyes and olive skin having a kid with pale skin, red hair, and green eyes was virtually impossible. Avery's DNA kit really just provided confirmation."

She smiled. "And I bet you *were* an A student. What did your parents say when you told them?"

"I never did. I think part of me didn't want to rock the boat. We were a happy family, you know? Why upset things over a simple question of genetic code?"

She took a sip from her glass. "That's pretty insightful for a fifteen-year-old kid, if I may be so bold. Too insightful for me to believe it's the whole truth."

"Maybe it isn't the whole truth, but that's what I convinced myself of for a long time."

She glanced past my shoulder a moment, seeming to gather her thoughts before she spoke. "I'm going to hazard a guess that you didn't tell them because you were afraid they'd love you less if the truth was out in the open. You worried it was easier for them to pretend you were their biological kid if you didn't know the truth."

I knitted my fingers in my lap. "That's also pretty insightful for someone who has spent less than an hour in my company."

"Well, even if I didn't have the chance to raise you, you have 50 percent of my DNA. There was bound to be a trace of me in your makeup."

I gestured to my face. "A bit more than a trace."

"Deeper than that. It's maybe not right for me to say it, but I know something about convincing myself that I was unworthy and allowing myself to accept things I shouldn't have. I hope you learn that sooner than I did."

"How do you mean?"

"I went through a bad couple of years after you were born and I entrusted you to the Strattons. Fell into, believe it or not, worse relationships than the one that gave me you. Took crap jobs because I didn't feel like I deserved better despite being qualified. It took me a long time to get my head right and not feel like I was the worst person in the history of mankind for not trying to raise you on my own."

"What changed?"

"Well, like you, I saw something. I saw a little redheaded girl on a bike when I was walking home after a spectacularly bad date. She was the same age you would have been. She seemed happy, but I followed her because I was worried she was going to stray into traffic. And she did before I could reach her. But the cars passed right through her and I could hear her giggling on the other side of the street."

At once visions of Aoife, Imogène, Carlotta, and Donatella returned to me. Ephemeral, glistening, just a shade too pale to be of this plane. And Tara—my birth mother—had seen the same. Whether she'd passed along some genetic form of delusion or a precious gift of sight, I couldn't be sure. But it was clearly a link we shared.

"Describe the bike?" I asked.

Her eyes flitted off to the distance, summoning the memory. "It was mostly a bright metallic magenta with little rainbows all over. And the girl wore a helmet shaped like a unicorn's head, complete with a foam horn."

"I loved that helmet. And the iridescent streamers on the handles. I got that bike for my fourth birthday." I could practically feel the heat rising from the asphalt as my dad taught me how to ride without training wheels as Mom watched from the porch, little Avery in her arms.

"I think it was you. Somehow sending me a message from Denver that you were fine and happy. It's what I chose to believe. And I clung to that. I let myself believe that you didn't want me to spend the rest of my life miserable because I tried to do what I thought was right at the time."

"Well, I can't say if I would have understood well enough at that age to absolve you of anything, but whatever it was you saw, I'm glad you did. You didn't need to spend the rest of your life atoning for making the choices you did. I am unreservedly glad you've had a good life."

"Thank you for that," she said. "And, as your birth mother, even if I haven't earned that title, I want nothing less than a stellar life for you."

I stood, and she followed suit. I think she expected I was going to leave again, but instead I enveloped her in another hug. I took a moment to feel the warmth of her and to take in the scent of jasmine and sandalwood. The familiarity of the powdery-floral scent filled me with a phantom memory of being held and safe so long ago, just before being placed in the arms of another who could love me without complication or regret. A woman who was, in many ways, far luckier than Tara had been but who was and always would be the woman I called Mother.

Avery's face filled my screen and her voice filled the apartment via FaceTime as I crossed the threshold of her door. She affected a tone of voice that begged me to divulge as much of the evening's events as I was comfortable doing—so long as I left out no detail. "There's a decent bottle of Cab in the bottom cabinet, and I insist you enjoy it."

"Yes to the wine. The dinner went great."

"And?"

I retrieved the bottle and hunted down a corkscrew, making a mental note to buy her a decent one when I was out the next day. She had her areas of expertise and I had mine. "I apologized for bailing on her."

"Unnecessary, but go on."

I considered torturing her by dragging out the details, as a gentle reminder that she was, in fact, prying, but everything began to seep into my skin with the weight of a sodden beach towel across the shoulders. I was too tired to put up any semblance of a wall with her just then.

"So what I saw at The Mercury? That was what happened. She recalled things in such detail, there was no way she could be making it up."

Avery sucked in a breath. "So what does this mean for you?"

I leaned my head against the back of the Ikea love seat, wineglass in hand, feeling the fatigue wash over me. "We promised to keep in touch. Email only for a while. If it gets weird, either of us can ghost for any reason. No explanations necessary."

"Are you okay with that?" Her voice was gentle, with her trademark pinch of insistence.

"I think it's the right place for us to start, yeah." And I meant it. There were no promises of another reunion or reintroducing her to Mom and Dad. I knew they'd love her simply by virtue of being the one who'd helped make them parents, but I wasn't ready for that yet. We kept the expectations manageable so there would be room to scale up our interactions later if we so chose. Only time would tell whether our relationship would flourish or fizzle.

And it didn't really matter which . . . I had some answers, and for now, that was enough.

"I promised Stephanie we'd add her to FaceTime if you're up to it," she said after a beat.

I paused. As exhausted as I was, going over the scene in the morning, when all my senses were sharp, sounded far worse than laboring through a call. "Sure. Let's patch her in."

Stephanie answered the call, looking as if she'd just come in from the office. Given that it was closing in on eight o'clock in Denver, it wasn't out of the question for her.

Avery and I took turns filling her in on the events of the evening while Stephanie nodded along like a diligent student in a lecture hall. "So now that you've made peace with Tara, what now? Are you coming home to Denver?"

"Soon. After a girls' weekend with Avery."

Avery turned bubbly. "I got us great tickets to a show. And dinner reservations to die for."

"Sounds amazing," I said, trying to summon the enthusiasm I'd feel when my energy returned.

"And let me play dress-up?" she pressed.

"Fine. As long as you choose shoes I can walk in." I shot her a no-nonsense older sister glare I hoped instilled fear in her soul, but I wasn't hopeful.

"Overrated, but fine."

Stephanie exhaled and rubbed her temples. She was in full-on PR problem-solving mode and had her boardroom voice on. "Okay, so do all the girly stuff with Avery. Eat amazing food and schmooze with the food gurus . . . but then what's for you here?"

"My job? I still need to answer Fairbanks."

Stephanie's face grew somber. "Listen, I am the career woman's career woman, but is your job really what's going to make you happy? I really want you to be honest. You have spent your whole career building other people's businesses. Isn't it time you do something for yourself?"

Avery chimed in. "And, Vero, as a person who has known you my whole life and most of yours, I've never seen you happier than when you were traveling."

I gave her a wary glance. "You want me to be a nomad? Spend my days wandering from one obscure village to another seeking wisdom or something?"

Stephanie rolled her eyes. "Not a nomad. I want you to pick someplace that speaks to you and create something new and exciting. For yourself."

I thought of the little red-haired girl Tara had seen bicycling on the streets of Manhattan. How she'd taken that vision as a sign of forgiveness from me. Part of me truly hoped it was the universe—and me—giving her much-deserved permission to lead a happy and fulfilling life. Giving her permission to forgive the world and herself for all that had happened.

And I wondered if, without a life-altering vision or any sort of inexplicable phenomenon, I could do the same for myself.

Chapter 40

My hands shook intermittently on the drive back up to Estes Park. The ghosts of memories that waited for me there were far more unnerving than any of the visions I'd seen on my travels. These ghosts were my own and I'd have to face them.

I pulled up in front of Mom and Dad's cabin, took several slow breaths, then grabbed my bag from the passenger seat before I opened the door to my Toyota SUV and swung my feet onto the driveway with the familiar, satisfying crunch of shoe rubber on gravel. True to my word, I'd worn some of my new clothes from Italy to show off and felt a smidge more confident for the added effort with my appearance.

Dad greeted me with a hug, like old times. He was one big smile in a flannel shirt, but I did notice a few extra creases around his eyes and a couple of extra gray hairs. Mom, who was usually on the porch before I could reach it, unless she was elbow deep in making a meal, hung back until I'd entered. Was she worried I wouldn't welcome her usual greeting embrace? She claimed that she didn't want things to be different just because I knew, but this was exactly *how* different happened.

I'd have to be the one to make things right. I'd have to make the gesture this time.

I removed my boots and hung my coat in the closet, debating my best approach. The living room felt stark without the Christmas decorations, and no wafting aroma was beckoning from the kitchen. Mom had been taking things badly if she wasn't baking. They both had, though Dad was better at putting on a brave face. My stomach lurched at the knowledge they'd been struggling. I wasn't a mother, but I could empathize enough to know that any sort of familial strife was the worst kind of torture for them both.

"You look great, shortcake." Dad gave me an appraising glance. "Travel suits you."

"Thanks, Dad. It's the new wardrobe. Avery just happens to have a knack with clothes, if you haven't heard." I shot him a wink.

His eyes crinkled with a smile. "Once or twice maybe. But it's not just the clothes."

I shrugged, not quite sure how to respond. "Well, it's been a whirlwind month, but I'm glad I went."

"Glad to hear it, kiddo." He wrapped his arm around me in another side hug. I crossed over to Mom, who looked like she was struggling to keep herself together. I wrapped my arms around her and took in the warmth of her cheek against the top of my head.

"Are you doing okay?" I asked.

Her voice was raspy. "Better now that you're back. I've missed being able to chat with you."

"Me too, Mom. Me too."

I felt the warmth of her tears sprinkle the top of my head, and I chuckled as she clumsily tried to dry them and stem the flow. She and Dad both dissolved into giggles as she did her best to restore her calm façade.

"Can we have a talk? I've got a lot to unpack with you."

Dad gestured to the sofas, and my head spun with where to start. Blackthorn? Niall? The email from Fairbanks? But I settled on the topic that, despite what I'd said to the contrary for years and years, mattered most.

I clasped my hands tight in my lap, forcing myself to breathe. "I didn't just go to New York to see Avery. I met my birth mom, Tara."

Dad's cheeks grew pale, and Mom's eyes didn't meet mine. They offered no comment, so I continued.

"The NDA expired, and she actually sought me out. She wanted the chance to explain . . . everything, and I decided it was time to know the truth."

Mom and Dad absorbed the information I spewed at them at the rate of a fire hose's spray with the grace and dignity I'd learned to expect from them. There weren't any real "bad guys" in my story— save for maybe my birth dad who was, as villains go, pretty mundane. He was just your basic rich guy who very much enjoyed getting his own way. The sort who was responsible for a lot of the problems in the world but utterly convinced of their benevolence and brilliance.

Tara's story led naturally into the rest of the trip. I waxed poetic about Westport, Beynac, and Piozzano. My stay in Copenhagen had been cut short and was definitely not the highlight of the trip, but I even managed to find a pleasant anecdote or two to share. I gathered the courage to tell them of the visions I'd seen throughout my travels, the echoes of the women from my past, and they listened with intensity and understanding. Even if what I'd seen had been some sort of manifestation of my imagination, they were experiences I'd needed to have.

"So what's next, shortcake?" Dad asked. "Helping Fairbanks through the Valentine's Day rush this weekend?"

I resisted the urge to run my fingers through my hair and instead leaned back into the sofa. "Oh, Fairbanks is probably set for this weekend. He does want to have a chat though, and it will likely lead to some sort of job offer, from the sound of it. I have some big decisions to make."

"Good," Mom interjected. "It's time for some big decisions. I am sick to death of my brilliant, darling girl making small ones. You're better than that."

I widened my eyes.

"I know. I know. I've always said that what makes you happy makes me happy, but I've been wrong to pretend that you weren't selling yourself short." She got up from her place on the sofa and handed me a kraft paper box wrapped with a green satin bow. "I should have given this back to you when your plans first wavered as a reminder of what you wanted for yourself."

I pulled the ribbon and opened the box to find the chef's jacket she'd given me roughly fifteen years before. *Chef Stratton* still proudly emblazoned above the pocket. I stood and put it on over my clothes. It fit like it was tailor-made for me. She'd ordered it in the large size when I was in middle school, knowing that even if I'd achieved my full height by then, I'd still have some filling out to do. She'd purchased it intending for me to wear it into adulthood, probably hoping this one and a few others would be worn out by now.

"Looks good on ya, shortcake."

"Darling, I don't often try to browbeat my girls into making the decisions I want them to, but please don't go to work for Fairbanks. I'm sure he's talented and has the sort of reputation that many chefs dream about, but you need your own kitchen."

I strode over to the entryway to inspect my reflection in the mirror. I looked like a chef. In time I might feel like one.

"We still have your culinary school fund intact. It's probably doubled by now. You could probably go to any culinary school in the world and it would be covered. I couldn't bear to cash it out and take the stiff tax penalties."

"Didn't I use that for college?" I turned away from the mirror.

Dad shook his head. "I had a separate fund for culinary school. Perhaps it was disloyal of me, but I couldn't be convinced it wasn't where you wanted to go."

"It pains me to admit it, but you're right. I do need to go." I gave my reflection a hard stare, daring her to argue with me.

Dad's face split into a grin and Mom clasped her hands and held them to her mouth in delight—the same sort of joy usually reserved for the announcement of an engagement or a baby. But this was every bit as momentous for me, and I was supremely lucky to have parents who understood that.

"I almost forgot, I have a present for you as well. For your collection." I fetched the tissue-filled gift bag and passed it over to Mom. Inside were little ceramic Santas. The one from the thrift store in Ireland, the outdoor market in Périgueux, the little village outside Milan, and even one I'd managed to find in my brief stay in Copenhagen.

Mom's eyes had gone from brimming to spilling over. "Oh, darling these are lovely. I didn't think they made them anymore."

"Thrift shopping for the win," I said. "They were a lucky find. Now they can bring Irish fruitcake, French nougat, Italian panettone, and Danish butter cookies for Christmas."

"We'll have a Christmas-around-the-world theme at the bakery next year," Mom proclaimed. "I can see it now."

"It'll be a hit." I patted her knee. "And I'll help you source ingredients from culinary school. The Kitchen Muse won't go away entirely."

"Where will you go?" Mom asked. "Culinary Institute of America? Johnson & Wales? The Escoffier School in Boulder is good, and you could even commute from here if you wanted to save money on rent." Mom's eyes fairly glistened at the idea of one of her chicks flying back to the nest.

I crossed back over to them, wrapped an arm around her, and placed a kiss on her temple. "A bit farther afield, I think. Apart from this trip, I've hardly spent any time out of Colorado. And when I have, it's been almost entirely in the American West. I think it's time to expand my range a little."

"Hear! Hear!" Dad said. "We know you'll come back to visit when you can."

"And *you* can come visit me too. Trust me, a bit of wandering is good for the soul."

Chapter 41

ONE WEEK LATER
WESTPORT, IRELAND

Castles were built to intimidate. This was true a thousand years ago, and no less true now as I walked up the gravel path to the front door of Blackthorn. The taxi had left me off at the road, as I'd requested, and while I was glad not to have an audience for what I was about to do, I began to wonder about the wisdom of sending away my only option for a speedy getaway. The idea of waltzing up to the castle door and hoping for admittance was growing all the more ridiculous in my mind. Would I just . . . knock? Wait for someone to yell, "Hark! Who goes there?" It was infinitely different when I'd been following Niall around like a duckling trailing its mother on our outings. I was ushered in and out and never had to think about gaining entry on my own.

Terror seized my stomach as Blackthorn grew larger in my field of view. What if there were guests? What if Niall had changed his mind about me altogether and he sent me on my merry way?

I tried, without much success, to take even breaths as I trekked the last thirty feet down the wandering walk and pushed the speech I'd been practicing in my head out of my thoughts completely. The more I tried to find reasonable words, the sillier they sounded.

Too soon, the massive oak door stood before me, and I had to decide what to do. After a few long and exceedingly awkward moments, I settled on knocking as I would have done if this were some suburban cookie-cutter house and not an ancient fortified castle. Reasonable.

Nothing.

For perhaps ten minutes I waited, knocking every minute or so, progressively louder.

He wasn't going to answer, and I was silly not to give him a heads-up. He was probably out for a pint or out seeing to something on the grounds. Maybe he wasn't even staying at the castle tonight, off on an errand while the low season permitted him an absence. It was growing colder and darker, and it would be a solid hour's walk back to Westport with my luggage in tow. I'd have to pray I had enough service to call a cab and hope I'd be able to find a room and an obliging pub with a warm meal and a pint of cider. Before I fired up my phone, I decided my despair and embarrassment deserved a moment. I turned my back to the door, slid down, rested my head on my knees, and let the sobs have me.

I was dumb to come to Ireland. Even dumber for coming unannounced and unbidden. I should have at least attempted to warn him before impetuously boarding a flight. As we were at the lowest point of low season, even last-minute airfare hadn't been exorbitant, but it turned out I wasn't entirely opposed to using Dad's Amex after all. At least not after some prodding from Avery. When Dad had called me personally to tell me he'd be *disappointed* if I didn't spend a bit of my inheritance before he kicked the bucket, I finally acquiesced.

I was about to dust myself off and head into town when I heard rattling behind me. Before I could react, the door gave way behind me, and I fell flat on my back against Blackthorn's cold stone floor.

"For future reference, Miss Stratton, it's nary impossible to hear someone knocking on this beast of a door unless you're already in the entryway. She's nearly a foot thick. You'd do better to text."

He offered me a hand up, which I accepted, wiping my tear-streaked face with my free hand.

I tried to giggle with some semblance of nonchalance but really only succeeded in making a strange croak like a deranged bullfrog. "Sorry, I suppose being in an environment like this makes me forget about these modern conveniences."

"Well, thankfully your sister is in New York and not under the spell of Blackthorn. She had my number from the vacation rental site and texted a few hours ago to let me know you'd be coming. I just had my timing off by a few minutes."

My jaw dropped involuntarily. "She did not. I will murder her later."

"I'd prefer you didn't. Of all the places you could choose to build a life, the jailhouse isn't one I'd recommend."

I unsuccessfully stifled a snort of laughter. "You're probably right."

He reached over and wiped an errant tear from my cheek with his thumb. I fought the urge to take his hand and keep it against my face a few moments longer. Perhaps sensing this, he lingered a few seconds, then smoothed a lock of my hair before he cleared his throat. "Come on in, Miss Stratton. I've got supper waiting for us."

"Oh, that sounds lovely." Even better than the greasy pub fare and pint I'd been envisioning moments before.

His eyes crinkled merrily as he smiled. I'd never noticed how their gray-blue color brightened when he was pleased. "Good. Perhaps you'll be willing to forgive young Avery for her interference. If she hadn't warned me, I wouldn't have known to put the proverbial kettle on."

I leaned into his embrace a moment before I stepped back. "You make a compelling argument. I'll forgive her if you share the sumptuous feast you've no doubt prepared."

"Sumptuous feast? I haven't told you what I made yet." He wrapped an arm around me as we walked down the corridor to the kitchens. "Who's to say I didn't whip up a box of that macaroni with powdered cheese sauce I see on American TV all the time?"

"I can't envision you stooping to such depths, but it doesn't matter. If you made it, I'm sure it's incredible." I leaned my head against his chest before he released me to open the kitchen door. "I'll bet you could even find a way to make powdered cheese palatable."

He threw his head back in a laugh. "I'm a fair cook, lass. Not a magician." He crossed to the kitchen table that was set for important company, rather than just an intimate dinner with me. "It's not quite the feast you cooked up in Beynac, but it's not half bad if you don't mind my boasting. Roasted game hens in burgundy sauce, potatoes au gratin, salad greens from my own hothouse, and if you speak sweetly enough, I might be able to scare up some of my famous millionaire's shortbread for dessert."

Steeling my courage, I met him at the table where he'd pulled out a chair for me. Instead of sitting, I placed a hand on his cheek and raised myself up on tiptoes to kiss the other.

I searched his eyes to gauge his response, hoping I'd not been too bold. He stared into mine just long enough I felt a tingling at the base of my knees. I saw the barest hint of color reach his cheeks.

"You can have two portions of dessert, then."

My confidence mounted a degree or two from his reaction. "That sweet?"

"If you stay around much longer, I'll be able to forgo beekeeping."

I took my seat, unable to suppress a groan. "With honeyed lines like that, I'm not sure you needed their help to begin with. But it would be a shame; bees are lovely."

"I wouldn't do without them." He took his own place. "There is something truly grand in keeping chickens and bees and tending a garden."

He served the meal that smelled of ambrosia itself. We made small talk about the village as we tucked in, but it wasn't long before weightier questions began to niggle at me.

"You're really glad I'm here?" I managed to ask.

He reached over and put his hand on mine. "Veronica, you flew back over an ocean to see me. Or at least that's what Avery said, at which point I refused the payment she offered for your room. I think that gesture alone is enough to compel me to accept your decision."

A smile pulled at my lips. "I was scared before I left for Italy. I wasn't sure I'd ever get to see you again . . . I was so concerned with protecting my feelings, I never stopped to ask myself what I really wanted."

"An astute observation. And, since we're in the business of confessing our innermost thoughts, I've been the worst sort of mope for the past few weeks. If I kept it up, Caitlin threatened to have Da fashion me a man-size brooding box like we use for our hens."

I smiled despite myself. "I'm glad. Not that you were mopey . . ."

"But that I cared enough to mope. I understand." He took his hand, the one not covering mine, and tucked another strand of hair behind my ear. "At the risk of being too direct, is there any way I'll be able to persuade you to stay, Veronica? You could stay here at Blackthorn and be the loveliest chatelaine since Aoife's mother. We'd have a raucous good time making lavish breakfasts for the tourists and all. Stay as long as you like without any obligation or expectation, but I'd like you to think on it."

"I have been thinking on it. More than you know. About you, Blackthorn, my future." I took a sip of the crisp white wine he'd poured to accompany the game hens, grateful for the refreshment and for something to steady my hands.

"You've had a lot to mull over the past few weeks. When you come to any conclusions, I hope you'll share them with me."

I angled my hand so I was holding his. "Of course. And the one thing I'm absolutely certain about is that I want you to be a part of whatever plans I make."

His face brightened and his hand squeezed mine. "You'll stay then? Here at Blackthorn and run it with me?"

"Yes . . . I mean no. Not exactly." I stammered. "It's just—you're destined to be the keeper here, and I want to help you with that. But not yet. I don't think you're ready for this life just yet, nor is your dad ready for this part of his life to be over."

Niall leaned back in his chair. "Be that as it may, he's retired now."

"So he can un-retire. It's not the Olympics. It's not like he's now ineligible to be the steward here because he went professional."

"A messy metaphor, but I see what you're saying. Ma always dreamed of travel. And not having the burden of this place on her shoulders all the time."

"Have they taken any trips?" Based on some of Caitlin's remarks, I could guess the answer.

He was pensive for a few long moments. "They went to go visit Ma's cousin Elsie out near Kilkenny last autumn."

"Quite the bold expedition from what I remember. Four hours away?"

He smiled. "Not quite that even. Maybe three and a half hours by car."

"And they were gone . . . ?"

"Four days. Da couldn't bear to be away much longer."

"Exactly. He isn't ready to hand things over to you, and your mom isn't exactly dragging him off to the Mediterranean for a two-month vacation. I think she misses it too."

"Perhaps so," he conceded.

"Definitely so. Taking a leave of absence made sense, but he's recovered now and miserable without this place. Your parents can ease out of the job over the next decade or three, rather than feeling foisted out after the heart attack."

Niall gazed out the window at the darkening sky as he considered my words. "You may have a solid case here, but you've sidestepped the real question with your usual grace. What is it *you* want?"

I took in a deep breath. "I want to go to culinary school. A good one. And I want you to come with me. Apparently my surplus college fund will cover the pair of us. When we graduate, I want to open a restaurant based on the same principles you adhere to in this very kitchen and the ones I used with The Kitchen Muse. Centered around the best ingredients we can source, solid techniques, and a generous dash of creativity."

I had rattled that laundry list out in the space of one breath as if I were confessing to some evil misdeed. It didn't feel all that different, really. Owning up to what I wanted, really and truly, was just as difficult as admitting to a felony because I'd become so unused to the sensation.

"You have given it thought, haven't you?"

"I have. And I want Caitlin to come with us wherever we go so she can get her degree too. It wouldn't be fair to leave her behind. Your parents can take on the help they need so neither of them has to exhaust themselves. And we'll come back as often as we can. We'll test out your Christmas feast ideas if your dad will let us. And when the time comes for your dad to really retire, we'll be here to take over the reins."

He lifted my hand to his lips and let them brush softly against my skin. "It seems you've got it all figured out, Miss Stratton."

I took my free hand and caressed the side of his face before leaning in for a kiss. "Not really, but I think I'm finally wandering in the right direction."

Chapter 42

The bunting is perfect, sweetheart." Mom stood next to me on the sidewalk across from the restaurant's façade where Dad and Niall stood on twin ladders affixing the green, white, and orange Irish flag bunting to commemorate the occasion. Stratton and Callahan's, the newest restaurant in Dublin, which we hoped would take the culinary world by storm, opened next week, and the soft opening for friends and family was tonight. I'd have been content with less of a fuss, but Niall was determined that if his father was to brave the train from Westport all the way to Dublin for the first time in six years, he was going to make it worthwhile.

"Thanks, Mom. It hardly feels real." I leaned my head against hers, taking a moment to let the significance of the day wash over me.

She brushed her lips against my forehead. "You've worked hard to make this happen, sweetheart. Your father and I are so proud of you."

I swallowed hard, feeling close to tears more often than not the last few days. "Thank you for investing in it. It couldn't have happened otherwise."

"I'm just glad you let us. And Tara too. It's what parents do for their children. Give them enough to do something but not enough to do nothing was my dad's motto."

"He was a wise man," Dad called from across the street, eliciting a smile from Mom.

It was a dream two years in the making. Much longer than that, really, but it had been two years since Niall and I had embarked on our journey to culinary school. We'd decided the old adage "Go big or go home" applied here, so we enrolled at the École de Cuisine Alain Ducasse for several intensive sessions. We had enough practical experience to forgo a full bachelor's program, so we each took the core diploma programs in culinary arts and pastry and then supplemented with a few shorter courses in more specialized areas like chocolate work and bread baking. We spent our downtime developing recipes for our future enterprise and eating like restaurant critics whenever the budget stretched to it.

Caitlin managed to get over her disappointment of not going to university in Dublin, finding Paris an acceptable substitute for her original plans. She still had two years to finish her art program and would be returning to France after the restaurant was launched. To appease her parents she took a healthy concentration of courses in graphic and digital design so she could do some corporate work to support herself as she got established in the field.

Molly, and especially Liam, weren't pleased that she stayed in Paris after we returned, but they knew once she'd flown from the nest, there'd be no getting her back. Ciaran Walsh had begun making frequent trips to Paris to help reassure the Callahans that Caitlin was well, of course. And from what we could tell, she didn't object to his attentions. He'd gratefully accepted the invitation to the restaurant launch when he heard Caitlin would be making the trip and hadn't strayed more than a few feet from her since he'd arrived.

Amid peals of laughter, Caitlin, Stephanie, and Avery emerged from the restaurant where they'd been busy perfecting every place setting and centerpiece, Ciaran trailing them. Introducing the three of the largest personalities I knew had been the most exhilarating and vaguely terrifying moment of our early days in France, but thankfully our small Parisian flat had survived the experience. And rather than feeling eclipsed by them, it felt as though they'd come to bask in my light for once. I found I rather enjoyed having a spot in the sun for myself.

Tara and her new boyfriend, Bryce, joined us on the street, followed by Molly and Liam, who passed out glasses of champagne to toast the opening. Tara and I managed to keep up regular emails for months, which evolved into the occasional phone call and FaceTime. We finally decided to meet up again last year, and I had great fun playing tour guide and showing her all our favorite haunts. She even took one of the short cooking courses for tourists and casual cooks that Ducasse offered to help bolster their income, and showed some real talent. I was more than a little proud when the instructor told me in confidence that she was miles ahead of the others in her class.

Mom and Dad had made a habit of coming over every six months or so, and while things would never be quite as they were before that fateful Christmas, I was glad. I was glad because things hadn't been right for a long time, and owning up to the circumstances of my birth was the only real path to healing. Knowing the full picture of how I'd come to be hadn't magically freed me from all the complicated feelings I had about it, but every day I felt a bit more comfortable in my own skin. A bit more worthy of love and success.

The bunting secured, Niall and Dad descended their ladders and joined us to admire the display and all it represented, made all the sweeter because our family and friends were able to join us for its opening.

"She's a right beaut, son," Liam pronounced. "And I couldn't be prouder of you, lad."

Liam's color and disposition were brighter for being back at Blackthorn, and Molly seemed happier for having a husband who wasn't a ghost of himself any longer.

"To Stratton and Callahan's." Caitlin lifted her glass. "The finest eatery in all of Ireland, or soon will be."

"Hear! Hear!" the rest chorused.

Niall wrapped an arm around me and kissed my cheek, then whispered low in my ear, "You're a marvel, you know that?"

"Naturally I am." I returned the kiss, nuzzling his neck before meeting his gaze. "Shall we get on with the show?"

His eyes sparkled with anticipation, and he raised his voice to call everyone to attention. "Let's get inside, shall we? I hear the chefs have quite the meal simmering for you."

This was met with enthusiasm from our gathering, who reentered the restaurant that we'd spent six months restoring from near ruin. We'd restained the peeling wood paneling and battered wood floors, repainted every surface, and polished everything until it glistened to the standard of the watchful eye of a Michelin-guide inspector. Not that we were ready for one of those, but hopefully someday before long we would be.

We'd brought in the waitstaff and the kitchen staff to give the family the full experience. The servers circulated, refilling champagne and passing amuse-bouches, each with truffles from the same farm we'd loved so well in Périgueux. The business card swapping in the markets had been a great use of time, as some of them became our regular vendors.

While everyone mingled merrily, Niall and I snuck into the kitchens and slipped into the back office that was still a jumble of boxes and invoices we'd have to sort later. "Are you ready, my love?" His voice was low, just above a whisper. He brushed his lips over mine and took me in his arms for a long moment, savoring slowly the beauty of all we'd built.

"More than ready. Stall them for five minutes, will you?"

"The way the first course is going over, I'd wager you have ten. Take your time." He grabbed a short garment bag with his suit jacket that he'd stashed in the kitchen, closer to the dining room.

When he left, I unzipped my own longer garment bag and removed the simple Ordaithe candle-glow lace dress. When I returned to Dublin, it had still been waiting in the thrift store I'd visited my very first day. I happened upon the shop completely at random, having largely forgotten about the place, the very day after Niall had proposed during a quiet candlelit dinner at home.

The shopkeeper recognized me right away, her face splitting into a grin as if I were the prodigal daughter returned. Before I opened my mouth beyond a simple greeting, she'd dashed to the rack and thrust the garment bag into my hands, insisting I try it on. "I do believe your time has come, dearie. I knew you'd be back."

It was long and fashioned of the finest cream lace, without frills and fuss. It clung to my curves in all the right places before gently flowing into a slender A-line skirt that brushed the floor, leaving a small sweep train in its wake. No alteration was needed, as though the gown was bespoken for me long before I was in need.

I liked to think it was.

When I admired myself in the mirror, she pronounced, "She's the very one for you, my dear. I'm so very glad of it." She wouldn't accept more than five euro for the dress and a bit more for an emerald-green ribbon sash with a bit of beading at the middle that added a lovely touch of color and definition to the waist.

That day my only jewelry was the silver medallion of Kilkenny silver Niall had given me before we'd left for France, my trademark emerald earrings, and the warrior's cuff I'd worn each day since Dublin. I'd been dressed for a party, with hair, makeup, underpinnings, and shoes to suit, so all I had to do was exchange my floral afternoon dress for the lace antique I'd found the day I met Niall.

I hadn't had another vision since the last one in New York, and while I didn't miss them, I did wish I could know more about what had happened to Aoife, Imogène, Carlotta, and Donatella. I mused over my vision of young Tara. Stephanie had deduced they'd all ended up on the East Coast. Aoife married and had children. Imogène gave birth to the baby she was expecting and went on to have more with a new husband. As it turned out, Carlotta, rather than Donatella, was my direct ancestor. Carlotta and Vincente were married shortly after their arrival in the States and had two children, one of whom was my great-to-some-degree-grandmother. Donatella never married, preferring to spend her days in the peace and quiet of her mother and stepfather's farmhouse in upstate New York. I didn't know about the blonde Danish woman, and it was fine if she remained a mystery lost to time. Some questions were all the lovelier for not having answers.

I didn't know if my ancestors lived happily ever after, but I do know they lived. Each was given a second chance at happiness, at life, and she took it in the New World. And knowing that had given me the courage to do the same in the Old.

I caught a glimpse of myself in the cockeyed office mirror. I slid the beaded headband in my hair, ensured the sash was straight, and picked up the dainty bouquet of cream roses interspersed with iris, lilies, daisies, and little sprigs of shamrock—the flowers of France, Italy, Denmark, and Ireland—as a remembrance for the women who had left all they knew for the hope of better things.

I took in a deep breath and crossed the kitchen, where Niall was waiting with the good-humored priest he'd snuck in the back door. Father O'Malley said a quick, quiet blessing over our heads before exiting the kitchen to ask that our friends and family be seated. They had no idea they'd come for a wedding as well as the christening of our restaurant, but all would see how the two events could never be truly distinct in our hearts.

Niall offered me his arm and we entered the dining room to the next chapter of our adventure together. And as we regarded a roomful of beaming faces, it felt that, with the love of Niall and our family and friends, I had finally wandered home.

Acknowledgments

My heart is filled with gratitude for all the following people, without whom this book would not be possible:

My incredible editor, Kimberly Carlton, for her guidance, her keen insight, and her trust in this project.

My incomparable agent, Kevan Lyon, for being a worthy champion for her authors and the written word.

My dear friend Kimberly Brock for helping me name this book and talking me off a proverbial ledge more times than I care to count.

Talented audiobook narrator and actress Caroline Hewitt, for her devotion to the craft and her uncanny ability to find the voice for my books.

My very first writer friend and one-woman hype squad, Jamie Raintree, for reading this manuscript in rough shape and helping me to connect with the story Veronica had to tell.

My amazing group of writer friends, including Heather Webb, Andrea Catalano, Kate Quinn, Stephanie Dray, J'nell Ciesielski, Rachel McMillan, and so many others, for your love and support.

The talented authors of The Tall Poppies, The Lyonesses, and the Business Hat—I appreciate your friendship and camaraderie more than I could ever adequately express.

My dear friends in the real world, Stephanie and Todd, Carol and Sam (thank you for letting me borrow your surname!), Danielle, Julie and Jim, and all the rest of my little squad: love you all!

All the amazing reader groups like Bloom with Tall Poppy Writers, Bookworms Anonymous, Reader's Coffeehouse, A Novel Bee, Great Thoughts, Great Readers, Women Writers Women's Books, Baer Books, and so, so many others—thank you for all the support.

Independent booksellers everywhere, especially my friends at Macdonald Book Shop (Estes Park, Colorado), Face in a Book (El Dorado Hills, Californa), The Poisoned Pen (Scottsdale, Arizona), FoxTale Books (Atlanta, Georgia), Litchfield Books (Pawleys Island, South Carolina), Cleary's Bookshop (Mount Holly, North Carolina), The King's English (Salt Lake City, Utah), The Ripped Bodice (Culver City, California), and so many others who are fighting the good fight to keep the local book scene not just alive but thriving.

And for all the readers who have enjoyed this and any of my other books, I am humbled that you've chosen to spend your time with me . . .

But most of all, my love and gratitude go to:

The wonderful Trumbly and Vetter clans for their tireless support and generosity.

My editor cat, Jiji, who insisted on more kitties in this book. You were right.

My darling children, Ciaran and Aria, for reminding me every day what truly matters.

And, as always, to my incredible husband, Jeremy, for the love and unwavering support you have shown for me, my career, and our family each and every day. I am so grateful to share my life with you.

Author's Note

I've been fascinated by DNA kits since their invention. For the
first time in history, we have the possibility of, for a modest sum,
uncovering hidden truths about family and genetic inheritance,
which can reshape the whole trajectory of our lives. While I was
on an extended road trip throughout Europe doing research for
A Bakery in Paris, *Mademoiselle Eiffel*, and *The Memory of Lavender
and Sage* (yes, I believe in multitasking, especially when it comes
to research travel), I got the inspiration to write a book about a
woman at loose ends in her life who is set adrift by the results of an
ill-timed DNA test. I didn't want her adoptive status to be a surprise
to her—it's a reality she'd been adjusting to for a while—nor did
I want this to be a journey for her to seek out her birth family.
Rather, I wanted her to have the chance to discover the places that
turned up in her tests, hoping she might find traces of *herself* in the
old buildings where she's sent to wander.

Gentle reader, you'll forgive this lack of creativity, but I've based
Veronica's DNA results largely on my own. While my results did
not reveal any surprises in parentage despite what I might have
believed as a child who was significantly shorter and lighter com-
plected than the rest of my family, they *did* reveal that there is

nothing more exotic in my background than an unexplained .7 percent Italian ancestry. Like Veronica, my makeup is mostly Irish with a healthy percentage of French and Danish, and the rest of the DNA is attributed to other countries in the general vicinity of those three. I chose to have Veronica's results emulate mine because it felt like the most personal way to connect with her and to eke out the story she wanted to tell us. It also served the story well to have the regions she visited in a more constrained area, rather than her voyage of self-discovery taking on a more global scale.

Veronica's quest to find herself once freed from the constraints from her daily life was one I delighted in bringing to life, and I hope you enjoyed wandering along with her.

Warmly,

Aimie

Discussion Questions

1. What do you feel is Veronica's general "vibe" with her family when we first see them together at Christmas? How does Veronica fit in with the group and each of her family members individually? Why does Veronica feel cowed by the big personalities in her family?

2. Why do you think Veronica's mother Elena intervenes on behalf of her father, sister, and best friend when the trip is proposed rather than letting them present a unified front? What does this say about their dynamic as a group?

3. Veronica states that Blackthorn is one of the first places she's been that truly felt like home on a fundamental level. Have you ever had this experience in a place you've never been, be it a building, a country, or an expanse of land? Do you think people feel the pull of places?

4. Food is obviously a recurring theme in this book, and something Veronica and Niall bond over. It was also a serious point of contention between Veronica and her ex-boyfriend Jonathan. While some argue that "opposites attract" (and that seems to be the case with

Veronica's parents), it would seem in this case that "birds of a feather flock together." Because of their shared passion, Veronica sees a kindred spirit in Niall that she didn't see in her ex. Do you think this is the more plausible scenario, or do you think it's more common (or preferable) to seek balance in one's counterpoint?

5. What was your first reaction to the vision or "echo" of Aoife? Did Veronica react the way you would have? What did you think was the significance of this vision?

6. In Beynac-et-Cazenac, Veronica finally lets her Kitchen Muse free and creates a sumptuous feast. We see hints of this before, but this is the first time she really lets loose in the kitchen. Why do you think she's kept her talents on a leash up to this point? Why do you think it was emotionally challenging for her to let herself create in the kitchen without restraint?

7. How are Aoife and Imogène's stories similar? How are they different? Did you find one woman's story more compelling than the other?

8. Why do you think Veronica doesn't want to continue to communicate with Niall once they part? Do you think she tells us the whole story behind her rationale? Why do you think she ultimately caves and agrees to continue to keep in touch with Niall once they part ways?

9. Clothing is another recurring theme. How does Veronica react to the prospect of a new wardrobe? Why do you think she's so reluctant to let her sister and best friend help her with new clothes? What is the significance/symbolism of Veronica being a thrift shopper?

10. Carlotta and Donatella's story is quite different from Aoife and Imogène's, and the earliest in the timeline (they're more distantly related to Veronica than the other two). What do you feel is the overarching theme between these three stories? Why does Veronica see these women at these specific moments in their history?

11. How is Veronica's vision of Tara different? Why do you think she sees this echo, despite Tara being a living person?

12. In the final chapter, what was the importance of the antique gown, despite all the emphasis on Veronica finding her own path?

Recipes

NIALL'S SODA BREAD (IRELAND)

*Do not add raisins unless you want to be
haunted by a banshee.*

Ingredients

    4 cups unbleached all-purpose flour

    1 teaspoon kosher salt

    1 teaspoon baking soda

    1 egg

    2 tablespoons melted Irish butter

    1½ cups buttermilk (This is important! If you don't have buttermilk, add 2 teaspoons lemon juice or vinegar to 2% milk and let stand 5 minutes.)

    Specialty equipment: 8–9-inch cast-iron skillet

Directions

    1. Preheat oven to 450°. Grease cast-iron skillet with softened butter.

    2. In large mixing bowl, whisk flour, salt, and baking soda to combine thoroughly.

3. Using your hands or wooden spoon, make well in center of dry ingredients. In separate bowl, whisk together buttermilk, egg, and melted butter. Add mixture to dry ingredients in well. Gently combine ingredients, starting at center of bowl and slowly working outward. Dough will be very sticky.

4. Lightly flour work surface. Use your hands to gently knead dough until it comes together and surface is somewhat smooth. Don't overwork!

5. Transfer dough to prepared skillet. Gently form into round cob shape. Lightly sprinkle top with flour. Use bread lame or sharp knife to slash large X on top of dough.

6. Bake 15 minutes at 450°. Lower temperature to 400°, rotate pan 180° in oven, and bake for another 25–30 minutes until deep golden brown. Allow bread to cool for 20 minutes or more, then serve warm with good Irish butter.

VERONICA'S CRÈME BRÛLÉE (FRANCE)

Always a delight, especially with a bespoke vanilla extract.

Ingredients
2 cups heavy cream
1 vanilla bean, split lengthwise, or 1 teaspoon vanilla extract (Preferably homemade!)
1/8 teaspoon salt
5 egg yolks (Save whites for meringue!)
1/2 cup granulated sugar
coarse sugar (raw or turbinado) for topping
truffle pearls (optional)
Specialty equipment: 4 ramekins, 1 culinary blowtorch (optional)

Directions

1. Preheat oven to 325°. In heavy saucepan, combine heavy cream, vanilla bean or extract, and salt. Simmer over low heat for several minutes to let flavors bloom. Remove vanilla bean and discard or save for another use.

2. In stand mixer or with hand mixer, beat yolks and sugar until color lightens. Stir about a quarter of vanilla cream into this mixture at a time, combining slowly. Pour mixture into four 6-ounce ramekins. Arrange ramekins in cake pan (8x8 should be big enough). Fill pan with boiling water until it reaches halfway up sides of ramekins, careful not to splash custard (bain-marie method).

3. Bake 30 to 40 minutes or until centers are just set. Remove ramekins from water (carefully) and cool completely on wire rack.

4. Just before serving, sprinkle custard tops with coarse sugar and truffle pearls and caramelize with culinary blowtorch or under oven broiler, watching attentively to avoid scorching.

VERO'S GIRLS' NIGHT TIRAMISU (ITALY)

A real pick-me-up!

Ingredients

1½ cups heavy whipping cream

8-ounce container mascarpone cheese, room temperature

1/3 cup granulated sugar

1 teaspoon vanilla extract (Homemade is best!)

1½ cups espresso, room temperature

3 tablespoons liqueur of choice (rum, brandy, Kahlua, etc.)

1 package premade ladyfingers or one batch from scratch

1–2 good-quality dark chocolate bars (Ghirardelli or similar), grated for dusting top

Pro tip: Grated chocolate is far tastier and less messy than cocoa powder that is traditionally used.

Specialty equipment: pretty 8x8 casserole dish suitable for presenting at the table

Directions

1. In stand mixer or with hand mixer, beat whipping cream on medium speed. Slowly add sugar and vanilla extract and continue to beat until stiff peaks form. Remove bowl from stand mixer and add mascarpone cheese. Fold in until combined but don't overwork. Set aside.

2. Add espresso and liqueur to shallow bowl. Quickly dip ladyfingers in mixture without letting them get soggy. Lay them in single layer on bottom of casserole dish.

3. Scoop half of mascarpone mixture over top and smooth with spatula. Add another layer of dipped ladyfingers. Smooth remaining mascarpone cream over top.

4. Sprinkle grated chocolate on top. Refrigerate 3–4 hours or overnight before serving.

Bonus Recipes at www.aimiekrunyan.com

About the Author

Internationally bestselling author Aimie K. Runyan writes to celebrate unsung heroines. She has written eight historical novels (and counting!) and is delving into the exciting world of contemporary women's fiction. She has been a finalist for the Colorado Book Award, a nominee for the Rocky Mountain Fiction Writers' "Writer of the Year," and a Historical Novel Society's Editors' Choice selection. Aimie is active as a speaker and educator in the writing community in Colorado and beyond. She lives in the beautiful Rocky Mountains with her wonderful husband, two (usually) adorable children, two very sweet cats, and a pet dragon.

Visit her online at aimiekrunyan.com
Instagram: @bookishaimie
Facebook: @aimiekrunyan
X: @aimiekrunyan
TikTok: @aimiekrunyan